Venture to
AFRICA

DAUGHTERS OF THE HIGH SEAS
BOOK 3

Venture to AFRICA

RACHEL CHERIE

Published in the United States of America

ISBN: 978-0-99988-182-8

1. Fiction / Action & Adventure

2. Fiction / Historical

Dedicated to my two little munchkins, DTW and NCW. And to KLR, hope you've enjoyed the journey.

Chapter 1

"Hurry, Alex! This way!" a voice commanded in a loud whisper.

A shadowy figure moved along a dim corridor.

"Jacq! Stop! Do you truly think it was best we sent Amy?" Alex asked in an equally hushed tone.

"For the fifth time, Alex, aye! Now hurry!" Stepping out of a shadowed part of the hall, Jacq motioned vehemently for her sister to follow.

Huffing in mild exasperation, Alex hustled over to where Jacq was gesturing. "I still say it was unthinkable what you said to that guard!"

Chuckling, Jacq shrugged as Alex stopped beside her. "I can't believe he believed me!"

"Well, I am certain he will feel like a fool when he awakens in our cell," Alex said, straightening her dress and nervously glancing about.

Grinning, Jacq nodded. "Shh. Let's go this way." She motioned to what looked like a bend in the dark dirt hallway.

"Why that way?" Alex asked, falling in step behind her sister, still brushing at the debris on her skirt.

"Shh." Jacq swatted at Alex. "I thought I heard…"

"Oi! Jacq! Is that you?" a voice called out from the direction in which the two girls were headed.

Tossing a sideways grin back at Alex, Jacq shook her head and said, "Come along."

As they turned the corner, they approached a dank cell, squinting in hopes they would recognize its occupants.

"Over here!" a secondary voice called out from the direction of the cell.

Slinking along the corridor, the girls arrived at the mediocrely barred hole.

"Miata," Jacq greeted the slightly ruffled lanky man gripping the bars of the cell door. Then looking past him, she exhaled in relief. "Dante?"

Shuffling forward, a roughed-up Dante winced at them. "Evening to you."

"Oh! Your eye!" Alex gasped, covering her mouth.

"Where be Amy?" Miata spoke up, leaning on the bars.

"A guard came to get one of us by request of our father," Alex returned, her voice tight as she glanced about them, anxiety heavy in her manner.

"Aye," Jacq confirmed, running her hands over the wooden and metal bars, trying, in the dark, to find the chain holding it shut. "We asked them to bring him Amy. We don't want anything to happen to her."

Shifting his weight while watching Jacq, Miata asked, "You be sure they'll be treatin' her proper?"

Jacq found the lock, and paused. "I'm certain the vice admiral will make sure of it."

Pawing at Jacq's elbow, Alex whispered, "Quickly! We do not have much time."

"We *never* have any time," Jacq replied in acknowledgment. "Where are the others?" She returned her attention to the lock, pulling the key ring she'd lifted from the guard out of her sash and trying different keys.

"We are fortunate you decided against wearing the sash with the coins," Alex noted.

"Aye. Somehow, after someone's severe insistence, I thought better than to bring it," Jacq grumbled, continuing with the keys.

Alex glowered at her. "I just said it was highly unfashionable."

A loud whisper interrupted the group chatter. "Oi! Jacq!"

Glancing around, Jacq asked, "Murtaugh? Is that you?"

"And Bahari," Murtaugh returned cheerfully as they both rounded a corner and passed under a beam of torchlight.

Grinning, Jacq turned once again to the lock. "How'd you get out?"

As the Irishman and Bahari came to a stop beside the girls, Murtaugh shrugged. "Would you expect any less from me?"

At his question, the lock clicked.

Jacq smirked at him then shrugged. "I suppose not."

Clearing his throat, Rackham retorted, "I was about to get us out."

Reaching forward and pulling the door open, Murtaugh nodded. "I'm sure you were, mate."

The two men glared at each other as Miata and Dante exited the cell.

"Where are we?" Alex asked, wringing her hands.

"In a dungeon," Miata answered.

"No," Bahari corrected. "But this is their prison. It is often where they hold slaves."

"Oh," Alex whimpered, hugging herself.

"We should try to find Amy and our father," Jacq said, shutting the now-empty cell door.

"I am not sure that is a good idea, Shakina," Bahari replied in a somber tone. "We should find an escape."

"I am in agreement with Jacq," Alex spoke up.

"Well, I'm sorry, but I agree with Bahari," Murtaugh said, halting slightly after getting a glare from Jacq.

Grinding his teeth, Dante nodded. "I also agree with Bahari." He sent a disgruntled glower toward Murtaugh, wishing he either had a different opinion or had stated it first.

Smirking, the Irishman nodded.

Miata opened his mouth to share his thoughts but was interrupted by the approaching sound of Dutch voices.

Stifling a gasp, Alex turned worried eyes to everyone else. Then everyone looked to Bahari.

Heaving a sigh, the burly man jerked his head to one side. "This way."

The company of six began scrambling down the mud-tunnel prison hallways with Bahari leading the way.

"There is usually an entrance towards the back for them to put their prisoners in when they are too cowardly to bring them in the front past those who might try and rise against them," Bahari explained. "I think I saw a corral near the east edge of this place when we were taken off the ship."

Stopping abruptly, he guided them off to the side, where they came upon a door. "Here. We leave two at a time."

Gesturing at Miata and Dante, he nodded. "You two first. The girls"—he motioned to the sisters—"will follow. Murtaugh and I will go last." Glancing about, he pulled the door open, not giving the young men a chance to argue with his course of action. "Go. Now!"

In accordance with Bahari's instructions, a grumbling Dante and a reluctant Miata darted out the door. Bahari watched the two

men duck and dash toward the corral, waiting for them to get about halfway there, and then he turned to the twins. "Ready?"

"Aye," Jacq answered for both of them, grasping Alex's hand and giving Bahari a nod.

"Be swift," he said, and then opened the door.

Scrambling out the dirt doorway, the girls hurried in the direction of the corral, which was barely lit by the partially clouded sky.

As they tripped over rocks, sticks, and debris, Alex growled. "How do Mr. O'Keeffe and Mr. Rackham move so quickly over this horrendous terrain?"

"It must be those bloody long legs of theirs," Jacq retorted, sharing the jealous feeling as she stumbled alongside her sister.

"Oh! Watch your language, Jacqueline! The language of the sailors is *not* befitting a lady!"

"Says the lass calling our Miata *Mr. O'Keeffe*!" Jacq shot back.

"If he is ever to be mistaken for a proper gentleman, *someone* has to address him by his proper name!" Alex argued.

Hopping over part of a small log, Jacq called, "Alex, watch out for—"

However, before she could finish her sentence, Alex's skirts caught on the log, tripping up her feet. Falling forward, she dragged Jacq to the ground with her.

As they tumbled down, Alex's head struck a rock buried beneath the muddy soil, knocking her unconscious.

Twelve months earlier…

"Africa?" Vice Admiral Luray asked, straightening up and staring curiously at Jacq, who stood confidently across the dining table from him.

"Aye. Africa." Jacq smiled over at a bewildered Alex and Miata. "Bahari risked his life to help secure my freedom and get me back to my family. I wish to return the favor."

His mouth tugging into a smile, Vice Admiral Luray tilted his head. "An honorable request. I will look into making arrangements, but no promises. I must warn you, we would also likely have to wait out the winter and go next spring."

Beaming, Jacq turned glittery eyes to Alex before nodding and replying in her calmest voice, "Thank you for the consideration, Father. Your generosity alone on entertaining the matter is invaluable to me."

Then whirling about, she exited the door back into the garden.

As she departed, leaving Vice Admiral Luray wearing an unmistakable look of pride, Alex turned back to James. "Leave it to my sister to impress everyone in the room in one fell swoop."

James chuckled and shrugged. "She does have a way about her, that is certain. But, you, Miss Alex." He paused, admiring her face and golden tresses. "You are exquisite in a manner all your own."

A coy smile upturned her lips. "Well, to have a good man believe so, whether I was to agree or not, is positively flattering."

The two shared a warm, smiling moment, but it was cut short when James's face began to cloud over with a look of distress.

Noticing immediately, Alex touched his hand. "James? Are you quite all right? What was it you wanted to speak to me about?"

James lifted his usually peaceful blue eyes to hers, wordlessly acknowledging he was indeed troubled.

"Oh." She cringed, having had a sense that something was amiss. "James, what is it?"

"Miss Alex," he said in a solemn tone, "I received some very unexpected news from my parents about two months back."

"Are they well?" she asked, touching his fingers.

"They are, aye," he replied, nodding. Then placing his hand over hers, he sighed.

A sense of dread crept over Alex's heart as she waited, searching his eyes for an explanation.

"They've sent word saying they've found a lass they wish for me t-to-to marry."

Alex felt her breath catch in her throat, and her skin went ashen. "O-oh... A-and you have accepted the arrangement?"

"W-well, no. I-I am making plans to go in person and deal with the matter formally. As a gentleman, I intend not to offend my parents or the lass' family." James stopped awkwardly, watching her hold back every thought and emotion with the refinement of a monarch. "I had only mentioned you a few times in my letters home, so my mother must have just assumed..." He paused again, gulping. "You-you understand my position?"

"Of course," Alex answered, pulling away her hand while holding herself in perfect stoic demeanor. "I would not want you putting your parents in any kind of undesirable position."

Clearing his throat, he examined her in earnest. "Should things be arranged, I may not be back in time to join you on your trip to Africa."

"Of course. I understand. I wish you the best on your journey, Mr. Monroe. Though I cannot completely comprehend why this is only coming up now. A gentleman should stand by his word." Pausing, she glanced at Amy and Miata. "Please excuse me."

Before James could stop her, Alex rose from her chair.

"Alex! Alex!" Jacq's voice whispered loudly into her sister's ears.

Alex blinked, then squinted. "Jacq? What?"

"Come on! Up! Up! We've got to go!" As she spoke, Jacq dragged Alex to her feet, and they began stumbling forward again.

"W-what happened?" Alex inquired, wincing at the pain she felt in her right ankle and head.

"You fell and hit your head, I think," Jacq answered.

They reached the corral, where Dante and Miata greeted them.

"You both well?" Miata asked in a tense voice, helping Jacq support Alex's weight.

"We saw the fall," Rackham added, coming up beside Jacq.

"It was just a tumble," Jacq insisted, shrugging it off.

"Oi, Jacq!" Murtaugh's voice interrupted as he and Bahari came up beside them. "Are you and Miss Alex unharmed?"

"Aye, no thanks to that log out there," Jacq responded. "We best make our escape and then see how bad off we are." She looked over at her sister. "Are you well, Alex?"

Wincing, Alex forced a weak smile. "Yes. Well enough. We should go."

"Right," Dante spoke up. "We should head into the woods before we've been missed and the alarm's been sounded."

Eyeing him, Murtaugh chimed in, "We should take a couple of the pack animals and set the rest loose."

"The animals will make too much noise," Rackham countered, returning the disapproving glare.

"It will slow their pursuit once they've realized our absence," Murtaugh said. "But it won't be much use either way if we stand here arguing until they raise the alarm."

Rackham's lip curled into a snarl, but before he could speak, Murtaugh spoke. "Bahari! What say you?"

After sending Murtaugh another glare, Rackham took a long breath. "Aye, Bahari," he said with a growl. "What say you?"

Bahari glanced skeptically between the two men. "Very well. I say we take two mules and scatter the rest. We do not want them able to follow, except on foot. We can release them on the morrow, to further their confusion." He looked between them again. "Agreed?"

Nodding, the fiver younger party members agreed. "Aye!"

"I'll get the mules," Murtaugh volunteered.

Dante shot Murtaugh another glare before speaking up. "Come along, Miata. Let's scatter the rest of them."

"Shakina, Miss Alex," Bahari started. "Stay with me. We look for our escape route."

The girls followed him as he investigated the perimeter of the ramshackle pen.

"We want to head north," he commented, concentrating on his examination of the varying terrain there.

"Two mules," Murtaugh reported, coming up behind them, a mule on a rope in each hand. "As requested."

"*All* other mules scattered," Rackham commented, joining them and snatching a lead from Murtaugh's hand as Miata stopped beside them.

"Nicely done, Skippy," the Irishman commended him in thinly veiled sarcasm.

"Oh, save it, Crevan," Rackham retorted with a growl. "And I don't go by Skippy anymore."

"Fine." Murtaugh's demeanor vibrated with sardonic amusement. "Rackham."

At this, Bahari and both sisters turned around, looking thoroughly unimpressed with their hostile attempt at conversation. However, before anything could be said, yells began rising from the small fort, and a bell began to toll.

Shaking his head, Bahari pointed at each of the two. "We do not have time for this. Follow in order: me, Shakina, Crevan, Miss Alex, Miata, and Rackham."

Glancing between themselves like scolded children, they nodded and fell in line, Murtaugh and Rackham each with an agitated mule in tow. As they scurried and picked their way north, they all began to feel a little relief when they hit the tree line. Yet the farther they got in the quickly thickening vegetation, the less at ease they felt.

"This be like trudgin' through wet hay!" Miata complained.

"Oh, quit complaining," Alex snapped as she hobbled along in front of him. "With Mr. Murtaugh and Mr. Rackham at each other's throats for who knows what reason, the last thing we need is for you to be whining about every little inconven—aaah!"

She managed to stifle most of her scream as she went lurching forward, landing on her already throbbing ankle and then dropping to the jungle floor.

"What happened?" Jacq asked.

The entire caravan halted.

Grimacing, Miata knelt beside Alex. "No worries, Jacq. She'll be fine. Keep going. We can't all be stoppin'. Dante and me have this."

Dante cleared his throat at being volunteered but didn't object. "Aye."

With a trace of a smirk adorning his handsome face, Murtaugh nudged Jacq. "Miata's right, Jacqs. If we separate and all head straight north, they'll catch up, but all six of us shouldn't stop here. We should split into two groups."

"Alex?" Jacq asked, all but ignoring the other remarks.

"Just keep moving," Alex returned, managing to keep her voice steady though it wanted to tremble and whimper in both pain and frustration. "I just need to rest a moment or two. We cannot all of us be captured."

When Jacq still did not look convinced, Bahari put his hand on her shoulder. "Come, Shakina. We will travel slow. Your friends will keep her safe, but they are right. It is easier to hide the few than it is the many."

Hesitating, Jacq nodded, still frowning at the plan. "Very well. We will wait for them at your village if they do not catch up with us before we arrive."

"Agreed," Bahari returned. "Remember what I told you of these lands on ship. It is how we will eat and stay safe."

With trepidation tugging at her every motion, Jacq moved to continue forward with Murtaugh and Bahari. However, in doing so, she left a wretched Alex feeling completely pitiful and useless.

Taking a seat next to her, Miata sighed. "It'll be fine, Alex. You'll see." Then he looked after those pushing forward, and a small, sneaky smile stretched across his lips.

Something in his voice caught Alex's attention. "What do you mean by that, Miata O'Keeffe?"

"W-what do you mean? Be meanin' by what?" Miata asked in a barely contained sputter, turning to stare at her innocently.

Whipping around, bringing them nose to nose, she narrowed her eyes at him. "Did-did you trip me?"

17

"Wha—? Me, trip you? No!" He scoffed, shaking his head and rolling his eyes.

"Shhh!" Dante scolded. "I'm going to tether this mule and see what we have following us. You two keep quiet until I get back."

Alex gasped. "You did!"

Miata shook his head adamantly.

"Shhh!" Rackham repeated hoarsely. "Both of you!"

Folding her arms across her chest, she shook her head. "I hate you."

Miata scoffed. "Alex!"

"Shhh!" Dante repeated as he trudged off with the animal.

As Jacq, Crevan, and Bahari moved off and their rustlings merged with the movements caused by the sea breeze, the jungle's nocturnal residents began again to stir.

Around Alex and Miata, quiet settled in, nesting for the night. It tucked them away in the dense forest vegetation, not caring that they were strangers. The longer they sat silent, the more afraid they were to move lest the sound attract unwanted wildlife attention or, worse, make the trees go silent.

Glancing over at Miata, who was wringing his hands with all his combined nervousness, Alex felt a twinge in her mind, and a scowl formed around her pleasant mouth. *Why, of all people, must I get stuck with him?* Ever since this business with Jim had come up, she found herself less patient and less trusting. Watching Miata quell a panic attack beside her, she found, made her wonder where his apprehension actually stemmed from.

With the jungle static murmuring about them, Alex leaned toward the lanky young man and whispered, "Mr. O'Keeffe. What ever is the matter?"

Miata turned his blue eyes to her. They were wide with anxiety. "How can you be askin' that question? Our impendin' doom not a

good enough reason? This jungle be smellin' of death." He studied her face as she observed him intensely.

She tilted her chin up, as though to challenge him. "Oh, truly? That is why you are wringing your hands like a girl wrings water from her finest dress?"

"Be that not reason enough?" he asked, incredulous at her response to him. "I be havin' a strong desire to be keepin' meself alive, Miss Alex." He eyed her. "What of you, Miss Alex? Why be you not concerned with our circumstance, hmm?"

"Oh, I have my misgivings. But tell me," Alex asked between clenched teeth, "why were you not more concerned at hearing Jacq sent Amy away?"

"What?" Miata scowled. "What kind of fool question be that?"

"A sincere one!" Alex returned, huffing. She checked her ankle.

Glaring at her, he curled his lip. "It just happens I be trustin' Jacq to be takin' care of her own, Miss Alex."

"You are not secretly reveling in having the company of one sister without the interference of another?" she questioned in a testy tone.

Leaning close to her, his features clouded in irritation, he countered, "And what sister be that, Miss Alex? You?" He scoffed. "Don't be fancyin' yourself so."

Grinding her teeth, Alex retorted, "You know very well who I mean, Mr. O'Keeffe! Do not mock my intelligence by pretending you do not understand my reference as to who you fancy."

"Jacq and me were ne'er meant to be, if that be what you be suggestin'." He cleared his throat. "She be me closest mate, and I be fine with that. Besides"—he folded his arms—"I've grown mighty fond of our Amy, and I fancy her more every day."

This comment made Alex lift her eyebrows. "Truly?"

"Aye! And I plan to be fancyin' her more and more till the day I pass on. She be the sweetest thing that ever be carin' for me, and I be intent on makin' it worth her while."

Alex's throat constricted, choking her. "Well, it should be no other way. Should a gentleman be so keen on a lady, she should feel herself to be quite lucky, indeed." She dabbed at one eye.

Shifting his weight, he nodded. "Aye. That be the same sentiments I be hopin' Jacq be comin' to realize while she be out with Crevan."

"J—what?" Alex straightened up. Suddenly, she began to understand. "You!"

"Hush, the both of you!" Dante snapped as he rejoined them. "Are you trying to get us apprehended?"

Miata and Alex narrowed their eyes at each other but obliged to Rackham's command.

As the trio went silent, they heard rustling in the distance. The sound of men shouting and arguing, trading off between English and Dutch, was much closer than they were hoping for.

"Gregor! Mogens! This way! *Debiel!* They are headed north... Or east."

"Find them, Barend!" a different voice shouted back. "They can't get too far!"

Alex, Dante, and Miata exchanged nervous glances.

"We lay low," Dante whispered. "We'll move when we have a bit more light to help us find our way, but we'll have to be careful and move slow."

"Agreed," both Alex and Miata replied.

"For once," Alex added in a grumble.

"You've agreed with me afore, lass," Miata retorted.

"Give it a rest," Rackham said in a growl. "Hope and pray Bahari's trail is easy for me to follow, or you two might be stuck together a very long time."

The other two nodded before doing their best to get comfortable for the night.

Meanwhile, at the small stronghold from which they had fled, Amy, after being escorted up from the earthy cells, found herself in a rough but sturdy sort of fort. It was outfitted with quite an assortment of furnishings from varying countries. As she came to an open door, she saw Vice Admiral Luray standing off to one side, straight and stately as ever.

"Father!" she called, running to him and throwing her arms about his waist. "Oh, Father! What is going on?"

"Everything is fine, my darling. Just fine. Our new friend, Sergeant Tuinstra"—he gestured toward a rough-looking man a few years his junior with a thick, bushy beard that fell to his chest—"assures me this was all a grand misunderstanding, which he is going to help rectify immediately."

"Truly?" Amy asked, straightening up and watching the bearded man.

"Aye." Her father eyed the sergeant.

"I told you, sir," Tuinstra said in a heavily Dutch-accented voice, stroking his beard. "This is indeed a misunderstanding. You can be sure we here at van Draenweg don't want the trouble from startin' a war. We would profit very little from it, and it would bring"—he paused, looking over the pretty girl—"unwanted attention our direction."

Vice Admiral Luray cleared his throat and tapped his boot on the floor, wordlessly conveying his disapproval of Tuinstra's glance.

Diverting his eyes, Tuinstra smirked. "Come now, Admiral. No harm, no harm. We all get deprived of delicate company here, always gettin' passed over for Whydah. But a chap can't complain

too much. They let us to it and stay out of it, you know?" He chuckled at the vice admiral's unwavering stare of displeasure.

Moving away from the wall upon which he'd been leaning, the sergeant sat at a moderately elegant desk—easily one of the nicest pieces in the room. "Come now, sir. We needn't be enemies. I've kept my word"—he gestured toward Amy—"and summoned for you one of your lovely daughters. I am not a disagreeable chap, truly. Put it out of your mind that I'd have anythin' to gain that would be worth findin' ill-favor with you, sir."

"Very well. Then let us leave this place. Grant myself and all those I'd arrived with safe passage out of van Draenweg, and we shall never look back or give you a second thought."

"Tch!" Tuinstra chuckled. "Nary a second, eh? Well, while that may seem the most direct resolution, it cannot be done, sir."

A frown etched itself deeply into the vice admiral's face. "And why is that, *sir?*"

As he held his hands up in the air as if to show them empty of tricks, Tuinstra shrugged. "Your ship isn't the lass she used to be."

The vice admiral's brow rose up, and his expression demanded explanation.

"Against my better judgment, I agreed to take on a few *Fransen*—er, Frenchmen, to build my numbers here." He paused, again contemplating the decision. "To say the least, I won't be doin' that again."

At this, despite the tension in the room, Amy had to repress a giggle.

Amy! she scolded herself inwardly.

"The ship, Sergeant," the vice admiral demanded in a remarkable display of disciplined stoic countenance. "Where is my ship?" He spoke each word with defined enunciation.

Bringing his hands down to rest on the top of the desk, Tuinstra sighed. "Those *idioot* French lackeys were sent aboard to have a look around, and"—he paused again, trying to assess the vice admiral's temperament. "Well, the bloody fools... They burned her down, sir."

Vice Admiral Luray's face turned red, and his eyes widened. "What?" He moved to a window, and though he was unable to see the remnants of smoke hanging in the dark evening air, he could smell it. He turned back to Tuinstra. "What?"

"I would assure you they'd be punished, but the daft *idioots* either drowned or burned to death at sea." The sergeant massaged his temples. "This is all quite embarrassing, sir, I assure you."

Scoffing, Vice Admiral Luray returned to his daughter's side. "This was supposed to be an easy thing. We had arrangements made with this Mr. Carloff to give us sanctuary in Cabo Corso. We should still like to travel there and receive some form of recompense for the destruction of our personal property! So, Sergeant, what do you suggest, hmmm?"

As he pointed at the vice admiral, as though to acknowledge him, Tuinstra thought a moment.

"You know, before we entertain any of your schemes, I'd like my other two daughters brought up. If we are not your prisoners, we shouldn't be condemned to your slave holds." Vice Admiral Luray's tone alone would have been convincing, but his height and the gleam in his eyes added in giving flight to any need for persuasion.

"Certainly, sir." Tuinstra nodded. "Barend! Bring up the other two lasses, eh? No need to leave our unfortunate guests locked away." He chuckled.

Another bearded man stepped into the room, nodded, and then vanished from sight.

Then turning back to Vice Admiral Luray, Tuinstra nodded, wearing a reassuring smile. "He'll fetch 'em straight away. Straight away, he will, sir."

As Tuinstra continued with his niceties and attempts to convince Vice Admiral Luray of his good intentions, Barend lumbered down to the yard. "Gregor! Come with me, ya lout!"

"What is it, Barend?" A hefty man pulled himself off the wall he was leaning against and fell in step behind Barend. "What are we out for?"

"Tuinstra wants us to retrieve the frocks for his lordship whose ship those French buffoons sank after it were stupidly attacked at the first." Barend snorted. "Foul luck, to be sure. Now the boss has to fix up the mess." Scoffing, he shook his head as he swung open the door to the holding cells.

The two trudged down to where the girls had been stashed away, grumbling all the while about the trouble caused by the French hirelings.

"*Vloek!*" Gregor exclaimed. "Is that Mogens?"

"Mogens!" Barend yelled, grabbing fistfuls of his shaggy chestnut hair. "Ya fool! What are ya doin' layin' about the holding, eh?" He flung open the door, the noise of which startled awake the unconscious Mogens. "Ya blitherin' fool!" Reaching down, he yanked the disoriented man off the ground.

"Aye! What're ya doin' down thar, Mogens?" Gregor asked, laughing incredulously.

"And the frocks! Where are they, hmm?" Barend's face turned red at this as he glanced about, awaiting a reply.

"I-I… Well, I…" Mogens stammered, trying to get his bearings. "I don't rightly know what happened, sir."

"Don't know what happened," Barend repeated with grand sarcasm, his dark eyes teeming with irritation. "What say ya to that, Gregor? Now, where are the lasses?"

"They-they must've…" He touched his waist. "They made off with me keys, sir."

"Oh, perfect! How utterly perfect of ya, ya lout! Check the other holds, men! Hurry it up! I'm to fetch the frocks up to the fort for the boss! Find them!" Shoving both Gregor and Mogens out the door before him, Barend roared out, "Find them! Find them, or ya'll wish I'd had ya flogged!"

Growling, as Gregor and Mogens dashed away to look for the girls, Barend stomped over to the other cells in which Miata, Murtaugh, Bahari, and Rackham had been stowed, and found them empty.

"Blast it! Blast that bilge rat Mogens! I'll not be flogged on his behalf, no sir!"

Upon finding both cells empty, Barend let out an angry roar. "Engels! Sound the alarm! We're leakin' prisoners faster than the *Anna Clara* sank off the west point! Fife! Where's Fife? What a bleedin' joke! I should've asked for more money."

Up at the fort, Tuinstra and the vice admiral looked at each other when the alarm began to sound. Vice Admiral Luray's already somber expression turned to stone, and all manner of irritation and mistrust began to steam off him. His calm eyes heated up with the flame of indignation. "What is that?"

Choking down a nervous laugh, Tuinstra shook his head, doing his utmost to hide a small panic attack. "Some minor issue, I'm sure, sir. Let me just…" Gesturing to the door, he then grabbed up his hat and hurried out, slamming it shut behind him.

"Wh-what is going on, Father?" Amy asked in a timid voice.

Tightening his arm around her, Vice Admiral Luray shook his head. "I don't know, and I'd rather not raise anxieties by speculating." Noticing her hand gripped tightly around something, he asked, "And what is this?"

Amy opened her hand, revealing the medallion Jacq had been wearing about her neck. "It's Jacq's. From Esperanza. She-she told me to hold it for her."

"Of course." The vice admiral forced a smile, and his eyes moved to the window. He saw the moon appear and then vanish among the cloudy sky. "Of course she did."

Minutes passed as they listened to shouts and hollers from the yard, but by and by, a breathless red-faced Tuinstra returned, his beard looking even wilder than before. Seeing his unhappy guests, he began pacing on the floor, pausing occasionally to look at the vice admiral before pacing again.

Finally, removing his hat and coming to a stop, he cleared his throat and said in a solemn voice, "It appears that my poor excuse of a crew has now managed to lose not only your ship, sir, but your daughters and four additional crewmen as well."

Clenching his fists, Vice Admiral Luray took several deep breaths as he stared down the sergeant with a look that would have made an ordinary grown man cry. "Is that so?"

Sergeant Tuinstra, holding motionless in fear that any movement might result in the loss of his life, replied, "Aye, sir."

"And where have they been lost to?" the vice admiral asked, maintaining a very composed exterior.

"They've run off into the jungle, sir. We think maybe they've gone east, but it could be north."

At this, the vice admiral turned to his remaining daughter. "Amy? Amy, please tell me this was not planned."

Attempting to find a place to tether her gaze other than her father's eyes, the girl shrugged. "I would not say so exactly, sir. It may have been the overhasty scheme of certain persons. However, I believe *planned* might be too severe a word." Her fist tightened on its contents, and she peeked up at him, offering up an innocent smile.

Closing his eyes, he shook his head. "Jacq. They're too used to having to fend for themselves." Sighing, he softened a small measure toward Tuinstra. "Take heart, Sergeant. This was not entirely the ineptitude of your men."

Giving the vice admiral a perplexed and incredulous look, Tuinstra returned, "Surely, sir, you're not suggesting—they are, after all, just lasses."

"In that," Vice Admiral Luray replied, a hint of both pride and exasperation in his voice, "you are egregiously mistaken."

Tilting his head in curiosity but not daring to request an explanation, Tuinstra inquired, "So what would you have me do, sir?"

"Fetch my first mate, Mr. Ellard. Hopefully you've not misplaced him as well."

Tuinstra's eye twitched at the remark. Normally he was content to run a mediocre operation, but this was just down right shameful. Clearing his throat, he nodded. "To what end, sir?"

"You will escort my man to Cabo Corso, where we had originally intended to make port. He will return to England and notify an associate of mine, apprising him of our... predicament." Watching Tuinstra shift his weight, Vice Admiral Luray added, "Off the record, as agreed. He will then sail down to retrieve us from Cabo Corso. We will wait here, under your roof, as your guests, for a fortnight, and then we shall travel to Cabo Corso, under your protection. Once we are safely arrived and we meet up with my contact, Mr. Carloff, you may go about your own business.

If, however, any of my missing crew or daughters should chance to darken your doorstep, I would expect you to feel obliged to bring them on to Cabo Corso as well." Straightening to his full, intimidating height, he held out his hand. "Agreed?"

"Agreed?" Tuinstra repeated, his heart beginning to beat more rhythmically again. "Aye, sir! Aye, sir! O' course, sir! Most generous of you!" He grabbed the vice admiral's hand to shake it heartily as though the vice admiral might change his mind. Relief washed over Tuinstra like high tide.

As soon as their hands were clasped, however, Vice Admiral Luray pulled Tuinstra close, startling him silent.

"Do not cross me, Tuinstra," he said, capturing the Dutchman's gaze. "Hear me. If I so much as sense deception from you, the king himself will be made privy to your actions, and you alone will be responsible for whatever is levied against you by your monarchy to keep the peace between us. Your little overlooked enterprise will be the center of the court's attention, your coffers will be emptied, and you will be utterly ruined. Are we clear?"

"Perfectly, sir," Tuinstra said in a breathless reply. "Believe me, sir, when I say that crossing you is furthest from my mind."

"Good." Vice Admiral Luray gave him back his space and his hand. "Very good. Then fetch me my Mr. Ellard, and we will get underway."

"Right away, sir!" Tuinstra agreed, hurrying out the door.

As soon as he was gone, Amy smiled. "Oh, Papa. I think you gave him a fright."

"You think so?" he asked, flexing his hand. "You don't think it was too much?"

"Not at all," she returned, looping her arm through his. "I think you seemed very commanding, very domineering."

Smiling down at her, he patted her hand. "Good. Very good. Now we just need to hope and pray those sisters of yours don't get

themselves killed. We'll send out searches for them first thing in the morning."

Chapter 2

The following morning found the leading trio of Jacq, Murtaugh, and Bahari sleeping on the low-hanging branches of a tree, several feet off the jungle floor.

Though the early sunlight danced on her eyelids through the leafy roof, it was Bahari's hand on her arm that roused Jacq from her slumber. Yawning and rubbing at the sleepiness lingering in her eyes, she sighed. "Did they find us? Are they here?"

"Miss Alex? No, Shakina. The jungle was filled with *umugo*. They should have hid themselves away and prayed not to be found," Bahari said, patting her arm.

"Of course," Jacq agreed, sitting up and straightening her waistcoat. "I knew that, I was just… hoping." A smile twitched at her lips.

Nodding, Bahari smiled back before turning and ducking into the large-leafed vegetation all about them. Everything was bigger here than in England, like she remembered Martinique Isle. Lush, green, warm, and enormous. Her friend, however, already seemed at home. The blousy shirt he'd been given was tied about his midsection, exposing his dark skin to gleam and glow beneath the sun's rays. A sad sort of gladness filled her heart.

However, the rustling of the leaves from a spot slightly elevated and to her right stopped her reverie.

"Oi, Jacq," Murtaugh's voice, gravelly from sleep, started. "Tell me again why"—he paused as he wriggled down from the branch—"we are in this tree."

Once his feet were firmly on the ground, he looked up at her—his eyes a perfect day's sky blue and his dark hair a wild, handsome mess. He smiled, an expression she wished she could behold every moment of the day, save an occasional gaze out at the sea.

"The, uh, Bahari. Bahari said we might be eaten otherwise." She cleared her throat, hoping it would help her brain functionality improve.

"Right. Eaten." Murtaugh nodded, glancing about them. "So the tree was the obvious preference."

"Mmmm," Jacq agreed, enjoying a moment to observe him without anyone—especially him—to scrutinize her shameless stare.

"Well"—he returned his gaze to her—"let me help you down, lass." He opened his arms for her and gave her an inviting smile of encouragement.

Despite the fact she could have gotten down on her own, Jacq grinned devilishly to herself. "Very well."

Repressing the delight from her expression as she took his hands, she felt confident. She was not, however, prepared for the rush that ran through her when she dropped down to him and his hands slid first up her arms and then down her ribs to her waist. And when she looked up in want of catching her breath, she found it was stolen away at finding his picturesque face mere inches from her own.

He was not unaffected either, finding himself breathless as well in such close proximity to her. Clearing his throat, he managed a sort of smirk. "Very well, indeed." Then using all the willpower he possessed, he released his hold on her body, exhaling a half laugh.

Mirroring his sentiments with a heavily exhaled half laugh of her own, Jacq's nervousness unleashed a set of giggles that was rather more like tittering as she backed away from him, dusting herself off. "Perhaps we can find a better place to rest tonight." She touched at her braided hair to feel for leaves, twigs, or anything to distract her.

"Aye," Murtaugh agreed, flexing his hands to try and dispel his own dose of adrenaline as discreetly as possible. "Perhaps Bahari will have mercy on us."

"You are alive," Bahari's voice intruded upon them as he broke through vegetation to the south, the way they'd come, effectively extinguishing their heated troubles. "We should move now. I have marked the trail for Rackham, as agreed. No one else should take notice."

Clearing his throat and rubbing at the light stubble shading his jaw, Murtaugh nodded. "Where's our mule?"

"I sent him away, as agreed," Bahari answered.

"And you doubled back so no one could follow you?" Murtaugh continued, casting a glance at Jacq.

Having composed herself, she dared look his direction, only to catch his gaze and feel her heart quicken at the sight of him.

Folding his thick arms, Bahari eyed the two younger travelers. "As agreed. What is going on here?"

"Nothing," Murtaugh responded emphatically, rolling his eyes and snorting at the suggestion. "This jungle is just... confusing."

Jacq's brow furrowed. *Nothing? Confusing?* Feeling injured by the enormity of emphasis he put on the question being ludicrous

and utterly ridiculous, she huffed and turned to Bahari. "When do we set out? It is of no use to linger here."

Observing her reaction, Murtaugh felt a pang of regret on his level of insistence as to the nothing. *Surely she must know I was merely diverting.* However, as soon as he had the thought, doubt pushed into his mind as a result of the cold look she gave him.

"We should go," Bahari said. "We have a three-day walk through this forest to reach the village. It would be best we waste as little time as possible. But here. I've brought you breakfast." And with that, he dropped a dead snake in front of them, his smile full of pride. "Oh, and star fruit."

Jacq inhaled sharply as both she and Murtaugh hopped back away from it. "Oh." She forced a smile through her grimace.

Meanwhile, a few miles behind them, Miata stirred in his sleep, snuggling against the warm, soft—

His eyes flipped open to find himself cozied up beside Alex. Pushing away from her with the speed and silence of a cat, he glanced around to find Dante sleeping sitting against a tree. Miata and Alex were propped up on a few logs they had pushed together and covered with some large leaves. They had both started on the edge, but clearly they had scooted to the middle during the night.

Getting up off the makeshift bed, Miata began fidgeting with his waistcoat—a relatively new item just weeks before, now smattered with mud and jungle debris.

"No good, no good," he muttered to himself. "Food. Food and water."

He glanced about, wanting to busy himself. "Eggs. Eggs be nice. Plums. Plumlike, bunches of plumlikes."

He tried recalling what Bahari had told them about while they were on ship. "Yellow flowers. Star-shaped fruit. Nuts inside."

He began visually searching the green canopy, continuously muttering to himself. "Keep all the nuts you find."

Squinting in the light, Dante's eyes opened to see Miata, his face pointed to the sky. Blinking, he scratched at his unshaven jaw. "Miata, mate. Wha-what are you doing?"

"Food!" Miata replied in a voice louder than he intended. Then taking a glance at the still-slumbering girl, he repeated, "Food. I-I be…" He gestured to the trees. "Food."

Giving Miata an incredulous smirk, Rackham tilted his head to one side. "You unwell?"

"No! No, no, no. No, indeed. I be fine. Quite, quite fine, I be assurin' you." Miata grinned, an attempt to be more convincing.

A doubtful expression forming on his face, Dante forced himself up. "If you say so, mate. I must release the mule from the tether." Touching at his purplish eye, he huffed a sigh.

Noticing Rackham pressing at his bruised eye, Miata's mouth picked up at the corner. "Just when it were healin' up nice too."

"I don't know what you all have against me," Rackham returned in frank irritation. "Have I wronged you in some way?"

"Oh, don't be tryin' to be playin' coy with me," Miata said, turning away from his search. "You be knowin' perfectly well."

However, before the conversation could continue, Alex groaned and began to stir. She stretched her slender limbs and yawned. Sitting up, she was displeased to see the sad state of her dress and feel the aches that whispered around both her ankles and head. Frowning at her attire, she let out a long, deep breath of air. Then looking up, she was a little surprised to see both Dante and Miata standing nearby, completely silent.

Glancing between them, she touched at her hair. "Mr. Rackham. Mr. O'Keeffe."

"Miss Alex," they both returned in unison.

"Is everything well?" Gasping internally, her fingers touched a leaf in her hair. "Oh, I must look utterly dreadful!" She moved to cover her face with her hands but stopped upon seeing the dirt that remained from the night before. "Oh!"

"No, no!" both men replied, giving her gentle smiles.

"Rackham were just about to set the mule on his way," Miata spoke up.

Throwing Miata a disgruntled scowl, Dante added, "And O'Keeffe was looking for breakfast."

At this, Miata gave Dante a wide-eyed look, wordlessly demanding to know why Rackham had said such a thing. However, when Alex lifted her gaze to them again, both donned innocent smiles and nodded agreeably.

"Truly?" she asked barely above a whimper. Touching at her heart, she mustered a tremulous smile of her own. "I am grateful for your attempts at making this undeniably abhorrent situation bearable. It is very noble of you."

"Truly?" Miata asked, his voice ringing with disbelief.

Clearing his throat, Dante threw the other man a warning glance. "Miss Alex, we'll find Jacq soon enough. Don't want her wandering around too long with a wastrel such as Crevan." His eyes darkened at the notion.

"What? Mr. Murtaugh?" Scoffing, Alex rose to her feet, dusting herself off. "Mr. Rackham! You are one to talk! Here I am stuck in the forest with both a prior sea pirate and a prior common thief. Wastrels the both of you, if any such blame were to be laid! While Mr. Murtaugh may not have a past of the highest order, he has thus far been the only one of you three not to have sullied my good opinion of himself."

Dante and Miata exchanged deflated glances.

"Now then," she said, straightening her battered skirts, "how shall we proceed, gentlemen?"

"Tell me, Bahari," Jacq requested as she trudged through thick underbrush, "what did you miss the most, besides your family, about this place?"

Bahari, who was up ahead of her, looked over his shoulder and smiled. "The trees."

As if they heard him, the leaves rustled in a light breeze.

"How do you fare?" Bahari asked.

"I worry about Alex, but that is all," Jacq responded. "I'm certain my father will take care of things. We agreed if we ever got separated to meet back at Cabo Corso, so I think that's where we should go once we've secured your family."

"Agreed," the stoic giant returned. "And how is Master Murtaugh?" He glanced past Jacq to glimpse Murtaugh bringing up the back of their tiny caravan.

"No need to call me *master*, Bahari," he called up. "If you wish to, of course, by all means. However, I'd rather consider you a mate where such formalities are unnecessary, and should like to think you feel the same."

"You are known widely as Crevan," Bahari noted. "Perhaps I could start there."

Jacq tossed Murtaugh a grin in appreciation of his friendliness. "I should think we'll all be friends after being together in this place."

"Or something far less amiable," Murtaugh said with a laugh.

Smirking at his audacious remark, Jacq turned back to follow Bahari. "Come now, lads. Things might yet work themselves out

very favorably. All we have to do is find Bahari's family, meet up with the rest of our company, secure our ship, and sail for home."

Bahari chuckled and snorted at the ease and brevity of her outline of events, while Murtaugh laughed aloud heartily. "Only? Is that all? With any luck, we'll be done by sunset tomorrow. You are quite the idealist, Jacq," Murtaugh said.

"I daresay, better to hope for the best than to feel sorry for oneself by constantly recounting all the evils of a particular situation," Jacq retorted, throwing the Irishman a good-natured glare. "Besides, we've you along, don't we? You seem to have a manner of luck about you."

Scoffing, Murtaugh shook his head. "But the nature of the luck is not always as favorable as you seem to believe."

Smiling to herself, Jacq sighed, continuing to trudge after Bahari, who seemed engrossed in his thoughts. *I wonder how much it has changed since he was last here. Perhaps he often visited in his dreams.*

Sadness tugged at her heart, an emotion she did not welcome, but in the silence, she could not shoo it away. For distraction, she asked, "Is it much changed since you were last here?"

Bahari remained silent a moment as he kept moving forward. *Did he hear me?* she wondered.

However, before she could repeat her question, he said in a deep, distant tone, "The forest changes every day, and I have been gone for a lifetime."

Her soul shuddered at his answer. *What do I say to that? How about...? No. I could say... No. Perhaps if I suggest his family...*

She stared at his large form clearing a path for them, marking a trail every so often by ripping leaves in half. *No.*

"My *ọmọkunrin*, my boy, will be a man," Bahari spoke up. "My *iyawo*, my wife, Aladia, has been a widow. Though I have hoped

every day to return to them, they have lived every day abandoned by me."

"You are afraid they will not welcome you home?" Jacq asked, aghast at the notion. Though in a strange way, she could relate. How she had pondered the reasons her parents had given her up for adoption.

"The heart," Bahari spoke again, his voice still shrouded in despair, "is like the forest. Every day it changes. If you are with it, the change is so small you do not notice. But if you are away for too long, when you return, you no longer know it."

Jacq and Murtaugh traded somber, doleful glances.

"Not to worry, mate," he said to her. "We'll find his kin, and when we do, all they'll want to know is why it took him so long to find his way home."

A ragged, tearful exhale escaped Jacq's lungs. "Who's the idealist now, mate?" She smiled through her sadness. "I hope you're right, though. I truly do."

For three days they pushed on, nobody feeling especially lighthearted or talkative, save for some friendly chatter between Jacq and Murtaugh. Then on the afternoon of the third day, they came upon a clearing surrounded by mud huts and hovels.

Scanning the dwellings, Bahari muttered to himself and asked in a low tone, "What is this place?"

As they approached the fire pit in the center, the embers still smoldering in its depths, Jacq noted, "Well, that is strange. No one is to be found?"

"Oh, I wouldn't say that, mate," Murtaugh returned, watching less-than-happy-looking indigenous persons materialize from out of the surrounding trees.

Holding up his hands, Bahari began addressing the locals in their native tongue—words he probably had not spoken aloud in seven years. Jacq watched, her emotions bouncing back and forth

between fear and excitement. Even after he had finished speaking, he remained with his hands in the air as the villagers assessed him in silence.

After perhaps a minute had passed, an elderly man came forward, a carved wooden mask, painted and adorned with beads, mounted atop his head. The mask had long dried grasses attached to the back, so they flowed about his head like golden hair. Poking at Bahari, he asked a few questions in the native language, to which Bahari answered in short, stoic statements.

I wish I had stood closer to Michael, Jacq thought, feeling increasingly less comfortable the longer she stood there, wondering what was being said.

At her thought, she felt something brush against her arm. Turning, she was surprised to see Murtaugh just a few inches away from her, constantly watching the locals.

He dared move? she asked internally, wanting to rebuff him and hug him simultaneously.

Casting a glance toward her, he offered a reassuring smile.

Finally, the older man put one hand over his heart and one hand over Bahari's. Bahari clasped both his hands over the one the old man put to his chest, and the man yelled, "Bahari! *O si ti pada!*"

The two hugged, and then began to move away together when one of the younger men came forward from the trees.

Pointing at Jacq, he yelled, "*Mo beere yi ọkan! Mo beere yi ọkan! Mo beere yi ọkan!*"

At this, the old man began shouting back at him and Bahari shook his head, saying, "*Shakina ni pẹlu mi.*"

Watching it all unfold, Jacq's heart quickened, and she felt a little light-headed. "What's going on?" she asked Murtaugh in a strained tone.

"I don't know. If they were speaking Dutch or Irish I could understand, but not this, Jacq." He glanced down at her, surprised

to see her shrinking away from the heated conversation. However, before he could ask her about it, Bahari was turning back to them.

"Wha-what's going on?" she asked.

"The old man is the *alàgbà*—the elder of this village. It would seem the younger man, Jokotade, wants you for his wife," Bahari answered in a dull voice.

Both Jacq and Murtaugh stood in astonished silence a moment before bursting into laughter. Slapping at their knees and clapping their hands, they felt a surge of relief at the ridiculousness and the absurdity of such a blatant statement.

Gasping for air and dabbing at tears welling in her eyes, Jacq shook her head. "My apologies! I thought it was something horrifying. Please inform Mr. Jokotade that I am uninterested at this time."

Looking over at him, she smiled and shook her head, still composing herself after her fit of giggles.

"For an outsider to turn down a Yoruba man's request of marriage, you must defeat him," Bahari explained with a solemn expression.

"Wha—?" Jacq and Murtaugh peeked around Bahari's massive frame at the tall, muscled young man now standing with his arms crossed.

"I can't fight him," she said in an anxious tone. "What a hideous rule!"

"It is because you have no standing with the tribe," Bahari informed her.

Murtaugh began chuckling to himself.

Glowering at her Irish friend, Jacq turned back to Bahari. "Can-can you? Can you fight him on my behalf?"

"I could, if I were not married myself."

"Ah!" Gasping, Jacq begged with her eyes. "Are you certain?"

He nodded, his expression never changing.

"Sorry chap has no idea what he's asking for," Murtaugh said with a repressed chuckle.

"It is not laughable," Jacq retorted, fidgeting.

Chuckling more, Murtaugh shook his head. "It is a fine joke, Jacq. This bloke wants you for his wife, but you wouldn't be any good for him. And now they want you to find some fool chap to fight him on your behalf because he can't take no for an answer."

Suddenly feeling utterly humorless, Jacq turned to him and snapped, "Laugh all you like, *Crevan*, but the joke is on you. It falls on *you* to save me."

Hearing her use his pseudonym rather than his real name, the mirth fell from his demeanor. "A-are you serious?"

Bahari nodded. "They will not tell me of my family until the matter is settled."

Clicking his tongue, Murtaugh crossed his arms. "I'll stand up for you, but I won't fight until you ask me nicely." At his statement, he saw Jacq's eyes spark.

That's my girl, he thought with an impish smirk.

"Don't be ridiculous!" Jacq returned. "You're just going to stand there and let him hit you?"

Scoffing, Murtaugh looked insulted. "What kind of daft fool do you take me for?" Then pushing past her, he nodded at the man, still awaiting a response.

Pulling his shirt over his head, Jokotade slapped his chest with both hands and roared. All the surrounding villagers whooped and cheered for him. Somewhere, a few of the tribesmen got out drums and started pounding out a rhythm for them.

Taking in his surroundings, Murtaugh followed suit, casting off his shirt and slapping his chest in reply.

As soon as his shirt came off, Jacq diverted her eyes, her brain swooning at his athletic, sculpted musculature wrapped in tight lightly tanned skin. Try as she might, though, her eyes wandered

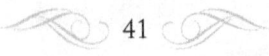

back to this handsome Irishman, fighting for her in the jungle forest of Africa. He looked lean and wild as he and Jokotade circled each other, the latter taking swipes at the former.

She was snapped out of her ogling, however, when she realized he wasn't actually landing any punches. She watched in confusion as he ducked and danced circles around Jokotade, making the crowd shout and roar all the more.

"What are you doing?" she yelled. "You're supposed to be fighting with him, not dancing with him!"

Grinning over at her, his dark hair falling rakishly across his forehead, he called back, "And you're supposed to ask me nicely! Is it really such a difficult task?"

As Murtaugh saw Jacq narrow her eyes at him, he thought back to a conversation he'd had with Miata.

Nine months earlier...

"Ye know," Miata said with a chuckle, "when most lasses be gettin' upset, ye be havin' to be worryin' about plates flyin' at ye, or bad cookin'."

Murtaugh looked across the table at him. "You need to find a better lass, mate." Laughing, he took a drink from the mug in his hand.

"Now, just be imaginin' what a lass the likes o' Jacq be doin', hmmm?" Shuddering, he reached for his own pint at the table.

Shaking his head, Murtaugh leaned forward, resting his forearms against the edge of the table. "You know what Jacq is, mate?" He set down his cup and began running his finger around the edge of it. "She's a selkie—well, *my* selkie, the bane of my existence."

Miata leaned forward too. "Sorry, a what?"

"A selkie. A faery woman of Irish lore. She's said to have a love by which no mortal woman can compare but who will always return to the sea, unless her husband steals and hides her seal skin." Pushing away his mug, Murtaugh interlaced his fingers. "I won't capture her, mate. She must choose to stay, but she never will."

"I wouldn't be so sure, mate," Miata said, examining his friend's downcast countenance. "But I be warnin' ye, don't be seemin' indifferent. Jacq be puttin' on airs o' toughness, but inside, I be thinkin' she be just as uncertain sometimes as the rest o' us mortal folk." He grinned.

Huffing out a laugh, Murtaugh shrugged and rose from the table. "If only I were a blackbird."

Standing with him, Miata tilted his head. "What?"

"Forget it," Murtaugh replied. "Come on."

"Watch out!" Jacq's voice interrupted Murtaugh's thoughts.

Murtaugh pivoted just in time for his face to connect with Jokotade's fist, knocking him back. Staggering backward and touching at his mouth and finding blood, he looked up to discover a crowd cheering, save for Jacq, Bahari, and the old man.

"So, you can land a blow after all," he muttered, spitting on the ground. "I bet you can't do that again!"

"Would you just hit him, please?" Jacq shouted.

"Well, that was very nice, but you have to use my real name," Murtaugh answered.

"What?" An incredulous laugh escaped her. "Why?"

"Because then I'll know you're not still vexed at me!" He threw her a lopsided blood-tinted grin that was still somehow completely charming.

However, before Jacq could respond, Jokotade came running across the open area, tackling Murtaugh to the ground.

Plucking half a leaf off a bush, Dante paused and twirled it in his fingers. "We are fortunate Bahari is excellent at leaving this trail."

Turning around, he found Alex and Miata sitting together on a log.

"We can't be too far behind them," Dante continued. "This leaf is still wet from being torn."

"I do not understand why those men have been so diligent in trying to seek us out," Alex said, rubbing at her ankle. "None of this was supposed to happen. No one was to get separated, or kidnapped, or-or left behind!" Taking a deep breath, she regained her composure. "What if we left Amy and our father in distress, in need of aid and rescue? All the while, we are out here trudging through"—she glanced about them, her expression twisting in disgust—"this savage wilderness."

"You be likin' walkin' the ground o' yer father's estate," Miata said. "Be this so much worse?"

Frowning at him with a mien of disbelief, Alex replied, "At my father's estate there is no worry of snakes falling onto one's head, or spiders the size of one's hand, or the need to consider eating"— she paused, gagging—"grub worms." She covered her mouth with her fingers, willing her stomach not to shame her by purging itself.

Gulping down a bubble of anxiety, Miata nodded. "She be right, Rackham. They be findin' us afore we be findin' our crew!"

Rolling his eyes, Dante shook the partial leaf at them. "What did I just say? We are close behind. If we can continue evading these pursuers of ours, I should think we could catch them by tomorrow's end."

"At least Jacq is with people who actually care about her," Alex said with a bite in her inflection.

"Miss Alex," Miata responded, "be not worryin' about that. Rackham and me won't be lettin' harm be comin' to ye."

Alex looked at him wearing a guarded, distrusting expression. "Truly?"

Nodding, he added, "Aye. 'Twould be upsettin' Jacq."

A furious rage burned in her eyes. "And to think, Mr. O'Keeffe, that I had considered counting you amongst my friends..." She lifted her chin to better glower at him. "What a fool I would have proved to be."

"I ne'er be doin' anythin' to ye but offerin' kindness," Miata retorted, suddenly feeling affronted by her attitude. "To be suggestin' otherwise 'twould be lyin' and downright unchristian."

"Oh, and who are you to judge a person on the points of honesty, integrity, and good Christian behavior?" Alex asked of him, an infuriated tone coating every syllable she spoke.

"You and me be gettin' on just fine until your blessed Mr. Monroe be takin' his leave o' ye," he said back to her in just as heated a tone, an equal feeling of justification behind every word exiting his mouth.

At this, Alex choked up. Touching at her chest and throat as though they might burst, she gasped several ragged breaths, barely holding herself together. With tears threatening to pour down her face, she stood and looked at a stunned Miata. "You, sir, know nothing of what you speak." Then with the composure of a queen, she walked away, disappearing behind some trees.

Once out of sight, Alex crumpled to the ground and pulled her knees to her chest. Wrapping her arms about her legs, she dropped her forehead to her knees and sobbed.

Dante, who'd been watching the whole thing unfold in perplexed silence, ran his fingers through his hair. "Miata, what-what-what just happened?"

Turning a bewildered expression Rackham's direction, Miata shrugged. "I don't rightly be knowin'. If I be sayin' I did, 'twould surely be a lie."

Glancing about them and sending a scowl skyward, Dante sighed. "We'll give her a moment, but then we must be off again, else we'll never catch them." He started to take a seat but then rose and began pacing back and forth.

Observing Dante's movements, Miata's eyebrow lifted in intrigue. "And what be you worryin' about so much?"

His mouth forming a firm line, Rackham lifted a shoulder in an effort to seem indifferent. "I don't like the thought of Jacq alone out here with only Crevan and Bahari as her companions. I know she trusts Bahari, and for understandable reason. However, I question her generosity to the Irishman."

"No doubt he be havin' the same to be sayin' about you," Miata retorted, folding his arms.

Rackham touched at his eye. "He's a might unstable, if you were to ask me."

Miata chuckled. "The lad's Irish! He be always up for a brawl, but I be sure he be takin' care o' Jacq and keepin' her safe."

"Oh!" Jacq gasped. She grimaced as Jokotade straddled Murtaugh on the ground and began beating on him, the Irishman holding his forearms over his face as a shield.

"Stop hitting him in the face!" she yelled.

Then as she watched in horror, Murtaugh escaped Jokotade, lumbering off to one side, blood dripping from his lip, and a gash now forming on his right cheekbone. He was smeared with dirt and sweat and blood, and his breathing appeared labored as he lifted those perfect blue eyes to stare at her.

Grinding her teeth, she jabbed her finger at him. "If you want to see me vexed—truly vexed—you will lose this fight, Michael Murtaugh, and I shall never speak to you again!"

As soon as she said his name, a roguish smirk picked up the corner of his mouth. Straightening, he spat out the excess fluid and turned back to Jokotade. "Ah! She fancies me, after all."

Jokotade ran to Murtaugh, but this time, the Irishman caught the man's swing. Shaking his head, he said, "Sorry, mate." Then he pushed Jokotade back and laid into him—all fists, elbows, and knees. In truth, putting off attacking Jokotade had allowed Murtaugh to learn about the larger man's fighting style and had exhausted him somewhat—both to Murtaugh's advantage.

After exchanging a number of swings for a few minutes and having a series of well-aimed hits, Murtaugh took a running start, jumped high in the air by pushing off a tree, and landed a solid blow right across Jokotade's jaw. The bulkier man took two dazed steps forward and then toppled to the ground. As he hit, displeased shouts sprang from the audience.

Exhaling, Jacq squealed in relief and pride. Rushing up to Murtaugh, who was doubled over and trying to regulate his breathing while keeping an eye on Jokotade, she threw her arms around him. "I can't believe you!"

Sputtering a noise that was a mixture of coughing and chuckling, he asked, "What do you mean?"

"Letting him beat on you just because you thought I was cross with you! It was reckless and daft, and-and what if you had lost?

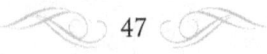

Ugh! Sometimes I loathe you, Michael Murtaugh!" Suddenly, she felt a rush of adrenaline as she contemplated the possible fallout of him actually losing the spar.

Straightening, Murtaugh pushed his hair out of his eyes and grinned down at her—fierce and fresh, no longer timid and shrinking. "No. No, you don't."

Narrowing her eyes at him, she reached up to shove at his shoulder. "I should! I should kill you myself!"

Catching her wrist in his hand, he examined her face, basking in the energy of her renewed spirits. "I would love to see you have a go at me."

Jacq's breath caught in her throat. Somehow, with that southern Irish accent, he made the brashest statements sound charming. Her face flushed at the rush she felt just looking at him and hearing his voice. His touch, his invasive stare into her soul, and the way he gave her that impish, confident grin as he spoke— he was enough to drive a girl mad.

However, the moment was broken by the elder pointing at them and shouting more things they could not understand. To this, though, the villagers seemed more receptive, cheering and smiling at them as two people came out and grabbed Jokotade off the ground. The pair of outsiders sent Bahari quizzical glances.

"Crevan has won the right to call Shakina his wife," he explained. "He insists you take the *igbeyawo* for the night." At seeing their still unclear expressions, he continued, "It is the celebratory hut for anniversaries, guests of honor, and"—he paused, smirking—"the newly wedded." With this, he motioned to a small dwelling across from them.

"But I didn't marry her, I won her," Murtaugh argued.

Jacq elbowed him, causing him to grunt in discomfort.

Bahari shrugged. "Interpretation. He also has proclaimed you *ikan jagunjagun*—a great warrior. They welcome our presence and

will now tell me of my family." Bahari gave Murtaugh a reverent nod. "I thank you."

Nodding back, Murtaugh shrugged. "My honor, mate."

Turning back to Jacq, Bahari motioned to the Irishman. "Perhaps you should tend to the wounds of your champion. I will speak with the *alàgbà* and tell you of what he says."

Jacq nodded. "Aye, that I can do." She glanced over at Murtaugh, assessing his condition. "Can you see that I be brought water and linens for his wounds?"

"Of course, Shakina," Bahari agreed, following her gaze to the injured Irishman before moving to leave.

"And, Bahari?"

"Shakina?" He stopped and rotated back to face her.

"Good luck." Then turning to Murtaugh, Jacq said, "Come along, *jagunjagun*."

"*Ìkan jagunjagun*," he corrected.

Bahari watched in minor amusement as Murtaugh limped along beside Jacq until she convinced him to allow her to help him walk. "Perhaps young Mr. O'Keeffe was correct." Then pivoting back to the old man, Bahari began asking him questions in the native dialogue.

Later that afternoon, when the sun was edging toward the horizon, casting an orange glow about the region, Miata sat himself down beside Alex as she sat alone on a log. He observed her in silence a moment, taking in the pink hue of her nose, the puffiness and redness about her eyes. He noticed her hands trembling and fidgeting in her lap and her deliberate effort to avoid eye contact.

Taking in a long, slow draw of air, he said in a gentle tone, "Miss Alex, I-I... I be feelin' a mite horrible for makin' ye so profoundly distressed. I-in truth, I be fool enough to not even be knowin' what it were I be sayin' to-to have such an effect on ye." He reached out to pat her hands but decided against it and retracted his. "I be sorry, Miss Alex. I-I do be carin' about yer life, honest." He remained a few seconds more in silence, then moved to stand.

"It is not entirely your fault," Alex spoke in a quiet tone. "Everything is so complicated. I thought I had found something simple, something pure, but I was mistaken. Nothing like that exists, not in this world." She finally lifted her eyes to him, revealing a red-gray glazed gaze—stained from an afternoon of secret tears.

"That be not true," he said, sitting back down. "I be thinkin' most things be not too complicated till we be makin' 'em so."

Her weary expression morphed into a scowl.

"Be thinkin' on this, mate. Even though we be not havin' the best o' relations and ye be likin' to be scoldin' me more than I be carin' to hear it, I still be thinkin' o' ye as a mate." He paused, considering his statement. "A mate o' sorts. Yer father, after so long thinkin' yer lost for good, be so glad to be havin' ye both back. The way ye be carin' for that confound monkey o' yers. All these be simple if ye be lookin' at the heart o' the thing." He smiled over at her. "Maybe they be not always makin' sense, but they be remainin' just the same."

"You consider me a friend?" she asked, her pitch heightening.

"Aye. Though ye be the poshest, most condescendin' person I e'er called as such." Miata grinned. "Probably best not to be tellin' folks, though. Might sully yer reputation, and mine."

Clasping his hand, and surprising him in doing so, she shook her head. "You are likely right, Mr. O'Keeffe. My being considered

to be on any sort of intimate relations with you of my own accord would certainly be a to-do in my social circles, but I thank you."

"I think we've lost the Dutchmen," Dante said, ambling up to them from beyond the trees. Out of the corner of his eye, he saw them pull their hands away from each other and hide them behind themselves. "Let us get some rest so we can catch up tomorrow, shall we?"

The other two nodded in agreement and moved nonchalantly away from each other.

"I just hope Jacq is safe," Alex commented.

"What danger could she be in that she, Crevan, or Bahari could be not savin' her from?" Miata returned.

Meanwhile, back at the village, Jacq was alternating dipping a wadded cloth into a bowl of water and cleaning off Murtaugh's chest, back, arms, and face. As she ran the cloth over his skin—exposing every scratch, gouge, scrape, and scar—she felt her heart pounding, her chest tight, and her fingers trembling.

Breathe, Jacq. Breathe! Don't linger! Stop staring into his eyes! She paused as they silently gazed at one another. *Stop…! Talk to him! Save yourself, and speak!*

As she helped clean and bandage him up, Murtaugh took care to focus on maintaining his breathing as he watched her. In the soft glow of the evening, her golden hair glinting like fire in the ruddy sunlight, all he could do was gawk at her. Her gentleness and careful approach served only to magnify the beauty he saw of her, both within and without.

"You must be exhausted," she noted in a hushed tone.

"Actually, I feel rather well." He grinned.

"Is that so?" she asked, smirking. She poked at the gash on his cheekbone.

"Ow! Well, save for when you do that!" He swatted at her hand, which she playfully retracted and returned to work. "To be sincere, it was good fun. Jokotade put up a good fight, but I've had worse when I was training with my uncle and when I was working with MacCarrick on my way to Fishguard."

"Truly?" Jacq mused over this. "Well, I thank you again, Murtaugh. To think you've saved me twice now..."

His expression remaining drawn in happiness, he nodded. "And I would do it again, Jackie." His eyes left no doubt to his sincerity.

"Jackie?" she asked with a giggle.

"Shakina," Bahari interrupted them, entering abruptly and causing both of them to start.

Clearing her throat, she stopped her task. "Bahari. You have word?" she asked, seeming indifferent to his arrival.

"I do. And clothes." Bahari paused in what seemed to be painful hesitation as he set their new attire down. "It would seem my village no longer exists. My people moved to be closer to Edo so the *oba* would keep them safe from the *erú alagidi*. This place is a hunting village and will only be occupied for the summer. Once *Ògún* comes, in two months' time, they will move on." His voice was grim.

"So your family went to this Edo?" Jacq asked, trying to determine if this was good or bad.

"It would have been best if they went to Edo or Oyo, but my eldest son, Kukoyi, does not trust Oba Etoade, Oba Ajagbo, or the *oloyes*. Because of this, they have formed a caravan and traveled north, further inland, to try and make a new home for themselves." Shaking his head, Bahari's blue eyes epitomized sorrow and angst.

"W-what does that mean?" Jacq asked, her brow furrowing in want of understanding.

"They have gone to Tenkodogo, about a seven-day journey without delay. I must set off tomorrow and hope they did not change course. They set out months ago, afore the rainy season, which is now upon us." Frowning, he shrugged. "I have come this far, thanks to you, and I will not give up now, but I can no longer accept your help."

"We told you we would help you find your kin," Murtaugh spoke up. "If Jacq wants to give further aid, I'll not stand by." He glanced between them. "Just wanted to make that clear."

"Wait for Alex and the others to arrive," Jacq requested. "Let me speak with my sister before I make a decision."

Taking a contemplative inhale, Bahari nodded. "I shall delay one day, but no longer."

"Very well," Jacq agreed. "Tomorrow we shall decide."

Sitting near a window, Amy searched the darkening horizon, running her thumbs over the engraved disc in her hands. "Where are you?" she asked in a whisper. "Why did you have to run away?" Leaning against the wall, she let out a heavy, pensive exhale. "Why did you run away?"

The sound of creaking on the floor grabbed her attention, and she spun about to see the vice admiral approaching her, followed by Tuinstra.

"What do you mean you lost them?" Vice Admiral Luray asked in a gruff voice. "Don't your men know the area? Are they *all* French?"

"Sir, the man with them—Bahari, you called him—he must know these lands. They have probably gone to Edo, sir, the vastest

empire of the region. Either that or Oyo—it is also a vast empire in this vicinage." Tuinstra shrugged. "I think, sir, they're hiding from us. Do not think my men are not looking hard enough. I have made an example of Mr. Barend for all his poor judgement and incompetency surrounding this unfortunate affair, but I cannot keep demoting or dismissing my men. I will have no one left!"

Rubbing the back of his neck, Vice Admiral Luray hung his head. "Aye, I've heard of this Edo and this Oyo." Crossing his arms, he turned his kind eyes to Amy. "If they don't want to be found, I don't see how we'd find them. The region is too infinite, too unexplored, and the indigenous population is too wary of outsiders."

"I could send out scouts, sir," Tuinstra offered. "I can send out men to check in at different locations to see if they've been seen or heard of. You can send your man to England, as agreed, and we'll wait a few days for my scouts to return with any word before escortin' you to Cabo Corso."

Nodding, Vice Admiral Luray consented. "That is the first good idea you've had, Tuinstra. Send them out. We'll get Mr. Ellard on his way and pray he has fair winds and following seas." At this, his gaze turned to stone. "If we suffer losses, it shall be on *your* head."

"Then we best pray there are no losses, sir," Tuinstra replied with a nervous chuckle. "I rather like my head where it is."

Chapter 3

After spending the day helping out around the camp—fishing, weaving, helping in the repair of a hut, and collecting water—Jacq and Murtaugh were sitting near the low-burning fire. The sun was crawling toward the western horizon, sending beams of light through the foliage to bid them farewell. Bahari and the elder were submerged in conversation, contributing to the sense of isolation in this unknown location felt by the two near the fire.

Drawing designs into the dirt with a stick as Murtaugh watched in tranquil silence, Jacq asked, "So, you would travel to Tenkodogo with Bahari?"

Shrugging, he answered, "For you, to help him find his kin? I see no reason why not."

"To help him find his kin?" she repeated, continuing to draw.

"For you," he corrected, maintaining his observation of her handiwork.

"You keep saying that," she said, running the stick over her art, erasing it to begin anew.

"It's true. You and Miata are my mates, not your sisters, not Bahari, and"—he chuckled—"certainly not Skippy." At this, he sat back.

Laughing, she shook her head. "I thought you two got on well enough? What's happened?"

"Maybe you should ask him," Murtaugh replied.

"Oh, very funny," she said in return. "As though he were here to inquire upon the matter."

"Actually, I was being rather serious," he said with a smug inflection.

"What?" Straightening, she turned to find his view.

"Jacq?" Alex's voice pierced the sky as the weary girl emerged hobbling from the forest.

"Alex!" Jacq jumped up and vaulted over the log bench, racing to catch her sister up in her arms.

"You're alive!" they both exclaimed between emotional laughs.

"Of course I am!" they both replied with a vaguely injured tone.

Murtaugh wasn't far behind her, shaking hands with Rackham and clapping Miata on the back. "Took you blokes long enough. This country not agree with you?"

"It was fine," Rackham assured him, his displeasure at seeing the Irishman thinly veiled behind politeness.

"What be happenin' to you, mate?" Miata asked, examining the damage to his face—the cut on his cheekbone, his split lip, and the purple hue around his eye.

"Nothing worth the hearing," he said, glancing at the girls as they chatted away.

Both men looked doubtful.

"Right," Miata said, lifting an eyebrow.

"As you wish," Rackham added, happy to oblige dismissing any derring-do on Murtaugh's part.

"You should see the other lad," Murtaugh said, giving them both an insinuating grin and a bob of his head.

"You have arrived," Bahari greeted, coming up behind them and giving Miata and Dante each a nod. "I have assured the *alàgbà* you are with us and have brought no trouble with you."

"It was lucky for us you left a good trail to follow," Rackham commented, crossing his arms.

"I'm sure you needed every portion of help afforded to you," Murtaugh said with a stifled chuckle.

Throwing Murtaugh an angry glance, Dante cleared his throat and added, "*We* were followed every day, save this one. The louts at that port really want us back."

"I'm sure it's the girls they want, not us," Murtaugh returned. "They'd probably fetch a handsome price."

"Miss Alex be wantin' to be returnin' as soon as possible for their sister and father," Miata said, pushing between the other two young men.

"That is a shame," Bahari said in a dreary tone. "We have learned that my family has left this place and journeyed north instead of to Edo." He shook his head. "I leave tomorrow to find them."

"A-and what of us? What of Jacq?" Miata asked, voicing the questions on everyone's minds.

"She requested me to wait until tomorrow in hope you would arrive today for these matters to be discussed. No doubt we shall do this after we eat." Giving them a respectful bow of his head, Bahari turned and moved off.

As he left, the sisters joined the three men arm in arm.

"So..." Jacq began gleefully.

All three pivoted to face her, wearing expressions in varying degrees of displeasure.

"Oh, he's told you, has he?" Jacq asked, assuming as much from their cheerless countenances.

Her happy expression wilting, Alex touched at her hair. "Told you what?"

Jacq looked at her, her mouth dipping down at the corner. "I very much doubt you shall be pleased."

Exhaling, she glanced at Miata and Dante. "I am becoming accustomed to expecting as much."

"Dante, mate, I be feelin' a might in need o' a drink," Miata said, disliking the look from Alex.

"Aye," Dante agreed, scowling. "A mighty long one."

Just as they started moving away, Jokotade appeared from behind some of the huts. He stopped at seeing Dante and Miata, but when he noticed Alex with Jacq, he paused to examine them. Noticing his lingering gaze, Murtaugh crossed over to him, catching Rackham's eye. "No, mate. You don't want to bother with her." Pointing at Dante, he added, "She is with that man. He is a warrior—a, uh, *jagunjagun*, even mightier than me." Murtaugh patted himself on the chest. "*Ìkan jagunjagun*."

Heaving a sigh and shaking his head, Jokotade sauntered off, muttering to himself as Rackham stormed up to Murtaugh. "What was that about, mate? Hmm?"

"Relax, Skippy," Murtaugh retorted. "Poor bloke thought you were a lass. I was just settin' him straight." He swayed and smiled, every detail of his deportment inviting Rackham to take a swing at him.

"How did you come by that black eye, huh?" the Englishman asked in a low, snide tone.

"I just wanted one to match yours, mate. Everything's about you, isn't it?" He huffed a sardonic laugh.

"You should stay out of the business of others, *mate*. Stay out of where you're not wanted," Rackham said in a growl, taking a step closer to Murtaugh.

The Irishman's mouth coiled in impish delight. "I do mind my own, *mate*. But my business includes *her* and anything that could hurt her—any*thing* or any*one*."

"Being a self-appointed guardian doesn't suit you, Irishman. You're a deserter. That's your history." Rackham sneered at him.

Insulted but uninhibited, Murtaugh returned, "And you… a pirate. Naught but a common thief with a boat and a sail. You have no claim to her *or* her affairs. You have just as little right to meddle as I have, probably less now."

The two leered at each other, threats and curses being exchanged wordlessly between them. However, before matters could escalate, Bahari stepped in and commented, "My people believe twins to be magical—a sign of good fortune. This will increase our favor with them." Smirking, he gestured to the girls and added, "It was good of you to tell Jokotade the second twin was also yours."

"Also?" Rackham repeated, his face scrunching up in confusion.

"Th-that's not what I said," Murtaugh replied, his smugness being immediately replaced with concern. "I did not say that, Bahari."

Rackham continued to look perplexed. "What?"

"It is better this way," Bahari returned, patting the Irishman on the back. "Because you have already defeated Jokotade, he shall not challenge you again." Then turning to the befuddled Englishman, he said, "Now, let us get you some water."

As they walked away, Murtaugh felt a wave of satisfaction pour over his soul. "Doesn't suit me. Ha! Not much is sweeter than

affirmation one is not seeking," he muttered to himself, touching at the wounds on his face.

"What was that about?" Jacq asked as she and Alex came to stand beside him.

Shrugging, Murtaugh tried to think of the easiest explanation. "Jokotade," he answered, immediately wondering if it would satisfy Jacq's curiosity.

"Jokotade?" Alex repeated. "What is a Jokotade?"

"Ugh! Not a what, a who," Jacq corrected, folding her arms. "Murtaugh had to… convince him"—she gestured at his eye—"I could not marry him."

"You were here ten minutes and got a suitor?" Alex scoffed. "If only you had been so charming while we were still in Swansea."

"Oh, Alex, you know very well that is highly doubtful," Jacq argued.

"Truly, I think not! You could easily have many eligible suitors if only you would heed societal protocols!" Huffing, Alex dusted at her skirts. The very thought of home reminded her she was abominably filthy.

"Are you speaking of that dress again?"

"I selected that dress very precisely for you, Jacq."

Rolling her eyes, Jacq let her hands drop to her sides. "I told you, Alex, that dress was…" She paused, searching for words. "Well, it wasn't *me*. It showed parts of me to the world that I don't even see of me save for when I chance to have a bath!"

At this, Murtaugh repressed an enormous smile that would have enveloped his entire face, advertising to the world exactly what he was thinking. He averted his eyes from the girls to his boots, hoping to diminish his imagination.

"The point is to look your most stunning, sister," Alex said. "To show off a bit."

Scoffing, Jacq held her sister's hand. "For what reason? So the self-proclaimed gentlemen can gawk at me from afar?"

Exhaling sharply in frustration, Alex pulled her hand away and thrust both fists down onto her hips. "The point is to be admired, and then they approach you to see if there is further interest."

Jacq's eyebrows came together. "Like a horse?"

"A what?" Alex covered her heart with her hand.

"Like a horse. They observe you from a distance, and if they see something they like, they come over to check your teeth, make certain they want to put their money on you."

Glowering at her sister's impertinence, Alex shook her head. "Why do I keep trying? For my own punishment?"

Shrugging, Jacq sighed. "I truly couldn't say."

"Surely you know it is out of love!"

Narrowing her eyes as if trying to ascertain the truth by visual inspection, Jacq returned, "Are you so certain?"

"Ugh!" Clenching her teeth together, Alex stomped over and took a seat near the fire.

As soon as she walked away, Murtaugh nudged Jacq with his elbow. "I like your teeth just fine."

Smirking to herself, Jacq kept her gaze fixed on Alex. "Thank you." Still, despite her sarcasm and sauciness, Jacq sighed inside—a deep, heavy sigh. *If I had your perfection, sister, your fineness, perhaps then I could manage to capture a man's love. But I am all rogue and roughness with no mind for etiquette and the tiresome way members of proper society play games with one another. I've enough trouble trying to understand the people I actually know without pretending to belong with folk whom I quite obviously do not.*

Dragging her gaze up to Murtaugh, she gestured toward the fire. "Come along. We best not leave her to herself."

A short while later, upon discovering they were hosting twins, the hunting village demonstrated their eagerness to help them—feeding them, clothing them. In fact, it seemed there was little they would not do to assist them. Of course, they believed their generosity would be rewarded by good fortune, but the group wasn't going to squabble on semantics. So after a strong meal, they sat around the warm, fragrant fire, discussing their plight as they watched the orange flames flicker and reach for the stars.

"No!" Alex objected. "No! No! This is insanity, Jacq! Insanity!"

"I agree with Miss Alex," Dante spoke up. "If I let you wander off into the wilderness with Bahari and no one to protect you properly, your father will have my head!"

"I say let him have it," Murtaugh said in a voice just loud enough for Rackham to hear, earning himself a glare. "Protect her properly," he repeated in an inaudible grumble, glowering at the insinuation he was incapable of doing so.

"*Let* me?" Jacq laughed at the very idea of Dante Rackham telling her what to do. "I thank you, but I do not need your permission, Mr. Rackham! I've a mind of my own, and it likes to be exercised."

"Be that the truth if ever there was," Miata commented.

"And what of Father and Amy, Jacq?" Alex asked. "Should we not ensure their safety? Is that not our duty and our right?" Frowning, she shook her head. "I will *not* lose our family now when we have only just found them!"

Pushing to her feet and pacing about the fire, Jacq massaged her temples, trying to keep her brain from exploding as everyone continued exchanging their thoughts. "Why must you all have valid points of view?" she questioned, her voice strained with the agony of attempting to evaluate and weigh the options everyone was bringing to light.

However, as they continued to bicker amongst themselves, Jacq found herself unable to focus, like trying to observe the movement of a single blade of grass in a meadow on a breezy day.

"If we continue in this way, we shall never come to a conclusion!" she declared in an elevated voice. Huffing in frustration, she marched back to the hut awarded to Murtaugh for his victory the day before.

As soon as she sat down, Alex limped into the tiny building to sit beside her. "Tell me, Jacq. Help me understand. Why is this of such import to you?"

Chuckling, Jacq shook her head. "I know what you're thinking, but this isn't just another adventure or treasure hunt. This is *the* treasure hunt. Bahari's family is *his* treasure. Surely you and I should understand that better than most!"

"But how shall you know when you have done enough on his behalf? I mean, you brought him here, did you not?" Alex laid a caring hand on her twin's shoulder.

"I know you mean well, but I shan't be satisfied until he is holding his children in his arms." Jacq's eyes teared up. "He saved me, Alex, at great risk to himself." Reaching up, she grasped Alex's hand. "Your thinking is sound, and I applaud it. I even agree with you. But I…" She sniffed back the threat of tears. "I can't, in good conscience, abandon him. Not now. Not with no one to help him."

Alex studied her sister's pensive face a moment. "Are you still having the nightmares?" Her brow was rife with concern. There was no evading the question.

"They come and go," Jacq admitted. "I've not had one since we landed. Perhaps they have gone for good."

"I worry for you," Alex returned, skepticism coloring her countenance. "Ever since the anniversary of—"

"Don't use the word *anniversary*," Jacq returned. "It should be reserved for pleasant memories."

"Jacq—"

"But truly," she interrupted, "you are well within reason to worry for Father and Amy. He will, no doubt, be anxious to learn you are well."

"That *we* are well," Alex corrected, a discontented expression blanketing her face. She sighed, her mouth twisting in contemplation, and she rested her head on Jacq's shoulder. "What is to be done? What are we to do?"

Leaning her head on her sister's, Jacq let out a slow exhale. "We do what we must."

Alex groaned. "I do not like the sound of that."

"For good reason," Jacq noted. "It seems to rarely coincide with what we want, and invariably someone is greatly disappointed."

Five months earlier…

"Did you hear Father saying how he elected not to attend the king's execution for treason three years ago? It is remarkable we survived without such connections before," Alex said as she sat beside Jacq on a quaint window bench overlooking the frosty garden. "Though we were not in any sort of proper society…"

"Aye, unthinkably remarkable," Jacq returned, unmoved by her sister's revelation.

"What do you want, Jacq?" Alex asked as she looked out at their father's beautiful grounds. "It is a new year, is it not?"

"What do you mean?" Jacq asked in return. "Do I not look perfectly content, sitting here in our father's house?"

"Something is amiss," Alex insisted, staring out at the estate.

"Father seems quite pleased with how quickly you have adjusted to these living arrangements," Jacq noted, moving away from the window to stand by the fire.

Pulling her shawl tighter around her shoulders, Alex tilted her head. "And you have not?"

Scoffing, Jacq smirked at her sister. "Like a cat to water, I'm afraid. Only with no claws to defend myself."

Giggling, Alex shook her head. "It is of no consequence. He seems taken with you, with your love of the sea. He has collected all necessary approvals for your venture to Africa, has he not? All that remains is gathering resources and awaiting the better season."

"Perhaps, but I fear I must be rather painfully deficient in every other respect. I have little in the way of manners and boast of no proper accomplishments with which to awe his friends and relations." A wry smile turned her mouth.

"These are things which can be learned," Alex pointed out matter-of-factly. "Having a heart in common is much more rare and valuable. Your interests are naturally aligned."

"But you, I'd wager, remind him of Mother," Jacq noted in a weighted tone, sauntering back to the window. "You, with all of your genteel nature and refinements, make a fine example of a gentleman's daughter. I also believe he finds your taste in prospective suitors a little more to his liking."

"Now, why would you say that?" Alex asked, brightening with curiosity and crossing over to stand

beside Jacq. "Has someone stated his intentions?" Her smile was all sweetness and hopefulness.

"Wha—no," Jacq replied with a chuckle. "And I doubt he would ever approve a suitor interested in me that I did not find utterly insufferable and horribly, horribly dull."

"Why ever would you say that?" Alex returned. "Mr. Monroe is a fine example of an engaging sort of man who is both adventurous and amiable with respectable breeding."

"If only I were to be so fortunate," Jacq returned, smirking. "But never mind. Forget I said anything on the matter."

"So, what shall you do?" Alex asked in earnest, touching at her sister's elbow.

Shaking her head, Jacq shrugged. "What I must."

"You know, I think I've come up with a solution," Jacq said after a few moments of silence.

"Oh, no." Alex's countenance became downcast.

"What?"

Gesturing at her face, Alex answered, "You have this look about you when you have devised a truly, truly abhorrent conspiracy and sincerely believe it to be a satisfactory scheme."

"Ugh!" Frowning, Jacq turned to face her and crossed her arms. "I do not devise abhorrent conspiracies! I-I... I actually have an expression for when that happens?"

"Oh, yes." Alex nodded. "I have become well acquainted with it these past ten years."

"Well, perhaps the men have come upon an astonishing solution which has thus far eluded us." Motioning to the door, Jacq invited, "Shall we?"

Upon exiting the house, the young women discovered the men still lounging about the fire, either engaged in mild discourse or sleeping. Night had besieged them, bursting with twittering and clicking from the surrounding forest. The trees only barely swayed in the tiny summer breeze, causing the leaves to very faintly sound like waves.

Approaching the group, they saw Miata kick Murtaugh's feet. "Lads."

"We've devised—er, well, conceived a plan," Jacq announced as everyone clambered to their feet. She threw Alex a wry smile in thanks for ruining the word *devised*.

"As have we," Miata said. "We be thinkin' it be best if we—"

"Stay together," Jacq blurted before anyone else had a chance to say, surprising Alex.

"But, Jacq," Miata started, scratching at his unshaven face, finally starting to bristle.

"We can't separate," Jacq said in a somber voice, eyeing Miata.

"Well, how can we be..." Miata stammered, and gestured toward the different directions that needed to be taken, north and west. "We can't be goin' two places at once."

Gulping, Jacq nodded. "I know." She glanced at Bahari.

A kind and understanding smile morphed his grim expression. "It is better this way, Shakina."

"Perhaps," she replied, her voice breaking. Her face twitched as it wanted to fall, but she fought to keep up the semblance of a smile. "Nevertheless, I am sorry, Bahari." Taking a deep, shaky breath, she held out her hand in an offering of farewell. "I cannot forsake Alex."

Grasping her forearm just below her elbow and setting his other hand on her shoulder, he nodded. "This is how the *jagunjagun* says good-bye." And he bowed his head.

Her eyes welling with tears that dared not stream down her face, she mirrored his respectful adieu though her body trembled from withholding her emotions. "I... I wish you the very best of luck, sir. You shall be forever in our prayers."

"Oh! Stop it! Just stop it!" Alex muttered as she observed the somber scene unfolding before them. "This will never do!" Huffing, she held her head and struggled against the onslaught of emotions assaulting her very sensible mind.

"Wha-what be happenin'?" Miata asked. "Be she possessed?"

Sending him an incredulous glare, Murtaugh slapped him in the back of the head. "Possessed? Judas!"

Miata sneered at him.

"This is pure lunacy," Alex said in a measured voice, "for which I blame you, Jacq."

Releasing Bahari, Jacq scowled. "Now, hang on! You've a bit of madness on your own account, Alex! Don't be giving me all the credit!"

"Well, I-I... I think you should go... with Bahari."

"By Jove," Murtaugh exclaimed in a hushed tone.

Jacq's eyes narrowed. "Is this a trick?"

Elbowing Murtaugh, Miata repeated, "Possessed."

Shaking her head, Alex shrugged. "We have sailed for buried treasure. We have found our sister and our father. We have learned about our past. We have forged for ourselves a future filled with prospects that I never would have believed possible just two years ago. And it is all *your* fault." She jabbed a finger at Jacq, her boiling emotions beginning to spill over. "This time, this risk, this shall be *my* decision." She stood tall, shoulders back, chin held high. "*I* say we separate, and we take it all."

Shocked but invigorated, Jacq grabbed Alex up in her arms. "You never cease to amaze me! But we must act quickly before you have time to reconsider your decision."

"You are probably accurate in that assessment," Alex agreed, hugging Jacq in return. "What do we do?"

An impish smirk stretching over her face as she backed away from Alex, Jacq laughed, biting her lower lip. "We use my truly, truly abhorrent conspiracy."

"I knew it!" Pursing her lips, Alex waggled her finger at her sister. "Did I not? I knew it."

Turning to the confused men standing about them, Jacq nodded. "She knew it."

Roused by the energy teeming off the girls, Murtaugh sprang to his feet and held out his hands in request. "So, please share."

"We split as we were to come here."

Miata and Murtaugh glowed with pleasure while Rackham glowered.

"Murtaugh and I will travel with Bahari to find his family," Jacq stated. "They are but a week's journey north. We shall fetch them and travel to Cabo Corso, as agreed. Miata, Mr. Rackham, and Alex will return to that dreadful fort we escaped from. You shall discover and reclaim our father, Amy, our crew, and our ship. You can then meet us in Cabo Corso."

"It be soundin' easy enough, save the reclaimin' bit," Miata commented, scratching at his head and licking his lower lip.

"Are you certain you want *Crevan* out in the wilderness watching out for you?" Dante asked, his inflection sounding skeptical as he bestowed a cold, menacing gaze on Murtaugh.

Clenching her teeth, Jacq looked from one handsome man to the other. However, even considering Rackham over Murtaugh made her feel like a fool. Keeping a guarded demeanor, though, allowed her motives to remain hidden, exactly as she wished them

to be. "I think I'll take my chances with the Irishman," she answered.

Bounding up from where he sat, Rackham grabbed her wrist. "You *must* speak with me," he insisted in a hushed tone. "Tell me what I have done to offend you and earn your ceaseless despise!"

"And you have treated me the same since your return from London?" she asked with a sneer.

"Come on, Jacq." He bore a look born of confusion and desperation.

Yanking her arm from his warm, pleading fingers, she shrugged. "Very well. I shall give you but a moment."

Murtaugh moved to stop them as they walked away, but Miata caught him. "No, no. Be lettin' it transpire, mate. Let him be the weasel."

The smugness dropped from Murtaugh's face and was replaced by uneasy anxiety. Still, he remained where he stood, and waited.

"You have been treating me with disdain for over a fortnight!" Rackham said, his voice fraught with agitation. He stood closer to Jacq, imploring her with everything in his countenance to explain her actions and forgive whatever indiscretion may have prompted them. "Tell me why."

"I heard a rumor—gossip—which you must confirm or deny," she answered, examining his face.

"Tell me," he pleaded, leaning closer.

"You are courting a lass—a lady—in London, but you have yet to mention it to me. Instead, you merely distance yourself wordlessly as though I might eventually disappear." She turned her big hazel eyes up to stare into his. "Tell me, is it true?"

His brow twitching, he shook his head and averted his eyes. "I-I'm..."

Assuming his reply, Jacq sniffed back angry tears and moved to leave, but before she could take a step, he latched onto her arm, pulling her ear nearly to his lips. "No. I'm not. I'm not courting anyone, Jacq. W-why would you suppose I was?"

Inhaling sharply, she looked at him out of the corner of her eye. "Strange behavior aside, one rarely receives a dinner invitation for absolutely no reason at all, and neutrality is not often a cause for a lady to extend an invitation of any kind to a gentleman. Our reputations, it seems, are too delicate."

"And a dinner invitation can never be given or received by friends or relations? They are merely a veiled romantic gesture?" Releasing his hold, he glanced back toward the fire. "Do not punish me for hearsay, Jacq. 'Tisn't right."

Touching at her arm where his hand had been burning her with his intensity, she shrugged. "Very well. I still require someone trustworthy to watch over Alex. I need you to get her to Cabo Corso."

He did not seem persuaded as he lingered, taking a close review of her face. "But who will look after you?"

"Bahari and Murtaugh," she answered easily. "Why would they not? Bahari is grateful, and Murtaugh is sincere."

Frowning at her word choice, Rackham shrugged. "As you wish, but I do not like it."

"It is fortunate then that your good opinion is not required." She moved to walk away, but paused to look at him once more. "I suppose you won't be finding me any zebras, after all." With that, she went around him and returned to the group.

As she left, Dante's mouth formed a thin line, and he closed his eyes, clenching his fists.

"Well?" Miata asked, licking his lips and fidgeting.

"We stick to the plot. Alex, if you must, please wait here a day or two to allow your ankle some rest," Jacq suggested.

"While we are to leave…" Murtaugh paused, awaiting the details.

"On the morrow, unless Bahari has altered his opinion. We shall follow his lead."

"There is another matter of import which I should mention," Bahari said.

All eyes swung to him.

"What matter?" Alex asked, her senses beginning to return to normal. "Of how much import?"

Clearing his throat, he simply answered, "The *erú alagidi*—slavers, evil men. These… men… are not easily dealt with and should not be trifled with, under any circumstance."

"So what do we do?" Rackham asked, rejoining the crew.

"When you see them, hide. There are also tribes and predators to watch for. Yoruba people are well-liked, but the *erú alagidi* has put a strain on even our best relations," Bahari explained, scooping up a pebble and turning it over in his hand. "We must tread with caution."

"Brilliant! And how are we to survive this land, this Africa, without such a savvy guide as yourself, Master Bahari?" Alex demanded, wringing her hands together.

"Where you go there will not be much in the way of man or beast," he explained. "The people who were settled there have moved farther inland, and so have many of the animals. Still, you must keep an eye keen for snakes, spiders, and all manner of hunter, just to be safe."

Whimpering, Alex sat down in hopes to more easily process the information.

Watching her sister wilt at this daunting proposition, Jacq nudged at Bahari. "Alex is right. What of a guide?"

Bahari eyed her with a pensive expression. "A guide?"

"Aye. Someone to walk with them and show them the dangers and food, and-and…"

"Aye! Food! A guide be a right smart notion!" Miata spoke up.

Stroking the beginnings of a beard outlining his jaw, Bahari pondered a moment before nodding. "It would provide much help. I shall speak to the *alàgbà*. The rest of you should get some sleep."

Dropping the pebble into the fire, he sauntered off to find the old man.

Morning pulled back the velvet blanket of stars too early for anyone's liking, replacing it with cheery shades of pink and yellow before the blue sky was unfurled. As those foreign to these lands awoke and came staggering out to the pit they'd been at just hours before, they were a little surprised to see Bahari sitting by the orange embers, cross-legged with his eyes closed. The rest of the village seemed empty as the others had already departed for their first hunt of the day.

Once all five had gathered by the fire, Bahari, eyes remaining shut, spoke. "Your loyalty and reverence have not gone unnoticed. With Crevan's victory and the twins, the *alàgbà* feels honored to grant your request for a guide." He opened his eyes, startling Alex and Miata. "He feels your willingness to acknowledge your weakness and defeat it shall make you great. Oduntan, cousin of Jokotade, has been appointed the privilege of being your guide.

"Jokotade himself wished for the honor, but because he does not know any of your language, it fell to Oduntan." Standing in one fluid motion, he beckoned for them to follow him. "They are preparing rations and weapons for our journey. We leave once they have returned from the morning hunt and completed the parting ceremony. Now we eat."

Within the hour, the hunting parties returned, kindly smiling and nodding at their visitors, particularly the twins. All the women greatly wished for the girls to breathe onto them or their fertility, wealth, or luck charms. In return, they happily supplied the travelers with some extra clothes, food, and water skins. Then in a final ceremonious act, they bestowed them their weapons.

As the elder made the presentation in the Yoruba language, Bahari translated. "These"—the old man held up a saber-shaped sword—"are *ida*, the preferred blade amongst the Yoruba warriors. They also send with us the smaller blade, the *obe*—a dagger. They wish us well on this journey and hope we are protected from harm. Oduntan will be your guide."

Bahari motioned to a tall, athletic man with high cheekbones and a stoic expression, his dark eyes sober with his task—a stately specimen of a man. Everyone's eyebrows rose at the pleasing sight of him. "They bid you, Shakina, carry Kehinde as a token of good fortune. Miss Alex, you will carry Tayewo as a token of safe travel. When they have been rejoined, it shall signify the journey's end."

As he spoke, the two girls were handed the tokens.

The sisters looked at each other, turning over the carved wooden pendants in their fingers.

"May it be ever so swiftly," Alex said in a quiet voice.

Jacq nodded, running her thumbs over the seashell-dotted leather-braided chain the wood charm hung from.

Minutes later, after all other strained well-wishes had been exchanged, Alex and Jacq stood facing each other.

"We can do this, you know," Jacq said, nodding.

"Oh." Alex let out a ragged breath. "To have your confidence. It must be reassuring."

Taking her worrying hands, Jacq donned a wry smile. "I doubt *reassuring* is the word. I fear rather it blinds me to the unfortunate consequences made possible by my decisions."

"Then I do not know which is worse," Alex returned with a halfhearted laugh. "To be blinded to the regrettable consequences or to be crippled by them."

"If our scheme does not utterly fail," Jacq said, giving Alex's hands a squeeze, "then we shall meet in Cabo Corso in three or four weeks' time, and we shall leave Africa together, just as we arrived."

Sniffling, Alex nodded. "Well, off with you then. The sooner we start, the sooner it ends, yes?"

Releasing her hands, Jacq nodded. "Alex, you are the most reluctant courageous person I know, and sometimes, you leave me in all astonishment."

"And you the most impish thoughtful person I know," Alex returned, her voice breaking. "Oh, Jacq." Lunging forward, she embraced Jacq, who returned the affectionate gesture with matched intensity. Then freeing her from her grasp, she took a deep breath. "Hurry back to me."

Taking a long, slow drag of the fresh air, Jacq smiled. "Indeed I shall." Glancing at Dante and Miata, who stood fidgeting nearby, she added, "You best take care of her, lads!" Then smiling once more at Alex, she about-faced and moved onward to where Bahari and Murtaugh were waiting at the tree line. Upon her arrival, Bahari walked into the forest, Murtaugh following after him. Glancing behind her at her sister and friends once more, Jacq lingered just a moment then plunged into the trees, vanishing in seconds.

Within minutes of their departure, a slight drizzle sputtered down onto them. The droplets were so fine they created almost a mist, but it seemed to have no effect on Bahari. They walked in silence, inclining their ears to any other human type sounds disrupting the hum of the wildlife. This proved to be greatly to their advantage as the day wore on, for they managed to avoid

detection twice—once from a group of slavers and once from a native hunting party. However, they were not the only ones in the forest being stealthy.

Late in the afternoon as they walked past a cluster of trees, four local-looking men appeared, pointing bows at them.

"Well, well. What have we here?" one of the middle ones asked, his tone taunting.

"They travel with me as companions," Bahari said, quick to intervene in their defense.

The man who had spoken initially stopped. Lowering his weapon, he inched nearer to Bahari, squinting at him. "Ba-Bahari? Bahari, is it truly you?" he asked with a chuckle.

Bahari's brow knotted into a quizzical expression.

The man slapped his chest. "It is I! Huru!" He then made additional remarks in their native language.

"Huru?" Bahari laughed, making a fist and holding it over his heart. "Huru, how are you? Perhaps you could tell your friends…" He gestured to the others who were still in a hostile stance.

Nodding, Huru waved his hand at the others, signaling for them to stand down. Then turning again to Bahari, Huru sighed. "Your friends are…" He paused, eyeing them. "English?"

Bahari nodded. "They are. They helped me escape my captivity."

Jacq and Murtaugh exchanged uneasy glances, and as Huru began engaging Bahari in banter using their language, Murtaugh inched over to Jacq. Nudging her, he whispered, "I don't like this. I don't like him, and I don't like"—he paused, scanning their surroundings—"this. Something feels amiss."

"Could it simply be the fault of discomfort in an unknown environment?" she asked, also plagued with unexplainable uneasiness.

"Would it be highly offensive if I question Bahari? I've always been a bit indifferent to these things, so I don't always give attention to proper etiquette," he said in a genuine confession tinted with regret for the latter. "But I'd rather not be left out here to rot for my lack of manners."

"Truly, I don't rightly know," Jacq admitted, fighting off the small smirk brought on by his honesty. "It is rather unsettling not having any inkling as to what they are saying." As she spoke, she watched them, trying to get clues as to conversation by body language.

As though sensing their growing anxiety, Bahari waved them over. "Shakina. Crevan. This is an old friend, Huru. He and his village are under Oloye Adetoun of Oba Ajagbo, Alaafin of Oyo— the Yoruba king. He heard of my family's journey north, but of no alteration. Hopefully this means they are in Tenkodogo, after all."

"Very good. Shall we carry on, then?" Murtaugh asked, concealing his eagerness to be rid of these new acquaintances.

"Huru has invited us for a meal," Bahari replied. "It would be offensive to dismiss the invitation of an old friend."

Murtaugh and Jacq traded uneasy glances. "If you think it best," she said, trying to rule out fear of the unknown as her objection. Without thinking, she reached up and began toying with the wooden piece hanging about her neck as was her habit with the locket she used to wear.

Seeing it, Huru pointed at it and asked Bahari, "Kehinde?"

Bahari nodded. "Tayewo is headed west. Kehinde travels with me. Crevan is her *alaabo*—her protector."

At this, Huru's expression darkened. "Very good. Come. Our camp is north."

As the group began moving, Murtaugh grabbed at Jacq's arm. "Do not leave my sight." His voice was all shades of somber.

She nodded. "Nor you mine."

The following morning found the handsome, virile Oduntan leading the other trio through the jungle back toward van Draenweg. As they trudged along single file, Alex found her ankle, though better, required a slower pace.

"What was I thinking?" she asked herself aloud. "Surely a madness must have overtaken me, giving me leave of my senses! What other reason would I have for agreeing to this-this-this *wretched* scheme!?"

"Were ye possessed?" Miata asked, turning to look over his shoulder at her and sounding overly interested.

"P-Possessed?" Alex repeated with a wry chuckle until she noticed the genuineness of his expression. Scoffing, she shook her head. "Do not be ridiculous! Unlike you, I am accustomed to having a very sound mind by which I come to decisions and conclusions in a logical manner. No, I blame this wilderness. It-it *addled* my mind. That is the only potential justification for this."

Smirking, Rackham cleared his throat and called from where he brought up the back of their caravan, "I doubt it is the *only* explanation."

"No? Hm! Well, what do *you* suggest, then?" She threw a somewhat well-humored scowl back at him, expecting some sarcastic response.

"Rather than possession or lunacy"—he paused, chuckling—"is it possible you simply had a moment of adventure lust?"

"Adventure—" Huffing and puffing at the very notion, Alex shook her head. "No, no. No, no, no! I do not... I do not crave such danger or reckless behavior!"

"Not even for one moment when you're in the middle of a vast wilderness and there's no one around to look poorly on your rash,

brazen desire?" he asked in a smooth inflection almost seductive in its delivery.

As the words slipped out of his mouth, Alex could feel her adrenaline climbing the tiniest bit, her mind frantically swatting it away, trying to subdue it. "It would be foolish," she retorted.

"As lusts so often are," he noted, his amused expression audible as he spoke.

While Alex fumbled for words with which to reply, Miata smiled to himself. *Miss Alex speechless. Miracles be happenin' even out here. Maybe there be hope for this scheme, after all.*

Before she was able to recover and come up with a response, Oduntan froze and held his hand in the air. "Be still!" he commanded in a deep voice that was both thick with accent and smooth.

As everyone came to a stop, he listened, peering through the vegetation. "Stay," he added in a hushed tone. Then he snuck off toward something or other, leaving them standing awkwardly in their tracks.

"What do we do?" Alex asked, looking between Miata and Rackham.

"Oduntan be sayin' to hide," Miata offered, shrugging.

Dante nodded and motioned to a spot a short ways from them. Hunkering down, they huddled together between some large ferns.

"What do you suppose it was?" Alex asked in a whisper.

Rackham shook his head. "People."

"What about those big cats they be talkin' about?" Miata inquired, peeking between the leaves.

"Jaguars?" Alex asked, trying to diminish the concern in her voice. She grasped the wood carving hanging from her neck. "Not jaguars. Please not jaguars."

Giving Miata a warning shove, Dante replied, "Doubtful. But do you see Odin anywhere?"

"Oduntan," the guide corrected.

"Ah!" they all gasped, spinning about to find him standing behind them.

"I thought we were well hidden!" Alex said, glancing about for any sign of whatever he had gone to investigate.

"Like elephant in savanna," he said, chuckling.

"Like elephant..." She looked at the boys.

"I'm fairly certain that means we were not," Rackham guessed, watching Oduntan laugh to himself.

Grinning, he beckoned to them. "Come. Quietly." Then he silently escorted them to a small stand of trees clumped closely together. There they saw a pair of men lounging on a log a short distance away.

"*Erú alagidi*," Oduntan said.

Squinting at them, Alex grabbed at Dante's sleeve. "Say, is that not—he resembles one of the guards we saw at van Draenweg. The one on the left."

"The porker?" Rackham asked, watching the men eat some food and talk. "You know, I think you might be correct."

"We must follow them," she said to Oduntan. "Follow."

"Follow?" Oduntan's face scrunched in dislike.

"Follow for"—she pointed at her head—"knowledge. Follow to learn."

Shrugging, Oduntan nodded. "Follow."

Chapter 4

The moist, earthy smell of rainfall filled the air, sweet and fresh. Raindrops pattered onto the leaves, serving as a steady, rhythmic background noise. Occasional birdcalls could be heard, but otherwise, the world was quiet. What sunlight there would have been was blocked by the clouds, making the sky a pale, light gray.

Gasping, Jacq sat up, clutching at the pendant and her blouse. Breathing heavily, she glanced around and relaxed a little when she saw Murtaugh a short distance away in the small hide and branch tent they'd borrowed. Her heart pounding wildly in her chest, she took several long, measured breaths to try and calm herself.

"It was just a dream. Just a dream."

Watching his body rise and fall with his respiration, she stifled a sob and brought the fist holding the wooden token to her mouth. "Just a dream."

"Shakina?"

"Ah! Bahari!" Regaining her composure, she smiled and responded, "What is it?"

"Are you unwell?" he asked, squatting to better examine her.

"I feel well enough," she said, discounting the state in which she awoke. "Do we leave today?"

"It was good to spend yesterday with Huru. He was able to tell me of my family. I have a son whom I have yet to become acquainted with." Shaking his head in awe, his mouth formed a distant smile. "It is much to take in."

Nodding, she offered up a supportive expression, pleased to see his spirits lifted despite her own reservations. "No doubt. So shall we depart today?"

"Huru knows of someone who may be able to assist us."

"How? All we have to do is travel to Tenkodogo. You know the way. What aid can he offer us?" she asked, trying to sound curious instead of distrusting and uneasy.

"He may have a map of camps to avoid," Bahari answered, studying her face. "Shakina, if there is trouble, you must tell me at once."

Meeting his gaze, which was genuine and kind, she shrugged. "I do not fancy the way Huru looks upon me. He has yet to be unkind, but he makes me feel ill at ease nevertheless."

"Huru is wary of outsiders," Bahari confessed. "Surely you can understand that. We were ọrẹ—friends—before Captain Ming threatened my family and stole me away. He is good people."

"Very well. If you trust him, then I will try and ignore my personal feelings." She forced a smile.

"I do not trust him in full, understand," Bahari said. "But thus far he has not deceived me. I know not how he would benefit from any such deception."

Rolling over to face them, Murtaugh commented, "That, mate, is the most effective type of deception there is."

"How long have you been awake?" Jacq asked, audibly surprised.

"Long enough to know this Huru chap has some mates he wants us to meet and you two don't share opinions as to the design of Huru himself." Pushing back his hair from his forehead, he smiled over at the girl. "Good morning, Jacq. You look very… fine this morning."

Her cheeks burned at his glowing approval and pleased expression. "You slept well, Murtaugh?" she asked, maintaining as indifferent of a demeanor as she was able while ensuring her shirt was not gaping open.

His grin inching wider, he nodded. "Quite."

"Well, rise for breakfast," Bahari said. "Huru wishes to depart before midday."

"How far away are these mates of Huru's?" Murtaugh asked, sitting up and gingerly rubbing at his bruised eye.

"About a day's journey. We should arrive by nightfall," Bahari answered, smiling. "Now, up!"

While Jacq and Murtaugh prepared to follow Bahari, Alex sat against a tree, watching Oduntan hunt for fish in a gentle side stream. He was up to his knees and acutely focused on his task. She found it mesmerizing how he moved slowly and then remained motionless until he struck with his spear. It was akin to watching a cat.

Approaching her, Miata was hesitant to interrupt. It was the first time she looked remotely peaceful since Jacq had left with Bahari. Sighing, he forced himself forward and sat beside her.

"Mr. Rackham send you?" she asked without even looking over at him.

"Aye. He did. The blokes, Greg and Fife, be on the move. Still headin' east," he replied. "Any luck here?" He pointed at Oduntan.

"Oh, yes. He should be finished soon," Alex said, her voice distant.

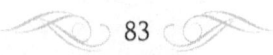

They sat in silence a few seconds then before she continued, "What came over me? Why would I suggest we separate? Why would I suggest following those scoundrels? Surely my mind has been addled by this place."

Looking her over, Miata contemplated how to respond. Maybe she had a point.

However, before he could say anything, she continued, "Observe Mr. Oduntan. See how he moves, so calm and confident. See how he waits, knowing the precise moment he will need to strike."

At that, he lunged for a catch, but came up with nothing.

"See how it does not always give him the results he is seeking. Yet he attempts again, because it is important. He deems it has value." Her countenance grew sullener.

"Aye, Alex," Miata returned, scoffing. "The lad be hungry. He be needin' to be feedin' four o' us, so—"

Scowling over at him, she retorted, "I was not speaking of fishing! Were you not listening?"

Complete confusion overtaking his expression, he alternated pointing between Alex and Oduntan. Rerunning the conversation through his mind, he tried to deduce where he had somehow misunderstood her. However, it was to no avail.

When she glanced over at him and saw the overwhelming puzzlement by which he had been ensnared, she shook her head and stood. "Why should I suppose you would ever understand my meaning!" Then she stormed off.

Watching her stalk away, Miata's confusion was compounded, his face displaying the fact shamelessly.

Laughing as he came up from the water, Oduntan shrugged and patted Miata on the shoulder. "Women," he said, walking back to their campsite.

"W-w—" Miata scratched his head. "What happened?" Staring a few minutes at the running water, he tried to reexamine the conversation again, but it didn't gain him any additional understanding. Pushing himself up, he trudged back to the camp, muttering under his breath. "Always the blinkin' laughin'stock. Always bein' assumed about. Well, who be she to be passin' her judgements on me? *Now* she be a proper gentleman's daughter, but afore that she were nothin'. She were not much better than me." Scoffing, he kicked at a rock.

Suddenly, he felt a push so hard it nearly knocked him off balance. As he stumbled to salvage his footing, Rackham grabbed him by the front of his shirt and shoved him against a tree.

"Poisoning Miss Alex against me now, eh?" His temper simmered, waiting for a reason to boil over.

"Unhand me, ya fool! Miss Alex were just chidin' me for thinkin' she were talkin' about fishin'!" he retorted, pushing back and ripping Dante's hand from his clothes.

Frowning, Rackham ran his fingers through his hair. "Well, what *was* she talking about?"

"Fishin'!" Miata answered, throwing his hands in the air. "It don't be makin' any sense! I reckon she's lost her mind!"

"Shh! Sh!" Dante signaled for him to be quiet. "Keep your voice down. She accused me of not doing my duties." He curled his lip. "What duties?"

"It were the same with fishin'!" Miata returned just above a whisper. "One minute she be talkin' about Oduntan's fishin', and the next she be vexed on account she weren't talkin' about fishin' at all!"

Before they could discuss the issue further, Oduntan sauntered up with a couple of gutted cooked fish on sticks. "Food. Eat. Madwoman almost done. Want to leave soon to follow."

"Madwoman," Dante repeated. "How accurate." Taking one fish and handing the other to Miata, he nodded. "We shall be ready. Just give us a minute. *E dupe*."

Smiling, Oduntan nodded. "*Ko Tope*."

"One phrase I doubt I should ever have the chance to say to our Mr. Oduntan," Rackham noted as the big man lumbered away. "Certainly not here, certainly not to him."

"Don't be jealous, mate," Miata said, clapping him on the back. "Maybe if you weren't shirkin' yer duties…" He started chuckling.

Glaring at him, Rackham's expression softened to a sneering smile. "Eat up, *mate*." Then he took a purposeful bite of the fish.

Late in the afternoon, the sky gushed down upon the northernmost travelers, forcing them to seek shelter rather than arrive at their intended destination. As Jacq and Murtaugh sat huddled together by their low-burning fire, they watched Bahari and Huru talking by theirs.

"It is a clever trick," Jacq noted, "to carry an ember with which to start a fire in this kind of weather."

Nodding, Murtaugh sighed. "Agreed. Though Huru seemed displeased to have to make camp here."

"And you're not?" she asked with a laugh, gesturing at the rain.

He turned to look at her. "I don't mind." He shrugged and glanced out at the rain. "It reminds me of Ireland."

Examining his face, she thought she spied some distant dolefulness in his manner. "Do you miss it? Ireland, I mean."

"Not much to miss most days," he replied, poking at their heat source with a twig. "But I always fancy a proper type of rain—a *báisteach*. Brings people together, you know?"

She smiled at him, certain he was only being partially truthful. She listened to the fire pop and snap and to the occasional hiss from a stray water droplet. The orange glow danced on his face, casting shadows to make his features appear even more severe.

Staring, Jacq! she snapped at herself. *Stop staring like a pining milkmaid!* Dragging her gaze from him to the fire, she sighed.

"What?" he asked, watching her for an answer.

"Oh, well, I…" She fumbled in her speech, frantically trying to make up something logical and clever. "I-I-I was just thinking. Thinking that surely you must miss something from Ireland. Besides, you know, besides the rain."

Shrugging, and entirely clueless as to her fabrication, he matter-of-factly said, "No, truly. For example, Irish women aren't very well balanced. They're either dull as a patch of dirt or completely mad."

Giggling, Jacq hugged herself to keep warm. "Dull as a patch of dirt." She giggled again, causing Murtaugh's expression to curl upward in a grin.

"It's true," he continued, the act of making her laugh proving unexpectedly rewarding. "I had a mate once, Colin O'Farrell, who was to marry this lass, Muireen."

"Muireen," she repeated, mimicking his accent.

"Aye, *Muireen*. And do you know what *Muireen* would go on about?" he asked, emphasizing Muireen's name each time he said it.

Jacq continued giggling. "What? What would she go on about?"

"Embroidery," he answered in a deadpan tone. "How can a person go on and on about *embroidery*?"

Laughing now, Jacq appreciated the warmth their conversation was filling her with and the smile on Murtaugh's face. "Embroidery," she repeated, attempting to mimic his accent but botching it with her snickering.

"Embroidery," he repeated, smirking as he observed her.

"Embroidery," she said again, this time failing her attempt due to an interrupting shiver.

Shaking his head, he dropped his twig on the fire. "Come here, Jackie," he said, putting his arm around her shoulders. "You should get some sleep."

"I-I'm a bit cold is all," she said, shivering and scooting up against his firm body. "Maybe it would help if I took up *embroidery*." She giggled to herself.

"I doubt it very much," he returned, tucking her in close under his arm.

As she snuggled up against his warmth, she felt him rest his head on top of hers. "Good night, Michael."

"Good night," he replied softly, watching Bahari's fire until his eyelids got too heavy to lift.

The rain continued on and off throughout the night, pitter-pattering on their hide tents and occasionally hissing on the fire until dawn. The sun rose to find them in the same sitting position, each propped up by the other. The air was quiet, save for the low trilling of forest insects, the light soft and pale. The earth seemed sated from the rain and was in no hurry to stir from its slumber.

"Ee-yaya-ya! Ee-yaya-ya! Ee-ya-ya!" shattered the peaceful morning stillness, shrill and piercing, startling everyone awake.

"What is that?" Jacq asked, shrinking against the tent wall.

"I don't know," Murtaugh answered, crawling forward to peek out of the entrance of the tent.

When he leaned to look, a painted mask appeared in the doorway, causing both of them to cry out. However, Murtaugh

instinctively threw a jab at it while the wearer of the mask reached in and grabbed him with both hands. Consequently, the two tumbled out onto the patchy ground, squirming in the mud and swinging at each other. As soon as they vanished from sight, Jacq turned and grabbed for the swords and daggers the Yoruba people had gifted them.

Twirling about with the weapons in hand, she scurried out to find Murtaugh struggling with a second masked assailant. The first man lay prostrate on the ground, groaning but not moving. Turning, she was horrified at seeing Bahari and Huru both engaged in a fight as well with Huru's friend laid out nearby.

Spinning back to Murtaugh, she took a deep breath. "Come on, Jacq. You can do this."

Rushing forward, she yelled, "Murtaugh!"

Hearing her voice, he moved to see her. As soon as he did, she tossed him the dagger she had in one hand.

"Ha!" He laughed as he caught it. "That's a good lass there!" he said, rotating back to continue his confrontation. "Now"—he brandished the blade at the masked man—"where were we?"

Reaching behind him, the assailant also pulled out a dagger.

Exhaling in disappointment, Murtaugh shrugged. "I suppose that's fair."

"Ee-yaya-ya! Ee-yaya-ya! Ee-ya-ya!" rang out again, and another group of the masked attackers emerged from the forest, this time with bows.

All the fighting ground to a halt. Then Bahari began talking to his sparring partner, shouting and gesturing to himself and the others. The man who had been tussling with Huru now moved to Bahari, yelling and pointing back at him.

"W-what is happening?" Jacq asked.

"I know not," Murtaugh replied.

Whatever the masked man said resulted in Bahari turning to Huru and proceeding to aggressively talk to him, using angry waves of his hand.

"Is he acting?" Murtaugh questioned.

"Bahari?" Jacq scoffed. "Do cats take to water?"

Sighing, Murtaugh looked at the two men he'd been fighting, the first of which was now sitting up. "Maybe you blokes'll let us go, eh?" He grinned and nodded persuasively.

The three bowmen near them stepped forward, giving commands in their native language.

"Maybe not," he said, putting his hands up. "Jacq, you stay close to me, you hear?"

"Likewise," she returned, copying his behavior.

The masked men escorted them over to Bahari, who was angrily glancing back and forth between Huru and the other man. Huru appeared very disenchanted with the whole of what was going on, rolling his eyes and shaking his head. However, the masked man who seemed to be the leader kept muttering and pointing at Huru.

"Bahari," Jacq asked meekly, "what is happening?"

"This is Nokware of a nearby Aṣanti tribe. He claims Huru makes deals and trades with *erú alagidi*." Bahari snorted. "It would seem impossible, but to my understanding, he has no motive to conjure this detailed account. He wishes to warn us, thinks Huru means to sell us off." He turned again to Huru and began shouting at him in the Yoruba language.

As they argued, Nokware looked at Jacq. Then as though seeing something inspiring, he took a few steps toward her. "Kehinde," he noted, gesturing at the charm.

Bahari stopped with Huru. "Kehinde," he repeated, pointing at Jacq.

This, the two foreigners observed, seemed to instigate an entirely new type of conversation, though they still had virtually no idea what was being said.

"That rain was merciless!" Alex said as they sat around a tiny ember fire finishing their breakfast. "I think it caught even Oduntan by surprise."

"I be doubtin' that. That be why he were stoppin' us afore a drop be hittin' the ground," Miata said with a somewhat glum inflection. "Seems like he be full aware all the time."

"I don't understand," Rackham spoke up. "He is our guide. Should we not wish him to be fully able to do his tasks?" He glanced between them, their logic escaping him.

"But he be laughin' at us!" Miata retorted, taking his final bite of food.

Alex nodded. "Yes. It is a bit insulting, to be truthful."

His eyebrows lifting, Dante rubbed the back of his neck. "I'm sure he does laugh at you."

"Oh, you do not believe he mocks you as well?" she asked, crossing her arms.

Rackham shrugged. "There is nothing to mock."

Alex and Miata exchanged glances. "Nothing to mock," she repeated, her voice incredulous.

"I know he's familiar with this land, not me. I give no undue credit to myself. I respect his knowledge in this place, as I would expect him to respect mine on ship." With an air of indifference, he reached his fingers toward the fire.

Miata and Alex looked at each other. "Why must you be so childish?" she asked with a scowl.

Scoffing, Miata pointed at Dante. "Why must he be actin' so noble? I be knowin' better!"

"You don't know anything!" Rackham retorted with a snap. "That's the point."

"No need to be insufferable, Mr. Rackham," Alex commented, dusting off her hands and skirt.

"Why must you be so superior even here, where there is no one to bask in your glory?" he asked, agitation from Miata shifting to her in reaction to the comment.

Miata's eyes grew wide at his condescending inquiry.

Taken aback by Rackham's remark, she sent him a scathing glare. "And who are you to pass judgement on me and my behavior when your moods and temper are clearly erratic?"

Holding up his hands in surrender, he sighed. "Forgive me. It was out of place to make such an uncouth statement. I admit this whole journey has transformed into a beast which puts me ill at ease."

"As it does for us all," Alex agreed.

Before more could be discussed, Oduntan walked up to them. "The man speaks of a meeting. Come. We must follow."

Standing, Rackham kicked dirt onto the fire. "You heard the man."

With groans and grumblings and stifled complaints, the other two pulled themselves to their feet.

"I have come to question nearly every position of this plan," Alex said.

His lips bunching together in lack of surprise, Miata shook his head. "Perfect. That be just... just perfect."

As the group followed along for a few hours, they kept quiet, remaining undetected thanks to Oduntan's advice. Equipped with his machete, he made quick work of the tangles in their way, permitting them to easily keep pace with Gregor and Fife.

Upon reaching a small village, the two men walked straight to one of the outlying buildings on the eastern edge. Sneaking around, the group huddled against the back wall and strained to listen.

Inside, Gregor sat himself down in a chair, scratching at his portly midsection. "Right then, Mr. Bolajoko. Mr. Fife here and I been sent to ask yous for some information we has." He gestured to Fife, who stood fidgeting by the door. "Sit, sit, Mr. Fife. Yous likely to make our friend Mr. Bolajoko nervous hoverin' by the door like that, you are."

"We are not friends," a tall man with a long beard corrected from behind a table. "What information do you seek?"

Fife timidly came forward and took the chair beside Gregor.

"Some runaways," Gregor answered once his companion was seated. "Four lads and two wenches, they are. And one o' the lads be one o' yorn, he is. The rest are English folk, they are."

Bolajoko leaned back and stroked his beard. "One of mine?"

"W-well," Gregor fumbled, "not someone from *your* village, Mr. Bolajoko. I just meant he be one o' you more savage types, he is." He gestured to Bolajoko's arm, where his dark skin was exposed.

Bolajoko forced a smile. "Of course. But no. I have not."

Sighing, Gregor looked over at Fife and motioned to the table. Obediently, Fife produced a pouch from which he extracted a few gold coins. Setting them on the wooden surface, he scooted them toward Bolajoko.

Smiling, the man picked the pieces up and began admiring them one at a time. "These runaways must be important."

"Aye, it would seem so," Gregor replied. "It's the boss's orders. I reckon they are sure to fetch a fair price. They are all young and strong, they are."

Alex gasped, but Dante and Miata were both quick to cover her mouth with a hand.

Sniffing at the coins, Bolajoko chuckled. "English folk. You tell your master that Bolajoko has not seen them, but if I do, I will be sure to inform him straight away."

"That"—Gregor moved uncomfortably in the chair and glanced at the weapons hanging on the walls—"that is all you have to tell us for that money?"

Bolajoko smiled a dark, devilish expression. "Some would find it a bargain, for that is all I know."

Clearing his throat, Gregor nodded and laughed uneasily. "Of course it is."

Waving them away, Bolajoko concluded, "See Folami for a meal, and then be on your way. I would hate for our savage ways to taint yours."

As Gregor and Fife rose from their chairs and clambered for the door, the four eavesdroppers slunk into the woods.

"He means to sell us!" Alex gasped in a panicked whisper.

"We don't know that," Dante said between clenched teeth.

"He were sayin' it!" Miata argued.

"That doesn't make it true!" Rackham countered. "Lots of people say things they don't mean just to get information!"

"We must get to van Draenweg. Posthaste! Mr. Oduntan, take us there as quickly as possible!" Alex implored.

"*Bẹẹni*, Tayewo," he said. "Quickly."

That evening, Jacq and Murtaugh once again sat by the fire of their tent, watching others in the camp argue and converse in a tongue still incredibly foreign to them.

"Next time we go on an adventure," he said, poking at the coals, "please be so kind as to select a place whose inhabitants speak a language we can understand."

Smiling over at him, she nodded. "I shall do my best." Moving her gaze over toward Bahari a moment before returning it to the fire, she sighed. "What do you make of this rubbish? Huru working with slave traders?"

"Bahari's been gone a long while. Much can change with the passage of time." He shrugged. "It is difficult to say what happened to bring him to it, if that is truly what he is up to, of course."

"Of course," she repeated, entrenched in thought. "Murtaugh, does Rackham strike you as an honest sort?"

Stopping his fidgeting, he looked over his shoulder at her. "In what respect do you mean?"

"Well, any in which you know him well enough to say," she answered.

A sardonic chuckled huffed out of his lungs before he could don a straight face. "Oh, umm. Well, I-I suppose in most respects. Though, I can't say that I'd recommend his company over my own." He winked at her. "Why do you ask?"

Smirking at his reply, Jacq shrugged. "I suppose I am still trying to make sense of his character, even after all this time. One day he is all attentiveness and happy manners, but the next he is all elusiveness and close hearted. What he truly thinks and feels, I may never know."

Murtaugh sat in silence a moment then said, "The best way to measure a man is by actions. His words are altogether meaningless unless he supports them with his deeds." He jabbed at the fire with his stick.

An appreciative expression pushed up the corners of her mouth. "Michael—" She reached out her hand to touch his arm.

"Shakina," Bahari's voice interrupted.

"Bahari!" she replied, withdrawing her hand in lightning speed. "What news have you?"

"The Aşanti people know of the Yoruba people's beliefs about the magic of twins. Because of this, Nokware wishes us to aide him in freeing some captives being held at the camp Huru was taking us to. If we help them, they will ensure us safe passage through their tribe's land to Tenkodogo." Bahari squatted beside them, clasping his hands. "I believe it to be a fair trade."

"What of Huru?" Jacq asked, toying with the end of her braid.

"He has agreed to help us," Bahari answered, relief audible in his voice. "He claims he was forced to make deals with the *erú alagidi*. We shall see!" He huffed and his mouth twitched with disdain.

Jacq and Murtaugh exchanged glances.

"Well, then," the Irishman said, "when do we leave?"

"We leave in the morning and attack by nightfall." Clapping Murtaugh on the back and nodding at Jacq, he added, "Best get some rest."

The following day, both Jacq and Alex trudged west, each with heavy steps and sullen expressions, each wondering what they would find upon arriving at their destination. However, as Alex bedded down for the night, Jacq sat still to accept her war paint application. Using his fingers, Nokware painted a pattern similar to the basic of the masks they had worn. A thick black stripe was drawn from the top of her forehead to her chin; another stripe from one ear, across her nose to her other ear; and black was smeared around her eyes. He then produced a white paint and accented the horizontal stripe top and bottom with tiny dots. This same design he repeated on all three of Murtaugh, Bahari, and Huru.

While they waited for the Aşanti to finish their final preparations, Bahari turned to Huru. "Before we engage in

96

combat, I want to say in front of my friend and ally, Shakina, that I have forgiven you for your deception."

"Ọrẹ." He chuckled. "You have no idea what is happening here. These Aṣanti are *omugọ*—fools. The, as you say, *erú alagidi* are powerful and can share their power with those so enlightened to see."

Deeply troubled by his friend's thoughts, Bahari shook his head. "So what they say is true? You are a traitor to our people?"

"Not our people," Huru corrected. "I would never give them one of our brothers or sisters."

"But you would give them someone else's? One man should never sell another!" Bahari yelled at him. "I gave myself up so my family could be free!"

"And where are they now?" Huru asked with a snide tone.

With only a second's hesitation, Bahari punched his old friend right in the nose. "No doubt hiding from cowards like you!"

Jacq moved to intervene, but Murtaugh stopped her, shaking his head. Reluctantly, she heeded his advice and sat back down.

"Where have your morals gone? You trade in blood and tears, and you care not for your beliefs! You are not the ọrẹ I left behind. You are more *alejò* to this place than the *erú alagidi*," Bahari declared with a growl.

"You know nothing of my beliefs!" Huru said with a snarl.

"I know nothing of you! The Huru I knew would never put Kehinde in harm's way. He would be reverent and wish to avoid angering orisha Sango, should anything happen to Kehinde," Bahari continued.

Huru's lip curled. "The gods of our people have forsaken us. You, of all people, should understand that."

Bahari shifted his weight. "Perhaps, but not all gods forsake their people."

"If that helps you find some comfort," Huru returned, his eyes gleaming with provocation.

Before Bahari could respond, Nokware approached, talking to Bahari about the impending raid. Subsequently, Bahari and Huru shared some terse words and threatening grunts before they returned back to the foreigners. "They are ready."

Ten minutes later, the group had snuck just a short distance from the edge of a very rough-looking collection of huts. There were five buildings in total—two for quarters, one for a sort of armament, one for food and dining, and one to house the captives being transported.

The warm night air was pleasant and peaceful, still fragrant from the recent rain. It was also alive with noises of the night—a much more advantageous background than silence. Nokware talked to the group, gesturing and pointing before Bahari turned to Jacq and Murtaugh.

"The building to the south has the captives. We shall run the raid to free everyone in there. Shakina, Nokware does not want to risk harm to you, and neither do I, so you and Crevan stay here to gather the captives," he instructed. "Crevan, it is your duty to keep her from getting even a scratch, or Nokware will take it as a bad omen. If we do this, we can continue on our own way tomorrow."

"So, no fighting?" she asked, gesturing at the paint.

Murtaugh shrugged. "Might be for the best. We won't know what's happening, anyway. We can't understand a ruddy word they say."

Bahari nodded. "Crevan is correct."

Running her tongue over her lip, Jacq sighed. "I find it a bit loathsome when the both of you agree to something and I do not."

A tiny smile flitted across Bahari's expression—the first sign of happiness she'd seen since they'd arrived, save his perhaps premature jubilation for seeing Huru. "Shakina, you are his battle

charm tonight. Tonight you must be Kehinde. You must uphold the morale, and you must give hope to the captives as they flee to the forest. Tonight you give us good luck." He set a small torch in her hand, and then he turned to Crevan. "You are *alaabo*. You must protect her as she holds the light. She must not have a scratch."

Murtaugh nodded. "Right. Not a scratch."

Patting him on the shoulder, Bahari turned and made his way back to Nokware.

Rolling her eyes, Jacq grumbled in frustration. "Such superstitious nonsense! A good luck charm?"

"I always thought you'd make a fine lucky charm," Murtaugh noted, smiling in self-derived amusement.

Shaking her head, Jacq laughed. "Your wit becomes you, Mr. Murtaugh." Then she saw the raiding party almost upon the targeted building. "Oh! Murtaugh!" She nudged him, and pointed.

Across the distance, Nokware, two of his men, Bahari, and Huru crept to the exterior wall, peering around and through cracks in the structure. Nokware motioned for his two men to check the sides for any additional manpower. As they moved out to follow his orders, he found a dry spot near the bottom of the wall. Using his machete, Bahari dug out the spot slowly and carefully so they could all peek inside.

Lined up along the wall sat five prisoners—three men and two women. Their hands and feet were bound, and their eyes and bodies looked weary. They hung their heads as if in shame, though they likely had done nothing wrong.

At seeing them, Nokware touched at the wall with a gentleness as though he might shatter the world. Bahari frowned. This was precisely what he'd left to save his family from. Had he succeeded? Huru took a glance, but immediately looked away.

"Hey!" a scruffy, unkempt man said as he walked through the front door of the poorly constructed building. "Make sure they get a meal and some water, huh? Don't want 'em wastin' away afore auction."

At this, outrage flared in Nokware's eyes. He stood and pulled his mask over his face, signifying he was preparing to attack. Nodding to Bahari, he yelled out, "Ee-yaya-ya!"

"Ee-yaya-ya! Ee-yaya-ya! Ee-yaya-ya!" rang out in a wild, chorus response.

As it did, the masked Aṣanti bowmen came pouring from the woods, shooting at the traders as they saw them.

In reply, the tradesmen pulled out their flintlocks and began returning fire. Whooping and yelling continued as the two groups collided, firing off their ammo of choice, swinging blades and fists. In the midst of the turmoil, Nokware and Bahari ducked into the hut, holding the captives, easily dispatching the two guards who stood to stop them.

Gasping and cringing, the prisoners shrunk away from the two newcomers. Nokware, however, continued with confidence and reassurance, communicating the escape plan for them to go to the girl with the light in the woods. Bahari knelt to help untie the captives, starting with the girl on the end. She lifted her thin face to look up at him with sad blue eyes.

Bahari froze and his heart nearly stopped. "Morenike?" he whispered.

"*Arakunrin?*" she asked, her lip trembling.

Shoving Bahari aside, Nokware cut her bindings and explained the plan again. Then he turned back to the stupefied giant he'd brought with him. "Bahari!"

Shaking off the debilitating astonishment, Bahari gave his attention back to the Aṣanti leader. When Nokware nodded, he took a deep breath and moved to his agreed-upon position at the entrance of the hovel. Shouts and grunts filled the air around him, but he said a quick prayer and made sure he was properly aligned. Then he yelled out, "Uu-ree! Uu-ree!"

In reply, he saw the soft glow of Jacq's torch become visible in the tree line.

Motioning for the nearest captive, he pointed him to the light and instructed him in his native tongue to run to it, not stop, and not look back.

As the man headed toward them, Jacq said, "Oh! There's the first one, Murtaugh! Here he comes!"

"Oi!" Murtaugh called softly as the man scrambled to them. "*Ailewu!*"

"*Ailewu! Ailewu!*" the man repeated in a whimper. Reaching them, he collapsed and huddled beside them on the ground, continually repeating the word. He eagerly accepted the food and water Murtaugh handed him, muttering other things they could not understand, but he kept returning to say, "*Ailewu!*"

"One out," Jacq said, smiling sadly at him. Then she flashed the torch twice and hid it, signaling his safe arrival.

Bahari reached for the next person, one of the girls. "Uu-ree! Uu-ree!" he called again.

Again, Jacq held up the torch, and again the prisoner fled, finding her way to them.

When Bahari summoned the next man, however, he shook his head and insisted, "I am Akinyemi. I will not be shamed any longer. I must stay and fight to regain my honor."

Clapping him on the back, Nokware put a blade in his hand. Then he motioned that he was free to go. With a wild yell, he disappeared into the all-encompassing brawl that was consuming the poor excuse for a village.

Beckoning the next person, Bahari again found himself looking into the eyes of a blue-eyed teenage girl, so much like his own. Pushing past his confusion and emotional reaction, he yelled, "Uu-ree! Uu-ree!" Then as soon as he saw the signal, giving her a reassuring squeeze to her shoulders, he sent her out.

With only one man left to send, Nokware and Bahari were beginning to feel the night was a success, until those engaged in the fisticuffs came crashing through one of the unkempt walls, causing the entire structure to tumble to the ground.

Seeing the building crumble, both Jacq and Murtaugh gasped. "Oh, Judas!" he muttered under his breath.

"That-that wasn't," Jacq stammered, pointing. "There were more-more people." Her heart pounded. "B-Bahari... Bahari was still..."

Putting his hand on her shoulder, Murtaugh whispered, "Just wait, eh? Just wait a moment."

Taking a deep breath, Jacq forced herself to remain calm, pushing her worry, fear, and impending sadness into a closet in her mind. "Just wait," she repeated. "Just wait."

As she tried to quell her anxiety, she heard, "Uu-ree-tah! Uu-ree-tah!"

Her heart leaping, she grinned over at Murtaugh. "That's the signal for the last one!"

"See, I told you," he returned confidently.

Uncovering the torch once more, she strained to see their final rescued hostage. "Oh! There," she said, pointing.

A lone figure was stumbling toward them, hesitation and trepidation hanging on every step he took.

"What's he doing?" Murtaugh asked, just as much to himself as to anyone else.

"Why is he so slow? Is he injured?" Jacq asked, fidgeting in her spot.

"He's stopping," Murtaugh noted as the man came to a halt.

"I'm going down there!" Jacq said, looking for a place to set the torch.

"No. No, you're not," Murtaugh argued. "Bahari said to stay here."

"Murtaugh, look at him. He needs help," she returned, cross with his disagreement with her.

As they squabbled, the man came to a nervous standstill and turned to look back. Doubt filling his mind, he started to return to the havoc-torn huts. Then he second-guessed himself again and headed back toward the safe location. However, before he got more than halfway, he paused again, and then began going an altogether different direction.

"Where is he going?" Jacq asked, bewildered as to his inability to adhere to his instructions.

Kawack! The man stumbled and fell.

Gasping, Jacq hid the flame. "Murtaugh!" she exclaimed in a whisper, her heart pounding.

"Sh! Shh! Shh! Shhhh!" he answered, urging her to keep silent, touching her cheek, shoulders, and hands in an attempt to reassure her.

When his fingers grazed her arm and hand, she involuntarily latched onto him, holding back the wave of anxiety threatening to crash down on her and wash away all logic. "What do we do?"

"We wait, like he said," Murtaugh replied firmly. "We keep these three safe, and we wait for either the signal or dawn."

Taking a long, slow inhale and exhale, she nodded. "You're right. Of course you're right. Bahari would want them safe."

"Bahari?" the blue-eyed girl asked. "You know Bahari?"

Jacq and Murtaugh glanced between themselves and her. "Aye. Do you?"

She smiled, and a tear rolled down her young cheek. "I am Morenike. He is my *arakunrin*—my uncle."

Back at the toppled building, Bahari and Nokware dusted themselves off and promptly threw themselves into the nearly concluded fight. With the two of them added, the tradesmen's already waning chances for victory were obliterated.

"I do not," Bahari yelled at one man, "like having a building dropped on my head! And I do not like the way you smell!"

As he dealt the man a final blow to knock him unconscious, he began noticing all the bodies—some injuries, some fatalities—strewn about the camp. Off to one side, he recognized Huru amongst the fallen. "Oh, no."

As Nokware's men began celebrating their triumph, Bahari trudged across the distance to check on his once good friend. His heart lurched, and his mouth frowned at seeing him—prostrate and lifeless. Kneeling beside him, Bahari closed his eyes and shook his head at seeing a flintlock wound to Huru's back. Muttering in his native Yoruba dialect, he wrote his friend's name in the dirt.

"You must believe he died well," Akinyemi said, coming up beside Bahari. Taking a knee, he continued, "*E dupe.*" Then he smoothed over Huru's name written in the earth.

"His sacrifice was not in vain. I only hope his redemption was secure," Bahari replied.

"Bolaji did not make it," Akinyemi said, "but the others, I believe, made it to your friends."

"Shakina," Bahari mumbled. "I must go."

"I will join you," Akinyemi said.

The two hurried to where the others had gathered in the trees, however, Bahari was surprised to see Nokware already there. He had his arms wrapped around the girl without the blue eyes, and he was stroking her hair with all the paternal affection a person could have.

"Bahari!" Jacq greeted him, giving him a quick hug. "This girl, Uchenna, was the daughter of his best friend. He cares for her like his own now, because her father died a few years ago." She smiled over at them.

Nokware looked up. "Bahari. Kehinde. Alaabo." Putting his arm around Uchenna, he talked to Bahari directly in their native dialect, extending a handshake, which Bahari took.

Then bowing at the group once more, Nokware and Uchenna turned and walked away.

"What did he say?" Jacq asked.

"He will keep his promise. We are to have safe passage from here to Tenkodogo. He offers many thanks and wishes us well on our journey." Then, glancing at Murtaugh, who was sitting alone off to one side, Bahari asked Jacq, "How are you? Did Crevan watch over you?"

Jacq smiled and looked over at the Irishman. "Of course he did. He always does." She shook her head. "He's always there when I need him most, even if only in my mind."

Bahari's face, covered in blood and dirt, tilted in confusion.

A rush of emotion jabbing at her heart and pricking at her eyes, Jacq lifted her shoulders in overwhelmed general appreciation. "He's my North Star."

Five months earlier...

"Your North Star?" Alex asked with an incredulous inflection, sitting beside Jacq on her bed.

Bill, Jacq's blue and gold macaw, walked over, clicking his tongue. "North Star. North Star."

"Aye," Jacq said, laughing and reaching out to pet Bill. "From the first time I met him, he showed me a man I could fancy didn't have to be a scoundrel."

"I have yet to see evidence of that," Alex returned teasingly.

Glaring at her, Jacq continued, "When he left, I forced myself to forget him. Then when I was stranded on that godforsaken island, I found that merely entertaining him in my mind gave me courage. I-I wished... I wished so desperately that he were there because I knew. I knew he would help me." She paused. "He would do everything he could to save me."

"Oh, Jacq." Alex's expression became sober.

"It's true! And he did, Alex! He brought you and Miata to me!" She touched her forehead. "I've fancied Mr. Rackham since I met him, but he's been naught but confusion. Mi—Murtaugh is like a light in the darkness. He is true and constant." She looked at Alex again, her entire countenance raw with sincerity.

"Perhaps he should receive sainthood," Alex suggested lightly.

Jacq frowned. "Honestly, Alex. Do be serious! He's... he's..."

"Your North Star," Alex repeated, a small smile breaching her face.

"My North Star." Shaking her head, Jacq smirked. "He's my North Star."

Touching at Jacq's cheek, Bahari smiled. "Tonight, you were the North Star." He glanced over at Morenike, and he was, once again, brought to a stop by those eyes of hers. Taking a step toward her, he said in a hushed tone, "I know your face."

"And I yours," she replied meekly. "I am your niece, Morenike." Tears began to stream down her cheeks. "You have been missed."

Hearing the words nearly burst Bahari's heart. He shuddered from the release of hidden anger, subdued fear, and stifled grief. She held out trembling hands to him, and in response, he engulfed her in a hug overcome with relief and racked with guilt.

"I was not supposed to be away so long!" he whispered into her ear.

She squeezed him, sniffling. "We know."

Shying away to give them some privacy, Jacq stared out at the destroyed town, silent beneath the moonlight. Every Aṣanti had vanished, and it seemed like no tradesman had been left alive. The brutality of it all began to sink in. "This… this is…"

"A tragedy," Murtaugh noted, coming up beside her. "But it is savage justice, the type of end that seems to find unsavory men."

She gazed upon him, so alluring in the darkness, especially compared to the ugly violence the makeshift village had succumbed to. She wanted to reach for his hand, to feel it warm and reassuringly holding her own. Temptation prevailed, and her fingers extended toward his, timid and shaking.

"We should leave," he said abruptly.

Her hand recoiled.

"You three come with us." He gestured to the two rescued men and Morenike.

Akinyemi covered his heart with his fist. "We thank you, but Wuraomo and me, we have work to do in this forest."

"And we have one more thing to do before we may be rid of this place," Bahari spoke up, releasing Morenike. "One more thing."

Chapter 5

Three days later, Oduntan and his trio of travelers snuck in close to the port of van Draenweg. All around the ramshackle fort was quiet, as though the forest and its inhabitants had to whisper among themselves. The port had men strewn about—wandering here, working there. The atmosphere reeked of idleness and desolation, as though it was in an indefinite waiting cycle while suffering perpetual exile.

"Looks like they fixed the fence," Miata said, gesturing to the livestock corral.

"Do you suppose the two mules made a safe return?" Alex asked, trying to get a good view of the animals.

"Say, there's Amy," Rackham said, pointing to the blond girl standing across the way by the water's edge.

"Oh! How well she looks!" Alex exclaimed softly, sighing in relief and finding herself instantly envious of Amy's clean, tidy appearance and posh clothes.

Alexandria! she scolded herself internally.

"She is your family?" Oduntan asked of Alex.

"Yes. My sister. Well, my other sister. We must rescue her and my father," Alex explained. "I am so grateful you brought us back, but do you suppose perhaps you could stay just a while longer?" She offered up a smile as her instrument of imploring and persuading.

He grinned. "Tayewo, I am your guide. If you need me, I am here."

"Oi!" Miata started. "That bloke be offerin' her a drink!"

They all watched as Amy smiled and laughed, accepting a cup from a bearded man.

"Oh. This is very bad," Rackham said.

"I be knowin', mate!" Miata touched at his lightly studded chin. "I be unable to be growin' a beard such as that!"

"No, our ship. She's nowhere to be found!" Rackham said, his voice rife with concern at this observation.

"We must find out what is happening!" Alex said firmly. "But how? How do we find out?"

Chuckling, Miata straightened his waistcoat. "That be somethin' I be havin' the skill to be doin'."

Scoffing, Alex shook her head. "On what notion do you make this assertion?" she asked, smiling to herself.

"It be just about two year ago I were a brilliant study o' the fine art o' movin' in secret," he said playfully.

"You mean sneaking around? For the purpose of stealing?" Alex asked, her voice painted with disgust. "Must you remind me of your sordid past?"

"More importantly," Rackham spoke up, "how do you believe this can be of use to us?"

"I can be overhearin' conversations and plans," he stated plainly, "without bein' caught."

"Truly?" Alex asked, interested though she didn't want to be.

"Let every man give the skill he has to offer," Oduntan said, dropping his hand on Miata's shoulder.

"He was not even very adept—" Alex began saying to Oduntan then turning to Miata, continued, "You were not even very adept, were you, Mr. O'Keeffe?"

"I reckon I rather was," he returned, sounding as though his pride was at stake.

"How adept?" she asked, crossing her arms.

"Seems I be makin' you vexed regardless of what my answer be," he returned.

"Well?" she asked, lifting an eyebrow.

An impish smile plucked at the corners of his mouth. "Quite."

His smug expression and the way he leered at her, oozing with confidence on the matter, put Alex ill at ease. "Truly? But you are all clumsiness and two left feet."

"On a ship, a bit, and in the forest, perhaps. But it isn't like I be tryin', Alex. Besides, who be believin' a clumsy oaf be a thief, hmm?" He eyed her. "A little trust, eh?"

She sat in silence, glancing between the other two. "Only a very little," she returned.

He nodded. "Don't be worryin'. You won't be gettin' disappointed." Beaming with sureness, he leaned against a tree branch, which immediately gave way, dropping him to the forest floor.

"Pride goeth before the fall," Alex noted with a grim tone.

"Oh, be sparin' me," Miata said, groaning as he sat up.

"You there! Mogens!" one of the ambling men shouted. "Go see what that sound was!" In response, another man grunted and headed straight for them.

"Brilliant," Rackham commented. "Someone's noticed your discreet attempts at waltzing with the tree. Move!"

Helping them hide away, Oduntan positioned himself as look out while the man lumbered over to investigate.

"Mogens," he mocked, "go see what that sound was! Mogens, clean up the slop! Mogens, fetch me shirt! Mogens, get the lass her tea!" Glancing about, he paused and looked back toward the fort. "Bad bunch o' bloody luck for Mogens, that's what they are. Makin' deals with the boss and all." He looked around to be sure he was alone, and then pulled a small flask of rum from his jacket.

Alex scowled and pointed in protest, but Miata pulled her hand down and covered her mouth, just to be safe.

"Ever since they made off with themselves, disappearin' into the woods." He shook his head and took a drink. "'Tisn't right. 'Tisn't fair."

"Mogens! You get lost?" a different man yelled, laughing.

Growling, Mogens put the flask away. "*Ik kom eraan, je achterbakse deerne van een hond!*" he yelled back, stomping out of the woods.

The two men continued insulting each other and their relations in Dutch as they walked back toward the fort.

Once they were gone, Oduntan motioned for the rest to come out.

"He was talking of us!" Alex exclaimed, slapping away Miata's hands.

"And yer father," Miata added in equal angst.

"My father is making deals with the lord of this insufferable, pathetic excuse for a port?" Alex shook her head. "How can it be?"

"I'm sure it's nothing of the like you two are squawking about," Dante spoke up. "We just need more information."

At this, all eyes turned to Miata.

Meanwhile, Jacq trudged along with Morenike and Murtaugh, still following Bahari. Catching up to the Irishman, Jacq said in a quiet voice, "He's hardly put three words together since we left that place, and we've been walking three days. Do you suppose he is unwell?"

"How should I know?" Murtaugh inquired back in an equally hushed tone. "He had us bury Huru and all the tradesmen. That can have an effect on a man."

"The whole incident was such a tragedy." Jacq sighed and looked at Bahari. "I think it's time I speak with him."

Murtaugh grimaced. "Are you certain?"

Shaking her head, she replied, "No, but-but it matters not. He mustn't be allowed to think he is alone in this."

"You think he blames himself for Huru's death?"

"I don't rightly know. He said everything to him in their native language. I couldn't understand a word." She huffed. "Wish me luck, eh?"

"Best of luck, Jacq," he said, smirking. "You'll be needing it."

Elbowing him playfully, she put her chin in the air and hurried to catch up to Bahari. "Bahari!" she called. "Bahari!"

"Shakina," he said, in a voice duller than ever before.

"How-how are you?" She was practically jogging to keep up with his long, stomping strides.

"Well enough," he answered, terse in inflection as well as words.

"Why..." She paused, trying to read him. *Go for something different, just to get him speaking*, she thought. "Why had you never afore mentioned the beliefs of your people?"

Glancing over at her, he was surprised as to the topic of her inquiry. "Well, they are just that—the beliefs of my people, not mine. I discovered quickly that their gods could not hear me on the ocean, but Father Brandon—rest his soul, the priest on Ming's ship—his god could."

"How do you know?" Jacq asked, now genuinely interested.

"His god gave him peace, regardless of his circumstance. This was something I needed. The orishas could never grant me that request, but Father Brandon's god, Cristo, he could."

"He gave you peace? About what?"

"Aye. About my decisions, my choices. I asked him to forgive me, and he did. I asked him to help me find my family." He gestured around him and to her. "He is."

"And he forgave you?" Jacq asked, taking a personal interest as to his insights on the subject.

"Aye. But to have complete peace I had to forgive myself as well." Finally slowing his pace, he looked over at her. "Why do you ask?"

"Oh." She shrugged and forced a laugh. "Just curious."

"Mmmm." He eyed her contemplatively before returning his gaze to what was ahead of him.

"Bahari?" she spoke again.

"Shakina." He stopped to give her his full attention, leaning on a spear he had brought with and was using as a walking stick.

"I just wanted to say burying the departed was honorable, putting up a memorial stone was noble, and I'm sorry about Huru. Losing someone you thought was a mate... someone you thought you knew, but are no longer certain of..." She paused, her expression tensing, relaxing, tensing, and relaxing in thought. "It's-it's-it's difficult." She lifted her eyes to his, expressing wordless heartfelt empathetic sympathies.

His hardened demeanor softened a smidgen, and his frown lessened just a little. Nodding, he agreed, "It is." Taking a deep breath, he glanced back at Murtaugh and Morenike, who had come to a stop a short distance back. "Well, we best keep moving. We don't want to be out in open savanna when night falls."

When he turned to push onward, Murtaugh smiled over at Jacq. "He'll come around. It just takes a bit of time is all."

"A bit of time," she repeated, nodding. "And a measure of self-respect so one knows when to cease with self-loathing."

His brow furrowing at this, he tilted his head, trying to deduce where such a statement derived from.

Noticing his study of her, she forced a laugh and waved away her comment. "I suppose everyone knows that."

Watching her pivot and follow after Bahari, he sighed. "Not everyone, Jackie. Not everyone."

As night fell across the savanna where the northern travelers tucked themselves away amid some trees, it stretched south with long, lackadaisical fingers to van Draenweg. Once darkness cloaked the oceanside fort, Miata slunk through town, keeping to the shadows as men ambled past on the way to whatever destination they had. The night life was dismal, considering it was predominately a small trade port. The centrally located main building was reminiscent of the inn where he originally came to know the twins. It was two–story, with the lower level being a sort of tavern-eating establishment while the upper was, unbeknownst to him, officer's quarters and Tuinstra's base of operations—where Vice Admiral Luray and Amy spent much of their time. To the west, a long single-story building served as the quarters for the majority of the port's workers while a smaller structure to the east seemed to be the port's auction house.

Taking note of the other small buildings sprinkled around, he decided to obtain his information from the loose-jawed boys in the tavern. Making his way over, he snatched up a few unsupervised items along the way—a hat, a coat, and a limp.

Lumbering inside, he was relieved when nobody lifted an eye to him. Scoping out the place, he selected a spot near some men who appeared to be dedicated patrons as one lay face-first on the table, and nobody seemed to mind or notice.

Setting up the coat and hat on the chair nearest the men, he sat across from it and listened to them as he sipped on a mead he pinched off the end of the bar. Minutes dragged by as they argued first over the best type of knot and then over the most irritating habits of their fellow crewmen. Just as Miata began to give up hope on them proving useful, however, their conversation pivoted to their involuntary guests.

"Have ya seen the way she walks 'round here? Like a princess, says I!" one man said, guffawing and slurping down his mead.

"We'll be glad to see 'em gone, we will," a different one said. "Though none as much as Barend."

They glanced across the room at a table where a bedraggled man sat in a brooding posture, hovering over his drink and a plate of food that was hardly touched.

"Maybe Mogens'll go wif 'em," the first one said, chortling.

"They can't be leavin' soon enough," the second returned. "We be wantin' fings back t'normal, we be."

"Aye. 'Tain't like the boss to be so careful and gen'rous," the first one noted, drinking another gulp.

"Well, we did burn down his boat," the third nondrooling man pointed out dismally.

Miata had to stop himself from choking on his sip of mead.

The first man shook his head. "Not us! Them French louts it were!"

"Still don't explain the boss. Maybe he's sweet on the princess." Chuckling, the second man took the sleeping man's half-empty pint.

"Maybe they's royalty after all, huh?" the first man asked.

"Likely not," the third man said with a sigh. "The wench be pretty, but that isn't it. It's somethin' 'bout that lord. Some sort o' nobility, I reckon. Either way, struck a deal he has, for her and him and his crew. They ship out tomorrow. I say good riddance." He lifted his mug.

"Good riddance!" the other two agreed, raising their pints in hearty agreement.

"See her dance!" the drooling man yelled, jolting upright and lifting his hand with theirs.

"Oi!" a man yelled as he walked in the door. "Some *dwaas juggins* nipped me coat!"

Looking up, Miata scooted away from his table and slunk into the dim corner nearby.

Then seeing it near the drooling man, the new arrival pointed an accusatory finger. "You there!"

"Wasn't him, no, sir!" the second man at the table spoke up.

"Well, it's me coat, for certain!" yelled the newcomer as he picked up the hat to take the coat off the chair.

"What're you doin' with my hat, Janssen?" a different man yelled, gesturing to the tricorn in Janssen's hand as he came roaring over.

"'Tisn't mine, Hendriks!" he retorted.

"You're right about that!" Hendriks shouted back, leaning back and punching Janssen in the jaw.

Within seconds, one punch led to another, and the entire room was embroiled in a free-for-all fracas.

Smirking to himself, Miata sauntered uninhibited and unquestioned out of the tavern without the coat, the hat, or the limp. "I still be havin' it," he applauded himself. He paused just a second to glance over at the brown-haired man he assumed they'd been speaking of, still slumped over his table in the opposite corner, seemingly unaffected by the outbreak in the room.

As he distanced himself from the building, he took a moment to look back and admire his work, but came to an abrupt halt. There, in the window above, Amy sat, nearly silhouetted against the candlelight. His heart sinking as he watched her dab at her eyes, he snuck closer, hoping to get her attention.

However, before he was close enough to call out to her, he heard the vice admiral say, "Amy, my dear, step away from the window."

Miata watched in dismay as she slumped her shoulders and obeyed.

"There, there, darling. Tomorrow we leave for Cabo Corso, and this will begin to become simply a horrible memory."

"Cabo Corso," Miata muttered. Then heaving a sigh, he hurried back to find his companions.

As he crashed into the forest, he was all but tackled and shoved against a tree with a stick pressed against his throat.

"Oduntan! Oduntan, be that you?" He coughed.

"The password," Oduntan demanded.

"Frankincense! Frankincense!" he said, pulling away from the stick. "Come now, release me!"

"You said—" Oduntan returned as he let Miata go.

"I be knowin' what I be sayin'," he said, touching at his throat. "I just be glad ye be helpin' us, not against us." He forced a smile.

"What's the word?" Dante asked, walking up to meet them, Alex at his heels.

"They be leavin' tomorrow for Cabo Corso. I be thinkin' we be needin' to be acquirin' some supplies and followin'," Miata said, straightening and trying to appear unaffected.

"You were able to procure information? Useful information?" Alex asked in unbridled astonishment.

Miata scowled. "Be it so hard to be believin' I can be doin' somethin' well?" he asked.

"W-well," Alex started, searching for polite words.

Holding up his hand, he interrupted, "Don't be answerin' that."

"Well, what of Amy and my father? Are they well? Did you see them?" Alex asked, pressing forward in earnest.

"They seem well enough," he said awkwardly.

"Why can we not simply join them?" she questioned.

"And where's our ship?" Rackham added.

Taking a moment to glance between them, Miata sighed. "It be seemin' the vice admiral be makin' a deal with the port boss for his freedom. I be not knowin' if it be includin' us or if we be puttin' them in jeopardy if we be just appearin'. An' it be seemin' as though some bilge rat be burnin' our ship!"

Dante and Alex started at this. "Burned?" they asked in unison.

Miata's face remained grim.

"We must set out for Cabo Corso," Alex said in a confident voice. "That was the agreement."

"We rest tomorrow and gather supplies," Dante added, nodding at Miata. "We'll just follow the beach."

"It would be best if we were to have a guide," Alex noted.

Everyone turned to Oduntan, who'd been thus far silent. He gazed between them. "You wish to go to Cabo Corso? I do not know the forest as I do here."

"You would have vaster knowledge than we have," Alex pointed out. "We could make it worth your while."

He looked intrigued. "You would give Oduntan a wife?"

"A w——?" Alex repeated, tripping up on the word. "I… uh… No. No, not a-a… not a wife." She laughed uncomfortably.

"How about gold, mate?" Dante offered, giving him a knowing smile.

"Tayewo, you give Oduntan fair trade?" he asked Alex.

"How does a gold coin for every day it takes to get from here to Cabo Corso sound?" she asked. "We could also grant you safe return when we depart, if you wish."

Oduntan smiled. "Two gold coins a day, but I will find my own way home."

"Agreed," she said, holding out her hand.

"We have an accord," Dante declared cheerfully.

Grinning, Oduntan spat in his hand and grabbed Alex's in a firm shake, squishing his saliva into her palm. It was all she could do to keep herself from vomiting.

The following morning, Jacq and Murtaugh were walking through some outcropping of forest that ran along the edge of the savanna. Antelope and elephants dotted the tall grass, grazing and roaming at their leisure. However, with the forest edge close by, the group decided to turn there for food.

While they trudged along, examining leaves and plants, Murtaugh found his eyes kept wandering to her. Clearing his throat, he noted, "So, the big bloke seems better."

"Aye," Jacq agreed, tapping the trunk of a tree with a stick she was carrying.

"Do you suppose he's ceased with his self-loathing?" he asked, kneeling to check for edible roots.

"I imagine he'll be coming about," she replied, leaning against the tree and watching him work. "Find anything?"

Shaking his head, he sat back on his heels. "No. We should head back toward the river. I'm better at fishing than searching for food over half buried in the earth," he said, muttering and grumbling while dusting off his hands.

Giggling, she nodded. "I can't imagine you a gardener."

"Tsk!" He snorted as though insulted. "I can do what I need to!" He stood, gesturing to the ground around him.

"Truly?" She eyed him, still ever so attractive despite the added roughness of the wilderness.

Smirking, he sensed her impending mischievousness. "Jacq—"

"Catch me!" she said, leaping away and charging deeper into the jungle.

"Jacq!" he yelled after her, shaking his head. "Jackie!" he called again, jogging further in to find her when she did not respond.

Giggling, she darted from tree to tree, keeping an eye out for him. "Come, come, Murtaugh! Must you leave me in such suspense?" Seeing him, she began circling back around.

"Jackie," he said again, scanning the forest and listening. The movements of leaves and branches caught his eye. "When I do catch you—" He laughed, his mind giving him suggestions he would never dare speak aloud.

"You'll what, Murtaugh?" she asked, taunting him. "You'll teach me a lesson? How to be a proper lady?" Quietly and quickly, she snuck around behind him.

He waited, listening and not responding. His breathing remained calm and his mind clear.

She slid out from behind a tree, silent and pleased as she approached him.

Whipping around, he grabbed her by the wrist and waist, shoving her into the tree she'd been using as cover. "Aye," he whispered. "A lesson." He grinned down at her.

Gasping, she squirmed beneath his hold but stopped when she met his gaze. "Nobody else calls me Jackie," she said in a low tone.

"No?" he asked in a breathless whisper.

Biting her lip, she shook her head. "No."

"Does it bother you?" he asked, watching her chew her lower lip and the rise and fall of her chest as she breathed.

A hint of a demure smile perking up her lips, she shook her head again. "Sharing something, just you and me—it's not so bad, is it?"

Shrugging, he answered in a husky voice, "No."

Across from them, they heard some rustling.

Pulling away from her, Murtaugh glanced about. "Did you hear that?"

"I did." She searched the vegetation for movement.

Snap! The twig breaking rang out loud, followed by a much-quieter *crunch, crunch, crunch.*

"This way," Jacq said, beckoning Murtaugh to follow her.

The two moved ahead laden with trepidation.

"Maybe," he whispered, "it's a really, really fat mouse."

Sending him a playful glare, she wrinkled her nose. "I very much doubt that. It's probably just a wayward—"

Before she could finish her sentence, she moved some leaves to reveal the mystery.

"Boar!" she squealed, tearing off in the direction of the savanna.

Murtaugh glanced over to find a highly agitated, bristly, tusked wild pig snorting at them. "Oh, Judas." Jumping back, he ran after Jacq.

However, the hostile animal decided to give chase despite their fleeing attempts. As the two ran, leaped, and crashed back to the grassland, the boar snorted and bashed his way right for them. Once they entered the grassy terrain, Murtaugh shouted, "I'll lead him away." Then he gallantly veered off a different direction.

"Murtaugh!" she yelled. "He's still after me!"

"Dodge it! Dodge it!" he shouted, chasing after the boar.

"I can't run forever!" she called back, zigzagging.

"Climb a tree!"

"I won't be fast enough!"

"Lose the sash! Maybe he doesn't like red! I hear it vexes a bull like mad!"

While racing for her life, Jacq undid her sash and let it float off behind her, completely ineffective. "Murtaugh!" she shouted, sincere fear beginning to take over as she became increasingly exhausted.

He paused, grabbing fists of his hair while trying to think. As he stood, unable to generate more ideas, Bahari came running up beside him, causing the Irishman to jump. No sooner did his feet stop than he was launching the spear at the boar with such force and aim it slayed the beast instantly.

Panting, Jacq came to a halt, her legs feeling like jelly. Then smiling over at the men, she collapsed. Running to her side, Murtaugh propped her up and handed her the water strapped to her body. After taking a drink and leaning her head back onto his shoulder, the two looked up to see Bahari approaching them.

"I said roots." Shaking his head, he pointed at the fallen animal. "I said find food. This was not what I meant." Grumbling, he snorted and sighed. "This was food finding you!" Continuing to mutter and mumble to himself, he marched off to assess the condition of the boar.

Between ragged breaths, Jacq said, "I've changed my mind. I no longer wish to be out here. Kill me now." She let out a weak giggle.

Chuckling, Murtaugh slung his arm around her shoulders. "And have that cheerful chap all to myself? I don't think so, mate."

She laughed with him, closing her eyes against the sun. "Maybe tomorrow."

"Probably not." Grinning, he rested his chin on the top of her head.

Trudging back up to them, huffing and sighing, Bahari said, "He's a younger male, probably trying to prove himself. But what's done is done. He will provide all of us much needed food for many days. I will prepare him tonight."

"You're welcome," Murtaugh said as Bahari left to tend to the slain boar.

"Don't be insufferable," Jacq said, taking a long breath. "It doesn't suit you, and you don't want him cross at you."

"That I know," Murtaugh returned. "I saw what happened to the boar."

Across the miles, Alex sat down beside Rackham, preparing to eat some food Miata had procured from the van Draenweg mess hall. "I keep thinking of Jacq out there in the wilderness. It puts me so ill at ease." She poked at her food.

"Crevan nor Bahari be lettin' anythin' happen to her," Miata spoke up. "She be in mighty carin' hands."

"Tsk! Do not trifle with my feelings or consider me too delicate to speak of such robust topics of conversation!" Alex retorted. "I am being sincere."

"As be I!" Miata retorted, injury echoing in his inflection.

"You are Tayewo. She is Kehinde," Oduntan said, holding up both hands. "You belong together." He clasped his hands. "You are not whole when you are apart."

"Perhaps," Alex replied, contemplating his input.

"Perhaps it is her choice of companion that troubles you," Dante suggested, taking a bite of his food. "I dislike her out in the wilds with Crevan."

Finishing his own meal, Miata scoffed. "You be one to be carin', mate." He laughed, wiping at his mouth.

"What are you suggesting?" Alex asked, glancing between them.

Miata smirked at Dante, who was glaring at him. "Should I be tellin' her?" He paused a beat. "Oh, I think I be." Turning back to Alex, he said, "You know he be fancyin' another—"

Gasping, Alex stared over at Dante in astonishment—an action that caused him great embarrassment. Clearing his throat, he spoke, "Well, I... I..."

Placing her food delicately on her knees, she crossed her arms. "I tell you, Mr. Rackham, a gentleman who professes empty affections or declines to correct misunderstanding is no gentleman at all. In fact, he is one of the most vile, insufferable, deceitful kind of man a person might have the unhappy chance to come across. He is, in a word, reprehensible."

Taken aback by her frank outburst, Dante scoffed and searched for some sort of reply.

"You do not wish to be such a man, do you, Mr. Rackham?" Alex asked, glowering at him expectantly for a response.

Dedicating a few moments to collecting his thoughts, Dante cleared his throat again and shook his head. "Certainly not. Though I should, in return, suggest you not be so hasty as to cast a man in such a lot afore he's had time to determine his intentions." With that, he finished off his food and stood.

"How long can it possibly take?" she asked in an incredulous tone.

Rackham shrugged. "I suppose it is determined by the man and his circumstance, as well as the inducement. One cannot expect every situation to be uniform."

"No, I suppose you are right on that score." Alex eyed him a moment more then returned to her meal. "If only it were simpler than that."

Fidgeting, Rackham looked over at a confused Oduntan and skeptical Miata. "If only," he reiterated in a mumble.

Oduntan scratched at his head. "Were we not speaking of her sister?" he asked, looking at Miata.

Shrugging, Miata laughed. "Don't be lookin' at me, mate. I be understandin' Alex like you be understandin' French."

His brow wrinkling, Oduntan shook his head. "But I do not— oh!" He grinned, pointing at Miata and chuckling. "Very good. You jest." He chuckled again.

A grin split Miata's mouth. "Aye." He laughed along with Oduntan. "Glad someone be appreciatin' me opinions."

Their laughter and remarks fell on deaf ears, however, as Alex was hundreds of miles away while she slowly ate her food. Rackham's words echoed in her mind: *Afore he's had time to determine his intentions.*

"They seemed perfectly clear to me," she muttered to herself, staring helplessly at the hot embers. "I-I... I am certain of it."

Two months earlier...

"Must you go?" Alex asked, taking a seat in her father's garden.

"I have put it off far too long," James said, sitting beside her.

"Have you not done your duty, writing the letters?" she asked, her voice strained with refrained emotions.

"I have tried, but they will not rest until they speak to me face-to-face on the matter," he explained. "They are very keen on seeing me married, and they have made it clear they suppose me utterly inept at procuring a wife of my own. Truly, they must believe me a complete fool." He laughed in embarrassment.

"Dear sweet James. Perhaps I should join you," she suggested with a timid voice and a small smile.

Shaking his head with a downcast demeanor, he sighed. "No, no. That is most generous and kind of you, but this must all be handled properly. You are a lady, and I shall not drag you with me in order that I may use you to defend myself against my own family." He reached for her hand. "I have to confront the issue alone, and when they see what I am saying is true, I shall bring you in with all the grandness you deserve. But I refuse to allow them the opportunity of conjecturing I have brought you along as a ploy to sate them."

"That is utterly ridiculous! Who would do such a thing?" she asked in disbelief.

"My, uh... my cousin, actually," he answered awkwardly, clearing his throat. "But you are real. It will be different."

Pulling her hands away tearfully, Alex asked, "What if it is not? What if they insist on you marrying this girl they have found for you? What if she is lovely?"

Retracting his hand, he shook his head. "No. No, they shall not continue imposing this girl's hand upon me once they hear what I have to say, and her loveliness is of no consequence because she will pale compared to you—in every way possibly imaginable. They *will* desist."

Sniffling, she wrung her hands as she watched him speak in all sincerity and passion. "But what if they do not?"

His jaw clenching, he stared at her with eyes clouded in emotions she could not determine. "They will."

"So I am to wait here, hoping you shall return for me?" she asked, a bitterness swelling in her tone.

"Not hoping. *Knowing*," he insisted vehemently, grasping her worrying hands in his. "Alexandria, you carry more doubt about your importance than anyone else I have ever known, but I-I… I love…" He choked a little on the word, as if his emotions were overwhelming his throat. "I love you."

"Then stay!" she begged. "Let us confront this together."

Standing, he massaged his forehead. "I cannot. I leave tomorrow."

Inhaling sharply, Alex stood and rushed into the house, fighting back tears she had promised herself would not fall in front of him. As she ran inside, James a few steps behind her, the butler asked, "Everything well with you, ma'am?"

"Yes! Mr. Monroe was just leaving!" she answered, climbing the stairs in a desperate hurry.

"Alex!" James called after her, but he was stopped by a firm hand on his arm. Glancing over, he saw the butler wearing a grim expression. "Mr. Edwards, please."

"I'm sorry, Mr. Monroe," Edwards replied simply.

"Ugh!" Tugging his arm free, he backed down the stairs. "Alexandria!" he yelled, looking after her. "I am coming back for you!"

However, she was already shut in her room, doubled over in a large armchair. Her body trembled with stifled sobs. As she cried, her monkey friend came to sit near her feet.

"He is leaving me, Frankincense," she whimpered to the little monkey. "He is leaving me."

The following morning found Jacq braiding her hair as she observed Murtaugh splash some water on his naked upper body and give himself a light shave. He caught her stare, and she turned away in embarrassment, coming face-to-face with Morenike. He smiled to himself.

"Oh! You surprised me," Jacq said, laughing.

"You fancy him? Alaabo?" the younger girl asked.

"Well, I…" Jacq smiled to disguise her unrest as she scrambled to think of some dull, reasonable excuse for her behavior. However, the bright, inquisitive stare of Morenike's eyes derailed her efforts. "He-he… he is a fine lad."

"He cares for you?" She tilted her head in curiosity.

Jacq's cheeks burned at the question and its directness. "Well, we're… we're, uh, good mates, so… he cares about me, you know, as a-as a mate." Clearing her throat, she tossed her braid over her shoulder. "How, uh, how are you and Bahari getting on?"

Shrugging, she sighed. "He is family, but I do not know him. My mother would tell me stories of her brother who went off to save his family. I did not… I could not see him until today when he…" She paused and did the motion of throwing the spear. "When he saved you." She smiled. "Then I saw him again."

Nodding, Jacq smiled back at her and gestured for them to walk back toward their campsite. "You speak very good English. How did you come to learn it?"

"The missionaries. They come to the village, but the traders do not fancy them and send them away. It is a short time after this I am taken away." She sniffled and then muzzled her emotions. "*Arakunrin*—Bahari, he says they have gone away—my family."

"We are going to find them," Jacq said with confidence.

"How do you know this? Because you are Kehinde?" Morenike touched at Jacq's hair and arms.

"No, I believe it, and I hope for it, and I pray for it," Jacq returned, smiling as she came to a stop at the site.

"Bahari says the orishas cannot hear," Morenike noted.

Exhaling, Jacq nodded. "Well, lucky for us, it is not to the orishas that I send my prayers."

Smiling, Morenike pointed a long, bony finger at the older girl. "You think my, uh…" She paused, trying to recall the word.

"Uncle?" Jacq filled in for her.

"Yes, Uncle. My uncle. You think my uncle to be a good man?"

An empathetic smile lightened Jacq's face. "I certainly have found him to possess quality of character and a strong moral code to which he remains faithful." At Morenike's confused expression, she added, "Aye. I think he is a good man."

"Mama always says he is. But he has seen so much."

"I believe he would say he's seen a bit too much."

They glanced toward him, kneeling beside the fire where he'd cooked the boar all night long. Feeling their stares, he said, "We leave once Crevan returns from the river."

Gathering her supplies, Jacq inquired, "How far do we walk today, Bahari?"

Looking to the sky, he answered, "We walk until the sun bids us stop. Moyo will cry until Morenike is returned."

Jacq turned to Morenike with a quizzical expression.

"Moyo is my mother," she said with a tense voice.

"She travels with his wife and children," Jacq explained. "He now has two reasons to find them." She smiled. "He will not be stopped."

As soon as Murtaugh rejoined them, they set out again across the savanna, continuing ever northward. The grassy plains occasionally traded off with small forest groves, but were otherwise vast, like the sea. Simultaneously, Oduntan and those with him struck out west for Cabo Corso through thick jungle forest teeming with life and rife with peril.

As they pressed on, both Jacq and Alex pondered of and worried for the other, clutching the little carved tokens and recalling Bahari's translated words: *When they have been rejoined, it shall signify the journey's end.*

Watching Alex trudge along in somber silence, Dante caught up to Miata and nudged him. "You really think Jacq is well with your mate, Crevan?"

Glancing over at him and trying to assess the motive for his question, Miata shrugged. "Aye. I imagine he be doin' everythin' in his power to be securin' her safety."

Scoffing, Rackham shook his head. "You certainly hold his dedication and loyalty in high esteem."

"For Jacq?" Miata grinned. "O' course I do."

Dante's brow furrowed. "On what grounds? Does he owe her a great debt?" he asked, troubled by the depth of Miata's certainty.

"Oh, no," Miata replied, chuckling. "It be far worse than that." He looked over at Dante again, discovering an expression of sincere confusion. Pausing, he studied Rackham, who had also stopped walking. "You truly be unaware?"

Rackham glanced about uncomfortably as if the trees might mock him. "Unaware of what?"

Resting his hand on Dante's shoulder, Miata whispered, "Murtaugh, the poor bloke. He be in love with her."

Blinking in astonishment, Dante scratched his head. "Are you certain?"

"As certain as I be that if we e'er be escapin' this place I ne'er be returnin'," he said without hesitation. Patting Rackham's shoulder, he started walking again.

Moving forward with Miata, Dante asked, "What of her inclinations?"

Miata shrugged. "I don't be supposin' to be knowin' Jacq's heart, mate." He looked over at Rackham. "Do you love her?"

Dante looked surprised at the question. "Well, I-I… I…"

"If you don't be lovin' her, you don't be standin' a chance," Miata stated firmly. "And I be thinkin' you should be havin' nothin' else to be sayin' about it either."

At that, the two continued on in silence, one trying to sort out his feelings like one tries to separate tangled necklace chains, and the other inwardly smirking like the cat who had eaten the canary.

Meanwhile, back at van Draenweg, the man Miata had assumed to be Barend sat at the same table in the tavern in the same brooding demeanor he'd been wearing the night before. Fishing an envelope out of his coat, he opened it and reread its contents to himself:

Dear Mr. Barend,

As requested upon your visit, I have spoken with H. C.. He feels that, under the circumstances, he does not owe you as you did not deliver upon the agreement you had therein. He additionally requests you not contact him again in the future about the matter as he has no intention of changing his position on it.

He extends his regrets regarding the unfortunate consequences of your actions and wishes you well on your future endeavors.

Please refrain from any further contact with H. C. as we feel publicly being an associate of yours might have ill effects on the reputation he is building with new prospects.

Sincerely,

Snarling, Barend crumpled the note in his fist. "Unfortunate consequences of my actions... future endeavors... bein' an associate of yers might have ill effects." He drummed his fingers on the table. "I'll show him. Thinks he's got rid of me, does he? I've lost too much to give up what's owed me."

Grabbing the drink in front of him, he gulped it down and returned it to the table with a heavy hand. "Thinks he's a gentleman, he does. No more than my aunt Myrtle. But I can be clever too, I can." His expression darkened. "Ruin him's what I'll do. Rot his boat from the bottom up."

A derisive smile altered his expression. "From the bottom up," he said again, smoothing the wrinkled paper. He sat back in his chair, refolding the note and stuffing it back in his coat pocket with a wicked air of satisfaction.

Chapter 6

"Here we are, lads!" a burly man called out. "We dock at Swansea by nightfall!" Turning around, he found a thin man with a thick beard staring out across the water as if he could get them there faster with sheer will power. "Just like I said, eh, Mr. Ellard?"

"Indeed, sir," the thin man agreed. "Your expediency has never been so deserved as it has been this voyage."

"My pleasure, Mr. Ellard," the man said with a hint of pride. "My pleasure."

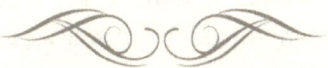

As rain gushed from the heavens, the travelers bound for Tenkodogo marched along, mostly protected under the canopy of a wooded area. Occasional drops of water dripped onto them, but most of it was captured by the leaves and poured down the trees. The balmy weather proved rather pleasant for walking in, despite the periodic heavy showers that forced them to seek shelter. Still, to keep herself entertained, Jacq sang quietly to herself:

So merry, so merry, so merry are we,
No matter who's laughing at sailors at sea.
E is the ensign, the red, white, and blue.
F is the fo'c'sle, holds the ship's crew,
G is the gangway on which the mate takes his stand,
H is the hawser that seldom does strand.
Oh, hi derry, hey derry, ho derry down,
Give sailors their grog and there's nothing goes wrong,
So merry, so merry, so merry are we,
No matter who's laughing at sailors at sea.
I is the irons where the stuns'l boom sits,
J is the jib-boom that often does dip,
K are the keelsons of which you've told, and
L are the lanyards that always will hold.

Stopping abruptly, Jacq caught up to Murtaugh and asked, nudging him with her elbow, "Tell us a tale of a lad who hailed from Ireland and rose from meager beginnings to a coveted fortune."

Chuckling, he shrugged. "I know of no such lad, mate. We Irish lads are a stubborn lot, but foolish too. No doubt many an Irishman would consider a store of ale a coveted fortune. So perhaps the question should be raised as to what manner of fortune you speak."

"Well, fortunes aside, perhaps you should entertain me with the tale you are more familiar with. Your own, perchance?" She gave him a hopeful, pleading smile.

Grinning down at her, he shook his head. "And you claim to have no wiles."

"Come now! A lass cannot tell all her secrets!" She nudged him again. "Astonish me."

"Fine then. The tale of a lad from south Ireland, mm? When I was but fourteen, I left home in Enniscorthy to go to England," he said, sighing as an afterthought. "I did not wish to go because I thought England more grand. I wished to go because I didn't want to fight in a war I did not agree with, and I didn't want to see my mates dying for nothing.

"Eventually, a fella by name of MacCarrick helped send me to Fishguard. He gave me the nickname of Crevan after I caught a lout trying to swindle him. I was there, in Fishguard, about six months' time, doing almost anything there was to be done just to feed myself." He paused, touching at the coin bound around his neck. "I became embarrassed with myself and began to believe I had made the worst possible choice of my life."

"But what of your parents?" Jacq asked, acutely interested in his personal history.

Scoffing, he rubbed at his jaw. "My parents are dead, Jackie."

"Oh." Her brain flinched. "I-I'm sorry. I-I didn't realize. If I would have known—"

"If you'd known, what? You'd not asked about my life?" A wry smile bent his lips. "Come now, mate. We both know you wouldn't be so refrained."

"Murtaugh!" she gasped, gaping over at him. "What an utterly abhorrent thing to say! It is a pity it is true."

Laughing, he shrugged. "Truly, Jacq, I don't mind telling you."

She smiled over at him, pleased at his statement.

"Now, where was I? Ah! So, my uncle took in me and my sister, but he was obsessed with the possibility of war. All the old man wanted to do was ready me for it. I was certain it was the only thing that brought him joy when he wasn't scuttered—teaching me to use a sword."

Giggling, Jacq nodded. "It is good you can smile despite your misfortunes. So many cannot."

"On what account could I make my complaints?" he asked, looking over at her. "How else could I have found my way here, with you? To Africa, of all places?" He laughed.

Her cheeks turned pink. "You surely know how to flatter a lass," she returned.

"I would claim it to be an Irish fault, but if you ever met Gearalt Mooney, you would just as soon call me a liar."

Giggling again, Jacq looked up to see Bahari standing still, staring out across the grassland now speckled with trees but having no forest left in sight. He glanced up at the churning clouds then to the other three, who came to a stop next to him.

"What is it?" Morenike asked, looking about as he was.

"When the trees become scarce," he said, gesturing to the horizon, where the golden grasses rose to meet the sky, "it means we arrive to Tenkodogo soon, in maybe three or four days."

"And we left that hunting village…" Murtaugh said aloud, trying to recall how long they'd been on the road.

"Twelve days ago," Jacq and Bahari said in unison.

"Almost a fortnight," she noted, sighing.

"How do you suppose the others are getting on?" Murtaugh asked.

"Oduntan will keep them safe," Bahari remarked immediately.

"Aye. No doubt they are well on their way to Cabo Corso by now," Jacq agreed, nodding.

"Probably already arrived, sitting in a proper chair by a proper fire with a pint of ale," Murtaugh said, jealousy obvious in his inflection.

"What I would give for a pint of ale," Rackham said, looking out at the sea as they walked along the edge of where the beach met the jungle.

"Must ye be carryin' on about it?" Miata asked, giving Rackham an agitated glance.

"Says the lad who had one just three days ago!" Dante replied with a sneer.

"Oi! It were mead, and I be earnin' that, mate!" Miata spun around to jab a finger at him. "I were riskin' me life for us. You should've been seein' the chap in the corner, glarin' at me as I were walkin' out like he were hatin' the world."

"I reckon I could've got us on that boat!" Rackham argued, slapping Miata's hand away. "Then we wouldn't be walking on this bloody beach talking about ale!"

"I weren't about to be riskin' Amy's life on account o' savin' yer feet a few days o' walkin'!" Miata exclaimed.

"A fine time to be turning gallant, mate! Right after you were the one to get yourself a pint of ale!" Rackham shouted, stabbing his long finger into Miata's shoulder.

Grabbing Dante's fist, Miata's nostrils flared, and his eyes narrowed. "It were mead."

Realizing they were no longer walking, Alex stopped and turned back, seeing Dante and Miata beginning to push each other, still arguing. Rolling her eyes, she marched back to them, grumbling with every step. Once she got into hearing distance again, she cleared her throat, but that didn't stop their volatile conversation about which of them would be eating the first piece of pie once they'd returned to civilization.

"Lads!" she yelled.

"What?" they shouted back, turning to see her and instantly regretting their behavior.

"If you ever want ale or pie again, I suggest you quit squabbling like schoolgirls over a bonnet and keep up. We are to pass around that Dutch port Whydah any day now, and I would rather not be discovered because you two cannot stop yourselves from behaving like a pair of silly girls!" Spinning about, she stomped off after Oduntan.

"And cheese," Miata said quietly after she was out of earshot.

"Aye," Dante mumbled, feeling foolish. "Ale, cheese, and pie."

Exchanging embarrassed glances, they followed after Alex without another word. Once they caught up with the girl and the guide, Oduntan motioned to the sky. "Rain. We continue in the trees. They give some—" He held his hand over his head.

"Protection?" Alex guessed, taking a peek skyward.

"Uh, yes. Protection. Protection from the rain," Oduntan stated.

"If you believe it best," Alex said, dusting at her clothes. "I am certain my inclination would be to never set foot in these woods again."

"You do not fancy Africa, Tayewo?" Oduntan asked, sounding rather surprised and slightly injured as he led them deeper into the jungle.

"I would not make so harsh a statement," Alex said in a polite and sincere tone. "It is that I do not understand this place. I do not know it. How can I have a proper opinion of that which I do not truly comprehend?"

"Such wisdom, Tayewo," Oduntan returned, seemingly pleased with her response.

"Do you think he be understandin' her?" Miata asked, smirking.

"Did you?" Rackham asked in return.

Scowling over at him, Miata snorted. "Ay!" Then he scratched at his head, recalling her comment just to be sure.

"This place," Oduntan said, sighing in appreciation, "she is like you, Tayewo." At this, he had everyone's attention. "She is… fierce and… cruel, but she is beautiful to the eye."

The boys nodded.

"She has many… secrets, but those who come to know her… they find she is full of… love and… protection. She keeps these secrets to keep those she cares for safe from harm."

Alex's lower lip trembled. "Your good opinion is most generous, Oduntan. If I should ever truly reflect your forest, I would consider it a great accomplishment. No doubt I shall spend my life trying to do so."

He beamed. "As you should. Come. This way."

They pushed farther into the jungle, and a drizzle began sputtering down, gradually working up to a steady rain. However, the canopy of leaves reduced it to more of a misty spray, dampening them slowly without completely drenching them.

"Show care," Oduntan said. "The earth will soften."

"If Jacq were here," Miata noted, "she'd be givin' us a song."

"She would," Alex and Dante agreed in a fleeting moment of cheerfulness.

"She'd be makin' us sing," he continued, thinking aloud.

"She would," the other two agreed again, smiling.

"What be you supposin' she be selectin' for this venture, Alex?" he asked, grinning at the prospect of Alex initiating a shanty.

"I am afraid I do not know as broad a selection as no doubt Mr. Rackham has the happy pleasure of being familiar with," she returned cleverly, pleased with her quick wit.

Laughing, Dante shook his head upon seeing them gazing back at him. "I could not lead you with due justice," he said. However, a few moments after they turned to face forward again, he began quietly singing:

A is the anchor that holds a bold ship,
B is the bowsprit that often does dip,
C is the capstan on which we do wind, and
D is the davits on which the jolly boat hangs.
Oh, hi derry, hey derry, ho derry down,
Give sailors their grog and there's nothing goes wrong,
So merry, so merry, so merry are we,
No matter who's laughing at sailors at sea.

Up north, Jacq and Morenike stood smiling up at a leggy long-necked creature with brown splotches and large moist eyes. It nibbled on some leaves with a long, nimble tongue and seemed indifferent to their awestruck observations.

"What is it?" Jacq asked in a whisper.

"It is *agunfọn*," Morenike answered in kind. "I never saw one before. I have only ever heard stories. They are so—"

"Tall," Jacq finished. "Say, do you think there are zebras here? I long to see one!" She was flooded with childhood memories and promises.

"A zebra? I-I don't..." Morenike returned, shrugging.

"Oh. Right. They, uh, they look like mules or donkeys, I think. They are white with black stripes all over their bodies, faces, and legs," she explained, bursting with hopefulness.

"Ah! You speak of the *abila*!" Morenike exclaimed, gleeful to understand. "But sadly, no. I have heard of them, but not here."

Jacq's bright demeanor darkened with disappointment. "Oh. 'Tis a shame, to be sure."

Touching at the older girl's shoulder, Morenike added, "But I am unfamiliar this far north. Perhaps we shall both be surprised, hmm?"

Jacq smiled and nodded. "Perhaps." Then she gazed once more upon the tall beast before them as it moved off to join others of its likeness.

"Oi, Jacq!" Murtaugh called to her. "What're you doing?"

She smirked. Hearing his accent, she realized, caused her to find him extra charming on occasion. "Will you tell me more of the life of Mr. Michael Murtaugh, rogue Irishman?" she yelled back.

Laughing, he shrugged. "If you insist, lass."

Smiling in happy anticipation over at Morenike, she nodded. "I do indeed, sir!" Beckoning the younger girl, she hastened to catch up to him. "Tell me of your preoccupations once in Fishguard."

"Well," he said, rotating to walk with the two girls, "after six months' time, I met a gentleman, an English blacksmith and swordsman renowned for his skills. He offered me an apprenticeship in Swansea as the one he was to have had been unable to join with him. He had high expectations, but he was fair."

"What was his name?" Jacq asked, running her fingers through the grass as they walked.

"Mr. Smith. I was there a year when I met Miata, and later, a lad you're acquainted with, Mr. Audric Schellden, on a trip to Penzance. It was all very well until I got word, after being there three and a half years, that my uncle died and my sister had been married off. Very soon thereafter, Audric found me and invited me on for some adventures and fun. Being the fool I am, I left with him." Sighing, Murtaugh rubbed the back of his neck.

"Audric—er, Mr. Schellden—has a way," Jacq noted, "of convincing you he is a good person with some faults, but I am certain he is truly a devilish rascal. He just happens to have some fine qualities. You are not the only one deceived of the truth."

"Believe me," Murtaugh responded, shaking his head, "I came to see him for the scoundrel he was. Six months after we left Swansea, I met you." He smiled over at her. "I wondered how he could have captured your heart."

At this, she glanced up at him and their gazes lingered awkwardly until Murtaugh looked away.

"You are not alone in that inquiry," she said in a depressed tone, moving her eyes to stare ahead of her.

"Well, as you know, a few months later, Audric wanted us to do that merchant job."

Groaning, Jacq nodded. "I remember. I was all rage and astonishment. I thought perhaps he had transformed and you had somehow aided it."

A wishful chuckle escaping him, Murtaugh sighed. "How I wish I had been so righteous. Instead, your vexation at the very idea caused me to reflect and become sorely disappointed in my actions. It helped me see how far I'd fallen and gave me cause to question my very character. Of course, I declined the job. And Audric... well, we went our separate ways. I desired to confess it all to you then, but I was so ashamed."

"You left. That's when you left," Jacq filled in, stunned and saddened. "You went away without a word, without any explanation at all!"

He stopped and stared down at her with sullen, overcast eyes. "Have you never been so ashamed you wished you could just disappear? Hmmm? Well, I was, and I could... so I did. I returned to Mr. Smith to complete my apprenticeship and become some sort of an honorable man. He took pity on me and welcomed me back."

Jacq felt a pang in her heart as she watched him speak, all manner of self-loathing, shame, guilt, and remorse whirling around just below the surface. His calm exterior was sealed tight, but it did not prevent her from glimpsing his struggle.

"Murtaugh," she said in a tight voice, "I always knew you to be a good sort of man. You have a kindness about you that is deeper than all your charms and happy manners." She reached out a hesitant hand to touch his and smiled.

A hint of a smile banished his downcast demeanor. "I believe that," he said in a whisper, "I can claim to be an Irish fault."

Smiling to herself, Morenike kept walking. "I knew she cared for him."

"Shakina! Crevan! Morenike!" Bahari shouted, approaching from the north. "I have scouted ahead. There are no lions or heynas—as you call them—nearby that I saw, but we must be wary."

"Wary?" Murtaugh repeated, an uneasy expression shaping his face. "Wary of what?"

"The *ẹsín-omi* with their big mouths and large teeth, the *erin* with their ivory, and the *ẹfọn* with their horns and their anger," he said as he rejoined them.

"Oh," Murtaugh said sardonically. "Is that all?"

"No," Bahari answered frankly.

"No," Murtaugh echoed, massaging his forehead. "I would like to meet something that didn't want to eat us or slay us for its own enjoyment."

"In the wild, you are either hunting or hunted," Bahari pointed out. "Many times you are both."

"Were you able to spot Tenkodogo?" Jacq asked.

"No. I scaled the tallest tree I found, but it is savanna for miles, as far as the eye can see," he admitted. "Maybe we will catch sight of her tomorrow." Then he nodded at Morenike. "Let us go!"

"Watch your step!" Rackham said loudly to Alex, trying to talk over the thunderous sound of the rainstorm.

"This rain!" she shouted back, clinging to his arm. "It is unlike anything I have ever seen!"

"I agree!" Dante returned. "It is unrelenting!"

"For two days!" Miata added, coming up beside them.

"There you are!" Alex said, leaning around Dante to see him. "Where is Oduntan?"

"He be sayin' to keep goin' this way. He were goin' for somethin', but I were unable to be hearin' him," Miata replied.

"Probably looking for shelter," Rackham guessed.

As they picked their way along a tree line that led farther inland, the oversaturated soil began to slip and shift beneath their feet.

"This is insanity! Perhaps we should seek refuge at Whydah!" Alex suggested, wiping at the hair plastered to her face.

"I wouldn't be trustin' it, Miss Alex," Miata said.

"Why not?" she asked. "Because I am the one who made the recommendation?" She attempted a glare, but all the water turned it into more of a squint.

"Not at all!" Miata snorted, finding her rationale to be altogether nonsensical. "It just be a Dutch port, with whom we be in questionable relations as it be."

"Not only that," Rackham spoke up, "but they are in the slave trade as well. I wouldn't want to risk Oduntan."

"I suppose you are both correct in your wariness. It is a shame, though. I should very much like a—" Her foot began sliding. "I should like to have a—"

As she tried to secure her footing, her other foot began falling as well. Catching onto a nearby branch, she was able to steady herself before the boys took notice.

"A what?" Dante asked, looking back for her.

"A fire," she said, adjusting her footing.

"Don't we all," Rackham said, nodding and moving onward.

Shuddering, Alex moved to follow, but the ground beneath her feet that she had worked so hard to regain suddenly gave way. She attempted to call out for help, but she gasped instead, which resulted in a sort of squeaky exclamation as she plummeted.

"Alex!" Miata yelled, lunging forward and grasping her arm before she completely disappeared from view.

"Oh! Miata!" She gasped, her toes catching on some protruding roots as she frantically tried to get a good grip on his hand.

"You be mighty slippery!" he shouted, using one hand to try and stay her and the other to hold onto a tree as an anchor. "Oi, Rackham! Mate! Give us a hand, eh?"

Turning about at hearing his name, Dante doubled back. "Miss Alex! O'Keeffe! What happened?" He knelt beside Miata, trying to assess the situation as fast as possible.

"The ground fell away!" she answered.

"Are you injured?" Rackham asked, still scanning the area.

"Not yet!" she said, her grip on Miata's arm slipping as she tried to dig her toes into the mud about the roots she was standing on. "I am falling," she whimpered to Miata in a desperate tone, panic lashing at her heart.

"Don't be worryin', Jacq!" he returned. "Yer fine. We'll be getting' ye up in no time."

Though vaguely surprised by the use of her sister's name, she disregarded it immediately, focusing on the reassurance and sincerity in Miata's eyes. No matter what he called her, that look did not lie.

"Just hurry," she pleaded.

"Astonishing! Murtaugh, look at that!" Jacq said, pointing over at some large black cowlike animals with big horns that curled on the sides of their heads. "Bahari! What are they?"

"They are *efǫn*," Bahari answered. "I have heard stories, but seeing one… they are magnificent."

"Oi, beasty!" Murtaugh yelled, waving at it.

Immediately, it turned to look at him.

"I don't think it cares for you," Jacq said, giggling.

"What? Sure it does! What's not to fancy?" He grinned engagingly at her.

They watched it begin to move toward him.

"Shakina might be correct," Bahari commented. "I have heard they can be very protective."

"Is it moving faster?" Morenike asked, squinting to see better.

"Mu-Murtaugh, I think you should run, mate," Jacq said, concern sprouting in her expression.

"So should we all," Bahari declared. "Go!"

All four spun about and began racing toward a small spread out stand of trees.

"First a wild boar and now a monstrous cow? Is there nothing friendly in this land?" Jacq yelled over to Bahari.

"I told you, it is a wilderness! You are either hunting or hunted, and oftentimes both!" he shouted back.

"Morenike," Jacq called, grabbing at the other girl. "Run this way!"

Nodding, Morenike followed Jacq's lead, and they put some distance between themselves and the men. As suspected, the buffalo was still keen to get itself a piece of the Irishman. Upping its speed, it was closing in on them as Murtaugh and Bahari scaled a tree so they were just out of reach when it came to a snorting stop below them.

Off to the side, the two girls slowly circled back to be near the boys, wanting to avoid angering the volatile animal. It stood snuffling and munching on some grass, bumping into the tree to scratch its shoulder. Every time Murtaugh or Bahari moved, a leaf rustled, or a twig snapped, it stared up at Murtaugh, wordlessly daring him to come down.

"Well," Jacq called to the treed men, sighing. "What do you propose we do now?"

"He will soon join his herd," Bahari answered. "Until then, do nothing to make him cross."

"I don't understand what vexed him in the first place," Jacq returned. "Is he just naturally a contentious animal?"

The buffalo snorted and pawed at the ground.

"Shh!" Murtaugh and Bahari responded.

Swishing its tail, the buffalo looked up at him and head-butted the tree with an agitated look in its eye.

"Oh, because we should follow the recommendation of the two gentlemen stranded atop a tree." Jacq began giggling.

"It's not funny," Murtaugh said in a flat tone.

"Oh, my dear Mr. Murtaugh," she replied between snickers. "It is, in fact, quite funny."

"If it would only leave." He turned to Bahari. "You send it away. Send it running back to its mates. As soon as it turns away, I'll pop down and make a run for it."

Bahari's brow creased. "No! This is *efọn*. I shall not be held responsible for you being gutted."

"Gutted?" Scowling, Murtaugh peeked down at the animal. "Very well. We wait."

As if in punctuation, the cloudy sky murmured and cracked. There was complete silence for four seconds, and then rain began drenching the earth. Everyone, even the buffalo, exclaimed in disapproval. However, the buffalo trotted off to reclaim its place in its herd, giving Murtaugh and Bahari the chance to jump to the ground, catch up to the girls, and make a mad dash for a thicker stand of trees.

"Once I leave this place," Murtaugh declared as they ran, "I wish never to return!"

Farther south, Miata was doing his best to hang on to Alex, whose feet were on tiptoe on a muddy water-covered root protruding from the hillside. The rain was still pelting them mercilessly as Dante searched for something—anything—to use to help bring the dangling girl topside. It was, however, in vain.

"I can't find anything!" he shouted to them. "Come on! Mr. O'Keeffe and I can pull you up."

When he reached down for one of her arms, the waterlogged terrain laughed at them and dumped all three tumbling down the hillside. Dante fell first, inadvertently dragging Alex with him. Alex, in turn, pulled along Miata. They spilled onto the ground, several feet below, coming to stop in a three-inch-deep mud puddle.

While they were all gasping and checking themselves over, both boys turned to Alex.

"Are you unharmed?" they asked in unison.

Sitting on her knees in the middle of the puddle, Alex's shoulders slumped. However, pushing away the overwhelming desire to break down and cry, she tried to breathe. Her shoulders began to tremble and shake, but when she lifted her face to look at a very concerned Maita, she began to laugh. "No! No, I am not well! I just fell down a muddy hill in the middle of a rainstorm!"

Chuckling along with her, Miata shook his head. "Why be ye laughin'?"

"If I do not laugh, I shall surely cry," she answered. "Have I lost my mind? Am I completely mad?"

He touched her cheek with the back of his hand. "O' course not. Yer Miss Alex Luray. You were born to be surprisin' us all. It be not madness ye be sufferin' from. It be courage."

"Ay!" a different voice called.

The trio looked up to find Oduntan staring down at them.

"What are you doing?" he asked, peering over the edge.

"What's it look like?" Dante yelled back, sounding incredulous. "We're having a bath!"

"We should put up shelter! Wait out rain!" Oduntan shouted.

The three glanced at each other.

"Very well!" Rackham called back, nodding.

Oduntan pointed north. "You go this way. I will come to you." Then he was gone from the hill's edge.

Pushing to his feet, Dante offered a hand to Alex. "You heard him. Let's go."

Taking his hand, she pulled herself to her feet. "Thank you, Mr. Rackham." She smiled as she looked over his handsome mud-splattered face and matted hair.

As she walked ahead, Miata stumbled to stand up. Grabbing him by the arm, Rackham asked, "How is she?"

Looking after her, Miata chuckled. "She be completely mad."

Dante's expression warped to concern. "What?"

"It be not so bad," Miata said, trudging past him. "I be thinkin' a little madness be just what she be needin'."

When they caught up to Oduntan, he led them to a ramshackle sort of lean-to not too far from where they'd fallen.

"How did you know this was here?" Alex asked as they piled beneath the leafy roof.

"I built it," he said. "That is what I told O'Keeffe." He pointed at Miata. "The supplies were many."

Dante and Alex turned to glare at Miata.

"I be sayin' I were unsure o' what he be sayin'!" Miata returned in his own defense.

"Well, what do we do now?" Dante asked.

"Oh, clothes off!" Oduntan said, gleeful that he had the answer. "Clothes off and come together." He made a motion with his hands as though he were squishing them all together.

The other three exchanged greatly displeased glances.

As night fell and they crowded together, Morenike smiled over at Bahari. "The stories they tell of you... they are true."

"Stories are often exaggerated one way or another," Bahari said, looking thoughtfully at her.

"Not these. Not you," she said, shaking her head.

"I'd wager the lass to be right," Murtaugh spoke up.

"What do you know of it, Crevan?" Bahari asked.

"I haven't known you long," he said easily. "But I know your type. You always do more than is asked of you and never ask anything in return. It's difficult to exaggerate about that, mate."

Shifting his weight uncomfortably, Bahari gestured to the Irishman. "Enough about an old man. Finish your tale, hmm?"

"Well, I… I-I don't…" He waved his hand away at the notion of speaking to more than Jacq.

"Aye," Jacq spoke up, nudging him. "What became of you once you returned to Mr. Smith?"

"Well, he kindly took me back to finish my apprenticeship. But after I was there just a year or so, he packed his bags and was off for Northampton. He had some sort of relation he needed to care for, so he left me to tend to his shop. I did some traveling for some custom work, but I kept the shop running two and a half years, waiting for Mr. Smith to return. He wrote now and again, making sure all was well. But one day, I got a letter saying he wouldn't be coming back." Laughing, he touched at the coin hung around his throat.

"So," Jacq paused, thinking. "So, that was…"

"Nigh on a year and a half ago, aye. I decided to close up shop and find something better. A few months later, I meet Miata in Penzance, looking for you, of all people in the world." He turned large soulful eyes to her. "And there was nothing I wanted to do more than help find you."

Jacq fidgeted under his intense gaze, her heart fluttering wildly in her chest and her insides trembling. "And so you did," she acknowledged, barely able to keep her voice steady.

He grinned triumphantly. "Of course I did!"

"What of your sister?" Morenike asked.

The glee rushing out of his demeanor, Murtaugh shrugged. "I doubt I'll ever see her again. I'm as good as dead to her, runnin' off the way I did. It was shameful, but I was…" He paused, his expression writhing at the recollection. "I was knackered, I suppose. Knackered and afraid."

"Afraid of what?" Morenike asked in suspense, speaking the question before Jacq could open her mouth.

He glanced up, his dark hair falling across his blue eyes in a way that made him seem worn, brooding yet enticing. "Afraid of dying, and afraid of being a bleedin' gimp." His eyes turned to Jacq. "I expect I became the latter." At this, his mouth twisted in a rueful smile.

"You're not a fool, Murtaugh," Jacq said, her defensive tone catching Bahari's attention. "I've told you before, you are a *good* man. You think so little of yourself, but it's rubbish."

Chuckling, he ran his fingers through his hair, pulling the locks off his eyes and forehead. "The same to you, mate."

Scoffing, Jacq studied him. "What do you mean?"

Eyeing her, he shrugged and shook his head. "Nothing. I didn't mean anything." Then he looked to Bahari. "Let's hear more of Bahari, eh?" He grinned persuasively.

As Bahari guffawed and objected, Morenike enthusiastically insisted he share more about himself. However, despite the smiles and the laughing surrounding her, Jacq couldn't stop herself from dwelling on Murtaugh's remark. The look in his eyes suggested he thought he knew something—something dark and secret, hidden away. The more she sat wondering, the more she despised herself for having such an abhorrent darkness buried in the back of her mind. And even more, she loathed how it haunted her.

Meanwhile, Alex, feeling thoroughly underdressed, sat huddled together in the makeshift shelter with Dante and Miata beneath a blanket. They were all wet but no longer utterly slathered with mud. Thanks to the warmth of the season, they were not cold despite the fact they did not have a fire. However, their own lack of clothing lent nothing to their present discomfort compared to

Oduntan's comfortability of stripping down to naught but a loincloth.

"Mr. Rackham, Mr. O'Keeffe," Alex whispered as she stared at the ground while Oduntan crouched by the entrance, humming. "We must *never* speak of this."

"Agreed," they both replied, nodding.

"I wanted to do something brave," she commented, still fixing her gaze to the ground. "But more and more, I believe this to be foolhardy, and I..." She paused, gulping. "I am truly, truly apologetic."

"Oh, Miss Alex," Miata said, chuckling. "Don't go bein' so hard on yourself, mate. Everyone be testin' their limits one day or another."

"You called me *Jacq*," she retorted, looking up at him. "This *is* something *Jacq* would do, but I am not her. I am *not* Jacq! I am Alex, and Alex does not go about the wilderness making rash decisions that result in her having to bunch together with acquaintances not of intimate relations in nothing but her undergarments!"

Frowning, Miata sighed. "No, I be callin' you Jacq because I..." His expression deepened to a grimace.

"You what?" Alex asked, scowling back at him.

"I be..." Scoffing, he shrugged. "I be comin' to admire ye."

She looked shocked.

"I know yer not Jacq, but you be doin' yer best out here, and even if yer not always nice to be around, I can see you be tryin'. *That* be admirable."

Her expression transformed to confusion then to a small smile. "Well, if you are to wed Amy, I suppose having a brother one is fond of is preferable."

Coughing, Dante shifted his weight and glanced at them awkwardly.

"If you are uncomfortable, Mr. Rackham," she spoke up, "perhaps you should leave."

"If that I could…" he said in a grumble.

"The rain seems to be less," Oduntan spoke up.

The three turned to listen to him, discovering he had stood and walked up to where they were sitting. "Ugh!" they groaned in unison, all spinning around in different directions to avert their gazes from his covering cloth, eye level and only an arm's length away.

The following afternoon, succeeding another long day of walking, when dusk was nearly upon them, Morenike pointed at a glimmer on the horizon. "Do you see that?"

"Aye!" Jacq said, anticipation lifting her voice.

Murtaugh nodded. "Bahari, please, is it the place?"

"It ought to be," he answered, anxiety and excitement vying for control over his tone and demeanor. "Let us make haste to discover the truth!"

Bahari trotted on ahead, with Morenike quickening behind him, though not as fast. Jacq and Murtaugh continued on at a steady pace, which bordered on being uncomfortably fast.

"Do you think we've arrived?" Murtaugh asked.

"I certainly hope so," she replied, her voice more sullen than usual as she recalled their conversation the night before.

Sensing something amiss, and taking into account her lackluster attitude throughout the day, he suspected he knew the root of her displeasure.

"Jacq, look." He paused, trying to get his words right, "I didn't mean offense when I asked more about Bahari last night. I just… I didn't want to talk about myself any more with them around."

Shrugging, Jacq nodded. "That was of no offense."

"No?" He scratched at his lightly bearded jaw. "Then what?"

She looked over at him—at his healing, scruffy face, his disarming eyes, his provocative mouth, his wild hair. She considered avoiding his question, thinking, *I should just keep quiet, let him wonder. But-but to what end?* She could see the sincerity behind his inquiry. *I can answer without being entirely transparent.*

"Jacq?" he asked, uneasy with her silence.

"Your remark. When you said, 'Same to you.' Why tell me that?" she asked.

"Oh, come on, Jacq." He smirked over at her. "I may not be a wit, but I know of your nightmares." He stopped walking and grabbed her arm to stall her. "I see your self-loathing when you think no one is watching."

Pulling her arm free, she quivered down to her core. "You know not of what you speak!"

"And who does, Jacq? You must confide in someone, must you not? Or do you carry it around alone, letting it eat at your soul and suffocate your heart?"

"Alex knows what haunts me," Jacq said with a snort. "Something I wish to forget."

"Just Miss Alex? Maybe you need more," he returned, softening slightly and taking a small step toward her.

"Miata and Rackham know too," she continued.

Stopping in his tracks, he scoffed. "Skippy. Of course."

"Stop it!" Jacq exclaimed, stepping in front of him when he moved to walk away. "It's not like that. He-he-he was there when it happened." She sniffed back tears. "They all were there. I-I've never told… I've never talked…" She choked, taking a deep breath and calming herself. "I've never spoken of it with someone who didn't know. Even that wretched pirate who kidnapped me… he knew of it, and he used it to torment me."

"Well, I don't go around telling my shameful history to folks either, love," he said gently. "When you want to tell me, if you ever do, just know I won't think any less of you."

As she chuckled at the notion, a rueful smile shaped her lips. "That's easy for you to say now without knowing."

He stared at her, standing in the fading light, dirty and exhausted from their journey for her friend. Her golden hair was a mess of a braid, her hazel eyes moist with pent-up emotion, and her lips twitched anxiously as she hugged herself.

Taking a few slow, deliberate steps forward, he was mere inches away from her, and in a low, husky Irish-accented voice, he said, "It's easy for me to say because I'm saying it about *you*, Jackie."

She lifted her eyes to stare into his. "Murtaugh—"

"Kehinde!" Morenike was yelling as she came running back to them. "Kehinde! We have arrived! Kehinde!"

Walking slowly away from her, Murtaugh let their gazes linger. "I won't, mate. You have my word."

"Did you hear?" Morenike asked, breathlessly coming to a stop between them. "We have arrived!"

A surge of hope sparking life back into her usual mien, Jacq laughed. "Show us the way!"

As she and Morenike passed him, hurrying to Tenkodogo, Murtaugh smiled to himself. "That's my girl."

Miles away, Mr. Ellard was tromping through the evening streets of Carmarthen, a day's journey from where he'd come ashore in Swansea. Looking up, he saw a wooden sign hanging out front of a large middle-class building, and read aloud, "The Rose Wood Inn." Then heaving a sigh, he took the short staircase two at a time and ducked inside. Once beyond the door, he found the building had a rather upscale atmosphere.

Immediately, a man approached, looking a bit displeased at Ellard's somewhat rugged appearance. "Hello, sir. May I be of assistance to you?"

"Aye, I hope so, sir," he replied, removing his hat. "I'm looking for Captain Turner. I was told I might find him here, sir. It's a matter of some urgency."

"Mmm. I see." He gave Mr. Ellard another disapproving once-over. "I will go ask if he is accepting visitors."

"I don't have time for that, sir. As I said, it is a matter of some urgency, and I must speak with him now," Mr. Ellard said, glancing about in earnest.

"Right. Of course, sir. Just wait here and—"

"No," Mr. Ellard interrupted forcefully. "Take me to him now, or I swear to you I will storm all about this inn looking like this and shouting his name as loud as a church bell." He smiled. "Please, sir."

His expression darkening with disgusted horror, the man politely gestured and said, "Right this way, sir."

Adjusting his cloak, Mr. Ellard followed after the man into a large room dotted with tables. At the tables sat sophisticated-looking men with their fine clothes and their tasteful foods and beverages, all smoking and chatting away. There was no doubt Mr. Ellard and his apparel was out of place, and every head turning as he walked past was a testament to the fact.

Finally, near the back of the room, they approached a table with two men enjoying a meal and bottle of wine.

"And do you know what he said then?" one of the men, whose back was turned, asked in a stiff, stuffy voice.

"What did he say?" the other man asked in return.

"He said, 'It was a pair of noisy snails!' That's what he said!"

Both men chuckled at this, the stuffy one patting his leg, displaying the magnitude of his amusement.

"Excuse me, Captain," the man escorting Mr. Ellard said, irritation vaguely detectable in his stodgy voice. "A man to see you. A Mr...."

"Ellard. Mr. Thurston Ellard," he introduced himself. "First mate to Vice Admiral Bartholomew Luray."

"Ah! Yes, yes!" the captain said, standing to take his hand. "Mr. Ellard, allow me to introduce my good friend, Mr. Bibbs."

"How do you do, sir?" Bibbs asked with a smile, turning and shaking Ellard's hand as well.

"Pleased to make your acquaintance, I'm sure, sir," Mr. Ellard returned, smiling nervously between them.

"Tell me, what can I do for you, Mr. Ellard?" Turner asked. "Would you care to sit?"

"Thank you, sir. No, sir. I..." He took a long breath. "I am here to request your aid. The vice admiral and all his crew are stranded down in Africa. We are to meet them down at Cabo Corso."

"Stranded? What of his ship?" Turner asked, confused.

"She was burned down by a fool bunch of blame French—"

"Ugh! French mercenaries?" he guessed.

"I was going to call them something else, sir."

Bibbs chuckled. "I like this fellow."

"Aye. Is everyone well and unharmed then, Mr. Ellard? However did you get here?" Turner asked.

"I don't know how everyone is, sir. The vice admiral made the arrangements to send me here to tell you the birds are in the air but they can't fly."

Turner's expression clouded. "We must leave at once. Mr. Bibbs, I apologize."

"Nonsense," Bibbs returned, standing. "The new Mrs. Pierce wanted a young staff attending her. So thanks to the new mistress, Mr. Pierce is no longer under my charge, and I am no longer his valet and butler. I am coming with you."

Chapter 7

In the darkness, Jacq saw a hooded figure stumble and stagger down the empty street lined with buildings constructed of earth blocks resembling bricks. The lanes were nothing more than dirt and had an eerie feel to them, with only the moon and stars lighting the way.

"Murtaugh?" Jacq called after the figure. "Murtaugh, is that you?" She hastened after him, but when she looked down the street, she didn't see him. "Murtaugh?" she called again, her voice betraying her uneasiness.

"Jacq?"

She spun around to see Murtaugh standing there wearing no hood or cloak whatsoever.

"Murtaugh! Did you see…" She gestured behind her where the phantom had seemed to vanish. At his confused expression, she laughed. "Forget it. My mind is playing tricks on me."

When she went to walk away, he snatched her wrist and pulled her close to him, only an inch or two separating them. "Don't leave me here, Jackie."

"I should find Bahari," she pointed out, struggling to concentrate with his mouth so close to hers.

Pushing her back with slow, easy steps, he returned, "The lad needs a few to himself. He'll find us when he's ready."

Her back hit the wall of the building behind her. She inhaled sharply. "Is that so?" she asked in a breathy voice.

He nodded, grinning. "It be." He touched his nose to hers.

"So what do we do while we await his return?" she asked, closing her eyes as he nuzzled her neck.

"What do you want, Jackie?" he asked, daring to plant a tiny kiss in the curve of her neck.

Jacq trembled but remained silent, her brain crackling with adrenaline and fuzzy with stimulation.

"Tell me, Jackie," he said again, placing a bolder kiss just below her jaw.

"Ol' Tom be wantin' ye to come with him," a different voice whispered in her ear.

"No!" Her eyes flying open, she was horrified to see a different dark-haired man looming over her. He was difficult to make out in the dark, but she knew who he was. Pushing him away, she shook her head and vehemently yelled, "No!"

"Ol' Tom be demandin' ye to choose," he said, giving her a sinister grin.

"No! My answer will *always* be no!" she shouted, tears forming in her eyes.

"It be too late for that, mate!" he said, a thin stream of red liquid trickling out the corner of his mouth.

Panting, she looked down to see her palms coated in blood. "No, Tom! Stop it!" Lifting her eyes, she gasped at seeing him sprawled on the ground, a gunshot wound in his chest having drenched his white shirt. Gulping, she whimpered and closed her eyes.

"It be on yer hands. Ol' Tom's blood be on yer hands," he said in a gagging voice.

Looking at her hands again, she saw the flintlock, still smoking from recent use. "I didn't have a choice!" she cried, dropping the gun.

"Sure you did," Murtaugh said, appearing suddenly beside her.

"No," she insisted, sniffling and shaking her head. "He was… he was going to shoot Miata!"

Rolling his eyes, Murtaugh shook his head. "You're not who I thought you were. You're not a lady. You're hardly an adventurer. What you are is a murderer."

"No." She leaned against the wall and sank to the ground. "No. I can't… I can't have you think that of me."

He laughed. "Why not? Everyone else does."

Gasping, she shook her head. "No. No, no, no—"

"Oi, Jacq," Murtaugh said, pushing on her shoulder.

Her eyes snapping open, she took in a long, sharp breath, her heart pounding wildly. "Did I fall asleep?"

"Aye, lass," he answered, looking her over. "Bad dream?"

Glancing over at him, she felt her eyes were drawn to his lips, and she recalled the start of her dream. Clearing her throat, she shrugged. "Part of it."

Giving her a skeptical look, he let his eyes roam about them. Tenkodogo was to their left, just north, but otherwise it was all sprawling savanna. "Bahari's been out all night," he said. "I say we wake the lass and find him."

"Do you think he discovered them?" Jacq asked, adjusting how she'd sort of slumped down while she slept.

"If that chap woke me in the middle of the night looking for his family and I knew where they were, I'd bleedin' tell him," Murtaugh said, shuddering at the notion.

"What?" Jacq giggled. "He intimidates you?"

"I have a natural inclination for self-preservation," he answered.

"You? The mighty *jagunjagun*?" She grinned.

"We don't become mighty for nothing," he retorted. "It's about strategy." Looking over and finding her amused expression, he glowered at her. "Go on! Wake the lass!"

After rousing Morenike from her sleep, the three went into town, and it wasn't long before someone admitted to hearing Bahari during the night. After several people confessed they had been unable to help him, a middle-aged woman set them off in the direction of Bahari's alleged family.

When they arrived, they were a little surprised at seeing the big man seated against a building, knees drawn and elbows resting on them.

"Bahari?" Jacq spoke as they approached.

"Shakina," he replied without looking at her.

"Did you—" She stopped, contemplating her words. "Are they here?"

"They are," he returned, jamming his thumbs over his eyes.

Grimacing, Jacq looked back at Murtaugh, who shook his head, and Morenike, who shrugged. "H-Have you seen them?" she asked, trying to be delicate.

"I have," he answered. "I have been here since before the sun began to rise. I saw my wife and sister leave for market with their baskets, but I hid in the alley like a coward." Pulling his thumbs from his eyes, he let out a ragged breath. "I should not have come." Dragging himself upright, he turned to the three. "Morenike can stay, but we should go."

"Bahari?" a woman's voice interrupted, built entirely of trepidation and neglected hope.

They all turned to find two beautiful women in their midthirties, lean and strong from toil. Each was carrying a filled basket, which was promptly dropped to the ground, the contents spilling into the street, forgotten.

Putting her hands up to cover her mouth, one desperately fought a losing battle to tears, and the other held out her hands, salty droplets streaming down her cheeks. "Morenike! *Tanna ti ọkàn mi!*"

"Mama!" Morenike exclaimed, racing into her mother's outstretched arms. "*Arakunrin* and Kehinde and Alaabo! They saved me! *Nwọn si ti o ti fipamọ mi!*"

While the mother and daughter embraced, Bahari looked awkwardly over at the other woman. "Aladia," he said weakly, opening his arms wide as though to make himself transparent and vulnerable. "I am returned to you, *mi ayeraye itansan oorun.*" He continued choking out words to her in their native language, taking one tiny cautious step toward her after another.

As she listened and watched him, she was constantly wiping away the tears pouring down her sculpted face. When he was close enough to her, she tipped forward and curled into his chest, her body shaking with sobs as she clung to his shirt. "Oh, *ifẹ mi,*" she said in a whimper. "We never thought we would see you again. It has been—"

"Eight years last month," he said, his voice tight as he held her close.

"So long," she breathed in wonderment. "Far too long."

"You speak English now," he noted.

"Me and the children," she added, nodding. "I thought it be making us have more value… just in case."

Shaking his head, he leaned back to take her in. Cupping her face, he wiped at her tears with his thumbs. "I am so sorry, Aladia. But I have returned to rescue you from this life."

Stepping back, her eyebrows came together. "What do you mean?"

"I have come to bring you and the children to England." He looked over at his sister and niece. "You are welcome to join us, Moyo."

"Oh, my dear Bahari," Aladia muttered in Yoruba. "So much has changed since you went away." She placed her hands in his and squeezed, staring up into his eyes as if she were afraid it was all a dream.

"How do you mean?" he asked, a nervous tone to his voice.

She looked over at Moyo and Morenike. "Baruti died, just a year after you went away, and I—"

"Mama," a little boy's voice interrupted.

Everyone turned to see a young boy standing in the doorway of the house. He frowned and tilted his head at seeing his mother so close to Bahari. "Mama?"

"*Mi ọwọn ọmọ!*" She hurried to him, wrapping her arms around his small shoulders.

Bahari's face became overcast, stormy with feelings of betrayal, regret, guilt, and anger all vying to be his primary emotion. "Who is this?" he asked in a tense voice.

"Bahari, please," she pleaded, imploring with her eyes. She spoke Yoruba to him in a hushed tone then took a deep breath. "I was with child when you left."

Relief washed over him. "Huru spoke the truth. I discounted all he said after—"

"You've seen Huru?" she asked, her eyebrows coming together.

"Never mind that," he said, crossing over to them. Kneeling in front of the child, he smiled. "What is your name?"

The boy looked at his mother, who smiled and nodded. Then looking back to his father, he answered, "I am Bakari."

"You look strong," Bahari commented in a tight voice, gently pressing on the boy's chest.

Bakari smiled. "Mama says I look like my baba," he said proudly. "He went away so we could stay."

As she watched Bahari's face twist painfully, Jacq leaned into Murtaugh, tears clawing at her eyes.

He put his arm around her and watched as the clouds above began churning and darkening. "Breathe, Jackie. Keep breathing."

Nodding, she sniffed back her tears and took a deep breath.

"Come," Aladia said, standing and motioning to a door near them. "See how your children have grown."

"Quiet, quiet!" Rackham said, crouching by a tree and motioning at Alex and Miata.

A short distance away, Oduntan stood peering around a tree, inclining his ear to catch any foreign sounds.

"What the devil did we do to be awarded this bloody assignment?" a man asked in a growl.

"You fell asleep on our watch, ya lout," a second man snapped in a hushed tone.

"I don't understand why we're lookin' for van Draenweg's escaped prisoners. Why does the boss care?" the first man asked, near Oduntan.

"Well, it's not your job to understand. Ya haven't the mind for it. But from what I heard, Tuinstra struck a deal with some well-to-do Englishman, and let's just say someone's not happy with the arrangements," the second man said, coming up next to him.

"Tuinstra rethinking his allegiance, hmm?" the first one asked, chuckling and scratching at his mop of hair.

Alex's lip curled in disgust.

"Can't say," the second man returned, shrugging. "But I reckon we'll not find 'em. They said it was a couple o' frocks that got away." He snorted. "Lord knows they wouldn't make it this far."

Chortling and shaking his head, the first man sighed. "Now we know what Tuinstra wants. They must be mighty pleasin' to the eye, eh?" Laughing and continuing to make their jokes and speculations, the two men moved back the way they'd come from.

Once they were no longer audible, Alex huffed. "Well, I never! How utterly vulgar!"

"You don't be supposin' Tuinstra be trickin' yer father, do ye?" Miata asked, worry echoing in his question.

"He'd be a fool to," Dante spoke up before Alex could make a fretting remark on the matter. "I reckon the vice admiral can read a man and take care of his own."

"Someone be spinnin' tales, Rackham," Miata replied. "Someone be sendin' out lads from Whydah."

"How do you know they hail from Whydah?" Alex returned.

"It be seemin' right as it be the nearest Dutch port," Miata said, shrugging. "Where else be Tuinstra askin' aid?"

"I agree," Dante said, glancing between them. "Perhaps we should follow these chaps and seek out just what *is* going on." He looked at Alex. "What say you?"

Taking a deep breath, she glanced toward their guide. "What do you think, Oduntan? Do you believe them to hail from the port town of Whydah?"

Joining the conversation with a perplexed expression, he asked, "Why my opinion, Tayewo?"

"I rather feel your insight is valuable. You know these lands, do you not?"

"Your humility is *imǫlẹ bí oòrùn*," Oduntan said with a smile. "You honor me with your request." Looking at the waiting young men, he nodded. "Let us see if they do come from Whydah. Keep pace, but I will scout ahead to be sure."

With that, he was off ahead of them.

"When we be gettin' to Whydah, I be goin' in to see what the feckless louts be about," Miata volunteered as they began to move onward after Oduntan.

Scoffing, Rackham shook his head. "No, mate. You went into town last time. It's my turn."

Snorting, Miata smirked. "You just be wantin' a pint."

"You're blasted right I want a ruddy pint!" he retorted. "Seems only just that since it got to be you last time it should fall to me this time."

"It weren't a reward," Miata returned, letting a large leaf go as Dante walked behind him. "It were dangerous."

Barely dodging being slapped in the face by a tree, Rackham grumbled. "I am far better suited for any danger than you are."

"You know," Alex spoke up, "I could—"

"No!" both men declared in unison.

Stopping short, Alex wore her offense plainly on her countenance. "I beg your pardon?"

Halting abruptly, they glanced at each other, wordlessly acknowledging the need to make amends immediately.

"They be lookin' for lasses," Miata pointed out, rotating to face her.

"In a place like this, everyone will notice you," Rackham added, sounding confident and smoothly complimentary.

Alex looked down at her dirty attire given her by the hunting village then back at the young men. "I sincerely doubt I would be any more noticeable than whatever ladies are there at present."

"That's what we mean," Rackham continued, sashaying up to her. "There might not be any womenfolk, let alone ladies."

She narrowed her eyes at him. "Are you simply telling me this to frighten me because you want to go?"

Chuckling nervously, Dante's face skewed into an awkward sort of half smile. "No! Preposterous!"

"Miss Alex," Miata chimed in, "Jacq be makin' it his duty to be lookin' after you and keepin' you safe."

Nodding in agreement, Dante smiled. "Aye."

"Well," Alex said, crossing her arms, "then should Mr. Rackham not remain with me if he is to ensure my safety?"

His mouth bunching together as he tried to refrain from snarling, Dante shrugged. "Perhaps."

Beaming like an overfed puppy, Miata patted Rackham on the back. "She be makin' a fair point, lad."

"Keep your hands off me," Rackham said in a bristling tone.

"Perhaps it is a matter best discussed upon our arrival," she commented nonchalantly, sauntering past them. As she pulled ahead, a pleased smile snuck onto her lips.

"Brilliant!" Rackham sneered at Miata as he stomped after her. "You scheming leech!"

"Schemin' leech?" Miata retorted, chasing after him. "Where be you gettin' off bein' so high an' mighty?"

"I don't skulk about these lasses lookin' for charity, mate! I am here in generosity!" He scoffed, glaring at Miata.

"Oh, be that right? The lad who be dippin' his hands in two pails o' water, eh? He be the one to be self-righteous?" Miata retorted.

"Two pails?" Dante snapped. "Explain yourself."

"We be knowin' you got two lasses, mate," Miata said, finally stepping out from behind his curtain of quips and metaphors.

"That"—Rackham stopped, jabbed his finger in Miata's face, and continued in a whisper—"that is not true."

"Well, if it weren't," Miata returned, cooling off a little, "then what be your purpose? In my experience, nobody be bein' so generous with their time as you be without some aim behind their actions. So what be it, Rackham?"

Rackham glanced at him with a mix of shrouded emotions Miata could not discern. "Come on," he said in a gravelly voice. "We mustn't let Miss Alex stray too far from us."

As he trudged off, Miata's brow knotted. "What be your purpose, boatswain?"

They huddled together in the corner of the small house nearly devoid of furniture. Jacq and Murtaugh watched in silence as Bahari stood in front of a line of boys. There were a total of seven—four his sons, three his nephews. Another boy and girl stood nervously off to one side with Moyo and Morenike. The boys' expressions ranged from stoic to borderline displeasure to nervous excitement.

As Bahari looked them over, he said, "*Rẹ ìyá yẹ ki o jẹ lọpọlọpọ bi awọn kiniun. Mo ti osi sile ọmọ, sugbon ti pada lati ri ọkunrin.*" He turned to Jacq. "I left behind boys but have returned to find men."

"Tell us their names," Jacq requested.

He smiled. "This"—he set his hand on the shoulder of the tallest boy at the far left of the line—"is Kukoyi, my eldest. It fell to him to care for his mother when I traded myself to the pirate captain, Ming." He moved along and set his hand on the shoulder of the next boy with a fierce haircut. "This is Akinlabi. He always had a warrior spirit. This is Nuru. He is curious like the lion cub. And this"—he looked at the smallest boy in the line—"is Bakari, whom I long to know. And these are my sister's children. The eldest, Adunni, then Ayotunde, and Enitan. Their father would be pleased with all of them."

"You should not have brought them," Akinlabi stated, gesturing at Jacq and Murtaugh.

"Akinlabi," Kukoyi snapped in a disapproving tone.

"It is true!" he continued, gaining all of Bahari's attention. "You have put us all in danger by bringing in outsiders to Tenkodogo. We have only just begun to build our reputation here, and now this? Kukoyi would never say so out of fear, but I am no coward!"

"I watch my tongue out of respect," Kukoyi shot back. "I suggest you learn to do the same, or you will be certain to bring dishonor to our family." He squared his shoulders and held his head high. There was perfection in his every manner.

Akinlabi glanced at Bahari. "I will not be the first."

Kukoyi sent him another warning glare.

"If I have put you in danger, we should leave tonight," Bahari said, studying his two oldest sons.

"That will not do," Kukoyi disagreed politely. "Those who traveled with us are many. We must gather and let them all decide to stay or go. But Akinlabi is not wrong. With the threat of slavers and us only newly arrived, to be seen with anyone of pale skin will put our honor to question. We will only be safe a day or two."

"Then tomorrow, Kukoyi," Bahari suggested. "Gather your people tonight. Let them have the day to decide, and then we leave at sunrise the morrow after."

"Why should we listen to what you say?" Akinlabi asked, anger bubbling just below the surface of his countenance.

"It is a good plan," Kukoyi spoke up as Bahari examined Akinlabi's face.

"You are angry," Bahari observed, his pale eyes confused.

"How did you think I would be"—Akinlabi paused, his expression teetering on being a sneer—"*Father*?"

"That is enough," Aladia said before Bahari or Kukoyi could react. "This is a happy surprise, and we are being offered safety away from this place. Safety from the fear of being stolen to be sold as slaves. Is that not what we pray for?" She turned dark, doleful eyes to her husband. "This is no longer our home."

"My home has always been with you," Bahari said in a solemn voice.

Jacq and Murtaugh, feeling awkward at witnessing such a private moment, looked at each other and instantly felt an entirely different uneasiness. However, they were saved by two new intruders. Two men in their late thirties stepped in, saw Bahari, and froze.

Bahari twisted to see them, smiling as his eyes came to rest on the one with a completely shaved head. "Gbeke," he said, opening his arms.

"Bahari!" Gbeke returned with a laugh, embracing him. "You are returned to us! Are you the madman everyone is talking about? Waking people up at all hours of the night?"

Shrugging, Bahari smiled. "I had to find my family. I had come so far, and I would not be stopped."

Patting the side of his face, Gbeke grinned at Bahari and motioned at the only boy present not in the lineup. "Do you remember my son, Olusegun?"

Bahari turned and looked at the boy as he came forward. "Olusegun! So it is!" He laughed and grabbed his shoulder. "Another boy who is now a man!"

"And this"—Gbeke motioned to the other man who'd entered with him—"is Durosinmi and his niece, Iremide."

With his gesture, Bahari watched the girl who'd been beside Olusegun come forward. She smiled at him and then glanced at Kukoyi, who looked away from her when Bahari followed her gaze to his oldest son.

"We have met before, I am sure," Durosinmi said, nodding at him and holding out his arm.

Bahari eyed the man, hesitantly grasping arms with him. "Perhaps. I am Bahari."

"Oh, trust me," he nodded to Aladia. "I know who you are. I am a friend of Gbeke."

"Gbeke was always too kind for my taste," Bahari returned, releasing Durosinmi's arm and smiling at Gbeke.

"With a world so full of hate, one can never show too much kindness," Gbeke reasoned with a mirthful expression.

"So you would say even if the world was new," Bahari returned.

Gbeke and Durosinmi laughed in approval of his remark but stopped suddenly upon seeing the other two newcomers in the corner.

"Prisoners?" Durosinmi asked, pointing at Jacq and Murtaugh.

"Friends," Bahari answered, looking to Gbeke. "They helped me escape the pirate ship, brought me to Africa, and saved Morenike." He motioned to Jacq. "Shakina is Kehinde."

"Kehinde?" Gbeke repeated, seeming intrigued at the concept.

Durosinmi laughed derisively. "The gods of this world have left us. Why should we believe in their superstitions?"

"She has brought him good luck so far," Gbeke returned.

"Well, what of the man?" Durosinmi asked, with a gleam in his eye that Murtaugh found quite discomfiting.

"*Ti o jẹ mejeji rẹ kiniun rẹ ati omi,*" Morenike spoke up.

"He is her *alaabo*," Bahari added as everyone eyed the Irishman. "He fought a Yoruba challenger on her behalf."

"Then they are to be married," Aladia remarked, perking up at this. "Or are they already?"

"No!" both Jacq and Murtaugh answered, firing each other injured glances.

"My father and sisters are awaiting our return," Jacq said.

"Oh! Then you marry!" Moyo spoke up with a whimsical smile, stroking Morenike's hair.

"I'm afraid not," Jacq replied. "In our world, lads fight over lasses rather frequently, but it does not mean they love them or want to marry them."

"Oh," both women returned with disappointed expressions. Then they scowled at Murtaugh.

First looking perplexedly at Jacq, Murtaugh then was a little surprised to see the disapproving women. "Oi! I did her a favor by fighting off that fella! I'm not going to force a lass to marry me against her will."

Jacq glanced over at him, hoping she had not insulted him or his noble efforts.

Scoffing, Aladia and Moyo turned to each other. "Is that not what the menfolk always think?" asked Moyo, shaking her head.

As the women chattered, Kukoyi turned to the newly arrived men. "We have something to discuss."

"Aside from the two *bia ẹmí èṣù?*" Durosinmi asked, still eyeing Jacq and Murtaugh.

"As you see, my father has returned to us," Kukoyi continued, ignoring Durosinmi's comment. "I have done my best to make decisions for my family, but now he has returned, and the honor and duty should fall to him." He smiled over at Bahari, who was marveling at his son's respectfulness and sense of duty. "It is a weight I do not envy."

Snorting and wearing an incredulous smirk, Akinlabi rolled his eyes. "He is a stranger in his own house!"

His lip curling, Kukoyi faced his brother. "If you challenge him, you challenge me, for I stand beside him. Is that truly what you wish?"

"No, brother," Akinlabi answered, looking down. "Like you, I want best for the family."

Kukoyi turned back to Gbeke and Durosinmi. "My father has offered us freedom."

"H-How?" Gbeke asked.

"We leave Africa and go with my friends"—Bahari motioned to the two in the corner—"to begin new lives. Build a new home, in England."

Miles and miles southwest of Tenkodogo and east of Whydah the following morning, Alex was tromping through some brush, muttering to herself. "Why forge an agreement? I knew we should have awaited instructions from Father instead of making a desperate, ill-conceived escape." She kicked at a leaf.

A little lizard scampered out from under the bushy plant.

"Oh! Well, hello," she said, feeling both curious and wary. "You are far too small to eat me, are you not?"

It ran to a nearby tree and scurried up the trunk until it was level with her shoulders. Turning its head round, it blinked at her with large inquisitive eyes.

Giggling, Alex found herself amused with the tiny creature. "Well, you are rather adorable of your own account."

Nearby, a bird flitted in some upper branches, twittering and chirping, catching her eye. Sighing, she looked back at the lizard. "Why cannot all the days here be like this moment?"

"Oi, Miss Alex!" Miata's voice shouted at her.

"That is why," Alex answered for the lizard. She rotated to find all three young men coming through the wall of vegetation.

"Why did you leave? Oduntan was showing us a new fishing technique," Dante said, his sincere lack of understanding evident in his inflection.

"Yes. Precisely," she responded.

"I be tellin' you she weren't bound to fancy it," Miata said in a low voice.

Elbowing him, Rackham smiled. "Well, what are you doing?"

"I was just admiring this little—" She turned back to discover the lizard was gone. "Oh! Well, I was admiring this lizard, but he has gone away." She leaned around the tree to see if she could find it.

Dante and Miata traded disbelieving glances.

"A lizard?" Rackham asked.

"She be losin' her mind," Miata said in a wary tone.

"Oh, here it—Aaaah!" Alex screamed, reeling away from the tree.

"What? What's wrong?" all three men asked in equal concern.

"My face! My face! Get it off!" She continued yelping and screaming, frantically waving her hands in the air.

As Rackham and Miata tried to carefully catch her arms, Oduntan came up from behind, grabbing her about the waist. Writhing, kicking, and flailing, she was still panicked and shrieking as they shouted, "Miss Alex! Alex! We don't see anything!"

"Oh! He's on my neck!" she cried, flinging her head back and hitting it on Oduntan's forehead.

Caught off guard by the knock, Oduntan stumbled but held her steady. His foot, however, snagged on some roots, and the two went crashing to the ground.

Miata and Dante did their best to prevent it, lunging forward and grabbing for them, but it proved useless. Then as they rushed over to help the two groaning on the ground, they all saw a little lizard go scampering away from them and disappear into the forest.

"Was that—" Rackham pointed in the direction of the escaped reptile.

"She were seein' somethin' after all," Miata said in amazement, straining to see where it went.

"Of course I saw something!" Alex retorted, furious at the suggestion. She felt a desire to slap him, a strange sensation even regarding Miata. "I am not suffering all forms of madness!"

"One can never be bein' too certain, eh?" Miata asked, holding out a hand to help her up.

Glowering at him, she took his hand and rose. "I can assure you the only ailment I suffer from in all its forms when I am with you is vexation."

Miata smirked. "I be thinkin' ye be likin' bein' cross with me. It be allowin' for ye to be kind to everyone else."

Sneering at him, she straightened her clothes and turned back to where Rackham was kneeling beside Oduntan. "Is he unwell?" she asked, dread threatening her calm.

"You hit him in the head… with your head," Rackham noted. "But it seems his arm is the trouble."

Dante checked it over as Oduntan sat up, wincing. "I've seen this injury afore. He'll need to mind his arm a few days, but it should heal so long as this cut doesn't get infection."

"We have some herbs to help with this," Oduntan said, reaching for the bag he always wore. "You mix with clay or mud and press onto cut. Will help protect from illness."

"Mud," Alex repeated, unimpressed. "Why must it always be something frightful or filthy?"

"Some days it be both," Miata noted. "Come along, Miss Alex. Let's be findin' you a stone to be grindin' up Oduntan's healin' plant. I'll fetch us the mud."

As they walked away, Rackham sat beside Oduntan, sighing and looking toward the sky.

"You search for purpose?" Oduntan asked.

"What?" Rackham returned, eyeing him.

Oduntan gestured to the sky. "He who looks to heaven searches for answers to questions he does not understand."

"Oh, I assure you, I understand the question, but the answer is still hidden from me," Dante said.

Oduntan smiled over at him. "If you truly understand the question, the answer will come to you."

Rackham looked again at the sky.

Eight weeks earlier…

"What do you search for, Mr. Rackham?" Bahari asked, walking up beside him.

Turning his gaze from the sky to Bahari, the lanky boatswain shrugged. "What?"

"You search for purpose?" the older man asked, sizing up the sailor with no reservation.

"Why would you say so?" he asked, folding his arms over his chest and returning the studious posture.

"He who looks to heaven searches for answers to questions he does not understand," Bahari said.

"What meaning does this have?" Dante asked, unimpressed and equally unconvinced.

"I suppose it is different to every man. For me, I always find I look to heaven, to God, when I have no place else to turn. That is not to say I recommend such behavior, but it is mine. I look to heaven when I do not understand—be it myself, my circumstance, or my purpose." Gesturing at Dante, he smiled. "You have the look of a man who knows himself. Your circumstances are favorable. So there remains only purpose."

"What do you know of my circumstances?" Dante asked, sounding indifferent and aloof.

"Enough to know your purpose should be your concern," Bahari replied.

Rackham scowled. "My concerns are my own."

"Perhaps, but hear this." Bahari closed the distance between them with the essence of command swirling about him like a whirlwind. "You *must* decide."

Rackham's face mellowed with an ignorant, quizzical expression.

"You either fight for Shakina or you set her free. Keeping her tethered is torture," he said firmly.

"Well, I... Well-well, I-I don't..." Rackham responded with stammerings and sputterings.

"You must decide before we return from Africa," Bahari said sternly.

"But-but, I..." Sighing, he stared at Bahari.

"You do not understand," Bahari repeated, nodding. "This is why you look to heaven, to seek your purpose."

Rackham began shifting his weight from one foot to the other. "I do understand your meaning, Bahari. Things are just a bit more complica—"

"No," Bahari interrupted firmly. "If you truly understand the question, the answer will come to you."

He paused his fidgeting. "How can you be so certain?" he asked in a voice laden with doubt and skepticism.

"You know the truth in your heart," Bahari replied. "But you do not yet truly understand the question. The question goes beyond, deeper, than the lass. It exists in your purpose—the purpose of your life. When you know the path you must take, you will understand the question, and the answer will come to you."

Frowning, Rackham shifted his weight again. "This is how you make your decisions? With this riddle?" His inflection was incredulous and his expression entirely unimpressed.

"Not always," Bahari said, glancing skyward. "But I am a fool, and walking the path is always more challenging than seeing it."

Taking a deep breath, Dante looked back at Oduntan. "Perhaps the question is more complex than I first believed."

Smiling, Oduntan nodded. "So it is with questions."

"Mr. Ellard, are you ready, sir?" Captain Turner asked.

"I am, sir. I'm sure the vice admiral will be waiting at Cabo Corso for us. He was mighty eager to put that place behind him. 'Tis a shame two of the girls took flight. The vice admiral weren't even able to make arrangements to secure safe passage afore they scampered off." The man shook his head.

"Miss Alexandria and Miss Jacqueline are missing?" Mr. Bibbs asked, coming up beside Captain Turner on the harbor deck.

"Aye, sir," Mr. Ellard answered. "I left afore much searching was underway, but that was the last report I heard."

"Oh! Those girls!" Mr. Bibbs said with a distressed sigh.

"No doubt they are recovered by now," Captain Turner said with well-meant confidence. "They best be with the unhappy news I'm bearing."

"One can certainly hope," Mr. Bibbs said with a huff. "They are formidable enough, but Miss Alexandria is not the sort to do well on a lengthy jaunt into some strange wilderness."

"And Miss Jacqueline is?" Mr. Ellard asked in disbelief.

"Miss Jacqueline is…" Mr. Bibbs glanced at Captain Turner. "Well, she is more, shall we say, adaptable."

"Aye, adaptable," Turner agreed, chuckling.

"And, if I may, what unhappy news, sir?" Mr. Ellard questioned.

"I've heard he is to be ordered back to the Caribbean since war has been declared with the Dutch," Turner confessed. "They want our ports secure."

"A trip to the Caribbean's what lost him the girls twenty years ago," Ellard said, shaking his head. "Will he go?"

"If what I hear is true, I don't know that he'll have a choice," Turner replied.

"Well, let us not linger needlessly. Let us be off," Mr. Ellard said, looking about. "The ship's ready, isn't she? Let us weigh anchor!" He gestured at the *Sea Dragon* near the end of the harbor.

"We await high tide. You know the procedure," Captain Turner said, pacing slowly about the dock.

"Ay!" Mr. Bibbs called out into the dark air. "Who goes there?"

A figure emerged from the shadows, a long coat billowing about him and a tricorn stationed securely on his head. "I was told I might find you lads here," he replied in an easy manner.

"Ah!" Captain Turner stepped forward to greet him. "I was hoping you would discover us before we left. We haven't much time. We sail within the hour."

"I am ready now, sir," he said without a hint of hesitation.

"Well, who is it then?" Mr. Bibbs asked, stepping up to the conversation.

"Mr. Bibbs, you remember my first mate, Mr. Monroe?"

Monroe turned to face Bibbs, extending his hand. "Sir."

"Ah! That I do, Captain. That I do." Chuckling, Bibbs shook Monroe's hand.

"Why the delay?" Ellard spoke up.

"I was away on business," Monroe answered. Then he turned back to Turner and Bibbs, his blue eyes glinting with resolve in the moonlight. "But I wouldn't miss this for a kingdom."

Chapter 8

Staring out at the dusty, neglected streets, Amy let out a long despairing exhale of air. The day was almost gone, being chased away by the night. Smells of smoke, animals, and rum filled the air, but nothing was as prevalent as the dirt, which was currently mud thanks to the rain.

Moving away from the window, she turned to observe her father, who sat pensively in a chair by another window. Leaning forward with his elbows on his knees, propping up his strong chin with knotted fingers, he was anything but relaxed. She took a step forward, wanting to console him, but stopped. Glancing down at the medallion in her hands, she suddenly found herself vexed. Clenching her teeth and the medallion, she moved back, muttering, "How could you do this to us?"

As she silently stepped away, however, the floor creaked. She froze, but without moving, her father asked, "What troubles you, my darling?"

Contemplating keeping her thoughts to herself, Amy decided she was not as stoic as that. "Everything! All of it! It is all wrong! None of it was meant to be this way!" Repressed tears tore at the backs of her eyes. "Look what they have done to you! To us! Why did they run?"

Exhaling, he dropped his head into his hands. "They are distrusting and independent," he answered. "They have, for so long, looked after themselves they forget others care. They do not consider"—he paused, wincing—"the pain or distress they may cause because they have never been in a position to do so before. If they have, it is forgotten. It is replaced by years of struggling to merely survive."

Some of the anger seeped out of the girl as she listened. "How dreadful. How awful! They are fortunate you are so understanding. I was so terribly hasty to become cross and injured by their actions."

Lifting his eyes to see the precious girl, he smiled. "You are fortunate that you do not understand, my dear. I am only so understanding because they are me. They are as I was when I lost each of your mothers and them." He held his hand out to her, and she glided forward to give hers to him. "I thank God he returned my senses in time to spare you this abhorrent feeling of helpless desperation—to feel as though there is no one in the world who truly cares. We saved each other, you and I."

The two smiled at one another, basking in comfort they provided each other. However, their tender moment was short-lived when a man about thirty entered the room carrying a covered plate of food.

"Hello there, Vice Admiral. I've got the best in the house here," he said with a moderate Swedish accent. As he set down the platter, he sensed the iciness of the atmosphere. "Is everything to your liking?"

"Mr. Carloff, I await a ship and two of my three daughters. There is much I would change that I could, but let us see what you have brought for us. We shall not be discourteous to your hospitality." The vice admiral stood and motioned for Amy to sit at the table. "I thank you for upholding your side of our arrangement."

Smiling at Amy who returned the expression in politeness only, Carloff shrugged. "I am a businessman, sir. It would certainly sully me and my reputation if I did not make good on my promises. You requested a safe place to stay while here. If I cannot meet such a simple request bought at such a fair price, I would surely lose my credibility. With no credibility, how could I possibly build the Cabo Corso castle? The Swedish Africa Company would suffer for my failures, and I would be ruined. So you see, it is in both of our interests for me to ensure your security and your comfortability." At this, he glanced again at Amy's done-up golden curls and pristine posture.

Though Amy remained oblivious, her father did not. "It is in our favor as well then that you rely so heavily on our good opinion of you and your comportment." He gave the man a knowing glance as he reached for the dome covering the food platter.

Clearing his throat and nodding to signal he'd received the warning, Carloff brought his eyes away from the girl. "Quite right, sir. Quite right." Making a show of checking over the room, he smiled and said, "Well, I will leave you to it. I'll be back personally in an hour to make sure all is well."

As he turned and exited, the vice admiral lifted the lid, exposing some assortment of meat, yams, and local vegetables. He looked up at Amy to find her staring languidly at her plate as though she were looking through it to someplace else entirely.

"You are still troubled," he commented, setting down the lid.

Glancing up, she forced a smile. "It is Mr. O'Keeffe. I miss him too, you know—just as much as my sisters."

The vice admiral's brow knotted. "Truly? I thought perhaps you were fascinated with him merely to worry me."

Giggling, her smile became sincere. "Of course not!"

Forcing a laugh, he shrugged. "Oh." Internally, he groaned.

"He is so many things I am not," she pointed out.

"Of that I am certain," he said, straining to maintain a placid demeanor.

"You may not believe it," she continued in a jollier mood. "But he helps me be a more thoughtful person, and he helps me appreciate all the wonderful things in my life—like you, for instance."

The vice admiral stopped. "Oh?"

"Oh, yes," she said, reaching for some food. "He often remarks on your good character and apologizes for not resembling you more in his manners and his demeanor. However, I tell him so long as he tries to always improve, he has nothing for which to be ashamed."

Watching his daughter, the vice admiral sat in awe of her purity of heart. "My darling, I know you were given to me out of grace, for I know I never did anything to deserve a daughter with so kind a heart as yours."

Smiling over at him, she shrugged. "It is I who am blessed, Papa."

"When I say my prayers tonight, I will be sure to include Mr. O'Keeffe on your behalf," he said in a benevolent warmth that was heating up his insides.

As they began to eat their supper, Miata squatted by the small campfire they had made near the beach. The fish had been eaten and the sun was beginning to set, but the breeze was low and soothing. Setting himself down on a rock, he kicked out his feet, letting his long legs stretch.

"Jacq would be green with envy if she knew we were here," Alex remarked, seating herself on another rock a few feet away from him.

Laughing, Miata rubbed at his thinly stubbled jaw. "There were ne'er a truer thing bein' said."

They shared a light moment with amused expressions. Alex found she was rather delighted with herself for getting a laugh out of him.

"How be our guide fairin'?" he asked.

"Mr. Rackham says he will be fit for travel on the morrow. I feel such a fool for bringing this delay upon us," she said, her mood wilting.

"Oh, don't be apologizin' again," he said with a groan. "If you do, I be throwin' myself in the sea in hopes o'bein' eaten by sharks."

Alex's eyes grew wide. "Truly?"

Staring over at her, Miata shook his head. "No! That'd be a ghastly way to be goin' out!"

Exhaling with relief, Alex shrugged. "You do not always have the most logical of reasons for what you do."

Chuckling, he sighed. "When it be about sharks, I do."

Giggling, she turned to watch the horizon. "I am relieved to hear it."

As they sat in amiable silence watching the sun dip lower into the sky, they each marveled a little at their company. To think, two years ago they couldn't stand to be in the same room with one another, and now here they sat enjoying a sunset together.

"Miss Alex?"

"Mr. O'Keeffe?"

He grinned at her use of his name and continued observing the sky. "What do you suppose be becomin' of us when we be returnin' to England?"

"What do you mean?" She looked over at him.

"Exactly that. What be becomin' of us? You be marryin' Mr. Monroe, Jacq be off on some adventure, and Miss Amy…" He paused then cleared his throat and went on. "Well, then there be us lads, o' course. Mr. Rackham be stayin' on with Captain Turner, to be sure. Murtaugh be on some brilliant scheme, and I be… I be what, Miss Alex?" He kept watching the colors in the sky alter their hues, preparing for the night.

"What do you want?" she asked.

Chuckling, he looked over at her, his face shadowed by the night and highlighted by the low fire. "Me? I be wantin' a dream, to be sure. Naught but a lovely dream."

She thought for a few seconds, recalling his improvements and his failures over the last couple of years. "If a dream is what you wish for, then perhaps it is what you should strive for."

Scoffing, he pulled in his legs to lean his elbows on his knees. "Don't be mockin' me, Miss Alex. That be easy for one to say when one be certain theirs be within their grasp."

An incredulous laugh eking out of her own lungs, Alex stared down at her feet. "Nothing is certain."

Miata gave her a curious glance. "Surely there be somethin'."

Meeting his gaze, she shrugged. "If there is, I know not of it." Heaving a sigh, she stared out at the ocean, glimmering in the dimming light like a sea of diamonds. "Well, I suppose there may be one thing."

"What be that?" he asked, following her line of sight.

"Jacq would be justified to be jealous of us in this moment." She grinned over at him.

Returning the expression, Miata chuckled. "Aye, that she would be."

"No… No, no!"

Murtaugh's eyes slid open with sluggish protest.

"No!"

Sitting up, he looked at the person sleeping about an arm's length away. "Oh, Jackie." He listened to her whimper and object a moment, but he couldn't abide it long. Scooting over to her, he placed his hand on her shoulder and gave it a firm shake. "Oi! Jacq!"

Bolting upright, she was gasping and flailing for something to hold on to. Her eyes were wild with confusion and distress while she shuddered and seemed on the verge of tears.

"Whoa! Easy!" he exclaimed in a whisper. Grabbing her by the shoulders, he caught her glance. "There, there now. Hush. All is well, Jacq. You're safe."

Continuing to take big gulps of air, she latched on to his shirtfront and leaned forward as though to be sure he were real. Sniffling, she trembled and touched at his face with one hand while the other held fast to his clothes. "H-h-hold me? P-p-please?"

His brow furrowing with concern, he nodded and opened his arms to her. "Shhh, Jackie. I'll keep you safe, love."

Shivering, she buried her face in his chest, soothed by the steady rhythm of his heart.

"Are they getting worse?" he asked, smoothing her hair.

"Would you believe me if I said no?" she asked, calming and regaining her usual attitude.

A wry smile formed his mouth. "It's been two days since we set out from Tenkodogo. Our new mates seem to be a mite superstitious. If their good luck charm is having nightmares, they might take it as a bad omen and turn back."

Sitting up, she sighed. "Do you not think that if I could be rid of them I would be?"

"Perhaps I could be of use to you," he said, touching at her elbow.

Shaking her head, she grimaced. "I can't. Not yet. I-I... I can't tell you yet." She looked down, shame for her actions and embarrassment of the consequential aftermath overtaking her.

Watching her, Murtaugh shrugged. "It's fine, Jacq. Just listen. Perhaps to be rid of your haunt, you should attempt one of two courses of action."

She gave him her attention. "Such as?"

"First." He cleared his throat and looked her square in the eye. "Perhaps you must accept what it is you are running from. You're Jacqueline Taylor Luray! You're a bleedin' treasure hunter, a bloomin' pirate treasure yourself, and now an African good luck charm!"

Her somber exterior began to crack. "Sh! You'll wake the others!"

"What you're running from, it can't be bigger than you. It just can't. So you must accept it and embrace it," he concluded firmly.

"And what if that does not do the trick, mate?" she asked, a smile whispering in her expression.

"Then you move to solution two." He lifted her chin with his finger. "You forgive yourself."

Tears pushed against the backs of her hazel eyes as she stared into his soulful blues. With mild trepidation, she reached up shaky fingers and touched at his wrist.

He started at the feel of her fingertips against his skin.

"Why are you so good to me?" she asked, a rare vulnerability and earnest curiosity to her question.

Tilting his head, he looked over her face. "Surely you must know."

Her eyebrow rose in question, but before she could verbalize it, Bahari sat up, grunting. Instantly both of them scurried to lie back down before he saw them. They watched in secret as he got to his feet, stretching in the sleepy morning air. He began collecting his things, but stopped abruptly and looked over at where Aladia slept, quiet and still a short distance away. Stealthy as a cat, he slunk over near her and crouched there in silence.

"*Emi ni ki binu, mi pipe esuro,*" he said in a whisper, his voice breaking. "I will fix this, I promise." He held his hand above her head, wanting to touch her but afraid to. "We will be *ọkan pọ* again."

Jacq closed her eyes, not wanting to intrude on Bahari.

Fortunately, one of the others began to stir, so Bahari returned to where he'd slept, allowing Jacq and Murtaugh to sit up without question. Sighing, Jacq looked at the Irishman. "Were his pain but a leaf, I would blow it away."

"His pain," Murtaugh observed, "is great because his love is great. It is a miserable thing, it is."

Smirking over at him, Jacq asked, "And what do you know of love, Michael Murtaugh?"

Returning the expression, he shrugged. "Not much, perhaps. But I know enough to know if you find it, you fight to keep it. After all, they say it's the best kind of misery there is, if you can find a fool to share it with."

"Is that what they say?" she asked, laughing.

As they chatted, Akinlabi awoke and, catching a glimpse of Bahari kneeling beside a freshly awakened Aladia, stomped off away from the group.

"Oi! Should we go after him?" Jacq asked.

"No," Murtaugh replied. "What could we do? Oh, look, Durotty is after him."

"Durosinmi," she corrected, giggling.

As they continued their banter, the older man went after the boy. Catching up to him, he cleared his throat. "*Ti o dara ilera*, Akinlabi."

The teenager glowered over at Durosinmi. "*Ti o dara ilera*."

"You grow weary of these outsiders?" the man asked.

"I grow weary of my brother treating them like gods," he answered, a bitter tone plain in his voice.

"He does not treat them as gods, but he does not heed the advice of those who have been close to him as maybe he should," Durosinmi returned, watching the boy stab the ground with a stick.

"My brother makes good choices, but he lets memories cloud his judgment. My father is just as much an outsider as those white snakes he brought back with him." Akinlabi's eyes burned with unattended rage.

"We are of the same mind, Akinlabi," Durosinmi said, chuckling and nodding in agreement. "But I think fate may yet smile upon us and return to us what we desire."

Akinlabi glanced at him. "What must be done?"

"When the time is right, opportunity will present itself," he said with a sly smile. "Trust me."

"Easy to say, hard to earn," Akinlabi said, looking out across the savanna.

"A wise statement. Where did you learn it?"

Giving him a final glance, the boy returned, "My father." Then he spun on his heel and trudged back toward the camp.

Back at the site, Bahari looked after Akinlabi and Durosinmi. The longer they were away, the more anxious he became until he threw down the sticks he was carrying and began marching out toward them.

However, Aladia sprang into action, jumping in front of him and stopping him in his tracks. "Bahari."

"Aladia." He was startled by her sudden closeness to him but managed to hide it, save for an eyebrow twitch.

"You must let him come to you," she said, admiring her husband's exposed chest and arms.

Disarmed by her attention, he simply replied, "Who is this Durosinmi that he thinks he can advise and counsel *my* son?"

"He has been a friend," she returned, gazing into his eyes. "Only a kind friend."

"No man is a friend to a woman like you without coming to find her company highly favorable," he said, delighting in her study of him.

Giggling at his indirect flattery, she shook her head. "By that measure no man would be safe for me to have as acquaintance."

A tiny bit of mirth shaping his face, he shrugged. "Am I not proof enough of that?"

"Come, *onírẹlẹ kiniun*. The rains are coming," she said, ignoring his demeaning remark regarding himself.

Taking a long inhale, he nodded. "The air is sweet with it. The sky is gray. We should hurry." Seeing Kukoyi talking with Iremide, he beckoned him. "Son, we should leave soon," he said as the boy approached. He motioned to the sky.

"You wish for me to lead?" Kukoyi grimaced.

"For now, my son. You have led well in my absence. If I take control now, some may believe me to be dishonoring you. I would not wish for this," he answered. "We will help one another."

Smiling reluctantly, Kukoyi nodded. "If you believe it to be best. I see the peril of not keeping an undeniable code of honor."

"Honor is important, as it should be, to your brothers," Bahari explained. "If we are to lose favor with someone, it will not be due to dishonorable behavior."

Nodding, Kukoyi smiled. "Very wise." Turning to the rest of the travelers ambling about the camp, he clapped his hands loudly. "Hail, friends!"

All eyes were his.

"The rains come. Make haste!"

In response, everyone stepped up their packing pace, peeking skyward periodically to check on the clouds. As Akinlabi rejoined them, scowling at the outsiders, the clouds began grumbling and spitting at them.

Bahari watched his son go past, but when Durosinmi walked by, he stepped in front of him. Almost of equal height, the two men eyed each other.

"My wife claims you a friend," Bahari said in a low, threatening tone. "I am not yet persuaded."

Durosinmi glanced over at Aladia, a crafty smirk carving his face. "She is beautiful. But only one *akọmalu kan erin* can lead the herd."

"You are lucky I do not squash you here and now," Bahari warned him.

"You are pathetic. Full of empty threats and muddy stories. You do not harm not because you are noble but because you are a coward." His face produced a smug, foolish sort of expression.

"I said I would not squash you, but I would be satisfied to pluck off a leg or two." With that, Bahari leaned back and then smashed his forehead into Durosinmi's nose.

As the man cried out in pain, covering his face as he moved away from the group, Bahari turned to discover Bakari and Nuru staring up at him. The little boys, eyes wide and mouths dropped open, gaped at him as one might watching a jaguar dispatch a crocodile. Donning an innocent smile, Bahari shrugged. "He will be fine."

"You must show us how!" Nuru said in hushed excitement.

"Yes! Can you do it again? We do not like him either!" Bakari agreed.

Stifling a delighted smile of glowing pride, Bahari nodded. "Perhaps later. Why don't you show me what you've been carving, hmm?"

"You like to carve?" Bakari asked, excited.

"Very much," Bahari returned, beaming as he followed his two youngest sons, oblivious to being observed by Jacq and Murtaugh.

As the father and sons walked off, Jacq and Murtaugh traded alarmed glances. "Did you see him…" Jacq touched at her nose.

"Aye, with the…" Murtaugh rubbed his forehead, grimacing. "And Dorsett's…"

"Durosinmi," she corrected, though still dazed. "Should we say anything?"

"No!" Murtaugh answered emphatically. "A thousand times no!"

They looked up to find Aladia watching with great pleasure as Bahari, Nuru, and Bakari sat and bonded over the carvings the boys were working on. As she observed them, Durosinmi stomped past her, covering his face.

"Durosinmi, what happened?" she asked when he brushed by.

"Nothing!" he growled. "That fool." He went on grumbling to himself as he returned to his belongings.

That day and the next, both groups traveled well. Both Alex and Jacq toyed with their charms, each thinking of the other and hoping things were going better for the other than they were for themselves. They observed the foreign wilderness around them, finding it strange how there was a familiarity they were developing toward it. Certainly it would never be home, yet it was somehow less intimidating than it was when their journey began just four weeks ago.

When dusk approached on the evening of the twenty-ninth day, Oduntan stopped and pointed at some lights in the distance. "Quick! To the shore!" he commanded.

Alex, Miata, and Dante were fast to obey, scrambling after him.

"What? What is it?" they were all asking.

"Perhaps... Whydah!" he said, gesturing grandly to a port easily visible from the beach.

"Well, this be where I be off," Miata said cheerfully.

"Actually," Rackham said, grinning, "I may have a scheme to get us all in." He looked over at Alex, who had tucked her hair up into Miata's hat and was sporting some dirt smears on her usually pretty face.

She gave him a distrusting glare. "What scheme?"

A couple of hours later, after the night had fully encompassed them, they arrived at Whydah, a bit cleaned up and put together, save for Alex who was still a little unkempt looking intentionally.

"Ready, Miss Alex?" Dante asked.

Shrugging, she sighed. Then in a lower tone than normal, she answered, "It is Mr. Thorpe tonight, lads. Let us make haste with this before I lose my courage."

"Right away, young Mr. Thorpe," Miata agreed, chuckling.

Scowling, Alex turned to Miata. "Mr. O'Keeffe, if you mock me while there, surely they will take notice."

"No," Rackham said with a sigh. "I'm afraid us lads rather enjoy mocking one another."

Alex groaned. "Wonderful."

"You'll be fine, Miss Alex," Miata spoke up. "Just be bein' yourself with all the meanness and none of the politeness or haughtiness. You be doin' just grand."

"What a hateful way to be!" She adjusted her clothes, huffing and fidgeting nervously.

"I don't know," Rackham said, shrugging. "You get to be more honest. You can say what you think. Perhaps you will find it freeing."

"I rather like politeness and manners," she retorted. "They keep us from being utterly beastly to one another with no sense of refinement. But it is a curious notion to say whatever comes to mind without consequence."

"I didn't say without consequence," Rackham said.

"She'll be bein' fine. Just be rememberin' he be your uncle," Miata said.

"That," Alex said with a laugh, "is the most ridiculous part of this entire conspiracy."

"I'm glad you think so," Dante said under his breath. Then clearing his throat, he continued, "Mind your manners, Mr. Thorpe! Come along. Just… just don't speak, if possible."

Glowering at him, Alex adjusted her attire and huffed. "I shall speak if I have a mind to," she said with a challenging tone.

Miata and Dante traded approving glances.

"Not too cheeky now," Rackham said, nodding. "But I wager you will deceive them all, *Mr. Thorpe*."

As they took a pause before entering Whydah, the clouds broke, pouring water onto them. Shouting in objection, the group raced for Whydah's gates. As they hurried inside, they immediately saw their destination. A midsized establishment called De Blauwe Paard stood just east of the center of the port town. Upon reaching the doors, they gave Alex a once-over and then walked inside.

Dante pushed through the door first, completely unnoticed, as were the others behind him. After they piled into the inn, he gestured to a table off to one side.

"We sit and observe," he instructed. "Once we have some food, we ask our questions. Understand?"

"Why not make our inquiries straight away and be done with it?" Alex asked, incredulous.

"We be wantin' to be eatin', Miss"—Miata fumbled—"*Mister* Thorpe." He cleared his throat. "Be that fine by you?"

Glaring over at him, she shrugged. "I suppose having a hot meal—"

"And a pint," Rackham interjected.

"A hot meal," she repeated pointedly, "would be a welcome end to our day."

"And a pint," Miata said in a grumble, nodding at Rackham.

"What is a pint?" Oduntan asked in a whisper.

Miata and Dante traded smiles.

"Come along, mate," Miata said, clapping him on the back.

After they had sat at their table of choice and eaten their food, Oduntan leaned back with a funny smile on his face.

"Pints. I like pints."

"Marvelous," Alex said with sarcasm. "Now you have managed to rob the most sensible of you lot of his wits. What about those questions?"

"Sh!" Rackham said. "The lads at the table over there are the ones we're after." He gestured to a couple of men sitting at a table off to their left.

"What?" She glanced around. "How do you know?"

"Don't be lookin' over!" Miata said, waving his hand to get her attention. "You be needin' to be less meddlesome!"

"I am not meddlesome, I am curious! There is a vast difference!"

"Not to them there's not," Rackham argued.

"*Unrẹrẹ ni o wa ti nhu*," Oduntan said with a big grin.

All three stopped their conversation and stared at him.

"How many did he have?" Alex asked, grimacing.

"Pints?" Miata shrugged. "I weren't countin'."

"*Kiniun omo wa ni joniloju*," Oduntan said, nodding and then slumping onto his hand to prop up his face.

"Just give the lad water," Rackham remarked, eyeing him.

"Well, what are the men saying?" Alex asked, gesturing at the table of interest.

"Don't point!" Rackham exclaimed in a whisper, swatting at her hand.

"Well, if we could get on with it, you would no longer be required to continue correcting my behavior!" she retorted with a hint of a snarl.

"You be needin' to be relaxin', M—" Miata stopped himself. "Mr. Thorpe."

"Relaxing?" she repeated, scoffing. However, her face drooped from incredulous disapproval to disappointment. "I have never excelled at relaxing."

"Now there be a bleedin' shock," Miata said in return.

"Allow me," Rackham said, standing. Purposefully staggering off with an empty mug, he bumped into one of the men at the table.

"Ay! Watch where you're goin', Mick!" the man shouted.

"I ain't no Mick!" Rackham retorted, slurring his words. "I'm English!"

"Well, shove off just the same," the man said with a snort.

"Sure, sure. But could you do a lad a favor and tell me who I can talk to about a job?" He swayed as he stood, the mug dangling at the end of his arm as though it weighed as much as fifty pounds. "A lad's got to pay somehow."

"A job, says you?" He scoffed. "Why would we share our work with the likes of you, Mr...."

"Rackham. Mr. Rackham. Truth be told, me and my mates are here for one job in particular." He gave them a dimwitted smile and nodded for further emphasis. "We just want to know if the employer is good on his word."

"Jolly good for you, *Mr.* Rackham. Now go away!" the man growled.

"What job?" the drunkest man at the table asked.

"Shut it!" the first man snorted.

"I-I d-doubt you've heard of it," he stammered. "We caught wind of it when we stopped by vonk Dragonwagon."

"Van Draenweg? Only thing we've heard of from there is those two wenches who got loose. Seems Barend is keen to get 'em back for his boss." The intoxicated man laughed. "Dedication and loyalty that are, but fool stupid too."

"Fool in what way?" Rackham asked.

"No doubt he wants the reward for findin' 'em that his boss is offerin', but it all seems a bit odd," the first man said, taking a drink.

"Odd?" Rackham asked in ultimate curiosity.

"Aye. Strange. What fool would offer to pay to find a couple of wenches who ran off into the wilderness? There must be more than we know about it, or he is a fool to his boss." The men at the table nodded, trading glances and murmuring.

"Ahem. Pardon, Mr. Rackham," Alex said.

Dante whirled about, startled to see her at his elbow. He scowled at Miata, who, still sitting at their table, lifted his hands helplessly. "M-M-M-Mr. Thorpe..."

"Mr. Rackham! You must rejoin us! It is so dull without you, and we are eager to continue our plans," she said in her faux voice.

"Aye, well, these lads were just filling me in on those two wenches we were contemplating searching for earlier. It seems *Barend* might not be good for the pay."

"Oh! Is that so?" she asked. "Tell me, where do you hear your rumors from? Are they reputable sources?"

"They are well enough," one man answered.

"Truly? Or are you, perhaps, simply trying to throw us off the search?" she asked, crossing her arms.

"W-what?" The man chortled, shaking his head. "Why would we do that?"

"To reduce competition, of course. Anyone dressed as poorly as you are likely goes to nearly any measure to try and secure accruing more money." As she concluded her observational statement, she immediately realized everyone was staring at her as though her clothes had abruptly vanished. That is, everyone except her own companions. They looked horrified.

Leaning forward on the table as he rose from his chair, the man eyed her. "You chatter on like a wench."

Scowling as severely as possible, she huffed. "I daresay! How rude!"

"Let's see how cheeky you are without your shirt, *boy*." He chortled, and reached for her.

Rackham, still wholly astonished and taken aback at Alex's unwanted involvement, was a little delayed in stepping between the man and Alex. While this shouldn't have been a problem, his pause allowed Alex the time to react as well. She, with all her quickness and might, grabbed Rackham's mug and swung it at the brute, knocking him right in the side of the head.

Consequently, much to Dante and Miata's wonder, the entire room exploded into a domino effect of volatile reactions. As fists were swinging and objects flying about the room, Dante grabbed Alex by the wrist and rushed back for Miata. Miata was struggling to get Oduntan on his feet. Each of them taking one of his arms around their shoulders, the two thin men hoisted the burly man to his feet.

"Miss Alex," Dante said, groaning from the strain, "you must help us clear a path if we are to escape!"

"Escape to where?" she asked. "It is night and raining! How far shall we get with Oduntan as he is?" She dodged a bottle that flew from elsewhere in the room.

"Do you have an alternative?" he asked, raising his voice above the din.

"We get a room to share," she shouted back.

"Wha—all of us?" Miata asked in great surprise, adjusting his hold on Oduntan. "How will we be payin' for it? None of us be carryin' gold, be we?"

"You could acquire some, could you not?" Alex asked, grimacing at the idea and hating herself for saying it.

"You be askin' me to be stealin' for you after you be hatin' me for years for it?" he asked, genuinely confused.

"Well, I…" She covered her mouth, ashamed.

"I be tellin' Amy I weren't to be doin' so again," he said, bewilderment still ringing in his voice.

"As it should be," she agreed, ducking to avoid part of a chair.

"They have a stable out back!" Rackham interjected. "I wager the animals won't charge us."

Disgusted with herself, Alex nodded. "Of course. Let us be off then."

However, as she turned to go, a couple of men came hurtling toward them, smashing into the three men and knocking them all over.

"Oh!" Alex gasped as they crashed to the ground. "Are you injured?"

As the other two men rolled away, Dante pushed himself up, groaning. "Just my pride."

"Well, come then. Quickly! Quickly!" She tugged at his arm. "Mr. O'Keeffe! Come! Come!"

Shaking his head, Miata opened his eyes and glanced around. "Oh, I were hopin' this were all a nightmare."

"I am afraid not," she said with a laugh. "Come on!"

Alex cheered Rackham and O'Keeffe up from the floor, with Oduntan suspended between them, out the door, down to the stable, and far to the back in some unused straw. But as they all flopped down, exhausted and weary, Alex found she was plagued with guilt whenever she looked at Miata. She contemplated the pros and cons of an unprompted apology until he caught one of her bothered glances.

"Miss Alex?"

"Hmmm? What? Yes, Mr. O'Keeffe?" she asked, wishing she was better at disguising such awkward feelings.

"What be troublin' you?" he asked, sitting beside her.

"I… Oh, I…" She looked at his eyes, the authenticity of his question unbearably obvious. "I am so disgusted with myself. Truly, I feel terribly for what I asked of you. To think I, of all people, would… I mean, here you are trying to do right, and I throw you back at the evils you are attempting to leave behind?" She shuddered. "It is unthinkable! I-I… I am ashamed."

Daring to put his hand on her shoulder, he said in a low voice, "Truth be told, I were a bit honored you be askin'. And I were considerin' it for a moment, just to be impressin' you. But I be realizin' not only were it not likely to be workin', but I don't be wantin' to be known for that. I be makin' a new life now, and I be makin' it right."

Huffing out a laugh, Alex shook her head. "In that, Mr. O'Keeffe, your logic is flawless."

"You be helpin' me see it." He kissed her on the top of her head so quickly neither had time to ponder or prepare for the action. He gave her a small smile. "G'night, Miss Alex."

As he moved off to get comfortable close to Oduntan, Dante took a turn sitting by the girl. "Tell me, Mr. Thorpe," he started, smirking, "why did you hit the man on the head?"

Refraining from giggling, she shrugged. "Is that not how you lads always make your grand escapes?"

"Some of us prefer a quiet exit," he said, grinning.

"I am terribly sorry. I do not know what came over me. I was afraid he knew I was no lad at all." She frowned as she reviewed the incident in her mind.

Reaching a thumb to her face, he wiped away some of the dirt. "Well, I wasn't going to let anything happen to you."

At the feel of his fingers, she closed her eyes then started away. "I made a mess of things."

"Oh, I don't know. I shall rather mourn the passing of young Mr. Thorpe. He's the best nephew I ever had."

"The *only* nephew, I suspect," she shot back, smiling.

Shrugging, he nodded. "Perhaps. Come on. Let's get some sleep."

The dawn rose gallantly into the sky with gold-encrusted wings. She smiled down at Jacq and Murtaugh, who sat quietly eating as the rest of the camp argued in Yoruba.

"How can they stand to quarrel so?" she asked.

"I have no explanation, but that is why the Irish appreciate their ale," he answered.

"Do you believe we made a mistake joining him?" she asked, rotating to observe his reaction.

"A mistake? No, lass. But these things are never easy." He sighed. "My uncle and I fought ceaselessly on occasion."

"Why?" she asked, finishing her food.

Shrugging, he plucked a stick from the ground and began poking at the earth. "He wasn't Papa."

"But Bahari is their father," she noted, watching him.

"By blood, perhaps, but he was gone a long while—one child's entire life. Akinlabi is angry, that is why he stirs the trouble."

"I know," she said dismally. "I wish I could be of use."

"You are," he returned. "You are a constant reminder to Bahari that his sons have a chance to have a father—*their* father—in their lives once again. If he is patient, perhaps they will love him as you love your father."

Smiling, she snatched up a stick of her own, tapping his when he tried to draw straight lines. "You know, I still miss Captain Taylor on occasion, but he is always with me."

"So it is with my parents," he returned, continuing to draw lines even with her interference.

Out of the corner of her eye, Jacq saw some birds take flight from the nearby forest that bordered the savanna. Nudging Murtaugh, she asked, "Did you see that?"

"See what?" he questioned, inspecting her eyes to know where to look.

"The birds," she said in a quiet voice.

As they watched the tree line, he nudged her back. "Do you see those branches swaying?"

"With no breeze," she noted.

They traded glances.

"Bahari," he said.

"Agreed." Nonchalantly, she rose and crossed over to where he stood by Gbeke whilst Murtaugh kept watch.

"Bahari?" she asked, loathing interrupting him.

"Shakina," he returned, glancing at her.

"There is movement in the tree line." She stared over at it, careful not to point or make a scene.

The arguing acutely diminished at her statement.

Bahari glanced at his sons. "What do you suggest we do?"

"Seek it out. It could be just a beast," Akinlabi recommended.

"It would be best to leave quietly at once, having one of ours trail behind to discover any possible followers," Kukoyi countered.

"Both are worthy options," Bahari noted. "But how will you choose? You cannot very well do both."

The boys traded glances.

"You must decide quickly," he continued. "There is no time to fight and argue. Someone must decide."

Murtaugh approached, exchanging uneasy shoulder shrugs with Jacq.

"I have done well with my leadership, I am told," Kukoyi replied. "But part of being a good leader is seeing when there is one better to lead. I would select you, Baba, to take my place as it once was yours, and I only held it to await your return. As you are now returned, I do not see why I should remain as the leader of our family."

Bahari looked at his other sons. "You gladden me with your honor and respect, Kukoyi. However, I do not wish to be forced upon your brothers if they will not receive me back with open hearts."

Scowling, Akinlabi looked at Nuru and Bakari, knowing by their hopeful expressions he was the one to whom Bahari had been referring. "If Kukoyi wishes to trust the man who abandoned us, he must see something I cannot." Glancing at his mother, he sighed. "I accept his leadership if Kukoyi is sincere in believing he can guide us safely to Cabo Corso."

Somehow, standing even taller, Bahari nodded. "Keeping you all safe is always my first priority." He glanced about, noting the expressions of all present. Durosinmi, with his swollen, purple nose, was the only one seemingly suffering from contempt at the decision. "We follow Kukoyi's plan. Akinlabi, you may select who should travel behind with intent to discover if we are followed."

Both boys nodded in agreement, and Aladia beamed.

"We will reach Cabo Corso," Bahari said to the group. "We must. Now, gather your belongings. We move now."

As they picked up their things, Jacq noticed Durosinmi talking quietly to Akinlabi off to the side. Seeing this, an uneasy, distrustful feeling welled up from deep within her being. It reminded her of the last time she had felt it.

Six weeks earlier…

Nabbing a biscuit, Jacq slid beneath the stairs which led from the ship's deck to the lower decks. Nestling between some ropes and bags, she sighed. "At sea again. You," she said to the bready morsel, "are always a proper mate."

"What's got your knickers pinched, Rackham?" a male voice inquired as footsteps began descending the stairs.

The sound of feet stopped, eye level with Jacq. "It's nothing, mate."

"Right. And I'm a plucky French lass," the man said in turn.

Chuckling, he shifted his weight on the stairs. "Truth be told, I met this lass a few weeks past—"

"Ah! Always a wench," the man observed.

"Well, the thing of it is, I cannot get my mind straight. She invited me for dinner with her parents, but I had already agreed to this voyage." He shrugged.

Jacq covered her mouth, shocked at what she was hearing. *Another lass? It cannot be!*

"Well, is she a pretty lass?" the other crewman asked.

"Oh, aye. Nicely accomplished, with very agreeable manners too, but eyes that rival the stars," Dante answered, a dreaminess in his inflection.

Jacq's lip curled, her heart rate increased, and she squeezed the biscuit so hard it crumbled.

"Your lass have a name?"

"Well, she's not mine," Dante answered, laughing. "But her name is Miss Wallace. Miss Emily Wallace."

"A fine name, sir. A fine name, to be sure."

"She's as fine as her name, that is certain."

"Very good, sir. I'm away with my duties. Best of luck to you, sir."

"Aye," he said as the other man's footsteps retreated. "I need a mighty sum of luck." Grumbling, he moved off to the kitchen.

A sickening feeling overcame Jacq as she emerged and slunk up the stairs. "And he said London was so dull there was naught to give an account of." Scoffing, she reached the upper deck. "I question which of us is the bigger fool."

"I'll not be a daft fool again," she said between her teeth as she watched Durosinmi. "Mark my words, your behavior shall not be dismissed or ignored."

Chapter 9

"Kukoyi! Kukoyi!" Akinlabi called in a loud whisper.

"What is it?" Kukoyi asked, rising from where he sat by Iremide.

Assembled in a forest clearing, the rest of the group turned to see him hurrying up with Olusegun behind him.

"I count thirteen now!" As he came to a stop, Morenike handed him a drink. He nodded his thanks to his cousin.

"They are persistent," Kukoyi noted. "Following us for two days! What is to be done? There are only seven of us men, including Nuru and Ayotunde who are barely more than children."

"We will stand beside you," Jacq spoke up.

Murtaugh nodded. "That would bring us to nine."

"Let womenfolk fight for us?" Durosinmi sneered. "I would rather perish a man than hide behind a woman."

"Oi, Durojin—"

"Durosinmi," she corrected quietly.

"Durosinmi. This lass can fight just as well as you or I," Murtaugh retorted, stepping forward. He looked to Bahari. "What say you?"

"You are welcome to stand with me, the both of you. But it may be to our advantage to send Shakina ahead with the women and children," he answered.

"W-why?" Jacq asked, a little injured.

"Who better to defend them than one who carries the luck of Kehinde and the ability of Shakina?" he returned.

Jacq and Murtaugh traded looks. Then turning back to Bahari, she nodded. "Very well. If that is where I am needed, that is where I shall go. I will go with Aladia and Moyo, to keep the children safe." She looked at the mothers, each holding her youngest child.

"Jacq," Murtaugh protested.

"No, truly, Murtaugh. This must be someone's responsibility." She looked over at Durosinmi. "Fortunately for me, the children are not so daft as to reject help out of fear of it diminishing their manhood."

Durosinmi glowered at her while Bahari and the boys snickered.

She turned back to Murtaugh, touching at his arm in appreciation of his defense. "Honestly, if this is how I can best be of service, then I should be honored."

Akinlabi watched them with interest, and Morenike smiled secretively. "Why cannot all the pale northerners be so kind?" she asked.

"No doubt everything would be quite different if they were," Akinlabi answered, turning away to go sit down, with Olusegun following after him.

"Are you so convinced they follow us?" Durosinmi asked.

"Quite," Akinlabi answered, agitated by the question.

"It would benefit us to learn why they do so," Jacq spoke up, nudging Murtaugh.

"Aye," he said, readily vouching for her. "We may better plan against them should they decide to attack us."

"True, but we have no proper way to go about it," Kukoyi objected with a contemplative air.

"On the contrary," Bahari said, his expression becoming a sly smirk. "We may have the perfect way. It rains tonight. We will use it to our advantage."

Just as he said, as the sky began to darken, rain began to fall. True to his word, Bahari snuck down to where their unwanted entourage had camped for the night. Quietly, he waited in the drizzly night until one unsuspecting individual strayed to the edge of their little encampment. Then with the decided quickness of a leopard, he snatched the poor man up.

Several minutes later, Bahari sat the man down across a sheltered fire from his fellow travelers. "I found this one. He may be willing to provide us the insight you were hopeful to learn."

"Aye, no doubt *finding* is one word for it," Jacq remarked.

"It does sound better than *kidnapping*," Murtaugh said.

"I suppose you are right," she agreed. "Well, hopefully he'll be of benefit to us. I haven't any idea what Bahari will do to him if he is uncooperative." She grimaced on behalf of the captive.

"Nor I," Murtaugh returned. "Bahari, what shall you do to this man if he does not assist us?"

Bahari, confused by their very overt banter, looked between Jacq and Murtaugh. "Well, I don't know."

"Oh!" they both responded, wincing at the painful notion.

"That often ends badly," Jacq started.

"Quite badly," Murtaugh added.

"For the person who would be, well, where you are now." She offered the stranger an apologetic smile.

Bahari was still lost as to their game, until he glanced at his captive. The way the man stared at him, he may as well have been a hungry lion.

"However," Murtaugh continued, "if you were to be of assistance, mate…"

"Aye," Jacq agreed. "Be of assistance, and I wager you shall be permitted to leave entirely unharmed." She nodded and smiled in an effort at persuasive emphasis.

The man turned anxious, panicky eyes back and forth between Jacq and Murtaugh, Bahari, and where everyone stood, decidedly confused by the situation.

"*Kí ni orúkọ rẹ?*" Bahari asked. He pointed at Jacq's charm. "Kehinde."

A gleam of hope lighting up his eyes, the man smiled. "*Emi ni Oluwaseun.*"

Bahari nodded. "Oluwaseun, why are you following us?" He repeated his question in Yoruba, and Oluwaseun was glad to answer.

The two remained in conversation for a minute or two, discussing whatever Bahari made into a topic for discussion.

Murtaugh and Jacq grinned at each other, pleased with how cooperative their new friend seemed to be.

"What was that?" Morenike asked them as they awaited Bahari's report.

"What was what?" Jacq asked back.

"Why were you saying those things? How did each of you know what the other was going to say?"

"We invent what we are saying as we are saying it," the Irishman explained. "It's not ideal for all situations—"

"But it is good fun," Jacq interrupted.

He smiled over at her. "So long as you and your partner have a common mind," he said.

"How marvelous," Morenike said with a wishful smile.

The lighthearted moment screeched to a halt, however, when Bahari rose and walked away from Oluwaseun. He paced a couple minutes, muttering to himself.

"Brother," Moyo finally spoke. "What did he say? What troubles you?"

"We are followed by friends of Huru," he answered.

"Huru! An old friend!" Aladia beamed in delight. "This should be easy to amend!"

"On the contrary," Kukoyi said warily. "Baba, I do not wish to be a messenger of evil news, but I'm afraid Huru has some questionable alliances."

"*Had*," Bahari corrected with a cold tone. "Huru is dead."

His family murmured and gasped.

"How?" Akinlabi asked, examining his father.

"I was there, but I do not know. His deception killed him." Bahari rubbed at his jaw. "He was to assist us, but he had other plans. It would seem he got in the way of someone else's schemes."

"Then he got what he deserved," Akinlabi said in assessment.

Bahari shrugged. "I cannot say, but it was marked for me as a sad day—a day I lost a friend forever."

Akinlabi nodded, looking sheepishly away. "Of course, sir."

"We never delight in the death of a soul," Aladia said to her son in a scolding inflection. "Every life is precious."

Jacq's stomach churned. Rather than succumb to the threat of mental anguish, she pushed it aside and questioned, "So what of Oluwaseun? How do their relations with Huru affect us?"

Bahari sighed, a somber expression overtaking his already serious demeanor. "They believe I killed him and have come to avenge his death."

"You know, that was the second occasion I have slept in a barn," Alex said with a disgusted flair as she stepped over a log.

"So you be sayin' for the last three days," Miata returned with agitation resounding in his statement.

"It was the seventh time for me," Dante added, dodging a low-hanging branch.

"So you be sayin' as well," he retorted. "Why be it a thing to be keepin' note of?"

"It's an easy occasion to remember so long as you don't"—Rackham looked over to see O'Keeffe nearly glaring at him—"make a habit of it."

Miata gave him a validated expression. "Aye."

Looking away sheepishly, Rackham shrugged. "My sincere apologies. I often forget your less-than-desirable beginnings, which, truly, is a credit to you."

"A credit? How?" Miata asked, forgiving him and moving onward.

"It means you behave in a manner which does not provoke one to instantly assume your previous occupation," Alex translated. "I do not know if I agree to this fully, but you make an admirable effort to seem unashamed of your disadvantage. This alone lends to others believing you have a more honorable history."

His countenance becoming cross, Miata frowned at them. "I be only ashamed when you be so Christianlike as to be goin' on about it and the way you be loathin' me, no matter how ye be tryin' to be seein' past it." Then he stomped away.

"I do not loathe you!" she yelled after him.

Rackham gave her an unconvinced glance.

"Well, I do not!" she snapped at him. "Not anymore," she added quietly, contemplating his outburst.

As Miata marched off, Oduntan looked between Rackham and Alex. "When we began this journey, I believed you all to be friends."

"And now?" she asked, disappointment hanging on her mien like a heavy fog.

"I would not know your word for it, but my people would say *kiniun ati akata*," Oduntan answered. "You are both different and the same. You fight for respect. You, Tayewo, are *kiniun*. You have the respect because it is yours by nature. Mr. O'Keeffe is *akata*. He only has it when there is no *kiniun*."

Heaving a sigh, Alex held her hands helplessly in the air. "It is not my wish, nor do I make designs to bring him misery and grief!" She shook her head, pushing the loose hair out of her face. "After all these years, I just…" Her voice broke, and she turned away. "I just do not know what to think on the subject of Mr. O'Keeffe."

"He has caused you injury?" Oduntan asked.

"Yes," she answered, gazing in the direction of the beach though she could not glimpse it. "Many, many years ago now. He altered my whole life. He changed everything."

She remembered that night she and her adopted mother, Mrs. Thorpe, arrived at the inn in Port de Couler de Beautaux. She could still feel the pull on her heart as she watched the ill woman look for her purse and the sinking feeling when it was revealed stolen.

"In mere moments, he ruined my life." She wiped at tiny streams trickling from her eyes. "But because of him, I met Jacq. I would not have gone in search of any sort of adventure. I would not have sought out a notorious pirate to attempt a rescue. And I certainly would *not* be here."

She rotated back to look at Oduntan, who was keenly listening, and Dante, who was trying to inch away.

"I have attempted to forgive him many times, but I cannot seem to be kind to him," she said in a whisper.

"You know," Rackham spoke up, "you don't *have* to be nice to him *all* the time. You certainly don't *have* to feel badly for him, and you don't even *have* to like him."

She stared at him, unimpressed with his input.

"Truly," he said, nodding. "Look at me and that ruddy Irishman. We were mighty amiable afore he started making moon eyes at Jacq. Now I don't like him. Not at all."

"And why, Mr. Rackham, should I accept any advice from you on the matter at hand?" Alex asked in a challenging tone. "You who torments my sister with obscurity and ambiguity. You who, to my knowledge, has never had the pleasure or displeasure of entering into any sort of relationship of a serious nature."

Pondering her comments a moment, Dante shrugged. "On these charges you may have sufficient evidence to stake your claims. However"—he looked at her with his dark, soulful eyes in a way that made her breath catch—"I can assure you of one thing. It is my aim to be at peace with all my relations, no matter the severity, the difficulty, or the obscurity. My intentions are to make things right. If I attempt this, will I not eventually arrive?"

Nodding, she sighed. "It is a worthy goal, though I certainly question your methods."

He bowed his head in appreciation of her concession.

"What do your people suggest on these matters?" Alex asked, casting a glance at Oduntan.

"My people," Oduntan said, continuing to study their expressions as he had been throughout the conversation, "believe that searching for balance in this life is a worthy aim, both for *kiniun* and *akata*."

"Well, we should find our Mr. O'Keeffe," Dante said with a sigh. "We don't want him sliding down a muddy hill or something."

Alex glared at him while Oduntan laughed. "That is what happened to Tayewo just seven days past."

Rackham nodded. "Aye! A reasonable concern," he said, looking over at Alex with a partially repressed grin.

"It would indeed be a grave misfortune," she said flatly. "Similar, perhaps, to awaking to discover pigs having selected you as their sleeping partner?"

"See if I permit you the safer sleeping location if ever we spend a night in a barn again!" Dante retorted playfully.

Oduntan continued chuckling. "Why do I not seem to recall these moments you mention of our visit to Whydah? What barn?"

Alex and Dante traded glances.

"Oduntan," Rackham started, "do you remember the pints?"

Oduntan looked confused. "The *ina omi*?"

"Aye," Rackham said. "We call it ale. Sometimes it puts smoke in your mind, and you cannot see the memories."

"Then it is poison!" Oduntan said, aghast.

"Uh, well," Dante stammered.

"Yes!" Alex said, jumping in. "Sometimes it will even rob a person of all their manners, leaving them to behave in the wildest behavior you can imagine."

"And you drink this for enjoyment?" he asked of Rackham.

"Well, if ingested in appropriate quantities, it is simply relaxing," Dante argued.

"Truly?" His interest was restored. "I simply had too much?" he questioned, looking to Alex.

"In my opinion, it is a foul drink that should not be given or received in polite company, nor should it be partaken of by oneself," she answered confidently.

Oduntan scratched his jaw. "Why are you in disagreement on it?" he asked. "It is either poison or it is not."

"Some of us less sophisticated persons enjoy a bit of poison on occasion. Some try to live on it," Rackham remarked.

"But not you," Oduntan said with a hopefulness in his voice.

"I considered it once," Dante said with a smirk, "but determined it would not secure my happiness." He grinned over at Alex, amused with her tight-lipped reaction.

"Perhaps we should focus on searching out Mr. O'Keeffe," she said in a clipped manner, trudging off ahead of them. "Mr. O'Keeffe!" she called out. "Mr. O'Keeffe!"

Still wearing his pleased expression, Dante moved off in another direction, yelling in cooperation with Alex, "Oi! Miata, mate!"

"O'Keeffe!" Oduntan joined in.

As they shouted for him, they moved in various directions, desiring to cover as much ground as possible.

Circling back around, Dante was approaching the shore when he heard a branch snap. Instinctively glancing above him, he shook his head at what sight met his eyes. "Miata? O'Keeffe, mate. What are you doing up there?"

"I be puttin' me previous trade to some use," he answered with snarky overtones.

"Listen, mate, like it or not, I understand you. Remember? Pirate." He gestured at himself.

"Yet she be not lookin' at you with disdain. It be near like I be the devil himself," Miata yelled down from the treetop.

"Well, I never stole anything from her," he pointed out.

"Not as such," Miata said in a grumble.

"What?" Dante shouted up.

"What I were about to say," Miata said, struggling down the tree, "be that…" Reaching the ground, he dusted himself off as he straightened in front of Dante who stood impatiently waiting.

"What did you climb up there for, anyway?" Rackham asked. "For sport?"

Glaring, Miata shook his head. "No, mate. I be lookin' for—"

He paused abruptly as a creature bigger than their hands came dropping down between them, stopping level with their heads. Both he and Rackham silently scooted back, each studying it with a disgusted grimace. It hung motionless, dangling precariously on…

"Is that a thread?" Rackham asked, inclining forward, squinting at it.

"Be-be it dead?" Miata added, following Dante's example.

Just as they were less than a foot away, it twitched.

They froze.

"Wha-what-what was…"

Suddenly, all eight of its long hairy legs stretched out, and both of the young men screamed, jumping backward.

In response, it dropped to the ground, lifted its two front legs, and scurried toward them.

"*Aaaaah!*" Shrieking and squealing, Miata and Dante tripped over themselves and each other as they made a mad dash toward the beach.

"What is it? What is it?" Rackham asked repeatedly in a panic induced rush.

"It be evil, to be sure! Evil with a dozen legs!" Miata whimpered, tripping and running alongside him.

"Wait," Rackham said, his head clearing a little. "Wait! There is a—"

Though Dante paused, Miata did not, and he slammed into his associate, causing them to tumble over the edge of a sandy berm, spilling onto the beach just as the tide carried in a wave to splash them right in the face.

Coughing and spitting up the gritty water, they scrambled up, still colliding into each other and stumbling about in a stupid fashion an observer might credit to an overconsumption of alcohol. Straightening their backs and their sandy soaked attire, they looked at each other with uncertainty of how to proceed.

Coughing again, Miata gestured to Dante. "You be a might wet, mate." He coughed again, smiling sheepishly as Rackham sent him a glare.

"You are one of the most apprehensive men I have *ever* been in acquaintance with," Dante remarked, displeasure coating his words like oil. Looking down at himself, he frowned and shook his head. "We are never to speak of this to anyone, understand?"

"Agreed," Miata said eagerly, nodding. "How be we explainin' ourselves to Miss Alex?" He dusted some sand off his shirt, grimacing at how he was completely covered with it.

"We'll tell her you tripped and grabbed my arm as you fell," Rackham answered flatly, examining his own clothes.

"Why me?" Miata asked, insulted.

"Because it were you that were up in that fool tree," he said, a growl underlining his statement. "What were you doing up there, anyway?"

"I be tryin' to tell you," Miata returned with a smug expression, "I be mostly certain I be seein' the flag o' Cabo Corso. It be maybe a day or two out."

Pointing a finger at him, Rackham smirked. "That is what we tell Miss Alex. We tell her straight away afore she can take too keen an interest on the state of our attire."

"You be mighty clever for a pirate," Miata noted, grinning.

His smirk growing, Rackham shrugged and headed back into the jungle. "You're not so bad yourself, mate."

"Baba," Kukoyi spoke as he and Akinlabi approached Bahari where he stood apart from the rest.

"What is it?" he asked, sullen and downcast.

"If you did not kill Huru, why can you not speak to them? Make them understand?" he asked, glancing at the cloudy sky.

Sighing, Bahari turned to face his sons. "They seek to blame someone, and they have chosen me. I only regret that by my presence you, your mother, and your brothers are in danger. You should go ahead without me. I will face these men alone."

"No," Kukoyi said firmly, surprising Akinlabi.

"Kukoyi, your heart is pure, but these men... they are like the angry *erinmi* who knows not mercy and forgets his gentle nature. He is wild and seeks only the taste of blood. These are not men who will listen," Bahari said, grasping his son's shoulder in a loving, appreciative hold.

"We will not leave you, will we, Akinlabi?" Kukoyi returned. "We made a plan. We shall keep to it."

Akinlabi looked between his brother and father, and he noticed something he hadn't before. He could actually see that his father cared. Behind his stoic exterior, there was pain—great pain. Pain that could only stem from love. It was a pain he understood. Feeling insecure in his own opinion, he looked to his brother, a shining star of reverence, respect, and loyalty—the perfect son. Together, they seemed somehow stronger, and he felt drawn toward that untainted strength.

"Akinlabi?" Kukoyi repeated, glancing back at his younger brother.

Taking a deep breath, Akinlabi nodded. "We shall," he said firmly, looking Bahari in the eye.

Bahari smiled, lifting his hand from Kukoyi's shoulder to Akinlabi's. "You honor me."

Suddenly, Akinlabi began to question everything he had ever assumed about his father. Perhaps his mother had not created a mythical figure of exaggerated greatness after all. Perhaps he truly did love his family. Perhaps he was a man of honor, not just a bedtime story. A tiny smile bent his mouth.

"So what do we do?" Kukoyi questioned.

"We prepare now," Bahari said, dropping his hand. "This pause in the rains will not remain, and they have likely noticed Oluwaseun missing from their company. We must hurry before the rain begins again."

"Why before the rain?" Akinlabi asked, more acutely interested in Bahari's reasons than before.

"Because that is when I would strike," he stated simply. "Just as the rain falls again."

As they rejoined the others, however, large drops of water began slowly falling from the clouds, splatting here and there in a warning of what was to come. Jacq and Murtaugh, standing near Aladia, Moyo, and Morenike, turned to see the boys rushing back with their father.

"Now, Shakina!" Bahari commanded. "Move them now!" His worried blue eyes and his voice conveyed even more than his words: they were coming.

Touching at Murtaugh's arm, Jacq immediately moved to spring into action. However, before she could dash away, he grabbed her wrist. Stopping, she turned a puzzled expression towards him. "Murtaugh?"

"Jackie." The corner of his mouth lifted as he tried to think of something—the right thing—to say. His eyes dropped as he searched for words.

Placing her free hand on the hand he had latched to her wrist, she smiled. "Michael."

He looked up, staring fixedly at her face.

Reaching out to run her thumb over the healing mark on his cheekbone, the mark now reduced to a scratch, she sighed. "Stay safe."

He nodded. "You too."

"Shakina!" Bahari bellowed over the commotion that had erupted around them.

She lingered a moment more, then Jacq tore herself away, gathering Aladia, Moyo, and the children.

Exhaling a long, ragged breath, Murtaugh stretched his neck and shoulders then turned to join the men. "Where would you have me?"

"Come, come!" Jacq was whispering. "This way! This way!" As she ushered the caravan of women and children, she found herself wishing Alex was there to help her.

She would know all the sweet and warm words to ease their souls, she thought. *What can I offer aside from assurance that I will jab a sword at anything that moves? What a jolly cheerful way to hearten people!*

Finding a nice grove of trees to hide in with lots of bushy, forest underbrush, Jacq signaled to them. "In here!"

As they filed in, she counted them off. "Aladia, Moyo, Iremide, Nuru, Bakari, Adunni, Enitan... seven..." She began going over the names in her mind.

"Morenike?" Moyo asked in a whisper. "Morenike, my child!"

Jacq's heart sank. "I shall find her, Miss Moyo. I shall! Everyone else, lie down as best as you can. Use the brush to hide yourselves away." Clasping Moyo's hands in the dark, she did her best to smile and give off every confidence. "I will fetch her."

"Please do," Moyo pleaded. "She is *awǫn tanna ti ǫkàn mi*— the flower of my soul."

Nodding, Jacq sighed. "Everyone, stay where you are. Allow me to—"

Snap!

Everything went silent.

"What was that?" Aladia whispered.

"I don't know," Jacq returned in an equally low voice. "Stay here. Let me look around. I shan't be far from you."

With that, she slunk around, performing a perimeter examination of their hiding spot then began spiraling outward in search of whatever had made the noise. With the darkly overcast sky, however, the evening sun was of minimal assistance to her. Still, she was able to see some movement, and she made her way toward it.

"Please be a bird, please be a bird," she mumbled as she got closer and closer.

Feeling a pair of eyes on her, she ran through the options in her mind, something she realized she should have done before venturing out this far.

"Run. Run away fast," she whispered to herself. "No, no. I am Kehinde. Kehinde is a bearer of good fortune. Right? Hide! I could hide… forever." Grimacing, she crouched down, disappointed at her inability to conjure a clearly brilliant scheme.

As she remained motionless, however, the decision was made for her when the being roaming the woods began approaching her from the side. Bracing herself, she listened to the rustling getting closer and closer. When a native tribesman appeared from the thick, leafy brush, she jumped to her feet, sword drawn. "Oi! What do you seek?"

Startled by her sudden appearance, he took a step back but instantly noticed her necklace charm. "Kehinde?" he asked, gesturing to the figurine and patting his chest.

Shifting her feet, she narrowed her eyes at him, trying to assess his affiliation. "Aye."

He smiled. "*Mo mọ* Akinyemi." He pointed again at the charm. "Kehinde."

"Akinyemi," she repeated. Then she recalled the giant of a man whom they had helped release the night Huru was killed and Morenike was discovered. "Aye! Akinyemi. You know him?" she asked, lowering her sword.

He continued smiling. "Akinyemi."

"You don't understand me," she guessed aloud, watching him remain in his expression. Gesturing in the direction she'd come from and where she planned to seek out Morenike, she said, "I am going this way." She patted her chest, unsure of proper communication technique.

Still smiling, he nodded, and then began walking in the same direction.

"No, no. Oh, no. No, you don't have to come—"

"Kehinde." He motioned for her to lead the way.

Sighing, she began walking with him, sword still drawn. "This would be much more agreeable if we could understand one another."

"Kehinde," he repeated, nodding and glancing about as they moved along.

As they drew closer to where their group had divided in two, they could hear shouts and clattering growing louder by the footstep.

Jacq's new friend looked concerned. "*Ti o ti wa ni ija nibi?*" he asked.

"Please understand," she said in return, unable to discern his words. "My mates are probably under attack this very moment. Bahari, Murtaugh, and—"

"Bahari!" he said, alarmed. Then he went charging forward, toward the fight.

"Mister! Ugh!" Jacq called after him, hurrying to catch him. "I'm looking for Morenike! Leave the lads alone!"

He paused under a tree close enough to get a view of the fracas that was in full swing. He motioned to it.

"No, I'm looking for a lass—Morenike," Jacq insisted.

Snap.

Jacq lifted her eyes to the upper branches of the tree. "Morenike?"

"I apologize, Kehinde. I just—"

"Never you mind!" Jacq retorted with a huff. "We just need to get you down from there quietly. Your mother is worried for your safety."

"Who is that with you?" Morenike asked, trying to reposition herself and see a good way down.

"I do not know. He knows Akinyemi and, identifying me as Kehinde, decided to join me." She looked over at him as he stood studying the fight just downhill from them. "I wish I knew his name. Perhaps I could call him Fred. How does Fred sound?"

"Bahari," he said, grinning.

Sighing, she turned to scan the mass altercation as well just in time to see Murtaugh pulling a man off Akinlabi and tossing him aside. Her heart swelled with pride. "If I were queen, I'd knight him just so I could keep him in my courtroom."

Morenike let out a dreamy sigh.

Suddenly realizing she'd spoke aloud, Jacq cleared her throat. "You know, as I believe he'd be a valiant defender of the throne, should his loyalty be mine."

Morenike smiled to herself. "Of course."

"Are you coming down or not?" Jacq asked impatiently. "I dislike standing here like a spectator at a Greek colosseum."

"*Ki, ti wa ni a dida wọn tabi ko?*" Fred asked, motioning to the brawling men.

"I can't understand you, mate," she replied, glancing back at the fighting.

When she did, she watched Bahari push a man who stumbled back, bumping into Murtaugh. Surprised, Murtaugh pivoted, only to come nose to nose with the man. Promptly dodging the blow intended for his face, Murtaugh was quick to administer his own series of well-placed punches. The Irishman smiled victoriously as the man slumped into an unconscious heap. However, he did not notice another assailant sneaking up behind him with a rock in his raised hand.

"Oh, no," Jacq whispered. "Murtaugh!" she yelled, charging down. "Murtaugh, behind you!"

"Murtaugh!" Fred echoed, racing after her.

Spinning about, Murtaugh barely caught the strike with his forearm. "Honestly, mate?" he asked, head butting the man in the nose. "Oh, my apologies. I think I hit your nose just there."

Calling out to Murtaugh had, however, caused unwanted attention to get channeled Jacq's direction, where she stood halfway down the incline. "Perfect," she muttered, pausing to reassess her next move with Fred stopped beside her.

However, before she moved a muscle, Fred rushed down the tiny hill, letting out a wild whoop.

"Fred! No! Bad Fred!" Jacq yelled after him. "Morenike, stay there! Fred! Get back here, Fred!"

However, as she observed him, he seemed to instinctively know who was who. He aligned himself with Bahari, who was armed with a stick rather than his sword.

Perplexed, she tumbled and picked her way over to Murtaugh. "What is going on here?"

"I don't exactly know," he answered. "Bahari wished us to fight without swords. He didn't want anyone to die. What of you? Who's that you brought? A new mate?" He pulled her away from the scuffle.

"I don't know. I discovered him when I was searching for Morenike. I can't understand a word he says, but he seems to want to assist us because he knows Akinyemi," she explained.

"The big bloke we rescued the night Huru died?"

"Aye." She nodded. "If you can use the word *rescued*. He fought alongside."

"How very fitting," the Irishman remarked with sarcastic undertones. Looking past her, his face tensed. "Give us a minute, love?" Confused, she watched him scoot around her and plunge back into the battle, making his way over to Kukoyi and helping him rescue Olusegun from a man twice his size.

"Aaaah!" a scream pierced the sky.

Everyone turned to see Morenike curled around her ankle at the bottom of the tree.

"She must have fallen! I told her to remain!" Jacq groaned, racing around the edge of the brawling mass that now had taken a pause to stare at the girl. However, to her surprise, she saw Bahari plowing through the midst of it—straight for his injured niece.

Bounding across the distance, he hoisted her back into the tree and stationed himself as her defender in front of it. Immediately, the fight moved toward him. As he engaged with one of the attackers, Jacq took an account of their numbers. The four younger men were paired together, defending against anyone who dared come near them. Murtaugh was making his way to her. Bahari was with Morenike, and Gbeke was wrestling some weighty man more than his size while Durosinmi was nowhere to be seen. Of course, Fred was…

"What is Fred doing?" she asked, pointing at where he stood by a rock formation near the tree holding Morenike.

"Who is Fred?" Murtaugh asked.

"There!" She pointed to his location.

"*Duro! Duro, gbogbo awọn ti o! Lẹsẹkẹsẹ!*" he yelled in Yoruba.

The fighting ground to a halt.

Fred proceeded to yell at Huru's friends, gesturing emphatically to Bahari, Jacq, and Murtaugh. The younger boys remained bunched together, Gbeke was still writhing beneath the clutches of his opponent, and Bahari and Morenike kept glancing between each other and Fred. Once Murtaugh reached Jacq, they remained motionless, wishing they knew what he was saying.

Pointing menacingly at the attackers, Fred made a few more berating-sounding statements and then stared expectantly.

In the silence that followed, one of the two men assaulting Bahari raised his arms, opening his palms for all to see his empty hands. He made a couple of somber-sounding declarations as everyone listened to him. Slowly, his cohorts began slinking away dejectedly as the sky darkened from dusk to night, leaving a veiled moon to barely shine down on them. Turning to Fred and Bahari, the assailant muttered a few more things and then vanished with his fellows into the growing darkness.

"How did he find us?" Kukoyi asked, gesturing to Fred.

Bahari smiled and motioned to Jacq. "Shakina. You may be more Kehinde than you could ever know."

Hopping down, Fred embraced Bahari and smiled again at Jacq. "*Alafia fun nyin,* Kehinde." Then he also disappeared into the night.

"W-wait!" Jacq called after him. Looking to Bahari, she shook her head. "I didn't even know his name! I called him *Fred!*"

Chuckling, Bahari turned and held out his hands for Morenike. "His name was Olujimi. Akinyemi is his cousin, a feared and respected warrior of this region. He said if any harm should befall us, they would never be able to rest again because Akinyemi would hunt them with his best men at his side."

"No wonder he kept walking about with that silly smile on his face," Jacq said, folding her arms.

"Aye. Now, return us to our womenfolk. Moyo will be anxious with Morenike's absence," Bahari noted.

"Oh! Aye! This way!" Jacq eagerly led them over to a joyous group still obediently hiding in the brush.

As they reunited, Morenike and the young men went on about the heroics of Bahari, Gbeke, and even Murtaugh. They delighted the younger boys with exaggerated tales as Iremide and Aladia each pulled aside Kukoyi and Bahari, respectively.

"Your bravery is beautiful, but you must know I am selfishly far more pleased you have returned mostly unharmed," Iremide said, smiling demurely.

Kukoyi discreetly touched at her hand. "Your pleasure is mine. Your belief in me is always my strength, like the roots of a great tree."

She smiled broader. "May I give you all you require to be as mighty as I know you can be."

Leaning forward, he rested his forehead against hers.

Simultaneously, Aladia was beaming up at Bahari. "You rescued our Morenike," she said in a whisper.

"What of it?" he asked, a cool, callous tone to his words.

"You have remained distant," she stated. "You fear bringing me close will push our children away, as the moon pushes away the sun."

"No," he said in a halfhearted attempt at denial.

"Do not forget," she whispered again, "that the sun teaches the moon to shine. Without the sun, the moon would fade away and forget how to light the night.

"Today you showed us all you are a man of honor. You are *my* man of honor. You are my *onírẹlẹ kiniun*. I chose you, Bahari, and I will continue to choose you until the sun forgets how to light the day, and fades away. Do not fear my love. Hold it tight. Never let it go." She stepped close to him, resting one hand over his heart. "Remind me how sweet it is to be loved by you in return."

Cupping her face in his hands, he fought back tears—the rarest of moments. "I do not deserve you, beautiful Aladia. But if you insist on loving me still, I cannot deny your wishes." Releasing her chin, he scooped her up into his arms.

"Look! There she be!" Miata said enthusiastically, rubbing his hands together. "Should we be goin' in now or waitin' until mornin'?"

"When have you ever been so eager to enter a place filled with people?" Alex asked.

"O'Keeffe does not like people?" Oduntan questioned.

Scoffing, Miata waved them off. "I be likin' people just fine. It be these two," he pointed between Alex and Dante, "who be less than fancyin' other folk."

"That's not true," Rackham spoke up. "I just don't fancy the way folks feel privileged to prevail on a lad just because he's in a public place." He gestured to Alex. "She's the one who's all judgement and condescension."

"Yet I am the one who has the least trouble with getting others to treat me kindly. Despite my preferences, I do my best to interact politely with everyone," she told Oduntan. "Besides, my opinion of most people is entirely inconsequential being as I do not even share an acquaintance with them."

"I don't think politeness earns you all of your kind treatment," Rackham remarked, observing her pretty figure, though it was partially disguised by her attire.

"Mr. Rackham!" Alex exclaimed in astonishment veiled appreciation. "Abominable reasoning!"

"I be in agreement," Miata said, winking at her.

She gasped. "Mr. O'Keeffe!" Her cheeks flushed at their studious glances.

"Truth be bein' told," Miata said with a sigh, "I be eager to be findin' Miss Amy. Lord be knowin' if she were apart from me too long she be findin' some other chap who be more deservin' o' her affections."

"Mr. O'Keeffe," Alex returned with discouraging tones. "She is already in acquaintance with many of those, and yet she continues to favor you."

"Thanks?" He grimaced at her attempt at encouragement. "But you be knowin' what I be meanin', Miss Alex. Lord be knowin' 'twouldn't be a hard feat," he said glumly. Rubbing the back of his neck, he gazed at the star-speckled sky.

Six weeks earlier...

The star-studded blanket of night was quiet. Miata leaned against the railing, staring out across the waters. "From a beggin' thief to a poor excuse for a proper gentleman," he said in wonderment. "What manner o' fortune be that?"

"Regardless of how pathetic you may be, I do expect a certain code of honor and manner of conduct," Vice

Admiral Luray interrupted, "to be followed by any young man interested in keeping company with any daughter of mine."

Miata spun about to find the vice admiral close by, watching him with disapproving eyes. "Sir," Miata started. "I be havin' every intention o' treatin' all o' your daughters with the respect and reverence they be deservin'."

"An impressive attempt for a man who never had the benefit of being brought up to learn these values to which I refer," the vice admiral commented.

"I were lucky to encounter a man or two who be havin' a code to his way," Miata said. "But I be knowin' it be nothin' to what I could be learnin' from you, sir."

"With this in consideration," the vice admiral continued, clasping his hands behind him and looking out to sea, "how do you intend to make good on your word if you have no connections and naught but squalor manners?"

Miata was silent a moment as he put together his reply. Then in a quiet, meek voice, he answered, "Sir, it be a mystery to you Miss Amy be carin' for me at all, and it be a mystery to me too. But she be all the same. I be all too knowin' my circumstances be inferior, but I be strivin' to become the kind o' man she be deservin'." Miata straightened as tall as possible. "I be intendin' to be doin' so till the day I be passin' on. Lord be knowin' I be still short o' the measure even then."

"It is astonishing you think you shall still be connected with her, unless you are planning an early death," the vice admiral said in a deadpan tone. Still, able to detect the sincerity in Miata's speech, he sighed. "Even so, let us hope you are as good a man in your heart as my dear Amy believes, else you shan't stand a chance. I cannot recover the time that was lost with my eldest girls, but I have every intention of doing my best by them, even if it means advising them against their wishes and pointing out to them the evils I see in a situation, regardless of the reasons for the circumstance. I do not presume to make their decisions for them, but I will make every acceptable effort to ensure them a secure and cherished future as free from scorn and ridicule as possible. Do you understand my meaning, Mr. O'Keeffe?"

A downcast countenance shadowing his expression, Miata nodded. "Aye, sir. You be wantin' them to be havin' the best. It be proper you be wishin' it, sir."

The vice admiral looked at him with maintained indifference. "Perhaps there is hope for you after all, Mr. O'Keeffe."

"Mr. O'Keeffe," Alex said, interrupting his reverie.

"Miss Alex, I—"

"Mr. O'Keeffe, if you please." She narrowed her eyes, lifted her eyebrows, and pointed at him—a look he had come to understand meant for him to be silent so she could speak. "We have our many, many"—she paused, laughing—"many differences."

He rolled his eyes.

"I seem to have a particular talent for finding faults and flaws in your motives, your methods, and even your character." She paused again, internally recalling her successes.

"This be wonderful, Miss Alex, but—"

"Bup, bup, bup, bup, bup!" she interrupted, repeating the shushing face. "Yet despite this, I can find no flaw in the care which you have expressed for my sister. And by sister, I mean Amy."

He glared at her for the clarification. "Care?" he asked, scoffing. "I... I love her," he said in a hoarse whisper.

A tearful smile pulled at her lips. "I know."

He opened his mouth to argue but realized there was no argument to be had. His expression stumbled from defensive to bewildered. Then a sort of shock lit up his face. "I love her!" he repeated, not in revelation but in freedom that he no longer had to keep it a secret.

Her smile broadening, Alex nodded. "For some time, I think."

He laughed as one might when a great pressure has been removed, just as the pain of adjusting to the liberation hits—a sort of broken laugh. He covered his mouth. "I were ne'er sure I be sayin' so aloud. Least of all to you."

Sniffling, Alex shrugged. "It seems our hearts have a mind of their own, does it not? We are destined, you and I, to love someone who is so decidedly apart from us by some circumstance we cannot control." Her voice broke. "At least you still have a chance. I have seen how she looks upon your face." She paused, sniffling. "She sees no one else."

Breaking both of their unstated no-touching policies, Miata stepped forward and embraced her. Being emotionally vulnerable, she accepted.

Nearby, Rackham was leaning against a tree, pondering their conversation. "Destined to love," he muttered. "What a bleedin' laugh." Kicking at the ground, he stomped away.

Chapter 10

"Murtaugh! Murtaugh!" Jacq called, glancing about the camp. "Murtaugh?" Seeing Bahari sharpening a stick, she hurried to him. "Bahari, have you seen Murtaugh?"

"He went for water," Bahari answered, glancing up. "He should have returned by now."

"The fool Irishman is probably having a swim," she remarked with a wry smile. "I'll fetch him."

Trying to maintain an indifferent exterior, she practiced her breathing and regulated her steps until she was out of easy visual range from the camp. Peeking about to be sure she was not followed, she broke into a run, eager to catch Murtaugh in whatever activity he was preoccupied in. As she neared the river, however, her excitement dimmed as she did not readily see him.

"Murtaugh?" she called out in a quiet voice. "Murtaugh?"

As she looked about the bank, she noticed something gleaming among the rocks. Kneeling, she picked it up, tilting her head to examine the little coin serving as a pendant. As she stared at it, some loose hair fell across her face, but she was not persuaded to move. "A James I shilling."

Dread filled her heart and seeped into her eyes. "No. Murtaugh... Michael, no."

Glancing about feverishly, her horror rose at seeing a fresh blood smear on a rock. "Oh, please no," she whispered. "He can't die. You can't die, Murtaugh."

Stumbling back up the bank, she searched for him, following a spotty blood trail. Not too far away, she saw him leaning against a tree, hidden by the tall grass.

"Murtaugh!" she gasped, racing to him.

As she dropped beside him, he sleepily opened his eyes. "I knew you would find me. I can't seem to be rid of you." Coughing, he weakly slumped over.

"You're bleeding! Where are you bleeding?" she asked, desperately examining him for a wound.

"It was grand, Jackie," he whispered. "The best was all the things we never said to each other."

"No!" Petting his face and squeezing his hand, she shook her head. "It will not end this way!"

"What?" a haunting voice asked. "With another man's blood on your hands?"

Stopping her panicked fretting, Jacq spun about to find Tom Thomas, handsome and devilish as he had been in real life.

"You," Jacq said.

He grinned. "Me. Always me, *Jackie*. Ol' Tom be likin' that one."

"You don't get to call me that," she said, strong resolve resounding in her words.

"Tsk! Ol' Tom be doin' what Ol' Tom wants. Wait." He grinned, approaching her and shaking his finger. "Ol' Tom can't be doin' much of anything. You made sure of that, lass."

Slapping him away, Jacq lifted her chin. "I'm not afraid of you anymore."

"Aye. Ol' Tom be seein' that. Thanks be to the Mick." He nodded toward Murtaugh. "That be why Ol' Tom were killin' him. 'Tonly seemed proper." He gave her a smug smile.

Clenching her teeth, she lifted her hand and was pointing her flintlock at him.

"Oh! Jacq." He laughed nervously. "Where'd ye be gettin' that? Hmm?"

"I'm truly sorry, Tom. I regret it, but I would do it again. You were going to kill Miata, and I was the only one who could stop you," she said with a shaky voice.

"Wrong again, lass! Ye weren't the only one," he said, mocking her.

"But I was," she said firmly. "No one else could have gotten to him in time."

"So what?" he asked, disappearing. "What do you do now?"

Following his voice, she whipped around to find him sitting beside Murtaugh. "Get away from him."

"No. Ol' Tom be wantin' an answer," he said, poking at the Irishman's still body.

"An answer to what?" she asked, pulling the hammer back. Murtaugh's advice to take ownership of her actions began whispering in her mind.

"If you truly be at peace with what you did to Ol' Tom." In a sudden, quick motion, he pulled a blade out of nowhere and began driving the tip straight for Murtaugh's heart.

"No!" she shouted, instantly squeezing the trigger.

The loud, horrible sound blasted. She felt the kick in her hands, smelled the smoke of the shot, and sat up sweaty and gasping. Blinking and taking large, ragged inhales of air, she felt herself, her clothes, her hair. "Murtaugh." Spinning to her left, she saw him sleeping peacefully just an arm's length away. Watching the rise and fall of his side as he breathed, she stifled a cry of relief, covering her face with both hands.

"Oh, Father God," she whimpered. "Forgive me." Tears streamed down her face. "I know I don't speak to you enough, but help me to forgive myself again and forever." Sniffling, she took long, ragged breaths to calm herself. "I know it's too late, but every day I wish I could have saved him. That has to count for something. I wish his goodness would have overpowered his evilness and greed." She paused, wiping at her eyes. "Keep me from such a dismal fate. Keep my soul from darkness. By your will, Amen."

Taking another heavy breath, she set her hands in her lap and glanced at Murtaugh. A lightness came over her, lifting away a weight that had been settled on her chest for months. Smiling, she whispered, "Thank you."

"There!" Brushing some sand off Miata's shoulder, Alex smiled. "Somehow you have all the pretense of moderate cleanliness. Ordinarily I would not be at all pleased"—she paused, straightening Rackham's necktie—"but I find I am quite satisfied."

As they smiled back at her—even Oduntan—a light, misty drizzle began descending upon them.

"Oh, no!" She touched anxiously at her hair. "As if my appearance was not completely shameful as it is!"

"I thought you were satisfied," Oduntan spoke up, watching her frantically grab a cloth to cover her head.

"For you! I am a lady! I am supposed to be a lady! The standards to which I am to measure myself are entirely different! I am a sham! An unforgivable sham! Pretense, indeed. Stupid!

Daft, ignorant, stupid girl!" she exclaimed, looking around desperately for something, anything, to improve her situation, but finding nothing.

"Miss Alex!" all three men shouted.

Stopping abruptly, she whirled about to look at them.

"You be lookin' grand," Miata said in a kind tone.

"A bit too much like Jacq," Dante remarked, smirking.

"I am certain," Oduntan added, "I shall always believe you to be the finest creature I ever saw. You have the heart of *awǫn kiniun* and the grace of *esuro*."

Her lips twitching and trembling, Alex placed her hand over her heart. "In case my courage to admit it later eludes me, I must now confess you are among the most excellent of traveling companions. I can think of few comparable."

All three men glowed a little at her approving remark—a rare gift from Miss Alexandria Luray—attestable by anyone who knew her.

"And on such a fine sentiment, let us be off!" Rackham said after an appreciative pause, motioning for them to move out. "Let us to Cabo Corso, mates!"

"He seems mighty jolly," Alex noted to Miata as she rejoined them to embark on the final part of their journey in the wilderness.

"I wager he be thinkin' on a hot meal… and a pint," he answered, grinning over at her.

"No pint for me," Oduntan said.

"Yes. What shall you do, Mr. Oduntan?" Alex asked.

"I am of benefit to my people. I shall return to them. No doubt my journey back to them will be much faster without you," he said in a flat tone.

"No doubt," Alex agreed, a rueful smile pulling her expression.

"Faster but far less worth the telling in the end, I imagine," he added, smiling.

Alex and Miata chuckled.

"Of that I am certain," she returned.

"When I have retold of this journey, it will be passed down for generations," he said, smiling. "Immortalized by the memory of my tribe."

"Hark!" a man's voice called, giving them pause. He approached them from ahead, the direction Dante had been going, carrying a lantern.

"Who be there?" Miata yelled back as he came into sight.

"Where ya bound, lad?" the bearded man asked, lifting the lamp to their faces in the overcast morning light.

"We be to Cabo Corso," Miata answered. "We be expected."

"There be just the three of ya, then?" he asked.

Miata and Alex glanced uneasily between each other.

"Nay. There be a fourth. He be ahead, alertin' our companions o' our arrival," O'Keeffe answered.

Alex's heart began to pound. She had been around Miata long enough to know the difference between reasonable cause for worry and paranoia. This was looking less and less like the latter. Even in the misty drizzle, she could sense the arid tension. Looking away to her right, she could see the wall surrounding Cabo Corso. The flag, fluttering in the uneven breeze, could be seen in the openings of the leafy canopy.

The bearded lantern man squinted at them. "Well—"

"Disperse! Run!" Rackham's voice commanded from somewhere in the trees.

The stranger stood silent almost as though holding his breath.

Hesitating only long enough to look at each other, the other three scattered.

"Argh!" he yelled. "All ya had to do was keep him silent!"

"He bit me!" a different man shouted back.

"Find 'em, lads!" the bearded man bellowed, growling. "Find 'em all!"

"If I can just get to the doors!" Alex whimpered to herself, stumbling and clawing through the dense vegetation as she dashed toward Cabo Corso. Leaves and twigs slapped her face and scratched at her arms, snagging her clothes and hair as she fought to break through.

Finally, the last of it gave way, and she fell out of the forest—mere feet from the wall. Tears mixed with the more steady rain that streamed down her face.

Forcing herself up, she hobbled forward and laid her hand on the stone wall. Nothing had ever seemed so glorious. Catching her breath, she pressed her cheek against it and closed her eyes just a moment. "I must get inside," she whispered breathlessly. "Just inside."

"Not today, lass."

Opening her eyes, she screamed. "No!"

The bearded stranger smiled.

Glancing up at the cloudy sky, Jacq smiled when a few tiny droplets dotted her face. However, a sudden feeling of anxiety overtook her. Pausing beside a tree, she glanced around. Their caravan was all accounted for and moving forward—even Morenike—after two days of slow going was nearly back to normal. Still, it was as if she couldn't breathe.

Moving to touch at her forehead, her thumb caught on the leather necklace holding her Kehinde charm. Looking at it, she became increasingly overwhelmed with worry. "How have I not been more concerned for her all this time? Five? Nearly six weeks?"

Her chest felt tight. "Something's wrong." She looked at the drizzly sky.

"Oi! Jacq!" Murtaugh called, noticing her fidgeting by the tree. "Are you well?" Trotting over, he examined her as he got closer. "What's wrong?"

"I-I don't know, Murtaugh. It's Alex. It has to be. She… she… I cannot explain it, but I fear her to be in utmost danger. Dire peril. I…" She grabbed at the branches as she wandered forward in the same general direction as the caravan.

The rain overhead increased from a drizzle to a steady pour.

Watching her in evident confusion, Murtaugh scratched at his stubbled jaw. "Perhaps you should sit down? You look a bit pale."

"No, no," she said, offering a weak smile. "I believe the exercise is of benefit. My mind is beginning to feel much clearer now, though I am still disturbed by that terrible sensation." Stopping, she leaned against a tree. "I tell you, it was like falling into a pit filled with anxiety and dread."

"Strange. Before that happened, I was going to mention you looked rather jolly this morning. I was pleased to see it," he said, extending his hand to her. "Come on, lass. Let's be off with our mates, eh?"

Smirking, she swatted at his hand, jumped up, and grabbed at the low-hanging tree branches. "I've got it, mate. You were right, though. I did feel a bit jollier than I have. Ow!"

Dropping abruptly to the ground, she stared at her forearm. Two bleeding puncture marks leaked her precious life in little red rivers down to her hand. "Wha—" she whimpered, grabbing at it.

"Judas, no!" Murtaugh said as soon as he saw it. "No, no, no. Where are you?" Instantly, he began scanning the tree where she'd been.

"Wha-what is it?" she asked, grimacing at the blood.

"It's a wretched snake is what it ruddy is, Jackie! We need to take it back to Bahari so he can tell us if it's poisonous."

Following him, she sighed. "You think of everything."

Glancing back at her, worry spreading across his countenance, he said, "If that that were true... Jackie, love, don't be walking about. Sit. Please." As she obeyed, he saw movement in the branches. "Ah! There you are!" Pulling out his sword, he hacked at the tree until he got what he was after.

When he was satisfied it no longer posed a threat to them, he wrapped the snake's head in a cloth. Turning to Jacq, who had been watching him in a trancelike state, he reached out for her. "Come now, Jacq. We must hurry back. If it is poison, we mustn't let it have time to get a hold on you."

With robotic obedience, she rose and walked beside him as he carried the lifeless reptile. "How is it you know so much about snakes?"

He laughed. "You know, we have no snakes in Ireland, but I heard my share of tales. When I arrived in England, they were one of the first things I wanted to see for myself." He chuckled again at the memory. "Like the fool boy I was, I got myself bit straight away."

"No snakes in Ireland?" she asked in a groggy tone.

"It is one of our boasts," he returned, looking over at her. Seeing her frequent blinking and droopy expressions, his heart fell. "No. No, no. Come on, Jackie." Stopping, he scooped her up and hurried towards their caravan, rain pouring down on them. "Bahari! Bahari!"

"I can walk, Murtaugh," she sleepily objected. "Just set me down. I can walk."

"I know, Jacq," he returned, ignoring her feeble request. "Bahari!"

"My legs are fine, you know," she continued. "I have good legs."

"You've got great legs, love," he agreed. "Bahari!"

Faintly hearing Murtaugh's voice through the rain, Bahari turned to see the drenched man running up with Jacq in his arms. "Crevan!" His eyes were drawn to the snake dangling from one hand. "She got—"

"Aye, mate. Help me!" If Murtaugh's inflection was not enough to give him reason to worry, his expression would have done the job. With his dark hair flattened by the rain, plastered carelessly about his face, his blue eyes large and pleading, and his mouth twitching like it wanted to beg and implore though it could not find the words, he was entirely convincing.

"Aladia!" Bahari yelled, snatching Jacq from the breathless Irishman. "Aladia! *Ejo ojola!*"

"Will Aladia know what to do?" Murtaugh asked, at Bahari's heels.

"Aye. She aided our village *oogun okunrin*. If she needs saving, Aladia is the only one who can help us," he answered, pushing to the front of the caravan. "Aladia!"

Turning to see them, she gasped. "What happened?"

"*Ejo ojola,*" Bahari answered.

"What *ejo?*" she asked.

Murtaugh held up the deceased reptile.

Squinting at it, she grew somber. "A *igi paramole*. We have work to do. Stop!" She waved her arms for the whole troop to pause. "Does anyone know how to find *krinkhout* and *kijani undongo?*"

"I do!" Durosinmi volunteered, stepping forward.

He and Bahari exchanged distrusting glances as Murtaugh muttered under his breath, "Duroshin."

Noticing, Akinlabi stepped forward as well. "I will accompany him."

"We can also look," Moyo volunteered, her arm around Morenike.

"Very good." Aladia nodded. Then turning to Bahari, she gestured to a nearby stand of trees. "Let us make camp there. We must hurry, my love."

Nodding, he and Murtaugh hastened to the location as she collected her things and followed them. Moyo and Morenike headed south toward the river while Durosinmi and Akinlabi went north.

"Stay with us, Jacq!" Murtaugh called as she blinked at him. "Stay with us, eh?"

"I'll be fine, Murtaugh. 'Tis only a flesh wound." She smiled.

Unconvinced, he grabbed her hand as Bahari set her down, and was relieved when she smiled and squeezed it.

"Just stay," he repeated.

Blinking slowly, Alex looked around. She was surrounded by some sort of wood and mud structure with a tiny window and…

She gasped. "The lantern." Rushing to rise up, she was horrified to be forced to a sudden stop. Looking down, she saw a cuff around her wrist, attached to a chain, attached to a post.

"Shackles?" She whimpered, pulling up her sleeve to have a closer look, finding two itchy red dots on her scratched-up arm. "What?"

"Miss Alex?" Miata asked. "You awake?"

"Y-yes." Spinning around, she was both relieved and grieved to see O'Keeffe sitting in a dark corner on the other side. "A-are you…" She jangled her chain.

"Oh, aye." He moved his foot, rattling the metal restraint attached to his ankle.

"Where are Mr. Rackham and Mr. Oduntan?" she asked.

"I be thinkin' Oduntan escaped," he said. "Lucky lout. As for Rackham, they been tryin' to bribe him."

"What? For what?" she asked, shuddering at the thought.

"They be under the belief there be more o' us than there be," Miata said dolefully.

"Wha—"

Before she could ask, the door squeaked open, and two men dragged a drenched Dante Rackham—dripping both water and blood—back into the hut.

Gasping, Alex reached for him, where he was slumped onto the floor. "You barbaric pigs!" she shouted, lifting his face to assess the damage. "You should be ashamed of yourselves! Making a living off of another person's misery!"

The men grumbled and chuckled, not necessarily remorseful of their actions but not pleased about being scolded either.

"He only had to tell the truth. That's all we asked of him," one of the men answered.

"Perhaps you'll be a bit more cooperative, hmm?" the other one asked, leering at her.

"Certainly!" she returned, indignant at their behavior. "But you had best fetch me linens and clean water to dress his wounds properly as need be!"

Her tone brought a smile to Miata's face.

"S-sure, ma'am," one said, uncertain of how to proceed with her demands.

The other man glared at him.

He shrugged and said, "It's a simple request, and the boss don't want none of 'em dyin'."

As they left, she returned her attention to Dante. "Poor dear."

Catching her wrist, he smiled weakly. "Don't say that."

"Hmm! Well, you should see yourself. Scoot closer to me if you can, please." She tugged at him for encouragement.

"I'm sure I've been worse," he said with a groan, obeying her. "Though I can't remember when."

"My condolences, if that is indeed true," she said, carefully checking him over.

"Speaking of true, I told 'em the truth—most of it, anyway. Look what they did to me," he returned, coughing and wincing.

"Yes. See, I am certain they disbelieve me to be clever or brave. So I intend to tell them the truth they are seeking, what they wish to hear," she explained quietly.

"The truth they wish to hear," Rackham repeated, scoffing.

"Precisely. Because they are convinced I would not attempt anything heroic, they have no reason to doubt my sincerity when I disclose to them the horrible tragedy of the death of my beloved sister, Alex," she continued.

"What?" both men asked, audibly shocked.

She smiled, pleased with herself. "Not to worry, lads. I have a scheme that should, in the end, work most brilliantly in our favor."

The door creaked as the men returned.

"We've got what you requested, but we want some information first," the man said, standing tall.

"I-I…" Sniffling, Alex held Dante's hand. "I… I do not know where to begin."

The captors grinned in misguided delight at their false success.

The rain had slowed to a misty drizzle. Murtaugh sat beside Jacq, where she had been situated under a thickly leaved tree.

"Why do you look so worried?" she asked him, her voice tired.

He glanced up, observing her paled skin and bluish lips. "I saw Aladia's face when she saw that bloody snake."

"She's a mother," Jacq rationalized. "Mothers fret and fuss."

"Jacq, this isn't to be trifled with," he returned in a grave tone, reaching up to move some stray hair off her face.

Watching his demeanor, Jacq's lightheartedness trembled. "What did she tell you?"

"I'm..." He looked away. "I'm to stay here and watch that you're still breathing, Jackie. She's making some tea and some other... I don't know."

"Oh." She gave a feeble laugh. "Is that all?"

"She said..." Gulping down his anxiety, he rotated back to her ashen face. "She said you may not be able to move or feel, that you might not be able to talk o-or breathe." He paused, looking at his hands. "That you—"

"Murtaugh?" Jacq interrupted.

He lifted his gaze to meet hers.

"Do you remember when we first met?" she asked.

"By the dock?" he asked, grinning. "As if it were yesterday."

"I saw you, you know? Before that..." She chuckled.

His interest grew. "Did you?"

"Aye. When you came to the *Midway Zebra* with Audric for a drink."

He laughed and rubbed the back of his neck.

"You wore a green waistcoat with a red sash round about you," she recalled. "You had some metal rings on it instead of tassels. And you wore that necklace." She pointed at the one about his throat. "When I saw you, first saw you, before Audric arrived, I thought to myself, 'How could such a handsome face turn up here? Could I be so fortunate?' Then Audric arrived, and I knew." She smiled. "I wore a sash after that too, but it never sounded as perfect as yours did."

His head whirred with conflicting emotions. He opened his mouth to respond, but no words exited it.

"You know, I have always greatly admired you," she continued with a tiny smile.

"J-J-Ja-Jacq," he stammered.

"I'm so tired," she whispered, her eyes concurring with long, heavy blinks.

"Oh, no. No, no. Jacq. Jackie, love, listen. You need to stay awake," he said sternly, grasping her shoulders.

"My lips are tingly. I-I can't lift my hand," she said in a troubled voice. "I-is that bad?"

Scooting to her head, he petted her hair and face. "No, no. You'll be fine. Can you feel my hand?"

She nodded, smiling. "It's warm." She was silent a moment, and then whispered, "Murtaugh?"

"Aye?"

"Which do you prefer? Murtaugh or Michael?" She searched his face as though it were the most important question in the whole world.

"Murtaugh is fine, but when you say my name, Michael, it sounds… it sounds grand." Wetting his lips, he tried not to fidget and expose the depth of his anxiety.

"Michael?" she whispered.

"Aye?"

"Would you… would you, before my lips have gone… would you kiss me? Just one time? I would never ask, but I shan't like to go without it—just one, from you." Her hazel eyes, despite her ghostly appearance, still shone warm and sincere as she stared up at him.

Clenching his teeth to hold back tears, he took a long, deep breath, willing himself to remain strong. "From me?"

She gave him a tired smile. "Only you."

Sniffling, he lifted her shoulders, propping her up with his body. "You know you're going to be fine, don't you? You can't scold me for this later."

"Your confidence is admirable," she said, constantly scanning his face as though to commit it to memory.

Brushing his thumb over her lips, he took a pause and then leaned down and kissed her brow just below her hairline. "I always imagined it to be a happier moment in far cheerier circumstances," he said in a husky voice, pressing his forehead to hers.

"We are together. One could say that is happy. I'm glad it's you. Could one not say that is happy too?" she whispered back.

"One could," he agreed. Cupping her face in his hands, he gave her a kiss from his heart—sweet, sorrowful, timid, and fervent. When she pushed into it as she was able, his heart soared, and for a tiny moment, they both forgot they were surrounded by people they hardly knew. They didn't care they were sopping wet in the middle of Africa, and they almost forgot she was waning.

When he sat back, he let out a nervous chuckle, petting her hair back from her face again. "M-my apologies."

"No apologies," she said in a breathless laugh. "My last should be my best, should it not?"

A rueful smirk pulled his lips.

"You know, Alex would be so furious with me. She would point out how improper my behavior, tell me how I act with such conceited independence. She would likely recommend me out of polite society entirely. But she would always care for me secretly, despite her being ashamed of my manners."

"No one's ashamed of you," he said, hugging her to his chest. "Even Miss Alex would forgive you this."

Resting her head in the crook of his neck, she sighed. "I just need to rest... for just a minute."

"I'll be here," he said in a low voice.

"Give us a shanty, eh?" she asked.

As he held her and her breathing shallowed, he buried his face in her hair. Then in the quietest of voices, he sang.

I am a young sailor, my story is sad
though once I was carefree, and a brave sailor lad.
I courted a maiden by night and by day,
ah, but now she has left me and sailed far away.
Oh, if I were a blackbird, could whistle and sing,
I'd follow the vessel my true love sails in.
And in the top rigging, I would there build my nest,
for without her I'll never be able to rest.
Or if I were a scholar and could handle a pen,
one sincere love letter to my true love I'd send.
And I'd tell of my sorrow, my grief and my pain
that can only be healed when she is mine again.
Oh, if I were a blackbird, could whistle and sing,
I'd follow the vessel my true love sails in.
And in the top rigging, I would there build my nest,
for without her I'll never be able to rest.

Holding her tight, he rocked her as he cradled her body.

"Don't be that maiden, Jackie. Stay with me. Stay with me always, Jackie love. I loathe my cowardice to say so aloud, but while there is breath in my body, you're the only one I will always love."

Six weeks earlier...

Standing against the mast, Murtaugh watched with a placid expression as the three sisters talked and tittered by the rail. He especially smiled when Jacq would make grand gestures about her current topic of conversation. As he observed them, however, his attention was ensnared by the quiet discussion of a couple crewmen mending a hammock just behind him.

"Oh, you know Rackham, always a favorite of the lasses," one commented.

"Aye, it's because he's tall," the second said dejectedly.

"Did you hear him say he had to turn down a dinner invitation to a proper lady's house in London? Poor fella," the first man continued.

"It's because he's tall," the second man reasoned again.

"What proper lady?" Murtaugh asked, coming around the mast and startling them.

"Uh, uh…"

"I know a lot of people in London," Murtaugh said in a friendly tone. "I just wonder if she and I share acquaintance."

"Oh. Right. It were… it were a Miss W-Wescott? W-Walsh?" the first man stammered.

"Shame. I don't believe I know her, after all," Murtaugh said, sounding disappointed. "Thanks anyway, lads."

As they nodded and went back to their work, Murtaugh marched off to find Rackham, his temper rising with every step. Noticing him near the stern with a few other crewmen, he stalked over and said in a commanding timbre, "I require an audience with Mr. Rackham *alone*."

The three other men dispersed with no argument.

Turning to look at Murtaugh, Rackham nodded. "What's the matter, Crevan? Is there a problem?"

"A problem?" Murtaugh laughed sarcastically. "A problem, Skippy?" Lunging forward, he grabbed Rackham by the front of his shirt.

"Oi, Crevan! What's your trouble, eh?" Rackham asked, pushing back.

"I heard you're receiving dinner invitations from a lass in London, mate," the Irishman hissed.

"Aye! What of it? Is being favored a crime?" Rackham asked through clenched teeth as he pried Murtaugh's hands off him.

"What about Jacq, eh?"

"What about her?"

"You best remove any claim to her," Murtaugh demanded.

"Why should I? I've not determined to have a design on either lass just yet," Rackham retorted.

"Ya ruddy plonker!" Murtaugh growled, punching him the face. "Ya can't have one foot on the boat and one on the dock! 'Tisn't right!"

"Lads!" Miata shouted, jumping between them. "The whole ship be takin' notice soon, and I be doubtful his vice admiralship be pleased for you two to be fightin' on his ship!"

Jabbing a menacing finger at Rackham, Murtaugh snorted. "If you hurt her, Skippy... if you hurt her I'll be sure to leave you bleedin' alone somewhere. Savvy?"

"Oh, you love her, do you?" Rackham scoffed, touching at his eye. "Can't stand a bit of competition?"

"My feelings are irrelevant!" the Irishman shot back with a snarl. "She deserves better than to be jilted by some cocky boatswain."

While Murtaugh sang his Irish melody, Aladia, Bahari, and Durosinmi stood near a tree to observe Jacq's well-being.

"Poor child," Aladia said in a discouraged tone. "Even a great *oogun okunrin* cannot save all who are bit by *igi paramole*."

"But the *tii* and *amo* are nearly finished," Durosinmi spoke up.

"She needs all speed and aid," Aladia said. "It is good she has Crevan. See how he breathes life into her with his whispers?"

"It is beautiful," Durosinmi agreed. "A man should always be there for the woman he loves." He glanced at Bahari.

Frowning, Bahari shook his head. "A person should not be sustained by another's love. And if they must be apart, and the reason is just, they should have the courage to continue."

"True," Aladia said, nodding. "But the love of another, or the love for another, can give one the will to live." Moving forward to check on the tea, she sighed. "I would know." Glancing over her shoulder, she gave Bahari a sad smile.

Sneering at Bahari when she left, Durosinmi scoffed. "How can she take you back after you abandoned her?"

Shaking his head, Bahari shrugged. "I will never know, but I do not underestimate my good fortune for having such a devoted wife." Smirking, he flicked Durosinmi's swollen nose, causing him to stifle a cry of pain. "You should find your own."

"Durosinmi?" Aladia asked. "Could you check the *amo*?" She gestured to a soupy, muddy bowl beside the fire.

Burying his outrage at Bahari for inflicting pain upon him, Durosinmi stomped forward to do as she'd requested. "Of course."

"May I be of assistance?" Bahari asked, pushing off the tree and approaching where Aladia sat with the tea.

"Murtaugh. He must get her to drink this," Aladia said, grinding some charcoal into the tea. "Once she does, we need to bleed her wound just a bit and then cover her skin with the *amọ*. We must let it dry and sit on her three hours. Then we wash it off and do it again."

Bahari's expression darkened. "For how long?"

Aladia shook her head and continued fidgeting with the tea. "Until she comes around again. Now, come on then." She held out the drink. "She is waiting, and so is her *alaabo*."

"Do you need more supplies?" Bahari asked, suddenly dreading taking a closer look at the deathly colored face of his friend.

"Moyo and Morenike are gathering more," Aladia insisted. "Now go! We must hurry!"

As Bahari and his family, alongside a desperate Murtaugh, fought to save Jacq's life, Alex rendered care to Rackham's newly acquired wounds. As Aladia and Murtaugh slathered on clay, Alex dabbed at Dante's face with water.

Sitting back after blotting him dry, Alex sighed. "They think they are so clever. Abusing one man to loosen the tongue of another." She shook her head. "They call these natives savage and barbaric, yet I do not see how they can be so condescending as they themselves define the terms."

Chuckling, Rackham shrugged. "Perhaps if the world was all as polite as you there would be little need for such brutish actions."

"Ugh! Aye, though it would be quite dull," Miata spoke up.

"Oh, you would rather a world of Jacq?" she asked in a quieter voice, somewhere between snide and serious.

"Oh, lord! No!" Miata said, laughing and scoffing. "We ne'er be knowin' peace."

Rackham and Alex chuckled along with him.

"Well, what are we to do?" Alex asked.

"Since you told him you, er, Miss Alex died, it seems they'll get on to making whatever arrangements that lout of a boss of theirs has designs for," Rackham noted, keeping his voice low. "They seemed to believe you. And I must admit, you were rather convincing."

She smiled, and even blushed a little at the sound of a compliment.

"Aye. For a lass who be so prideful o' bein' honest, you be mighty able to be spinnin' a tale," Miata remarked.

Huffing, Alex frowned. "Well, I—"

Scratch, scratch.

"What was that?" Alex asked, her bravery extinguished.

Miata sat quiet, nervous, and wide-eyed. "I don't be knowin'."

"Mr. Rackham?" she asked.

"Sshhh, sshhh, sshhh!" he said, waving her silent. "Listen."

Suddenly, there was a loud *crash* in the distance.

"What were that?" one of the men outside the door asked, his chair scraping as he jumped to his feet.

"I don't know," the other replied in a somewhat lazy inflection.

"You reckon we should infestigate?" the first man asked.

The three captives exchanged puzzled expressions.

"Investigate," the second corrected.

"Right, right. Well, should we?"

"I don't know." He yawned, moving in the chair.

"I think we better," the first one said, worry in his voice.

"You think too much," the second man chided.

"And you don't know anyfin'. Now come on!"

"Anythin'," the second corrected. "We get paid in two days when the boss comes. Until then, we just wait."

"Right, right. Well, come on, you. Come on!"

"Fine, fine. Just to get you to stop your blatherin'."

The prisoners listened to the pair get up and lumber away, arguing as they walked.

"What do you suppose that was?" Alex asked.

"I don't know," Rackham said, still listening. "Perhaps we should try to—"

Creak.

The door squeaked as it opened. A burly man was silhouetted in the moonlight, and the dim lantern light gave them no answers as to his identity.

Gasping, Alex grabbed onto Rackham's arm.

"Ow!" Rackham groaned, grasping and squeezing her hand.

"Oh! My apologies!" she responded, loosening her grip.

"Miss Alex?" the burly man asked.

"No, Miss Jacq. And that's Miss Luray to you!" she corrected.

"Oduntan?" Miata asked, straining to see.

"Mr. O'Keeffe?" he returned.

"Oh, for the love of—why are you here, mate?" Rackham asked in a hoarse whisper, sending him a disapproving glare. "We thought you'd gone. You could get caught!"

"A rescue seemed proper," Oduntan returned, entering the room and squinting around at everyone.

"You owe us nothing," Alex added. "You should go before they return."

"I have yet to take you safely to Cabo Corso," Oduntan said firmly. "My mission is unfulfilled."

"Well, unless you have a key, we are tethered by these rotten chains," Alex pointed out in a melancholy tone.

"One be not needin' a key," Miata said, stepping forward chainless. Grinning, he held up a thin metal nail.

"There's a good lad," Rackham said with great approval. Favoring his right arm, he sat up taller. "Get us loose then, eh?"

As Miata crossed over and knelt beside Rackham, they heard the approaching voices of the two guards.

"What do we do?" Alex whispered.

"Oduntan and O'Keeffe can overpower the guards," Rackham suggested, glancing between them.

"M-me?" O'Keeffe asked, disliking the suggestion.

"Surely you've had your share of tussles before?" Dante asked, incredulous.

"I rather be pridin' myself in the art o' escape," Miata returned. "The trouble be it were ever only myself I were tryin' to save."

"It is fine," Oduntan assured them. "Two against one I have won many times."

"But what about four, lad?" the bearded lantern man asked, wearing a wicked smile and holding a firearm. "'Tis a shame you be makin' your rescue attempt at the change o' the guard. To be fair, though, I'm sure you could have succeeded with these two louts." He gestured at the other two who were now rushing back to the door. "Too bad."

Then in one quick movement, he flipped his pistol around and struck Oduntan with the handle across the side of his head, knocking Oduntan unconscious.

"Crevan? Crevan?" Morenike whispered, pushing on his shoulder.

Inhaling sharply, Murtaugh opened his eyes, sitting up. "Did I fall asleep?" He rubbed his face with mud-encrusted fingers.

"It were bound to happen," she said, smiling at him. "It's been two days and nights."

Rolling his head to the side, he looked down at Jacq's still body, caked in dried clay.

"I just want her to wake," he said in a gravelly voice. Rubbing his hand down his dirt-flecked face, he squinted in the morning light.

"Crevan," Aladia said softly as she came up beside them, "it is time."

Groaning, he pulled himself up further into a fully upright position. "So soon?"

"If we hope to return her to you," Aladia said, offering an empathetic smile, "we must be steadfast."

He nodded, weariness eddying about his demeanor. "Of course."

"Why don't you take her face and shoulders this time?" Morenike suggested.

"I-I don't know, Miss Morenike," he returned. "If she wakes, I'd rather not wish her to think I'd behaved ungentlemanly or improper."

"Believe me," Aladia said, hugging Morenike, "she won't."

Nodding, he took the bowl of warm water Aladia held out for him. Grabbing out the cloth floating inside, he wrung out most of the excess water and began dabbing it over Jacq's face. Everything save her nose and mouth and eyes was slathered with Aladia's medicinal concoction. Gently rinsing her forehead and cheeks, he moved to her neck and then to her arms.

As he washed away the clay on her left shoulder, he noticed a ragged, circular scar.

"You were shot," he observed aloud to himself in a whisper. Running his thumb over it, he shook his head. "You never cease to amaze me, you know." Scooping up her hand, he laid her open palm against his cheek and continued, "I wish you would come back." Closing his eyes, he took a moment to feel the warmth of her skin.

As he sat there, exhausted and in angst, her hand twitched. His eyes snapping open, he stared at her face. Her thumb began slowly caressing his cheek as though trying to recall how to move properly.

"Aladia," he said, trying to call out but only managing a little more than a murmur.

Jacq's eyebrows moved.

"Aladia!" he shouted, squeezing Jacq's hand, afraid to look away in case she might stop stirring.

"What? What?" Aladia asked, coming over from the fire.

"She moved! Her hand," he said breathlessly. "Her face…"

Aladia watched her, but she did not move. "Her color is returning, but you are weary, Crevan. I—"

"No! I saw her!" he shouted desperately, getting everyone's attention. "I-I… I saw—I *felt* her!"

"Murtaugh?"

The Irishman and Aladia spun about.

"Jacq?" he exclaimed, dropping back to her side.

"A-are you well?" she asked.

"Ha!" He laughed, near tears. "Am I well? Oh, Jacq. Oh, Jackie, love." He kissed the back of her hand and her knuckles. "You're alive, mate. I've never been so well."

Laughing weakly, Jacq looked up to see Bahari standing with his arm around Aladia. Moyo and Morenike were hugging each other nearby, and all the boys and Iremide hovered around, smiling down at her. Smirking, she directed her gaze back to Bahari. "Was it truly so bad?"

Grinning, he started to laugh. "Shakina… I was certain of your recovery, but Crevan has never left your side."

Slapping his chest, Aladia shook her head. "He belittles his concern! We were, all of us, eagerly awaiting your return."

"And returned I have," she said, looking back to Murtaugh, who was still holding her hand. Giving his a squeeze, she sighed. "I'd rather stay a while."

"I'd rather you did too," he said, grinning.

Slowly, they sat Jacq up, testing her limbs and digits. Aladia served her a final cup of the *krinkhout* tea and some bread as Murtaugh sat beside her, eating as though he'd been starving for two weeks. Throughout the entirety of their meal, he kept taking pauses to beam over at her.

"Why do you continue to smile at me?" she asked, giggling.

"It's just... it's a relief to see you as you again—not you covered in strange mud and a cloth," he said, continuing to send her happy expressions. "How's your arm?"

"It hurts," she admitted, looking down at the bandage. "But I'm rather delighted to be able to feel it."

Grinning broader, he chuckled, overjoyed beyond words.

"I-I told you things..." she noted, a demure shade coloring her countenance. "Things I wanted you to know in case..."

"I know," he said, nodding, his expression sobering. "If you want me to put it out of my mind I would understand."

"On the contrary. I thought perhaps we have some talking to do, once we're returned to Swansea?" she asked, her eyes full of hope and her mouth forming a shy shape for asking.

At this, his demeanor perked back up. "A fine suggestion," he returned.

"You know, I also wanted to thank you," she added.

His head tilted in curiosity. "Thank me?"

"Aye. Now I have two counts for which you are owed. Murtaugh, you saved me. Again. Twice." Sipping her tea, she coughed. "Oh, this is horrible."

Sharing a laugh, they then enjoyed a moment of pleasant silence before Murtaugh returned, "You know, I would save you in every way possible every single day if the occasion called for it."

"Well, fortunate for you, I am not usually a damsel in great distress," she said. "And I do relish proving I can fend for myself, but I rather fancy having someone around to give me aid, should the need arise." She grimaced at the tea.

"I'm not rescuing you from that," he said, shaking his head.

She mock gasped, feigning insult. "Murtaugh!" Pausing, she then added in a more serious inflection, "You know, I want to tell you something."

He gave her his undivided attention. "As you wish."

"There was a man… a black-hearted, selfish scoundrel of a man." Her expression twitched and faltered. "He befriended then betrayed me. He promised me the world but offered me a cage." Touching at her shoulder, he watched her hand flit nervously about her throat and then drift down to join her other hand in her lap holding the cup. "It turned out he was a liar." She gulped and laughed uneasily. "H-he threatened to kill my mates—*our* mates."

"Jacq." He covered her fussing hands in her lap. "I—"

"Please, let me finish," she requested, grasping his hand. "I've never told anyone, never spoken of it to someone who did not already know the terrible truth. If I don't tell you now, my courage may desert me forever."

He nodded. "As you wish."

Sniffling, she recollected herself. "The first father I ever knew, Captain Taylor, taught me the basics of the sword and pistol. He said I was a natural." Scoffing, she shook her head. "I proved it that day, Murtaugh—the day I shot Tom Thomas. It was a perfect shot. I could have wavered and missed, but my aim was true. Tom Thomas died that day, and so did I."

"He is the one haunting your dreams?" Murtaugh asked, seemingly unshaken by the revelation of her darkest secret.

"Aye, though, thanks to you, he is gone." She glanced at the afternoon sky, buried beneath layers of gray clouds. "W-why are you not backing away from me in all horror and astonishment?"

"I told you it wouldn't affect my opinion of you," he said, smiling. "It doesn't. You are tortured by something you did— something unthinkable you did—to *save* your mates." Raking his fingers through his hair, he chuckled. "I've seen men kill for less and be glorified for their actions. Your remorse is your assurance you are still very much alive." He paused, catching her chin on his finger. "You may have your faults, Jackie, but needlessly delivering persons to the underworld is not one of them."

Grateful for his empathy and compassion on the subject, she smiled at him with an ever-growing affection and admiration. "If I may get so diverted, be so kind as to expound on your reference to my faults?"

A lazy grin stretching his expression, he shook his head. "Despite appearances, I am not entirely a fool. Now, finish your tea."

Grimacing down at the drink once again, she put the cup to her lips.

As night fell, Alex felt an anxious pit forming in her stomach. Her nose told her, beyond the dirty shack, they were likely in the jungle, probably within easy walking distance to Cabo Corso. She clutched the charm of Tayewo that still hung about her neck.

"Good fortune." She scoffed. "What a laugh. What a jolly laugh."

"Listen—"

"Keep quiet, Mr. O'Keeffe!" she growled. "You are the last person on this earth I wish to speak with."

"Well, that can't be bein' wholly true," he said, offended.

She sat a second, thinking over his remark. "True. You are the last person in this dreadful, filthy, shoddy little hut that I wish to speak with."

"My apologies again, Tayewo, for failing you," Oduntan said from over near Miata.

"Please, Mr. Oduntan. You gave a fine, valiant effort. It is far more than *some* can say." She tossed a snarky expression at Miata.

"I be seein' that, mate," he retorted.

"What?" she returned, snide and aloof.

"What be you havin' me do, eh? That bearded bloke be getting' the best o' Oduntan straightaway! There weren't no way I were bein' able to be takin' on all four myself! So, you be takin' yer self-righteous nose and be—"

"O'Keeffe, mate," Rackham interrupted. "No need to get nasty. And give the lad a rest, eh? A man can only do what he's able, lass." He coughed, holding his ribs.

Sighing, Alex nodded. "Of course you are correct, Mr. Rackham. They sent for their master two days ago, but every hour that passes only adds to my anxiety." Leaning her head against the wall, she paused, tugging at the chain about her wrist.

"You be not alone in that," Miata spoke up.

Her voice breaking, she continued, "We-we were so close to Cabo Corso."

"So very close," Rackham agreed.

Sniffling, Alex shifted from tearful to aggravated. "I tell you, I would like to give whomever he is a piece of my mind!"

"Is that so?" a voice interrupted, the shack door thudding open. "Pray tell me, Miss Luray, what's on yer mind?"

Miata's eyes grew. "You? B-but they be sayin' 'boss'!"

"You know him?" Alex asked.

"Aye. He were an unfortunate bloke in the tavern at van Draenweg."

Sashaying into the room, he grinned like a well-fed cat. "Sorry to disappoint, lad. Everyone's got a boss. You lot can call me Barend."

Chapter 11

"So," Barend spoke between bites of food, "your sister, Miss Alexandria, didn't make it, did she?"

"That is correct, sir," Alex said, nodding. She glanced about the forest. His men had brought a table out of the shack for him to eat his breakfast. In attempt, she assumed, to seem somewhat civilized, he had her brought out as well for a chat.

"Well, we both suffered a loss there," he remarked. "It's a shame, truly. A right shame."

"I-I... I do not understand why you have sought us out such as you have," Alex said, gripping her hands to try and counteract her nerves. "We have no association with you and have never slighted you or done you wrong."

"Ah! That, lass, is where you're mistaken," Barend said, chuckling and stroking his chestnut beard. "You two frocks have done me a great disservice. You cost me my position, my gold, my reputation, and skin from my own back."

"But... how is that possible?" she asked, not persuaded of his misfortunes.

"Let's just say your father and I have a mutual business partner who gets a might squeamish over particulars and is then prudish with his pay," Barend replied. "If the two of ya hadn't run off, it would have been sorted. But run ya did. And to be fair, I find yer pluck admirable and"—he leaned closer to Alex, making her grimace and hold her breath at the smell of him—"quite provocative."

"Ugh!" She shuddered in disgust.

"So I've gone about collectin' ya myself so I can get what's owed me," he concluded, reclining back into his chair and taking a long drink.

"You are going to *sell* me back to my father?" she asked.

"I'm sure ya find it despicable, miss, but I've been robbed myself, see? And someone's got to pay. I just don't much care who. It's a real pity about yer sister, though. I could've asked twice the price for discoverin' ya both," he noted casually.

Her eyes growing wide with astonishment and her skin flaming pink with indignation, Alex gasped and shot to her feet. "You, sir! How dare you belittle my sister with such blatant disregard! You hateful man! You must have buried your conscience with your integrity and decency, leaving you not only immoral but utterly, utterly devoid of any sort of human emotion!"

"I'll not argue I have my evils, Miss Luray," he said calmly, "but I am just a man."

"A horribly selfish, insufferable, repulsive man with an abominable sort of wretchedness!" she corrected, her heart racing with rage induced adrenaline.

"Ya do yer family proud, Miss Luray," Barend noted, pushing his plate away. "But I'm afraid the time has come for me to dispense with the pleasantries and get down to business."

Alex watched with a distrusting eye as he rose from his seat and rolled up his sleeves. "What business is that, Mr. Barend?"

"Well, I got to send a message, miss." He turned to one of his guards. "Bring me the lad."

"Which lad, boss?" he asked in a dimwitted inflection.

Rolling his eyes, Barend shrugged. "Whichever ya can get up easiest, eh?"

"Oh. Ri-right, sir."

As he moved off, Barend rotated back to Alex. "Why is it so bloomin' difficult to find quality help, eh? Quality."

Alex frowned. "Perhaps they prefer honest work."

"No. Perhaps higher wages is the key," he said, pondering aloud.

"Let go! Let go!" Miata's voice interrupted them.

Alex spun about to find two men dragging a straining Miata toward them.

He looked at her with an expression half wild with fear.

She glanced between Barend and Miata, uncertainty and worry mounting with every inch they drew closer together. "Please, Mr. Barend. Let us not be too hasty—"

"Too hasty?" He laughed.

"Please," she continued. "W-what do you intend to do with this man?"

Hearing the care in her voice, Miata found a little courage where he was usually so depleted. "Sir, I—"

"Bup! Bup! Bup!" Barend interrupted, holding his finger to his lips. "I need ya to deliver a message for me, lad."

He glanced at Alex. "I-I… I be thinkin' I'd rather not, sir," he stammered.

"Oh." Barend nodded in understanding. Then he laid a blow to Miata's stomach.

As Miata doubled over, coughing, Alex gasped. "Mr. O'Keeffe!" Turning to Barend, she went to move forward but was restrained by the bearded lantern man. "Mr. Barend, please! Mr.

Rackham has already endured abuse by your men! Could he not deliver the message just as well? You need not assault Mr. O'Keeffe for no reason!"

"No reason?" Barend chuckled. "On the contrary, Miss Luray. He's accepted the beatin' I owe ya and yer bloody sister, rest her soul, for ruinin' *my* life!" Grabbing a fistful of Miata's hair, he lifted his face. "Isn't that so, *Mr. O'Keeffe?*" he asked in mock politeness.

Glancing at Alex, who stood struggling and trembling in lantern man's arms, he saw her shake her head vehemently, giving him a shred of purpose. Smiling in appreciation of her efforts, he shrugged. "Sure, mate."

"No!" Alex cried, tears welling in her eyes as she thrashed against the lantern man's hold. "M-Miata, no!"

"Ah!" Barend turned and smiled at Alex. "See there, Miss Luray? A true gentleman." Then he pulled his fist back again and threw it against Miata's face.

Tears streamed down Alex's cheeks as she closed her eyes while Barend vented his anger on Miata's body.

Glancing about at the tall trees, Jacq sighed. "We are getting close, aren't we, Bahari?"

"The trees say we near the ocean," he said, smiling. "Soon all the trees of the savanna will be but a memory. Cabo Corso could be as little as seven days away." Looking over at her, he shook his head. "You are certain you feel well enough to walk?"

Touching at the leaves, she nodded. "Aye. With the poison gone, I feel nearly like new. And if I had to drink another sip of that tea…" She shuddered.

Chuckling, Bahari looked around to be sure they were alone. Seeing Murtaugh headed toward them from the front of the caravan, Bahari cleared his throat. "You know, Shakina, if you were my daughter, I could not have been more pleased with how Crevan attended to you."

Glancing up to see the Irishman hiking straight for them, she sighed. "He is my North Star. When he is with me, I have this inclination to rely on him and trust him in measures I find unsettling."

"*Àríwá Irawọ*," Bahari said with a smirk.

"Pardon?" Jacq asked, realizing she'd been distracted observing Murtaugh.

"It is Yoruba for North Star," Bahari said, smiling.

"*Àríwá Irawọ*," she repeated, a whimsical expression overtaking her countenance.

Joining them, Murtaugh grinned. "Jacq. Bahari, Aladia was hoping you might walk with her."

"I'm sure she does," he said. "Stay well, Shakina. Crevan."

They all exchanged pleasant smiles and nods as the men traded positions alongside Jacq. Then as Bahari moved ahead to find his wife, the recovering snakebite victim nudged Murtaugh. "Have you noticed how keen Kukoyi and Iremide are for each other?" She motioned to where they strolled together off to one side, conversing quietly and smiling sweetly.

"I can't say I had particularly. My attention has been more engaged elsewhere," he commented.

"Oh." She minimized her grin of delight at this possible insinuation to a small, appreciative smile.

Watching her reaction, Murtaugh put to memory how she exhibited such an unflappable level of self-control. Then he cleared his throat, raking his fingers through his hair. "Jacq? Might I be so bold as to ask you a personal question?"

With all the talk of his wonderfulness swirling about in her head, Jacq's heart swelled with curiosity. "Oh, of course, Murtaugh. What is it?"

"How—" He stopped, rethinking his words yet again. "How did you come by that scar? The one on your shoulder?" Gesturing to where it was hidden beneath her clothing, he added, "I-if you don't mind my asking, of course."

"Oh." Her brain tripped over itself and did a face-plant as her heart deflated. She covered her shoulder with her hand.

"Not from that Mr. Thomas bloke?" he asked in a highly defensive tone that made her smile internally.

"No. In truth, I am not precisely certain who did the shooting. It was likely one of Captain Burgess's men," she answered. "But it did happen that day on Martinique. That island was nobody's friend."

"You needn't be ashamed, Jacq. For most of us, our worst scars are on the inside." He grinned at her. "They are far less intriguing."

"Intriguing?" She gave him a wry smile. "You, sir, are incorrigible."

"Incorrigible?" he asked, feigning shock. "You must mean charming!"

"Charming indeed, you impish meddler," she retorted, shaking her head.

"Meddler? I don't meddle!" he disagreed.

"You certainly are meddlesome!" she said, playfully glaring at him.

"Mmm. Perhaps you are the one who is charming," he noted, clasping his hands behind him and eyeing her.

Caught off guard, Jacq's cheeks flushed. "Perhaps to someone who was ill-qualified to identify charm."

"Hmmm. You know, we Irish are the *worst*." Though his expression remained neutral, his eyes twinkled as he looked at her.

"Perhaps I should go to Ireland then," she returned, matching his manner. "I could charm the whole isle."

"That would be ill-advised, lass," he said, maintaining his demeanor and countenance.

"Why?" She pursed her lips to hide her amusement.

"We Irish can be a might jealous, you know. We can be driven mad by it," he explained matter-of-factly.

"So I should only be in close acquaintance with one Irishman?" she asked, peeking over at him.

"Aye. That would be my recommendation," he said, finally cracking a smile.

"I shall take your opinion under advisement," she returned, sounding serious despite her difficulty of preventing a gleeful expression. "Though I should inquire upon your credentials to make such claims."

His grin widened. "I've made a thorough study of it. You should consider everything I say to have the utmost accuracy."

Smirking, she nodded. "I shall bear that in mind."

"Miss Luray," a man spoke.

Looking up, Amy found Mr. Carloff standing near the door, his African native housekeeper beside him holding a tray with tea.

"Mr. Carloff. What can I do for you?" she asked, rising.

"I was hoping to entice you to share afternoon tea with me," he said, smiling. "You've been so quiet and withdrawn your entire stay here. I thought some company might lift your spirits." He gestured for the woman to place the tray on a table.

"Anythin' else, maste'?" the woman asked.

"No, no. That'll be all for now, Hasina. Thank you," he said kindly before turning back to Amy. "So what do you say, Miss Luray? Can I persuade you to join me?"

"I am afraid I am not good company, Mr. Carloff. Though I do appreciate your efforts in politeness, I fear my spirits are not likely to be lifted by your company." She moved to the window, watching people and carts go by in the streets below.

"Is it only your sisters you worry for?" he asked, inching closer to her. "Do you have a suitor at home whose company you long for?"

"Only?" she echoed bitterly. "As if they are not enough?" She spun to face him, a displeased expression marking her pretty face. "And though it is none of your business, my heart's interest is lost in the wilderness along with my sisters."

"Truly? Well, then, we are the both of us disheartened," he said, taking a step closer.

"Why should you share in my despair over my misfortunes?" she questioned, lifting her eyebrow.

"Can a gentleman not sympathize over the woes of a beautiful young woman?" Mr. Carloff returned.

"He may not if his intent is to prey on a vulnerable girl," she retorted.

Laughing awkwardly and scratching at his cleanly shaved jaw, Mr. Carloff took a step back. "My intent was never to prey, Miss Luray."

"I should hope not," she returned, examining the tea tray, "for all pretense of your remarkable gentlemanly behavior would be called into question, and my father would likely vilify you as easily as you exalt yourself. And should your character prove you to be anything less than honest and honorable, my father would take great pleasure in seeing you properly represented to the world and all your associates." She smiled sweetly. "Tea?"

"C-certainly, Miss Luray," he agreed uncomfortably.

As he reached for the teapot, however, there was a piercing shriek from downstairs. Glancing at each other, Amy and Carloff then rushed to the window. Everyone nearby was either peering at or hurrying toward Mr. Carloff's manor. Again trading glances, the two spun about and raced down to the first floor. Hasina was standing in the entryway panting and fanning herself as a host of people milled about the front of Carloff's home.

"What happened, Hasina?" Carloff asked her.

"Beggin' you' fo'giveness, maste'," she breathed, still gasping for air. "I opened the doo' and the'e he was."

Outside, Vice Admiral Luray, who'd been out getting some fresh air and exercise, heard Hasina's scream. Seeing the commotion, he sped over, pushing through the crowd as courteously as possible. "Excuse me, ma'am. Sir. Ma'am. Pardon," he said, scooting through.

As he broke into the center, he saw a burlap-wrapped body, spots of blood seeping through, lying on the bottom step with a note attached. With everyone standing about gasping and whispering, he knelt beside the still figure and plucked off the note. It was addressed to Carloff.

Suspicion rising from his already cultivated distrust, he moved his hand to expose what lay beneath the burlap. Bracing himself, he flipped it back, revealing a battered young man.

"Oh, good God," he muttered as a sort of unfinished plea for mercy. Holding his hand under the man's nose, he felt great relief to feel him exhale. "Oh, thank the Lord." Then looking at the gawking faces, he shouted, "Who did this? Did anyone see who did this?"

"Miss Luray, please!" Carloff's voice sounded. "Don't go until we've seen—"

The vice admiral looked over just as Amy shoved through to the center, coming to a stop across from him.

Her eyes widened in horror, and she opened her mouth to wail, but she could utter no sound. Instead, a strangled gagging sort of whimper emitted from her throat as she dropped to her knees. "Is-is… is he…?" she choked.

"He's alive," Vice Admiral Luray answered, reaching over to grasp his daughter's hand.

"Miss Luray, I beg of you," Carloff was saying as he too entered the center of the crowd. Seeing the partially exposed body, he jumped back. "Oh!"

"Pray tell me, Mr. Carloff," the vice admiral said, standing, "why Mr. O'Keeffe has been delivered addressed to you in this state? And while you are concocting an explanation, get this man your best physician *immediately*!" He held out the note, his hazel eyes burning with displeasure at the turn of events. "And if he dies…"

"I assure you, sir," Carloff said, taking the note with trepidation, "he shall receive the very best care I have at my disposal." Pointing to two able-bodied men in the crowd, he added, "You two! Bring this man inside at once!" Then, turning back to his house, he yelled, "Hasina! Fetch Dr. Lindgren! Tell him it's urgent!"

As night crept over the country and Miata remained unconscious, Bahari stood away from the fire, observing these people who had elected to travel with him. Noticing his watchful position, Aladia crossed over to him and whispered, "What is on your mind?"

Smiling in appreciation of her gentle, soft-spoken nature, he sighed. "After Shakina awoke from her fight against the snake's poison, I have thought how she faced death in our wilderness, for me. For us. She and Crevan are strangers here, but see them smile at each other, not complaining. See our son attempt to hide his interest in Iremide. See my sister and her daughter care for the younger boys. See Gbeke and Olusegun smile, assisting them." Shaking his head, he held her hand. "See my wife still loving me after being abandoned for years. I have been blessed, Aladia. You—all of you—are my treasure."

"When I look at you," Aladia said, teary-eyed, "I see the sunrise in the morning. I see the rain fall to quench the thirst of the earth. I see the tree in the forest in which all the birds wish to build their nests. You are future, you are hope, and you are family."

As Bahari and Aladia continued with their intimate conversation, Akinlabi watched his family interacting with each other. He frowned as he considered his position regarding his father's good character and his brother's leadership abilities. Was he understanding them better or just growing sympathetic to their situations and predicaments? Pushing aside his contemplation, he began sharpening the end of his stick.

"Look at him," Durosinmi said, coming up beside him. "It seems he has managed to convince her to forgive his abandonment of your family."

"Perhaps he truly believed he was doing right by us," Akinlabi said, a little surprised to hear himself say the words.

"Oh, come now. Don't let him fool you! We got to look out for each other, we do. I thought we was partners," said the man, leaning back against a tree.

Shaking his head, Akinlabi scowled at Durosinmi. "Not anymore. You would see my family in pieces so you can get at my mother. From what I've seen, he may not deserve her, but you deserve her even less. My father's friends are true to him and fond of him, just as my mother and Gbeke are. There must be a reason for it. As for you, you deserted us in the fight against Huru's friends while he was prepared to take them on by himself."

"Your father does have a way about him, that I grant you," Durosinmi said. "However, what's to keep him from leaving again, huh? What happens in England?"

"He came back for us, did he not? And now he attempts to take us to a new home. A safer home. And what do you do? Want for my mother's attentions?" The boy scoffed.

"These things are always a bit awkward in the beginning, son," Durosinmi insisted, shoving off the tree and grasping his shoulder.

"Do not call me son," Akinlabi retorted, shrugging free of him. "I already have a father, and I don't need someone lesser trying to take his place." As he pointed the sharpened stick at the man's face, the teenage boy added, "I am decided, and I do not wish to speak of it again. But I would suggest you stop making designs on my mother. She will never have you."

"Come on, boy. Don't do something you'll regret. Remember, I can help you get what you want," Durosinmi said in a threatening inflection.

"I am beginning to believe we do not share common interest as I first supposed. In truth, I don't think I ever should have listened to or made an alliance with you." His mind feeling confident, he moved forward toward the group.

"You're making a mistake!" Durosinmi called after him.

"We shall see about that!" Akinlabi yelled back.

"Aye," Durosinmi said with a growl. "That we shall."

Sitting at his desk, Carloff gazed at the note. It had a blood smear across one corner he couldn't stop staring at, and it remained unopened. His breakfast was nearly untouched beside him. Plucking the note gingerly from the desk, he glanced at the fire that crackled low in the hearth across from him. Standing, he crossed over and held the note toward the flames. His name, scrawled on the back, with the red smudge dragged above it, beckoned to him, making him hesitate.

"Wait, si', please!" Hasina's voice was saying just outside the door to his study.

Holding the message behind his back, he was not all too surprised to see Vice Admiral Luray come bursting into the room.

"Carloff," the vice admiral said, severity in his timbre.

"I'm so'y, Maste' Ca'loff," the housekeeper said. "He would not hea' me o' take no fo' an answe'."

"It's fine, Hasina. Truly. Leave us," Carloff assured her, switching the envelope to the hand farther from the fire while still behind his back.

As she closed the door, the vice admiral stepped forward. "I'd like to see that message, Mr. Carloff."

"How fortuitous, Vice Admiral, sir," Carloff said, pulling it from behind his back.

Vice Admiral Luray glanced at his tidy desk and uneaten breakfast. "You have not already opened and read it?"

"I was waiting for you, sir. This is, I'm afraid, just as much an attack on me as it is on you. It is abominable the lengths some will go to in an attempt to sully, ruin, or take advantage of us men of stature," he said, shaking his head in disappointment at the extent of human depravity.

Unconvinced of his good will or misfortune, the vice admiral snatched the paper from Carloff's hand. "Indeed. It would certainly have been a shame if you had misplaced or lost this. We might never had discovered the full design of our enemy's scheme or the depth of his ill will."

"Quite right, sir. Quite right. These bad eggs will do anything to spoil the barrel," Carloff agreed, wincing as he watched the vice admiral open the envelope in one swift move.

Still observing Carloff, the vice admiral pulled out the message. Then he glanced down and read the letter aloud:

Dear H. C.,

As you can see by the identity of the messenger, I am quite serious when I say I have located the persons gone missing from van Draenweg. I also have the daughter, Miss Jacqueline Luray, a Mr. Dante Rackham, and a man called Oduntan who Miss Luray wishes to keep.

I fully expect to be rewarded handsomely for my discovery in the amount of £60 as shillings.

Pausing, Vice Admiral Luray looked up to an anxious-looking Mr. Carloff. "That's a rather generous amount."

"He is obviously mad with greed," Carloff said. "It has probably addled his brain."

"Perhaps," the vice admiral said doubtfully. Returning his gaze to the paper, he read on.

I fully expect to be rewarded for my discovery in the amount of £60 as shillings. To benefit us all, I will have a man in Dread Roberts' Brews tomorrow eve to discuss the terms of our arrangement. He will have a white feather in his hat. I'd prefer Mr. Petersson and that he come alone.

If you do not find me worthy of your time, I shall be obliged to send another messenger, though I cannot guarantee they would arrive in as fine a state as this one.

Lastly, do not involve the authorities. We know you wouldn't want to risk a public scandal, considering the delicacy of your reputation.

Sincerely,

O. Barend

The vice admiral stood quiet, and Carloff found he was afraid to speak. However, his desire to preserve his repute outweighed his instinct to remain silent. "Well! I—"

In one adrenaline driven instant, Vice Admiral Luray lunged forward, grabbing Carloff off the ground by his shirt and slamming him into the wall.

"Why," he growled, "is this man demanding a reward for *my* daughter's safe return? Where is my other daughter? And why does he request your Mr. Petersson by name? Have you previously done business with Mr. Barend, Mr. Carloff?"

His toes barely touching the floor, Carloff shook his head, laughing nervously. "As I've said before, sir, I am a businessman. I do occasionally make acquaintances with men who turn out to be of less-than-desirable character, but I do not recognize Mr. Barend's name. I won't declare it impossible that I've made his acquaintance, but—"

"Maste'," Hasina started, opening the door to the study. "Oh!" She grasped at her dress collar in surprise.

"Please excuse us, Hasina," Carloff said awkwardly. "As you can see, we are very busy."

Wide-eyed, Hasina obediently closed the door.

Still seething, the vice admiral returned Carloff's feet to the floor. "We should get the authorities involved, despite his threats," he said. "I want this man Barend and all his associates arrested!"

"Well, sir, I-I... I'm afraid it's not so simple here. And with the time frame of tomorrow evening, I don't see how I could muster the forces needed to sufficiently pursue and retrieve him. And I, for one, would not wish to risk your precious daughter's life on the matter," Carloff stammered, cowering from the thinly veiled rage in the vice admiral's expression.

"Rest assured, Mr. Carloff, every man involved in this ill-conceived plot will pay the entirety of what the law will allow." He gave him a distrusting glare.

"Of course, sir," he agreed. "As it should be. Has your Mr.… Mr.…"

"Mr. O'Keeffe," the vice admiral supplied in a weary voice.

"Aye. Mr. O'Keeffe. How's he coming along?" Carloff asked, eager to deviate from the current subject.

Sighing, the vice admiral rubbed his jaw. "The lad has yet to wake and has barely stirred. My darling girl won't leave his side, the poor dear." He sat a moment in thoughtful silence before straightening and holding up the letter. "Now, shall we discuss how to proceed?"

Meanwhile, Amy sat beside where Miata lay in a clean, quiet room. He was bandaged and bruised, only one closed eye visible. Having barely left his side, Amy was laid back in her chair, fast asleep. A book she'd been reading to him lay open facedown on her lap.

Startling awake as the book slid off and hit the floor, she glanced over at him and yawned. "Come along, Miata. You've made it back to me, so please don't leave now. Jacq will be furious with you if you die, you know. Me crying and Jacq vexed—you don't want that, do you?"

Touching the exposed skin on his face, she shook her head. "My poor, poor dear," she whispered, sneaking his cheek a kiss. "Come back to me. Oh, please, come back to me."

The following evening, all the women—even Jacq—helped the children clean up after their supper and prepare for sleeping. Murtaugh smiled to himself when he noticed Kukoyi leaning against a tree and watching Iremide. Making his way over to him, the Irishman smiled and said, "They are fascinating, are they not?"

"Who?" Kukoyi asked, straightening.

"The womenfolk," Bahari said, joining them.

Both Murtaugh and Kukoyi chuckled nervously while the older man smirked at them.

"I... I was simply..." Murtaugh stammered, gesturing toward the fire.

"You are both young and have found one who makes your heart sing," Bahari filled in.

Both Murtaugh and Kukoyi looked sheepish.

"No need to feel shame," he said. "The chase, the hunt—they are exciting and merry, but they are also meant for you to learn. Unlike *kiniun*, er..." He looked to Murtaugh. "Lion?"

Murtaugh nodded.

"Unlike the lion, we are to keep *esuro*..." He looked to Murtaugh again. "Jazelle?"

"Gazelle," Murtaugh corrected, smiling.

Bahari nodded. "We are to keep the gazelle once she has been caught. And the gazelle, once she transforms into a lioness"—he looked at Aladia—"has more power than she will ever know."

"Fortunate for the lion his gazelle doesn't have a disapproving father," Murtaugh commented, sighing.

"Iremide only has her uncle, Durosinmi. He is more like *akata*—er, hyena," Kukoyi said, equally discouraged.

Bahari chuckled. "Aladia's father thought no one was keen enough for his daughter, and he was correct. But fate smiled on me, and Aladia had a greater fondness for me than the other *ọmọkunrin* in the village. She even told me once that her father wished I would give up."

"What did you say?" Kukoyi asked, grinning.

"I asked her what she would do if I listened to her father and did as he bade me." His blue eyes twinkled as he recalled the memories.

"And what was her reply?" Murtaugh asked in amused expectation.

"She said she would marry another man, one who was not afraid of her father, if she could find one." He laughed, and they chuckled along with him. "I tell you, lads, I could not abide the thought of her marrying another man. So I vowed that if she would have me, I would do my best to be the man she truly deserved." He gave Kukoyi a sad smile. "I know I have failed in many ways, but my intentions have never wavered."

"Someday," Kukoyi returned, "I hope to devote my life to such a task. Akinlabi thinks me a fool, but I haven't the heart for war."

Murtaugh sighed. "You're not alone on that, mate."

"Coveting war is not a thing to take pride in," Bahari said. "I have seen both of you stand and fight when the time demanded it. I am honored to know you. And, Kukoyi, I am proud to claim you as my son." He grasped Kukoyi's shoulder, and Kukoyi returned the gesture.

Looking back toward the campfire, Murtaugh saw Jacq take a seat and then look his general direction. The glow warmed her skin and cast shadows on her face that accentuated her pleasing features.

"Excuse me, fellas," he said, leaving the father and son to themselves. Approaching her, he donned his usual relaxed expression with a hint of a smile. "Jacq."

"Murtaugh! There you are!" She grinned.

"Have I told you yet that you are looking rather well since the snakebite?" he asked.

"Oh." She blushed, though it was hardly noticeable in the dim lighting. "Well, no. No, you hadn't. But thank you. You look well too, you know. This wilderness cannot mar Michael Murtaugh. That is certain." She forced an awkward chuckle.

Hiding his amusement, he nodded. "Your kindness is most generous, Jacq."

Regaining her usual nonchalant demeanor, Jacq shrugged. "It's hardly generous when it's a simple truth." She patted the spot beside her.

Accepting her invitation, he seated himself next to her. "What shall become of us, I wonder, once we return to civilization?"

Unsure of his meaning, Jacq shrugged and turned her gaze to the fire. "I wonder too."

Taking a moment more to admire her face in the firelight, he too stared into the flames, unknowingly joining her in a state of contemplation about the question he'd just asked.

All around them, chirps and croaks provided a soft background for the cracking and popping of the fire. The wind danced in the treetops, barely disturbing them down below but adding a gentle whooshing and rustling to the ambiance. The warmth of the evening reinforced a general peaceful feeling all about them, a great improvement over the tension that had been following them all the way from Tenkodogo.

Trouble, however, was not taking the night off. Instead, it loomed over Cabo Corso, particularly over Dread Roberts' Brews. At a table off to one side of the room, the bearded lantern man responsible for apprehending Alex sat with a pint in his hand and a white feather in his dingy brown hat. As he finished off his third mug, the door opened, and a short portly sort of a man with a white wig and a waistcoat that was nearly too tight, entered the room.

"Ah, Mr. Petersson. I believe youse have gotten fatter," lantern man muttered to himself.

After glancing around a minute, Mr. Petersson noticed the white feather and began heading over.

"There ya go, ol' boy," he said, smirking and shaking his head.

Making his way over, Mr. Petersson stopped and peered over his glasses at the bearded lantern man. "Good day, sir. I'm here on behalf of Mr. Carloff, as requested."

"Aye. Mr. Petersson. Glad to see your boss can follow the rules. Seems that were a might challengin' for him before," the man said.

Clearing his throat and adjusting his glasses, Mr. Petersson frowned. "I would not know anything about that, sir."

"Oh, I'm sure not. Have a seat, Mr. Petersson." He shoved a chair out with his foot.

Petersson looked disinclined to do so, but he sat anyway. "And what, pray tell, is your name, sir?"

"Muller, Mr. Petersson. But let's not be friendly, ay? I've got terms from my boss for yours. If they be followed proper, your Mr. Carloff gets the poor lost souls we found. We're callin' it a findin' fee, savvy?" He put a folded-up note on the table and pushed it to Mr. Petersson.

"A finding fee. Very clever, Mr. Muller," Petersson said, picking up the note. "My employer has terms of his own as well. He declares you, your boss, nor any associate are to speak of his previous arrangements with Mr. Barend. Not even the slightest indication."

"I shall pass along Mr. Carloff's request," Muller agreed. "The rest of the details are in his note. He wishes to make the exchange in two days' time."

"Very well. Is there anything more? Mr. Carloff is eager to discover Mr. Barend's instructions." Pushing up his glasses, he tucked the note into his pocket.

"I'm sure that'll be all, Mr. Petersson," Muller said with a smug expression.

Rising from the chair, Mr. Petersson straightened his snug vest and jacket. "Very good, Mr. Muller. I'll take my leave, sir."

"Oh, Mr. Petersson," Muller spoke as Petersson moved to leave. "I'd also recommend you avoid the biscuits with your afternoon tea." A self-amused grin stretched his mouth as he chuckled at his own remark.

Huffing at his impoliteness, Mr. Petersson squeezed his way back through the crowd and out of the Dread Roberts' Brews tavern. As soon as he was out, he grabbed the little one-man cart he'd driven over and hurried back to Carloff's property, where a very eager father and businessman were each awaiting his arrival. The instant he returned, they were upon him.

"Well?" Carloff was asking.

"Tell us, man!" the vice admiral demanded.

Holding up the note, Mr. Petersson cleared his throat. "For you, sir."

Both Carloff and the vice admiral grabbed it, immediately eyeing each other.

Glancing between them, Petersson said, "A good night to you both, sirs." Then he quickly vanished.

"We open it together," the vice admiral said sternly.

"Very well," Carloff agreed.

Neither moved.

"One of us must relinquish his hold," Vice Admiral Luray stated.

"It *is* addressed to me, after all," Carloff pointed out.

"It is *my* daughter's safety at stake," the vice admiral returned, obviously intent on keeping hold of the letter.

Though slightly infuriated, Carloff put on a placid expression. "But of course, sir." Carloff forced himself to loosen his grip just enough to let him yank it away.

Opening it, with Carloff practically sitting on his shoulder, Vice Admiral Luray shook his head. "Sixty pounds as shillings in two days' time. Do you have this kind of finances at the ready, Mr. Carloff?"

"I'd be lying if I said I did, sir. I would have to borrow from the company, but it would take longer than two days to get approval," Carloff admitted.

The vice admiral folded the paper up and rubbed his jaw. "How clever is this Mr. Barend, do you think?"

"If I were to guess, I would say ordinary—unlike you and me, sir. I'm sure we could devise a scheme—"

"I already have," the vice admiral interrupted. "Fetch me your trusted blacksmith." He grinned. "We have work to do."

The vice admiral spent all the following day working with Carloff's blacksmith of choice. They labored until night fell across Cabo Corso and the port town grew still—everywhere except the harbor.

"Here we are, lads. Welcome to Cabo Corso," Captain Turner announced. "May our fortune be great."

James Monroe smiled. "May it be great indeed."

Chapter 12

Knock, knock, knock!

Muttering to herself, Hasina went trudging toward the front door. "Who'd be callin' at this hou'?"

Knock, knock, knock!

"I'm comin'! I'm comin'!" she called out, checking that she was presentable. "Honestly." Opening the door, she didn't look impressed. "It's a bit ea'ly, gentlemen."

"I fear it's quite urgent, ma'am," Turner said, removing his hat. "We've just arrived a few hours ago by request of Vice Admiral Luray. This is where he is staying, is it not?"

"My apologies, si'." She gave him a courteous nod. "He ce'tainly is. Come in. I'll fetch him fo' you." Opening the door wider, she permitted the four men inside. "May I tell the vice admi'al who's callin'?"

"Of course, ma'am. Captain Turner, accompanied by Mr. Ellard, Mr. Monroe, and Mr. Bibbs." He gestured to each of his companions in turn as he spoke their names, each removing his hat when introduced.

"Tu'ne', Ella'd, Mon'oe, Bibbs. Ve'y good, si'. Please wait he'e," she said before marching off to the large staircase.

"What state do you suppose them in?" Monroe asked.

"It's difficult to say, Jim," Turner answered. "From what Mr. Ellard has told us, those two headstrong lasses ran off into the wilderness in pursuit of Bahari's family." He shook his head. "Unless they have been recovered, I'd expect the vice admiral to be most seriously displeased."

"I sincerely hope they have been recovered by now. If not, I wonder how Miss Amy's spirits are," Jim said, sighing.

"As do we all, lad," Bibbs spoke up. "As do we all."

"Turner, is that you?" the vice admiral's voice boomed as he came hurrying down the stairs. "Good God, man! You are a sight for sore eyes!" Grinning as he approached them, he sighed with relief. "Mr. Ellard, I never doubted you. It's good to have you back with us." Glancing at the other two, he nodded. "Mr. Bibbs. Mr. Monroe." He shook each man's hand with emphatic appreciation. "I am indebted to you all."

"Nonsense," Turner retorted immediately. "Unfortunately, it is not all happy news I bring."

"That seems to be the current trend," Vice Admiral Luray said, folding his arms. "What news have you?"

"It would seem war has been declared between England and Holland," he answered somberly.

"War?" Vice Admiral Luray repeated, grimacing. "That *is* unhappy news."

"That's not all, sir," Turner continued. "You've been commissioned to go to the Caribbean… indefinitely."

The vice admiral frowned. "That is… that is a topic best saved for another day." Clearing his throat, he rubbed his hands together. "Today we meet a man to trade gold for my daughter's freedom." He sneered, the notion deplorable.

"Just one? Have you already recovered one of them?" Monroe asked, sounding much keener than he'd intended. Realizing it, he cleared his throat. "S-sir…"

Vice Admiral Luray chuckled, clapping James on the back. "At ease, lad. I know you have friendly relations with my daughters. I'm glad you were able to join us."

Monroe smiled and nodded. "Aye, sir."

"Come now. We have preparations to finish, and I'm sure you lads would enjoy a hot meal. Mr. Carloff has been a gracious host to Amy and me. He also put the crew up at the inn just down the way. It is good to have someone on our side in these foreign lands."

Meanwhile, nestled in the jungle woods east of Cabo Corso, Alex sat in front of a smudged, cracked mirror. There were tear streaks down her cheeks, and she hated the sight of the girl staring back at her—filthy, frightened, and alone. However, it was time for her to play her part: pretend she was Jacq.

She pulled one corner of her lips back into her cheek. "No." She sighed and tried again.

"Put more heart into it," Dante said from where he sat chained to a tree with a bucket of water at his feet. "Remember, you're pert to your bones."

"I… I-I do not know that I possess…" She gave him a dejected frown and sighed helplessly.

"Sure you do," Rackham said, chuckling. "Think of when you've had a clever idea and you're just about to share it with someone who's been particularly vexing, and you are certain it will astonish them to silence."

Tittering in nervous embarrassment at the notion of her admitting to such feelings, Alex shook her head. "I do not—"

"Tsk! Tsk! Take that feeling and put it on your face," he directed, motioning and instantly wincing.

Frowning, she turned back to the mirror with renewed determination. Taking a moment to focus, Alex looked back at her reflection. She tried the expression again, but this time, her mouth coiled and her eyes engaged, and suddenly, she was wearing an entirely new countenance.

"Ah! Look at you!" he said in approval.

"You truly believe so?" she asked, turning and grinning delightedly.

"Oh. It's gone now."

Smirking, she shook her head. "I see why you two get on so well, you know."

His smug air faltered a second. "We do get on mighty well on a fine day."

She tried making the smirking face again. "That we do."

Dante tapped by his eyes. "A little more here, lass."

"Oi! Stop yer blatherin', lady and gentleman!" Barend bellowed as he approached them. "We can't have ya lookin' ill-treated now. O' course, wanderin' around in the wilderness helps lower expectations of yer appearance." He winked at Alex, who frowned at him.

Picking up the wet cloth out of the bucket beside her, she wrung it out and rubbed it on her cheeks. Staring at herself in the mirror, she watched as the dirt washed away, exposing tanner skin than she'd ever had before and a few freckles across her nose.

"Oh! I am brown," she whispered to herself, whimpering.

"Come along, now," Barend said, clapping his hands. "No time to waste. We have an appointment to keep, and I don't plan to be late. This bein' my first hostage exchange, I'd like to do it proper, see? So, get yerselves washed up." He splashed some water on

Rackham's face. "Hear me, lad? Quit carryin' on like an old wench!"

Scowling and wiping the water from his face, Dante nodded. "I hear you. I hear you."

"What of Mr. Oduntan?" Alex asked.

"Oh, one of the lads poured a bucket of water over him," Barend answered apathetically. "Now, hurry up! We've no time to waste."

Dante and Alex cleaned themselves up as best as they could, though still looking a bit bedraggled. Once Barend deemed them acceptably presentable, the three remaining captives were escorted a few miles through the forest to the beach a couple of miles east of Cabo Corso. They got comfortable in the tree line, able to see down the beach to the large port city.

While they awaited the arrival of their trading partners, Barend paced around, practicing his presentation as if it were lines in a play.

"They come," Mr. Muller announced, peering up the beach.

"Oh!" Barend straightened his cap. "Miss Luray? Would ya allow me to recite my proposition to ya just once?"

Scoffing, she wrinkled her nose. "Honestly? Mr. Barend, it is not your intellect I fear for. It is your sanity."

"Oh, Miss Luray, if we had more time, I could impart to ya all my misfortunes and then ya would understand," he returned. Then spinning around to look at his men, he said, "Come, come, lads. Take them to the beach and stand them on the boxes." He smiled at Alex. "This is a big day for us all, Miss Luray. Do us a favor and look a might less dejected, eh?"

She put on the expression she'd been practicing.

"Good! Very good! Lads! Get 'em all to the shore! Onto the crates! Onto the crates!" he shouted, bellowing out orders like a head chef in a kitchen.

While he was finishing assembling them, the incoming group trotted up on horseback. Coming to a halt and hopping down, they handed all the reins to Mr. Bibbs. Vice Admiral Luray, Carloff, Turner, Monroe, and Ellard lined up, ready to do business with Barend.

"You unharmed?" the vice admiral asked, looking at Alex.

She nodded.

Then he turned to Barend. "You?" Vice Admiral Luray asked, scoffing as he recognized him as Tuinstra's man.

"Aye. Me. I see ya brought yer mates. I brought mine too. Mr. Carloff." He grinned, and Carloff shifted his weight uneasily.

"What of Tuinstra? Does he know of your actions?" the vice admiral questioned.

Laughing, Barend shook his head. "No, sir. Now, no more inquiries. Do ya have the gold?"

"I do," the vice admiral said, nodding. "But I do have more questions. Where's my other daughter? What happened to her?"

"Truly, sir, I have not seen her. I wish I had, though. It would have made this a lot more profitable for me," Barend answered.

The vice admiral clenched his teeth, and outrage at Barend's flippant attitude rose in his chest. "Profitable?"

"Aye, sir. But alas, today I have only one Miss Luray, one Mr. Rackham, and one native named Oduntan. I sent ya one free of charge, as ya may recall. An act of goodwill. Unlike some men, I keep my word." He smiled again at Carloff.

Vice Admiral Luray took note of Barend's glance to Carloff, unsettling him all the more. "Let us not make a production of this, Mr. Barend."

As Barend and the vice admiral talked, Alex noticed Mr. Monroe in the row of men. Overwhelmed with emotions at the sight of him, she began to fidget and couldn't stop staring at him.

James too took note of her behavior, and even though he had been told she was Jacq, he couldn't stop studying her across the distance. Her posture, her shoulders, her chin—he could have sworn it was actually Alex.

Barend motioned for them to be brought forward as the vice admiral went to retrieve the payment off the horses.

As they stood, the ocean breeze blowing their hair about and tugging at their clothes, James watched Miss Luray touch at her hair as best as she could with her hands bound, trying to smooth it. Certainty flooded his nerves, and he took a step toward her. "Miss Alexandria? Is that you?"

Shuddering as she withheld a gasp, Alex slapped on her practiced face. "No."

Scoffing, James rubbed the back of his neck. "My apologies." However, continuing to watch her, he was not persuaded. "I-I'm sorry… a-are you—"

Looking away from him, she glanced at where her father and Barend stood now motionless, taking an interest in their conversation. "My apologies, Mr. Monroe. You are mistaken. I am Jacq." She looked at Rackham, her concern written all over her face.

"What's going on?" the vice admiral asked.

"Nothing," Alex answered, glancing again at James.

James came forward, confusion coloring his expression. "No, I—"

Rushing forward, Dante punched him across the jaw with his hands tied, surprising all in attendance.

Alex gasped, and James recovered, glancing at his shipmate. "Ow! What was that for?" he yelled, holding his jaw.

"Oh, come now, Jim," Dante said with an incredulous air. "That was for showing your face here after what you did!"

"Mr. Rackham!" Alex exclaimed in objection.

Everyone turned curious eyes to James.

"Mr. Monroe?" the vice admiral asked, confounded.

"He'll be fine, lads," Rackham spoke up. "Jacq here told me about you leaving Miss Alex, mate. And here I thought you to be a proper gentleman."

"I never!" Monroe retorted, glowering at Rackham.

"Aye. You never do much of anything, do you, mate? Save talking. You're mighty fine at that. You with your polite accent and your posh words. But you're a scurvy dog just like the rest of us, eh? You just wear a nicer costume." He laughed with sarcasm in James's face.

Barely keeping himself together, Monroe snarled and grabbed Dante by the front of his shirt. "See here, Rackham. I do not know what you're on about, but—"

Chuckling, Dante shook his head. "Oh, Jim. No need to be prudish, mate. You left her for that wench your parents found for you. More pence per petticoat, eh?"

As Dante began laughing again, Jim threw his fist against his cheek.

Jumping in surprise at James's outburst, Alex gasped. "Oh! Mr. Monroe!"

"Stop it! Stop it now!" Barend demanded, pulling out his flintlock. "No fightin' until after we've made the trade!" He motioned for Rackham to step back.

Pulling Dante close, James said in a growl, "Be she alive or dead, never speak about her in so ill a manner! I care not for pence per petticoat. I came back for her." He paused to look again at the girl atop the crate. "I don't know your game, but I know it's you."

Quivering with a refrained sob, Alex felt a tear roll down her tanned cheek. In search of strength, she clutched at her charm.

"Come now, chaps! This was meant to be a simple exchange! The wench and both lads for sixty pounds as agreed, no thanks to

Mr. Carloff," Barend said, glancing between the vice admiral and Carloff.

Still holding the bags in his hands, the vice admiral turned to Carloff. "What does he mean?"

"How should I know?" Carloff returned. "This man is quite obviously mad. He means to sully my good name and ruin my reputation out of misplaced blame for some misfortune he feels has unjustly befallen him."

"Unjustly befallen," Barend repeated, laughing maniacally. "Good name." He continued sniggering, and as the vice admiral gave Carloff a withering look that demanded explanation, Barend lunged forward, grabbed the gold bags, and bounded back, holding the pistol out at them. "Hands up! Hands up!"

Everyone obeyed.

He handed the bags to Muller. "Take a peek, Mr. Muller. We want to be sure we're not being cheated now."

Opening the bags and peering inside, Muller nodded. "Looks good, boss."

"Pleasure doin' business with ya, sirs," Barend said, grinning. "Now, kindly lay on yer bellies, lads. I'd ask ya not to follow me, but we both know ya'd be lyin' if ya agreed. Down, down, down."

As they all lay out on the sand, Barend and his men backed into the jungle, turned around, and vanished.

Once they'd disappeared from view, those lying on the ground scrambled to their feet.

"Should we after them, sir?" Ellard asked as he helped Bibbs gather the equines.

"No, Mr. Ellard. We'll alert the authorities of Mr. Barend and his fellows. They'll pursue him in due course, or at least restrict his operating abilities," the vice admiral said as he and James rushed forward to the girl.

Turner was quick to Rackham then Oduntan as Carloff dusted himself and whined. "What a foul man!"

"Alexandria, is it truly you?" Vice Admiral Luray asked.

She looked at him then James. "Yes." Sniffling, she covered her face with both hands.

James smiled to himself, proud he'd seen through her charade.

"Where's your sister? Where's Jacqueline?" her father questioned.

"She is with Bahari and Mr. Murtaugh. They went north for his family. We agreed to meet here in Cabo Corso. We did not know what was happening." Tears began to fall from her eyes. "I did not know if I would ever see you again!" She hugged her father like a terrified child. "They beat Mr. Rackham and… and poor Mr. O'Keeffe. Is he… is he…?"

"He's alive," her father whispered, kissing the top of her head. "Let's get you back, dear. You've had quite a shock."

Turner looked at Rackham. "How are you, lad?"

"I'm alive," he said, smiling through his bruises and healing split lip. "Captain, meet Oduntan. We wouldn't have come this far without the benefit of his company."

Oduntan, not without his own assortment of injuries, nodded. "Traveling with Tayewo and her companions has taught me many things."

"I'm sure of that, lad," Turner said, glancing at Alex as she tearfully explained their situation. "Come back with us. We'll feed and clean you up proper."

Oduntan nodded. "Very kind of you, sir. Very kind."

"And how is Mr. O'Keeffe?" Rackham asked of Turner as they moved toward the horses.

"Not very good, I'm afraid," Turner said, pausing to sigh. "Truth be told, lad, he has yet to awake since he was left on Mr. Carloff's front steps."

Dante grimaced, and his countenance darkened. "That feckless lout. How much did the vice admiral pay for our safe return?"

Turner grinned. "Oh, I wouldn't worry about that, lad."

As the Lurays and their friends made their way back to Cabo Corso, Barend and his men gathered in a clearing, gleefully clambering to have a look at their haul.

Holding out his hand, Barend beckoned Muller. "The bags, if you please, Mr. Muller."

Donning an expression akin to delight, Muller came forward and handed over the bags.

"Lads!" He held the bags up with great pride. "Lads, today we collected that which was promised me but not delivered! Today we retrieved the balance of a debt what cost me my position and my honor! And unlike them who think they're better, I uphold my promises and will grant each of ya the share ya were promised for helpin' me collect what was owed me!"

His men cheered and clapped, applauding his perseverance.

Reaching into one of the bags, he pulled out a fistful of coins. But his pleasure soon waned as, upon closer inspection, he saw most of it was not coins at all. Drawing his hand to his face, he shook his head. "No! No, no, no!"

His men abruptly stopped their adulation.

"What is it, boss?" Muller questioned.

Tossing the bags to the ground, Barend seethed. "It's iron! Scraps of iron pounded flat! They put a few honest coins on top to fool the likes of Mr. Muller, but the rest... the rest is iron!" He roared with rage. "Gather all our mates, lads! We are goin' to plunder everythin' Mr. Carloff owns in Cabo Corso, startin' with

that fancy house of his. And if we see those lasses, we're goin' to get rid of 'em once and for all!"

The men stood about, unsure of his instructions.

"Come on, men!" he bellowed wildly. "We tried to get what's owed us proper. We tried to trade for it. From now on, we take what's owed us! We take what we want, and we take it when we want it! Today, we become pirates!"

At this, a few men looked wary, but most cheered vigorously.

"Aye, lads! Gather yer fellows! We strike in three days!" Then Barend stormed off, leaving Muller to stare at the bag of spilled contents at his feet.

Back at Carloff's manor, Amy sat in a cushioned chair beside the still-unconscious Miata. She had fallen asleep again, this time sitting up with a book in one hand. As she slipped off to slumber, however, the book fell from her fingers, thumping on the floor and hitting a bowl near the chair, which clattered and jarred her awake.

"Oh!" She rubbed at her eyes, but they felt hot, dry, and heavy. "My sincerest apologies, darling. I am so weary, but I suffer as I watch you lie so still."

She touched his forehead, one of the least damaged places on his body. Running her fingers through his hair, she sniffled but was unable to cry. "Perhaps if you knew I was here, waiting for you, you would return to me." She laid her head beside his and closed her eyes. "I have cried all my tears, but I continue to wait."

Just as her breathing became shallow and rhythmic, the housekeeper knocked on the door. "Miss Lu'ay?"

Pushing it open, Hasina cleared her throat, feeling bad for disturbing Amy. "Miss Lu'ay? Miss Lu'ay, you asked me to tell you when the pa'ty retu'ned. They've just a'ived, miss."

Lifting her head, a hopeful expression cheered up Amy's countenance. "Have they?"

"Just now, miss," Hasina said, nodding. "Go on down. I'll wait with him."

"Thank you, Hasina. Bless you!" Amy said, a surge of energy at the prospect of her sister being returned lifting her spirits. Leaning over Miata, she said, "Do you hear that, darling? They've returned! I will go see them and then come straight back to you." She looked back at Hasina. "I shan't be long!"

"Of cou'se, miss," Hasina said, smiling and nodding again. She reached out, helping Amy to her feet.

"Am I presentable?" she asked, smoothing at her curls.

Toying with her hair just for a few seconds, Hasina smiled again. "The'e. You look pe'fect, miss."

"If he moves, so much as a finger or an eyelash—"

"I'll come st'aight fo' you, Miss Lu'ay," Hasina assured her.

Nodding her thanks, Amy turned and hurried from the room. She moved quickly down the corridor and was coming to the top of the grand stairwell when the front door swung wide. She held her breath as she watched two sets of men enter, each supporting a third man between them. After them, she recognized her father and Mr. Monroe accompanied by what looked to be one of her sisters.

"Oh!" She gasped. "Is it Jacq or Alex?" she asked, rushing down the stairs.

"It is Alexandria," the vice admiral answered. "We also reclaimed Mr. Rackham and freed a man named Oduntan to whom I seem to owe a great debt."

She covered her mouth, sniffling in both joy and dismay. Then throwing her arms about Alex, she whispered, "I am so glad you are safely recovered."

Returning the affectionate hug, Alex fought back tears. "As am I, dear Amy. As am I!"

"But where is Jacq?" Amy asked, straightening to see Alex's face. "Why is she not with you?"

Her mouth twitching with emotion and self-doubt, Alex shrugged. "We have been apart for several weeks. She went north with Bahari and Mr. Murtaugh. They are to meet us here in Cabo Corso with his family."

"Perhaps we can estimate their travel and arrival time," Vice Admiral Luray spoke up. "Mr. Carloff, have you a map of the region?"

"Uh… uh, well, aye, sir," Carloff said, grimacing as he slid out from under Oduntan's arm.

"Fetch it, will you?" the vice admiral requested. Then he turned back to Alex. "Perhaps between you, Mr. Rackham, and your friend Oduntan we can chart their course. We can see if there is cause for alarm that they have yet to reach us."

Alex smiled. "That sounds like a perfect plan."

"Aye." He beamed at her in a way only a father can—a mixture of pride and surprise. "Lads, let us get these two somewhere more comfortable. Carloff, be so good as to fetch Dr. Lindgren again, will you, please?"

"Oh, of course," Carloff said, still swatting at the parts of his jacket having been touched by Oduntan. "Hasina!"

"Oh! Let me relieve her, sir. She sat with Mr. O'Keeffe so I could come down." Giving Alex a quick peck on the cheek, Amy squeezed her hands. "I am revived upon seeing your face." Then she whirled away and vanished up the stairs.

"Bring the wounded this way," Carloff instructed, leading the men off. "Hasina!"

"And don't forget that map, Mr. Carloff," the vice admiral said, following after them.

As they moved away in a clamoring mass, only Alex and James Monroe were left still lingering by the door. In the deafening silence that followed, they eyed each other, both wanting to demand answers from the other and both deeply disguising their joy at seeing the other.

Still feeling troubled about her behavior earlier, however, Monroe ventured to attempt speaking first, "Miss Alex—"

"Mr. Monroe!" she said loudly—more so than she'd meant to. "I shall not stand for you continuing to rescue me."

Taken aback, he smirked. "Oh? Is that so, Miss Luray?"

Digging deep within herself, she nodded. "It is. In fact, I wish you had not come here at all."

His smirk fell. "No?"

"No. For I shall not permit a man to continue rushing to my aid when he has clear designs to marry someone else! Furthermore, I shall not condone a man following after me in such a manner unless he has every intention to marry me." She avoided eye contact with him, afraid looking into his kind eyes would extinguish her resolve.

His expression remained neutral. "Are you certain? This is your decision?"

Taking a deep breath, she nodded. "Yes. I have had an abundance of time to consider my thoughts while traipsing about in the wilderness, and I stand by my conclusion."

"Well then, Miss Luray," he said, circling behind her. "I suppose you should prepare yourself to only ever receive aid in such precarious situations from me." At this, he stopped in front of her, rotating to face her.

Her gaze darted up to meet his. "But... What..." She scowled. "It is beneath you to trifle with my feelings!"

"Indeed. An unthinkable act," he agreed.

She suddenly found it difficult to breathe. She began scratching at the two red dots on her forearm and touching self-consciously at her hair. "Oh. I-I must look a fright…" She paused, staring at him and trembling. "I-I-I should freshen up."

She moved to follow Amy, but he blocked her. "I believe we have more to discuss."

Still trembling, she eyed him. "What are you saying, Mr. Monroe? You are not suggesting… are you?"

"I am, if it pleases you," he answered with no hesitation. "Unless your interests lay elsewhere."

"No," she breathed.

"No?" he asked, taking a step forward but visibly confused.

"I… I-I mean no, my interests do not lay elsewhere."

"Ah." He nodded, still waiting. "And?"

She smiled, though she felt a bit dizzy. "It would please me very much."

Smiling back at her, he reached out in trepidation and took her hands in his. "Good."

"But what of your family and their wishes?" Alex asked, breathless.

"As I told you, Miss Alex, they were simply trying to assist me in the procurement of a bride. My father was especially glad when I requested to be released from the arrangement," he explained in kindness. "And I do apologize for being so dim-witted earlier at the beach."

Giggling, she shrugged. "No one else knew the difference."

"No one knows you as I do," he said, tugging her closer to him.

"How fortunate for them," she said with another tiny giggle.

Leaning forward, he whispered in her ear, "I would say quite the opposite."

"Kehinde! Kehinde!" Morenike called, racing up to her.

"Morenike," Jacq said. "What is it? Is something wrong?"

"Oh, no. Have you seen Murtaugh?" she asked.

"Well, not in a while. Why?" Jacq instantly began glancing about, the unknown status of his whereabouts immediately concerning her.

She sighed dreamily. "Do you not think him brave and thoughtful and every good thing?"

Chuckling, Jacq grinned. "You fancy him, I think."

Sighing dramatically, a starry-eyed expression overtook her. "What is there not to like, Kehinde?"

A coy smile teasing her lips, Jacq shrugged. "He is certainly one of the best I have ever known, faults and all."

"Faults?" Morenike asked, swooning. "They must be but sand amongst the rocks of his character."

Laughing, Jacq toyed with her hair. "Rocks of his character."

"Oi, Jacq!" Murtaugh's voice rang out.

She turned to find him with his shirt off, in a tree, holding up a piece of fruit. "What are you doing, mate?" she called out.

"These taste amazing, love! Would you fancy one or two?" he called down.

"What faults?" Morenike whispered in her ear.

Swatting at the younger girl, Jacq laughed. "Sure," she replied, walking up to the tree.

Plucking a few, he hopped down with the agility of a cat. "Two for you, Jacq. Oh, and two more for Miss Morenike."

He held them out to the girls. Jacq took hers with an understated smile, but Morenike snatched hers up and ran away squealing with delight.

Murtaugh gave Jacq a puzzled look. "She must really like those."

Giggling, Jacq nodded, though her eyes were distracted by his partial nakedness. "Aye, I believe she likes them very much." Then clearing her throat, she dragged her eyes away from his chiseled physique. "Thank you, Murtaugh. But be wary. You're liable to make every lass in Africa fall in love with you."

"Oh." Grabbing his leather jerkin, he slipped into it while chasing after her. "Jacq. Oi, Jacq!"

"Murtaugh?" She glanced back, both disappointed and relieved at seeing his covered chest.

"We, uh… we never came to a conclusion the other night at the campfire. We'll be in Cabo Corso any day now, and you'll be off with your father and sisters, but I—" He stopped, trying to think of what to say.

Jacq halted, listening to him. His repeated interest in what they would be doing upon returning gave her a surge of giddy hope that she tucked away in the corner of her mind. "Well, perhaps my father could assist you in locating some work in Swansea. With his connections, I would suppose he could benefit you in any way you require."

Murtaugh's mouth curved into a lazy smile. "Stay in Swansea?" Walking around to face her, he shrugged. "Why would I wish to stay there?"

She looked up at him from under her lashes. "Do you not find it to be a rather lovely town?"

He smirked. "It has its charms."

"Do you have an interest in remaining in any town in particular?" she asked, smiling demurely.

"Oh." He shrugged. "I don't know. One town is just as good as another."

"Is that so?"

"Aye." He leaned in a little. "It's the people that would give me reason to stay."

The giddy hope she'd tucked away crept back out of the corner, and she began toying with her hair. "Any people in particular?"

Grinning and stepping closer to her, he answered in a whisper, "Suppose I were to say there was. One person in particular, to be honest."

Pulling her bottom lip between her teeth, she was unable to stop a pleased smile from altering her expression. "I am certain such a person would be delighted to have you stay."

"Well, if that be the case." He ran the back of his hand from her elbow to her hand, where he danced his fingers against hers. "Perhaps I will stay, after all."

A rush flooded her brain at his touch, making her feel fuzzy. Forcing the effervescence down, she grinned playfully. "Well, what are we standing here for?" Pushing him back, she started walking again. "Sounds like we need to get you to Swansea."

The afternoon waned, giving way to a partially cloudy and sprinkling evening. As the sun sank, Amy lit the lamps and candles in Miata's room. Sitting in the chair beside his bed, she sighed. "So much excitement today, Miata. Alex is returned to us, as is your friend—well, I think he is your friend—Mr. Rackham, and an exotic native! It is all so scandalous and marvelous! If you would just join us, you would see." She grasped and squeezed his hand.

As he lay there, unresponsive, she was overcome with the severity of his circumstance. Pressing his hand to her cheek, she began to whimper and cry.

Hovering in the doorway, Alex's heart sank. Knocking softly, she walked in, causing Amy to sit up and dab at her eyes.

"Amy? Oh, darling."

"No, no. I am quite fine. You needn't concern yourself with me," she insisted, waving away Alex's outreached hands. "Mr. O'Keeffe is the only one suffering here."

"Amy," Alex said gently, taking her hands, "that is not true. There is no shame in your care for Mr. O'Keeffe's health and recovery."

Just then Vice Admiral Luray was passing by and, seeing his two daughters conversing, stopped to listen.

"Truly," Alex was saying, "I admire your courage in this."

"My courage?" Amy scoffed. "You walked across this side of Africa, facing all kinds of dangers while I sat here day after day drinking tea and eating biscuits and wondering why you lot left— ran away! That is neither brave nor courageous!" She covered her mouth. "My apologies."

"I meant your sitting with him day after day," Alex said, allowing the outburst. "I was horrified supposing Barend had killed him and so relieved to hear he was alive. But when I learned he had not yet opened his eyes, I was afraid—so afraid—to come see him." She sniffled.

"Why?" the younger girl asked.

"When-when that villain abused him—" She paused, her voice breaking. "He said he was giving Mr. O'Keeffe the punishment for all the pain and ruin Jacq and I had brought to his life. W-when he declared that was what was happening, Mr. O'Keeffe looked me in the eye and accepted it." She turned to him and reached out with trembling fingers, gingerly touching at his hand. "After all the condescension from me, he acted so noble." Sniffling, she leaned toward his ear. "I am so sorry."

At this, his fingers twitched.

"Did you see that?" Amy asked, pointing.

"What?" Alex asked.

A groan rose up from Miata's throat, and his head moved.

"Oh! Hasina! Get Dr. Lindgren! Quickly! Quickly!" Amy yelled, rushing out the door and past her father, indifferent to his presence.

"Has he not stirred at all?" Alex asked, hopeful of the possibilities.

"Not like this!" Amy called back. "Hasina! Hasina!"

The vice admiral entered the room and took up a post in the back corner to observe and be available upon request.

Amy, Alex, and Hasina fluttered about like hummingbirds, chattering and barking out orders. When Miata's eyes slid open for just a second, Amy threw herself down to embrace him, forgetting his bodily injuries.

Groaning, he weakly moved his hands in want of returning the gesture. "Amy," he whispered, eyes still closed. "Your sister… Miss Alex… She-she be…"

"Just here, Mr. O'Keeffe," Alex said softly, standing beside Amy as she knelt at his bedside.

"Oh." He chuckled feebly. "So you be."

Watching Alex smile down at Miata jarred the vice admiral's memory. Perhaps it was the fact she was not pristinely kept as usual or the fact she was smiling at Mr. O'Keeffe, but she reminded him intensely of Jacq.

Eight weeks earlier…

"Come now, Jacq! The lad is trouble. Your sister Alex sees that. I grant you, Amy's opinion is too easily persuaded, but you are a brilliant, clever young woman with so many options before you. Why weigh yourself down in society by forming attachments to the likes of Mr. O'Keeffe and Mr. Murtaugh?" he asked in sincere concern and lack of understanding as he watched her admire his telescope in the captain's cabin.

Shrugging, Jacq smiled. "I do not see why they are so unfit for society. They have always done right by me."

"Well, Mr. O'Keeffe is, by your admission, a man of questionable moral background with no connections at all. He has been, by all accounts, a scoundrel. As for Mr. Murtaugh, not only is he, by his own admission, a deserter, but he's a drifter with naught but a marginally completed blacksmith apprenticeship. And... he's Irish!"

"Papa." She laughed in exasperation, sitting on one of the extra beds he'd had installed for the girls.

"Darling, I know I cannot force you to do or be anything, and... and I do not wish for that. Truly. I care about you and your future." He paused and sighed. "Amy, however, I have a little more sway over. I know she could find a man to make her perfectly comfortable without tarnishing her social reputation."

A disappointed and rueful expression replaced her amusement. "Comfortable? Is that what you desired for my mother? For Amy's mother? Did you not seek to bring them joy?"

"Jacq, my dear, I-I do not wish to diminish the qualities your friends possess, I only mean to make certain you are content with their faults," he explained, still sincere.

"Aye, well, I will only be induced to matrimony if I feel something significantly stronger than *comfortable*. If I manage to secure that for myself, I do not intend to let go without a fight," she said calmly, standing and crossing her arms.

"While I do understand and appreciate your feelings," her father replied, looking out a window, "I must admit my wishes are unchanged. I would like Mr. O'Keeffe to give Amy space so she can consider all of her options with, God help us, some clarity. As for Mr. Murtaugh, I would recommend you do the same, but a recommendation is all I will force upon you." He rotated to look at her. "Are we agreed? One of us will speak to Mr. O'Keeffe?"

Looking completely crestfallen, it was Jacq's turn to stare out the window. "Can you wait until we've returned to England? To talk to him, I mean, if you must."

"I suppose. You do not wish to? I thought as his friend you might rather he hear it from you," the vice admiral said in surprise.

"As his friend," Jacq returned, continuing to stare out the window, "I do not have the heart."

Seeing Alex interact with him now, hearing her account, watching Amy's face light up at the prospect of him rejoining them, the vice admiral mused to himself. "Well, lad, seems fortune favors you. You've a long way to go, but perhaps you're worth the investment afterall."

The next instant, Dr. Lindgren came rushing into the room. "I heard the lad's awake."

"Open your eyes, darling," Amy whispered. "See that you are safe. The doctor is here to see you now and make sure everything is fine."

Everyone held their breath as he pried his lids back, but when he did, he grimaced. "I… I can't see."

A quiet morning greeted the party from Tenkodogo. Soft echoes of chirping birds and trilling insects filled the air. Jacq's eyelids fluttered open as her face was warmed by the sun. To her pleasant surprise, a large yellow flower was the first thing she saw. Sitting up, she plucked it off the ground and sniffed at it—just as enticing to the nose as to the eyes.

Noticing it, Morenike skipped over and asked, "A flower for you?"

"It is curious. I wonder who it could be from," she pondered aloud, leaning in to sniff its fragrance again.

"Some sappy bloke with poor judgment, I wager," Murtaugh said, walking by and winking.

The two girls giggled, and Jacq held up the Kehinde charm about her neck. "Perhaps today we will be reunited and we can end our journey here."

Just a few miles away, the crew at Mr. Carloff's was collected at the Cabo Corso harbor. Oduntan, still lightly bandaged but looking otherwise healthy, stood smiling at Alex. "Tayewo, the journey with you has been exciting and painful. You have enriched my soul, and your father has kindly and generously enriched my fortune."

Everyone standing to see him off snickered at his matter-of-fact remark.

"You are *awọn kiniun* and *esuro.* I am better for having known you. I hope Mr. O'Keeffe will see again one day," he concluded.

"I wish I knew what that meant," she said.

"It means 'the lioness' and 'the gazelle'—strength and grace," Mr. Carloff translated.

Alex's eyes brimmed with tears. "Thank you."

"Dr. Lindgren said O'Keeffe's already on the mend," Dante spoke up. "Seems he can see shapes and shadows now, so there's hope."

"Good luck to you, Mr. Rackham. May you understand the question."

They exchanged respectful nods.

"Thank you again, sir," the vice admiral spoke, "for helping take care of my daughter."

"Aye," James agreed heartily.

Bowing to them, Oduntan smiled. "I tell you, the honor was mine." Then as he gave a final round of handshakes and good-byes, Oduntan got on a boat bound for a beach just east of van Draenweg.

"Thank you again," the vice admiral said to Carloff. "It is very generous of you to offer a man and a boat to transport Mr. Oduntan back to his shore."

"What is it if I cannot assist a man who so generously brought the daughter of my good friend back?" he asked, brushing it aside.

"You have certainly proved yourself a resourceful ally, Mr. Carloff," the vice admiral said. "We do sincerely appreciate everything you have done for us."

"Of course, sir! Anything for a man like yourself!" he agreed zealously.

Giving him a nod, Vice Admiral Luray joined the group in waving good-bye to Oduntan as he sailed for home.

That night, as they all sat down for their evening meal, there was a knock at the door.

"Hasina!" Mr. Carloff yelled to her.

"On my way, si'! On my way!" she said, hurrying for the door. Upon opening it, her eyes grew wide. "Miste' Ca'loff, si'! You need to see this!"

Huffing in agitation, Carloff pushed to his feet. "Please excuse me."

His suspicions climbing, Vice Admiral Luray echoed, "Please excuse me as well."

Close behind, the vice admiral easily caught up to Carloff as he reached the doorway where Hasina waited. When they peered out, they both gasped. There on his front steps was gathered a filthy-looking crowd, with the person in front donning a larger-than-life smile. "Are we late?"

Chapter 13

A wide grin sprawled across the vice admiral's face. "Jacqueline."

The young woman laughed and cried at the same time. "I thought I might never see your face again!"

Rushing forward, she threw her arms around him, clinging tightly with all her strength. "Please tell me, did Alex arrive safely?"

Embracing her in return, he waved the others inside. "She did, but three days ago. Come. We've just sat down to eat." He looked at Carloff. "Do you mind?"

Frozen with some form of shock, Carloff laughed helplessly. "Of course, sir. Hasina!"

"Is that Jacq?" Alex asked, entering the room at the top speed she deemed to be ladylike.

"Alex!" Jacq exclaimed, releasing the vice admiral and flying over to her sister. "I cannot wait to hear your adventures!"

"Well, you must," Alex returned. "I do not know if I shall ever want to relive them." Then she pulled Jacq in for a hug, and their two charms clicked together.

Bahari smiled. "So the journey comes to an end."

Backing away from each other, Alex nodded at the newcomers she recognized. "Mr. Murtaugh. Mr. Bahari. And this is your family?" She smiled at the assortment of persons. "There are so many!"

"So many, indeed," Carloff muttered. "I do not have room to accommodate you all."

"Are your grounds protected?" Murtaugh spoke up. "We can camp outside. We have been for weeks. Another day or two as we prepare to leave will be of no consequence to us."

"Aye," Bahari agreed. "We do not wish to inconvenience you with our presence."

"Oh!" Jacq nudged Alex. "How are the lads?"

"Mr. Oduntan left just today. You missed his departure by mere hours. And Mr. Rackham and Mr. O'Keeffe, they are... uh..." She tried to think of the best term for their subpar conditions.

"Here," Dante rescued her. "We are here."

"Oh." Jacq winced. "Alex, what did you do to him?"

"Me?" Alex retorted.

"Did he make one too many careless remarks?" she asked, teasing, though her curiosity was genuine.

Rackham glanced at Murtaugh, jealousy instantly clawing at the back of his mind. "Nothing like that, Jacq," he said, smiling.

"And Miata, er, Mr. O'Keeffe?" she asked eagerly.

The room fell to a hush.

Glancing about, Jacq's fears began whispering in her mind. "W-where's Miata?"

"Here!" he called out. He came around the corner, with Amy guiding him to a stop beside Rackham. "Here I be, mate."

The moment she saw him, all joy she'd regained at hearing him left her expression. "Oh, Miata, mate. You look worse than you did the day Frederick Ellis saw you smile at his lass."

"That good, eh?" he asked, laughing awkwardly.

"What-what happened?" Jacq asked.

"Barend, that bloke that kidnapped us, did it to send a message," Rackham said in a flat tone.

"Kidnapped?" Murtaugh asked, scoffing.

"You were kidnapped?" Jacq asked, sending a look of astonishment to Alex.

"Mr. O'Keeffe suffered the worst of it," Alex said. "He only just awoke last night."

"Awoke?" Jacq repeated, her face contorting in horror.

"But I be startin' to be seein' now," Miata said in an attempt to make things seem better.

"Starting to see?" Murtaugh repeated in disbelief.

"It be mostly shadows and lights, but it be better than nothin' at all," Miata returned.

"What is this?" Alex asked, picking up Jacq's bandaged arm.

"Oh, that... that..." Jacq laughed uncomfortably. "That's just—"

"Mr. Murtaugh saved her!" Morenike spoke up, stepping forward. "She was bit by *igi paramǫlẹ—*"

"Heavens! What is that?" Alex asked, horrified.

"But Mr. Murtaugh was there, and he ended the beast and brought Kehinde to my aunt, Aladia, who was able to bring her back from death," Morenike finished.

All those new to this information stared in wide-eyed silence.

"Death?" Alex and their father repeated, aghast.

"It was not as bad as all that," Jacq said, laughing uneasily.

"You were supposed to take care of her!" Rackham shouted at Murtaugh.

"Oh, says the lout who got nabbed!" the Irishman retorted.

"She's here, is she not?" Rackham snapped.

"So is Jacq," Murtaugh argued tersely.

At this, the others who'd been left at the table joined the group.

"What's all the commotion?" James asked, pushing through to stand by Alex.

"What's he doing here?" Jacq asked, raising an eyebrow to Alex.

"He came with me," Captain Turner said from the edge of the room.

"Oh! Well, what are *you* doing here?" she asked, significantly more cheerful at seeing him than Mr. Monroe.

"Your father sent for us. Someone had to fetch you after your ship was burned down," Turner said, shaking his head at the outrageousness of it happening.

"B-burned...? What? Burned? What do you mean *burned*?" Jacq asked, stammering in disbelief.

"Oi! Someone said there was food, did they not?" Murtaugh interjected. "Let us talk over food!"

"Aye!" the vice admiral agreed. "Come, all of you. Let us eat. But, Jacqueline? Alexandria? A word?"

Everyone else filtered back toward the table, which was not big enough to accommodate the doubling of the previous company. As they found places to sit around the dining room, causing Mr. Carloff much grief, the vice admiral pulled the two girls aside. Sighing, he stared at them, unsure of where to begin.

After some thought and pacing, he finally came to a stop and said, "First, I want you to know how very relieved and gladdened I am to have you both returned."

They smiled brightly at him and each other.

"However." He paused, clearing his throat. "I want you to know that I know why you ran. Your sister, Amy, does not understand, but I do." He knelt in front of them, his eyes wet with heartache. "I want you to understand that you're not alone anymore. We are family. I was fighting for you—for us. You are a part of us now. And you making decisions like that…" He rubbed his hand down his face. "You making decisions like that reminds me of how alone you were for so long. And I-I am so sorry."

The girls traded tearful glances.

"We are sorry too, Papa," Alex said, sniffling.

"It was all my fault, really," Jacq spoke up. "You… you're right. I acted as though I was alone, even though in my head I knew I was not. I should have put more faith in you, and I promise, I will try harder."

"It's not your fault, darling," he said, taking each of them by the hand. "I will not hold this against you, nor will I punish you with it later. I just wanted you to know I was going to have us out of there if you would have let me."

"But it is partially my fault," Jacq insisted. "Sometimes we must choose to have faith in someone. Being with Bahari's family, I've been witness to what having faith in the right people can do." She sniffled. "And I… I want that. I want to surround myself with people I can put my faith in. You are certainly one of those people."

"Jacq is right," Alex spoke up, surprising her sister. "I am so afraid of letting new people close to me, but I believe it is preventing me from finding happiness."

"Then let us pursue faith and happiness together," their father said, giving their hands a squeeze. "Let us find them, as family and friends."

As they basked in the tenderness of their conversation, Jacq sighed. "I am still all astonishment. Who burned down our ship?"

Morning sun streamed down on Cabo Corso, making the town sparkle and gleam with the remnants of rain from the night before.

The whole town seemed a little extra sleepy, except Carloff's manor.

As soon as the sun peered onto the grounds, there was a hum of activity as Bahari's family rose to begin their final preparations to leave Africa for England. Upstairs, Jacq and Alex were sitting on a bed beside each other, examining the dots on Alex's arm.

"And they just appeared without any explanation?" Jacq was asking.

"Yes, and began to itch like mad."

"It's so strange," Jacq said, her brow furrowing. "They are not unlike the snakebite I received." She pulled out her arm, taking the bandage off.

To their surprise, the marks were identical.

"What could it mean?" Alex asked.

"I don't know," Jacq said, covering it back up. "So many things are strange in this land. I will be glad to go home."

Alex gestured to the medallion hanging around her neck. "Amy returned it to you?"

"Aye, after she made me apologize three times for running off. I feel so wretched about it now," Jacq said. "Papa seemed so downcast about the whole thing too."

"Yes. But we are all together now. I believe we should think on that and be merry," Alex said, yawning and reclining back onto the pillows.

Dropping back beside her, Jacq grinned. "I can't believe you were captured."

"I cannot believe you nearly died!" Alex returned, shaking her head. "Truly astonishing!"

"But here we are," Jacq said with a smile.

"Yes." Alex cozied into her pillow more.

"So tell me of Mr. Monroe. May I find obscure and ridiculous reasons to despise him, or are we mates again?" Jacq asked, smiling at Alex and hoping to spark a reaction.

"Actually," Alex said with a demure expression, "I believe he intends to marry me after all."

"What?" Jacq breathed, propping herself up on her elbow. "How do you know?"

"I told him he could no longer go about saving me unless he intended on marrying me. He said I should prepare to be only ever rescued by him," Alex recalled.

Giggling, Jacq flopped back down. "If that is his true intention, how can I fault his heart?" she asked, smiling.

Happily sighing, Alex shrugged. "I suppose you cannot. You know, on the beach, he recognized I was not you. No one else questioned it, but he knew."

"So you believe he knows you?" Jacq asked, seeking understanding.

"Yes. He has knowledge of small irrelevant things about me as well as personal, important things, but it is beyond that. He can perceive things about me—my inclinations, my worries. It is as if he has somehow gained access to a window into my soul." Alex curled a strand of hair around her finger as she pondered this.

"I wish someone knew me so well," Jacq said with a sigh.

"You may be surprised. Some may know you better than you give them credit." She grinned secretively.

Jacq turned a suspicious eye to her sister. "Why do you say so? Has Rackham said something? You and Miata do not count."

Alex's face scrunched up. "Mr. Rackham? He does not even know his own mind. But pray tell me, what of you and Mr. Murtaugh?"

"I do not know what you mean," Jacq returned, looking at the ceiling.

Alex sat up and watched her sister's face. "I believe you do. Something has changed between you. There is an unspoken closeness that was not there when last we were together."

"We are mates, Alex. Mates who have nigh on crossed Africa together, but nothing more. If he has intentions of there being more, he has not spoken of it," Jacq said in a frank, downcast inflection.

"Is that because he has not said or because you have not listened?" Alex asked, smiling down at her sister.

Giving her a distrusting glance, Jacq scoffed. "Since when are you Mr. Murtaugh's advocate?"

"Since he saved your life. Since I have noticed a happiness in you when you are with him that I have scarcely seen before. Since he behaved as a gentleman out in the wilderness," she answered readily.

"Miss Morenike is in love with him too, you know," Jacq remarked. "Perhaps you two should join together and make a secret society of lasses bewitched by Mr. Murtaugh."

"You jest," Alex returned, grinning broader now with gained confidence. "But I am convinced he would do almost anything for you."

"In that you are correct," Jacq said, conceding Alex's point. "Perhaps he'll favor me with a walk about Cabo Corso."

Smirking and shaking her head, Alex sighed. "Hide behind your walls of friendship as long as you must, but do not delude yourself with supposing a man devotes himself so fully with no meaningful intent."

"As I said before, Alex, we are mates," Jacq returned with a well-modulated tone of indifference. "Mates watch out for each other."

"And is that what you want, Jacqueline? Is that what you truly desire?" Alex asked, serious and direct.

Jacq stared over at her. "I'm going to see about that walk now," she answered, vaulting out of bed. "I don't like being disappointed, Alex. The grander the thing you wish for, the higher the chance of great disappointment."

"There is something to be said for hope, Miss Luray," Alex retorted as Jacq dressed herself.

"I know we have our differences, sister, but I believe we are the same in this," Jacq replied, pulling on her jerkin. "The closer to my heart a hope is, the more painful and frightening the rejection. Sometimes it is not worth the risk."

"Without some risk, there is little reward," Alex noted.

"And less chance of displeasure when it doesn't turn out," Jacq returned, laughing and tugging on her boots.

"When did I become the positive thinker of the two of us?" Alex asked, frowning. "I do not care for it."

"Since you are the one who seems to have love pledged to you," Jacq said, sighing.

"Seems?" Alex repeated, her face wrinkling at the word.

"I wouldn't get too excited until he makes a formal proposal," Jacq said. She kissed Alex on the forehead and then headed for the door. "Perhaps a walk alone would be best. If anyone asks, you can tell them I'll return before supper."

Flopping back onto her pillow, Alex sighed. "That was not how I imagined our conversation."

As Jacq hurried out of the house, a man standing across the street from Carloff's manor turned and headed out of town. He walked nonchalantly until he was beyond the Cabo Corso walls then he darted off the path into the jungle.

After walking about a mile, he came to a stop by a tree. "Fish eggs in a barrel!" he shouted.

Coming out from behind a different tree, Barend's friend Mr. Muller narrowed his eyes at him. "How many?"

"There was some fifteen showed last night," he answered. "But most o' thems was women and children. Maybe four men and two lads more is all. Mostly native folk too."

"Very good," Muller replied. "You'll be rewarded for your services after we drain Mr. Carloff like a strung-up goose."

The man nodded. "The boss want an extra hand?"

Muller grinned. "Sure, mate. We move at dusk and attack by cover of night."

"I'll be waiting," he said. Then tipping his hat, he made his way back to Cabo Corso.

"Bahari," Murtaugh spoke, approaching the burly man as he was assisting with the organization and cleaning of their small tribe's things.

"Crevan," Bahari returned, mostly disinterested.

"Have you seen Jacq?" he asked.

"I did. Earlier," Bahari answered.

Murtaugh watched him cleaning their tools and weapons while the women cleaned clothes. Gbeke assisted Moyo while Durosinmi sat off to one side, sharpening his own dagger. The smallest children played while the older ones were assigned other various tasks.

Gesturing at his work, the Irishman asked, "Would you like some help with that?"

A bit surprised at the offer, Bahari shrugged. "What could you do?"

Murtaugh chuckled. "I *am* a blacksmith by trade."

A contemplative expression reforming his countenance, Bahari nodded. "Very well." He offered Murtaugh a seat beside him and handed him a sword. "You are not the first to inquire after Shakina," he commented.

"No?" Murtaugh asked, forcing himself to remain where he was. "Who else?"

"Your friend, Mr. Rackham," Bahari responded, watching Murtaugh for a reaction.

"Oh, did he?" Murtaugh asked tensely, cringing inside. He picked up a whetstone and began gliding the blade along it.

"That he did, Mr. Murtaugh," Bahari answered, smirking.

The Irishman glanced up at him. "Mr. Murtaugh?"

"In life, we choose many things. Whom we call friend is one of them. Thank you for helping save my family," Bahari said.

Smiling, Murtaugh nodded. "It was my honor, Bahari."

As they set to working, Akinlabi approached his father. "May I speak with you?"

"Of course," Bahari agreed. He looked at Murtaugh. "Do you mind?"

"Not at all, mate," he said, nodding in confirmation.

Setting down his things, Bahari began walking with Akinlabi around Carloff's grounds. Once they were apart from the others, Akinlabi cleared his throat. "I have watched you and Kukoyi these last weeks. My brother, though loyalty and kindness sometimes make him weak, seems to have a gift of wisdom. This made him a good leader for us when you were gone."

"Loyalty and kindness are not weaknesses, Akinlabi," Bahari said, frowning at his son's sentiments.

"So says Kukoyi," Akinlabi returned pensively. "But I have not asked to speak with you for this. Instead, I wish to tell you that though I still doubt and distrust you, after seeing you with us these weeks since Tenkodogo, I am prepared to try."

Puzzled, Bahari shrugged. "Try what?"

"To trust you and accept your leadership," Akinlabi said, all seriousness and formality.

Smiling, Bahari nodded. "Akinlabi, know this. I expect nothing from you except honesty. I hope we can respect and honor each other and that perhaps, someday, you will know I do love you, your brothers, and your mother—more than I could ever say."

Touched by his father's gracious opinion of him, Akinlabi contemplated his words. Honesty. "If it is honesty you desire," the son spoke, "then I should tell you Durosinmi has some evil tendency. He has designs on Mama, though she would never have him. But he is filled with lies and trickery."

"I know," Bahari said. "He has revealed his intentions to me, though I knew even before that."

"Then why permit him journey with us?" Akinlabi asked, feeling self-conscious about having been tempted into a temporary alliance with Durosinmi.

Bahari chuckled. "It was not my decision to make."

"I would be wary of him," Akinlabi returned. "Unlike you, he cares little for what anyone else thinks or believes."

"Perhaps you could do us both a favor and keep an eye out for him," Bahari suggested.

Nodding, Akinlabi, ever serious, replied, "Aye. A wise plan. I will do as you say."

"There you are."

"I was wondering when you'd come find me," Jacq said, leaning on the railing of a fence post. Turning, her expression twisted. "Oh. I thought you were someone else."

"Your little Irishman?" Dante asked as he came to stand beside her.

Scoffing, she shook her head. "He is not little."

"What's that supposed to mean?" he asked, studying her face.

"Simply that he is not small," she returned, frowning at him.

"I'm sure we are of nearly equal size," he continued, completely serious about the matter.

"I never said you weren't!" she retorted, laughing.

"Well, what are you doing, anyway?" He glanced around. "Why are you by the auction house?"

"Look there," she whispered, pointing at a cluster of various animals.

"What?" He squinted at them.

"There! Just there! I thought Miata was the one with vision problems, not you. There! See the stripes!" She smiled, wholly enamored. "Isn't it beautiful?"

"What? What are you—"

Just then the animals moved about, revealing a pair of donkeylike creatures that were black and white with a striped coat pattern.

"Oh. Those... those are..."

"Zebras," she breathed. "Beautiful creatures. That one ate out of my hand twice." She pointed, beaming proudly. "Aren't they marvelous?"

Chuckling, he smiled at her. "How long have you been here?" he asked, leaning on the rail beside her.

"How long have you been searching for me?" she countered.

"Oh, an hour or two perhaps," he said, trying to guess.

"Longer than that," she said, still fixated on them. "If only Captain Taylor or old Mr. Bumbleridge could see me now." She laughed—a dry, rueful chuckle.

"I told you I would take you to see them, did I not?" Dante replied, elbowing her gently.

"Aye, you did, mate. Seems like a lifetime ago," she said in a doleful tone.

"It was," he agreed. "You have so many answers now."

"Aye," she said, eyeing him. "And so many more questions. What of us, Dante? What happens when Mr. Rackham, boatswain, and Miss Luray, daughter of a vice admiral, return to polite society?"

"We'll always be mates, Jacq," he said with confidence. "There's no reason for it to be any different."

"No reason for it to be different?" she repeated, her attention immediately halting on zebras and steaming ahead on Rackham.

Shrugging, he rubbed his palms together. "Everyone's been through quite a lot, Jacq. Once things have returned to some sort of order—"

"Oh, Rackham." She shook her head in despair. "Is it truly lack of order that troubles you?"

Grinning despite his face being sore, he sighed. "Jacq, I know not what else it could be. We are all together now. That Mick didn't get you killed, so—"

"Could it not, perhaps, be that you have intentions of going to London once we've returned?" she asked, baiting him.

Scoffing, he shook his head. "Jacq…"

Rolling her eyes, she glanced at the afternoon sky. "You know, I should be going. No doubt Alex has missed me. I wouldn't wish them to worry."

As she moved away, Dante grabbed at her arm, his handsome face contorted with conflict. "Jacq, please. Can we not be like this?"

Tugging her arm free, she scowled. "Well, therein lies the problem, mate. I don't know what we are anymore. Your manner and your intent never seem to match. One day you're attentive and kind, but the next you're lamenting to your shipmates about having to decline a dinner invitation from the very desirable Miss Wallace, who you then claim is nobody!"

As she fired out the words she hadn't intended to say, Jacq decided she may as well say them all. "What does it mean, Mr. Rackham? Do you have intentions for any of us? Or perhaps *all* of us?"

"Jacq! You know I care for you! You are a mate close to my heart!" he said.

"Ugh! Alongside Mr. Monroe and Mr. O'Keeffe, I suppose!" Huffing, she spun away from him and began marching back to the house.

"Jacq, stop! I don't know what the future holds," he continued, chasing after her, pushing past people walking by. "No one does!"

"Do not mock me," she returned, halting abruptly and facing him. "I care about you, Dante. I always have. From the moment I saw you, you fascinated me, but I will not wait for you forever. If you are not certain how you feel now, that's fine. But what if you never are? What if you are never certain enough?" As she spoke, she trembled, shuddering to her core.

Heaving a sigh, he hung his head. "You were right."

She narrowed at her eyes at him. "Pardon?"

Unable to look her in the face, he gazed away down the street. "Miss Wallace. When I was in London, I met her, and she reminded me of you. I grew to fancy her, though I did not intend it so."

Slap!

People nearby paused to stare before muttering to each other and continuing on their way.

Rackham touched at his cheek, the stinging hand print hot to his fingertips. "Jacq... Jacq, I—"

"No." She shook her head, tears clawing at her eyes. The clouds above swirled and churned. "Why did you insist it was nothing? All this time!" Her mouth twitched as she oscillated between anger and sorrow.

"I was confused, Jacq! You-you confuse me!" he said, grabbing her shoulders. "I thought I knew what I wanted, until we were together again. Then I wasn't sure if I care for Miss Wallace because she reminded me of you and you were who I truly cared for, or if it was, in fact, Miss Wallace."

"I will be second to no one," Jacq said, seething.

"I would never ask you to be," he returned. "Have you never had an interest in a person o-o-or something and then become interested in another? A part of you feels obligated to the first interest while part of you knows you are meant to move forward from the first to the second? Not because you value the first interest less but because you have a greater connection to the second and are unexplainably drawn to it?"

As he spoke, suddenly her mind cleared, and so did the sky. The tears on her face dried as she considered his words.

"I... I do," she said, sorting through her own feelings with the clarity of someone who's had a light shown for them in a dark room.

He was stunned. "Y-you do?"

"Aye." As she continued thinking, a half laugh eked out of her lungs. "Truly, truly. Mr. Rackham, you... you are so right. If there has been no permanent attachment to the first interest, why not move forward to the second?"

"W-well," he stammered, "you should be certain the second interest deserves attention."

"I agree completely," she said, nodding. Shrugging free of his grasp, she held his hands and smiled up at his abused face. "Do not feel an obligation to me, Dante Rackham. If you care for Miss Wallace as much as you claim, then you should go to her. I will find no fault with you so long as your actions are true."

Shaking his head, he chuckled. "It is not myself I worry for. Will you ever stop confounding me, Miss Luray?"

"I certainly hope not. Not so long as the sun brings the day, Mr. Rackham," she said, squeezing his hands and letting them fall.

"Mates then?" he asked, gesturing for them to proceed forward.

"Mates," she agreed, joining him in the walk back to Carloff's.

Meanwhile, Amy and Miata sat across from each other on a blanket out with Bahari's family.

"Can you see my hat?" Amy asked, hopeful and chipper.

"You be soundin' mighty cheery, Miss Amy," Miata noted.

"You are all returned to me! How could I not be filled with joy? We are to depart this place in two days' time and leave all this anguish behind us. I am ready for a new beginning, a true future. While I find the concept of adventure exhilarating, I dislike us being ripped asunder by another's whim. I missed you, Mr. O'Keeffe. I was frightened for your life when I saw you on those steps, and now here we sit," she said in a bright inflection. "Now, tell me, can you see my hat?"

Straining his eyes, he took a deep breath and focused. "Be it… orange?"

Scowling, knowing her hat was lavender, she turned to see anything orange. Behind her, Moyo was doubled over washing something, wearing a predominantly orange skirt. Turning back to Miata, she sighed. "No."

"Amy! Mr. O'Keeffe!" Alex called out as she approached them. "Have you seen Jacq?"

"No," Amy said, a wry smile forming her expression. "Perhaps Bahari knows where she is."

Clicking her tongue, Alex sighed. "I hope so. She said she was going for a walk, but that was hours ago. Oh! There is Mr. Murtaugh. Surely he will know." Gathering her skirts, she hurried over to where he was still assisting Bahari. "Mr. Murtaugh!"

Glancing up, he smiled. "Miss Alex."

"Mr. Murtaugh, my apologies for interrupting you. I was just curious if you had seen Jacq," she said, watching him work.

Looking up at her, he wiped his arm across his brow. "It would seem she went for a walk."

"Without you?" Alex asked, perplexed.

"Aye," he answered, returning his attention to the dagger he was sharpening.

"But… but that was hours ago," Alex objected, disliking this information.

"Aye, so it was, Miss Alex. Your point?" he asked, pausing to look at her again.

"How could you let her go alone?" Alex asked, irritated.

"Oi! She didn't invite me, lass. Sometimes she fancies a bit of time to think on her own, eh? Of course, Skippy went off for her, so perhaps she isn't alone after all," he said in a calm, sardonic tone. "Now, as you can see, I've got work to do."

She stood in silence a moment, trying to understand his reaction. Thinking over their brief conversation, she suddenly smiled to herself. "You know, sometimes I may seem fastidious and intolerant, but that does not mean I do not notice things, especially little things that are of great import."

"Miss Alex," he said, stopping again, "I thank you not to pretend to know me, and I—"

"You care for her," Alex stated.

He dropped his tools, and they clattered to the ground. "Miss Alex, I…" He laughed, embarrassed. "I don't know—"

"Why you have not told her yet? Neither do I. Now, listen here, Mr. Murtaugh. Let me tell you a secret I have learned about the daughters of Vice Admiral Luray," she said, demanding he listen by her inflection. "When we deem a person worthy of our friendship or our care, it is a rather difficult task to convince us otherwise. With Jacq, I have come to believe it is impossible unless the person betrays her, and even in that, there seems to be no absolutes. Do you intend to betray her trust, Mr. Murtaugh?"

"W-well, n-no," he answered, feeling uneasy.

"Well, I suggest you never do," she said.

"Alex! Alex, I saw them! I saw them! Zebras, Alex!" Jacq's voice bubbled over as she came running up to her sister, with Rackham hobbling close behind. Then, seeing Murtaugh, she gasped. "Oh! I thought you had come to accompany me, but it turned out to be Rackham."

"What a disappointment," he said flatly.

Laughing, she shrugged. "Perhaps it was for the best. We had a marvelous conversation, did we not, Mr. Rackham?"

"We did," he agreed, nodding and smiling at her. "It was liberating."

"Liberating?" Murtaugh snorted, stood, and stomped away.

Jacq turned to Alex. "What did you say to him?"

"Me?" Alex retorted. "You are the one who returned from an unchaperoned outing with Mr. Rackham, cooing about your *marvelous* conversation! The two of you are so daft!"

"I was not cooing!" Jacq objected, nearly sounding offended.

"You certainly were!" Alex argued.

"Well, I suppose you would know all about that, wouldn't you? All Mr. Monroe has to do is compliment you, and you're under the belief he has designs on you," Jacq said with a biting undertone.

At this, Rackham snuck away.

"Under the belief? You are not one to mock a person for entertaining a belief in someone! She who drags all of us out into the wilderness of Africa!" Alex exclaimed.

"You were agreed for it," Jacq shot back.

"I know," Alex said, huffing.

"So, why are we arguing?" Jacq asked, cooling off.

"I do not know," Alex said back, frowning.

"Well, did you hear me say I saw them?" Jacq asked.

"Were they as beautiful as you have always dreamed?" she asked.

"They were perfect," Jacq said, happy tears brimming in her eyes.

Smiling, Alex threw her arms around her sister. "I am glad. I know what it meant to you."

Hugging her back, Jacq let out a ragged sigh. "It meant the world."

As the sun began to sink in the western sky, Jacq found Murtaugh standing alone on the beach just beyond the Cabo Corso harbor.

"Red sky at night, sailors' delight," she said, coming to a stop beside him.

"Red sky at morning, sailors take warning," he returned without glancing at her.

She observed him in silence, his discontent bubbling just below the surface of his tranquil exterior. "Murtaugh—"

"I thought we had an understanding, Jacq," he said flatly.

"An understanding about what, Murtaugh?" she asked, a bitterness in her voice. "What did we discuss so plainly that I would know we had an understanding between us?"

Turning to look at her, a flustered sort of scowl took residence over his face. "Why were you out alone with Skippy?"

Choosing not to be sarcastic, Jacq sighed. "He came and found me. It seems he has a personal interest he wishes to pursue."

"Oh, does he?" Murtaugh's expression darkened.

"He does," she answered, eyeing him and his reaction.

"And you approve his pursuit of his interest?"

"I don't see how I should be in a position to approve or disapprove of Mr. Rackham's choices! I'm not his mother now, am I? I do hope they are happy together, and I see no issue with that," she said, her voice tense.

"Th-they?" Murtaugh repeated, his interest heightening.

"Aye. He and Miss Wallace," she stated indifferently, frowning at him.

Murtaugh took a step toward her. "Miss Wallace?" he repeated, taking another step.

"Aye." As he drew closer, her heart began to quicken. "N-now, w-what was this understanding you believed us to have?" she asked, chills rushing up and down her spine as his expression morphed into that rakish smile she reveled in. She stared out at the darkening water.

"Let me ask you, why would I wish to remain in Swansea, do you suppose, Jacq?"

"Pray tell me," she said in return, not daring to look up into his beautiful blue eyes.

"I think you know," he said, brushing his fingers down her arm.

His touch sending electric jolts across her skin, she closed her eyes. "You cannot let me to my imagination. You must be obvious, painfully obvious as to your meaning."

"Painfully?" He guided some stray hair off her face. "What do you think of me?"

"My sister believes you to be a gentleman," she answered.

"Is that what you wish?" he asked, running his finger under her jaw to tilt her face toward him.

Her eyes flitted open, her gaze instantly meeting his. "At times."

"And now? What do you want, Jackie?"

"I want you to tell me, Michael. Tell me what you want."

Letting his hand drop, he looked away. "If I say it, it can never be unsaid."

"Is that so bad?" she asked.

"People I care about. They get hurt, Jacq. They get torn away from me," he said in a defeated inflection.

"I know how that hurts," she said softly. "I have had to fight for all the people I care about. Even after I have them, I have to fight to keep them. If you care… if you care enough about a person, the fighting is worth it."

Glancing at the darkening sky, he sighed. "Come. We should return."

Disappointed, she obliged, walking with him back to Carloff's, chased by spitting raindrops. As they approached the manor, Jacq noticed some unsavory men loitering across the street. Nudging Murtaugh, she asked, "What do you suppose they're about?"

He followed her gaze and immediately began glancing about. "Jacq, get inside now. Now, now, now." He pushed her up the steps and into the house as the rain began to increase. Once inside, he locked the door, wrapped his arms around her, and stood with his back against the wall to peer out a window.

"Murtaugh," she whispered.

"Shhh!" he returned, still looking outside.

"Mr. Murtaugh?" Vice Admiral Luray's voice spoke. "What are you doing with my daughter?"

Trepidation taking over, the Irishman turned away from the window to discover almost everyone was gathered in the great room across from them, staring. Releasing Jacq instantly, he cleared his throat. "Mr. Carloff, sir, I do believe you are about to be invaded."

Before anyone could respond, a volley of shots pelted the building, breaking glass, splintering the door, sending bullets whizzing through the air.

Everyone began ducking and scattering.

"Aaah!" Carloff cried out. "My house! Oh! I've been hit! Make them stop shooting my house!"

Checking the arm Carloff held out toward him, the vice admiral scowled. "It's only a flesh wound!" Then he got Amy's attention. "Amy! Take Mr. O'Keeffe somewhere safe—upstairs to his room. Women, gather your children and go with her. Jacqueline, Alex—"

"We're with you, Papa," Jacq interrupted, watching the others retreat as they were told.

"Wha—" He glanced over at Alex, who reluctantly nodded.

Another volley of gunfire hit the house.

"Very well. Jacqueline, stay with Murtaugh. Lad, don't you lose her."

"Sir," Murtaugh returned, nodding.

"Mr. Monroe, Alexandria. The same for you," he ordered.

They nodded.

He looked back at Murtaugh. "How did you know?"

"I saw them, sir. They were all over the street, glancing at the sky, walking in twos and threes. They thought they were being mighty sneaky, but they're not so clever."

Another volley hit, more ricocheting and crashing into the room than before.

"How many?" the vice admiral asked.

"Oh. How many, Jacq? Seven or eight across the way. Another maybe five or six on this side. There could have been more," Murtaugh answered, trying to think.

"Lad, you may have saved our lives tonight," Vice Admiral Luray said with a sincerity and unspoken thanks that filled Murtaugh with pride. "Carloff? How many weapons do you have?"

"I'm a businessman!" he said, holding his arm. "I have but two swords, perhaps. Only a flintlock or two and a hunting rifle."

"Naturally," the vice admiral said, unimpressed. "Bahari? What of you?"

Bahari grinned over at Murtaugh. "How many do you need?"

Bang! Bang!

The front doors began to shake with what the men threw against it. "Carloff! I know you're in there!"

"Bahari, take two men with you. Bring back all can carry," the vice admiral instructed.

Bahari beckoned to his two sons, and they hurried to get their weapons cache.

"Lads, daughters." He nodded at his two girls. "We are going to defend this house."

"I should send for Dr. Lindgren," Carloff groaned, touching at the scratch on his arm.

Bang! Bang!

"Not unless you want him killed before he can tend to your *wound*," the vice admiral said, pronouncing 'wound' with a hint of sarcasm. "Now, Mr. Bibbs, are you up for this, old man?"

Bibbs chuckled, a wheezing sort of sound. "I shall imagine every one of them to be the mistress of my previous employer," he said.

Bang! Bang!

"Very well. Mr. Rackham, you go with Jacqueline and Mr. Murtaugh. Stay near the door. Mr. Carloff, you're with Captain Turner and Mr. Bibbs. Sorry, lads," he said directly to Turner. "You position yourselves across from the stairwell there."

Bang! Bang!

"Come on out, Carloff! You and your precious companions!"

"I will go with Alexandria and Mr. Monroe to guard the stairs," Vice Admiral Luray continued. "Bahari, you split your men into two groups as you see best, and defend this entry point into the rest of the house."

Bahari, who'd just returned with his two boys and with armloads of swords and daggers, nodded. "Agreed."

"Stay together! Watch each other's backs!" the vice admiral shouted.

Bang! Bang! Crack!

"My front doors!" Carloff cried.

Bahari, Kukoyi, and Akinlabi handed out the weapons as fast as possible.

"Knock, knock! Oh, Mr. Carloff! It is I, Octavius Barend and my band of buccaneers!" Barend laughed maniacally. "We come to collect what we're owed and anythin' else that strikes our fancy!"

Bang! Crack! Crunch! Bang! Crack!

Suddenly, the doors gave way to the mass behind them. A stream of rain and men came pouring in, whooping and chortling as they rushed into the manor. They stopped abruptly at finding themselves surrounded.

"What have we here?" Barend asked, coming out from the midst of the crowd. His observant eye noted both Alex and Jacq. "So there were two alive, after all. Pity ya didn't pay me for the safe return of one. Now I've come to collect on both." He dragged the tip of his sword across the floor, making a horrible scratching sound.

"You have no claim to anything here," Vice Admiral Luray said.

"That's where yer wrong." Barend paused, looking over the group. "Dead wrong. Lads! Mates! Attack!" Pointing his sword at Carloff, he led the charge, colliding his gaggle of ne'er-do-wells with those who were intent on defending the house.

The clanging of metal, crashing furniture, thudding against walls, and hostile shouting could be heard by those huddled together upstairs.

"Miss Amy," Miata whispered, "be findin' anythin' we can be usin' as a weapon."

Forcing herself to let go of his arm, she nodded. "To what end?"

"In the worst event that we be havin' to be defendin' ourselves, I'll be not havin' you defenseless," he answered somberly. "I'll not be havin''em takin' you from me."

Sighing, she touched at his cheek. "I assure you, I have no intention of leaving you—ever."

"It be a most kind thing of you to be sayin' afore I be facin' most certain death defendin' ye," he returned in a frank tone.

Down below, the groups tried to stay together, as designated by the vice admiral. Murtaugh and Rackham fought on either side of Jacq while Alex had Monroe to her right and her father to her left.

Carloff, going head-to-head with the disgruntled Barend, was making a spectacular show of swordsmanship alongside Mr. Bibbs and Captain Turner. However, things were less smooth at Bahari's end.

While Olusegun and Gbeke aided Alex's group in protecting the right of the stairwell, Bahari and Kukoyi were just a short distance to their right. Akinlabi and Durosinmi were along the wall where the room transformed into a corridor to the dining room. Akinlabi moved to join his kin, but Durosinmi caught him in an armhold.

"What are you doing? Let go of me!" Akinlabi shouted above the din.

"I made a terrible mistake trusting you," Durosinmi said, pulling him close enough so that Akinlabi could feel his breath. "I said you would be sorry you crossed me." With that, he jabbed a dagger into Akinlabi's back.

Gasping and exclaiming in agony, Akinlabi dropped his weapon and gave Durosinmi a pained look, begging an explanation.

"It's not personal, lad. Oh, actually, it is. I don't believe your mother will have me with Bahari and Kukoyi alive, and you... you betrayed me," he said into Akinlabi's ear. "*Ti o ti fi mi ati gbogbo awọn enia wa.*"

Taking a shaky breath, Akinlabi returned, "She will never have you. He has his faults, but my father is a man of honor. *Ti o wa ni nkankan.*" Then he spat in Durosinmi's face.

Pulling out the dagger, Durosinmi angrily pushed Akinlabi to the ground off in an empty corner, leaving him to bleed helplessly. Unfortunately for him, Bahari saw him shove the boy away, and when Akinlabi did not bounce back, he began brawling his way through the crowd.

A few of Barend's men raided the kitchen for silver and made a run for it, but many of them remained, enjoying the fight and hoping for greater riches. Mr. Muller caught Murtaugh's sword with his and took a swing at him, punishing the Irishman's jaw with his fist.

Jacq gasped. "Oh, you shouldn't have done that, mate."

"Aren't you supposed to be dead, lass?" he snorted back at her.

Quickly recovering, much to Muller's chagrin, Murtaugh reversed his hold on the hilt of his sword and brought it up to meet

Mr. Muller's nose. "Not hardly, mate." As Muller doubled over, he shoved him backward by introducing his foot to the ruffian's behind.

While Muller stumbled into his fellows, Barend was taunting Carloff, suggesting he may as well give up. Bibbs, however, was not in the mood for such prattle and shared in the chore of keeping the angry man at bay. Devotedly, Alex maintained the railing behind the vice admiral and Mr. Monroe. Dodging back and forth from side to side, jabbing at faces and smashing fingers with the hilt of her dagger.

Meanwhile, Bahari reached Durosinmi, grabbing him by the throat and ramming him against the wall, smashing someone else in the process. This allowed him to see Akinlabi lying on the ground with a puddle of blood beside him.

Anger igniting a furnace within him, Bahari tightened his grip on Durosinmi's throat. "How dare you! If you ever have thought you have suffered, you will find it a pleasant memory after what I do to you!" he growled between clenched teeth.

Noticing Bahari and Durosinmi, Kukoyi began making his way over to the two men.

Upstairs, Amy had found a curtain rod and tools for stoking the fire. "There. I think that's the best of it."

"Very good," Miata said, nodding and testing their weight in his hands. "You be bein' most brave about this, Miss Amy."

"What have I to worry for? My father and many able-bodied men are downstairs defending us as well as my sisters. You are here with me, something I wish never to change," she said in a chipper tone. "Why should I not find courage in these circumstances? Truly, I am sorry for our attackers."

"Sorry for them?" Miata asked, surprised.

"Well, yes. Mr. Bahari and we traveled hundreds of miles to get his family back. I hardly think a few greedy pirates will stand in his way." She giggled at the absurdity of the notion.

Miata sighed. "You be an angel, Miss Amy. Will you see to the others?"

"Of course," she agreed readily. Then she moved off to check on Aladia, the other women, and the children.

As she went off, Miata strained his eyes, trying to will his vision to improve. "A few greedy pirates, indeed," he said, listening to the clamor below.

Off to the right of the entrance hall, Rackham was defending himself with a chair. "Murtaugh! Jacq!"

Hearing his last name, Murtaugh perked up. "Oi, what are you doing with that chair, mate?"

"It seems I misplaced my sword," he returned, grunting as he moved the chair to block an attack.

"A fine time for that, mate," he retorted. "Jacq, get my back."

In one smooth rotation, Jacq and Murtaugh traded places. She continued slicing at arms and legs in hopes of persuading them to leave as Murtaugh located and returned Dante's weapon. As he handed it back, he paused. "Are we on the same side then, Rackham?"

Understanding his meaning, Rackham took the sword and nodded at Jacq. "I like to think we always were."

Grinning, Murtaugh grabbed the chair. "Allow me."

Together, they took the piece of furniture and went rushing forward, knocking men all over the place before it was cast aside and broken into pieces.

Seeing them, Jacq frowned. "Come back here, lads!"

Across the room, Kukoyi was calling out to Bahari. "Let him go! Let him go!"

"He is poison, Kukoyi. We should be rid of him." As he further tightened his hold, Durosinmi grabbed his wrist with both hands, gasping for air.

"On whose authority? He's Iremide's uncle. I… I-I intend to marry her, and I won't have you or anyone else dispatching the only family she has left," he argued.

"See what he has done to your brother?" Bahari cried. "I did not return to Africa only to have my family stolen from me, and that is all he has tried to do!"

"Then let us deal with him properly!" Kukoyi said, watching Durosinmi writhe. "Not like this, Baba. Not like this." He pushed his way between them. "Please."

Releasing his hold, Bahari immediately scurried to Akinlabi, Kukoyi right behind him. Feeling his son with trembling hands, a rush of optimism filled his heart. "He breathes!" He looked up with relief at Kukoyi, only to see Durosinmi staggering up behind him with a blade drawn.

"No!" Bahari roared, lunging forward and flinging his son out of the way. As a result, Durosinmi plunged his dagger into Bahari's muscled shoulder.

Scrambling to his feet as Bahari roared in pain, Kukoyi flew back to his father's side, pushing Durosinmi away. They watched as Durosinmi took three wobbly steps backward and slipped on the dagger Akinlabi had dropped when he'd stabbed him. His feet flew into the air, and his body came crashing back down on the splintered remains of the chair Murtaugh and Rackham had used as a battering ram, effectively piercing himself through the heart.

Kukoyi and Bahari exchanged astonished expressions.

"That, my son," Bahari said, groaning and touching at his shoulder, "is fate." Pulling the knife out and tossing it aside, he crawled back to his son. "Akinlabi? Can you hear me?"

"We will save him," Kukoyi said confidently, the reality of his brother's condition suddenly hitting him. "We will."

"Alex," the vice admiral yelled back. "Perhaps you should seek shelter with the others!"

"Aye!" James agreed. "I think you'd be safer there!"

"Safer and useless!" she said in objection. "Is that how you would have me, Mr. Monroe? Safe and useless?"

"What?" He scoffed. "What an outrageous thing to say!" He did his best to concentrate on her voice while continuing to block and parry the blows and thrusts of his current opponent.

"Well, it might be outrageous, but you have yet to deny it!" she argued, leaning over and smashing someone's fingers between the rails.

"This is really not the place for such a conversation," he said, grunting and hitting back at the man, making him back down the stairs a few steps.

"That may be, but I want an answer. A simple yes or no shall suffice," she said, completely serious.

Giving the man a hearty shove, making him topple off the steps and into his fellows, Monroe glanced over his shoulder. "Of course it's not what I want! You are brilliant and beautiful, and you astonish me with all that you are. Can a man simply wish to keep his future wife safe from harm?"

Gasping, she covered her mouth with her hands. "So you *do* intend to marry me?"

"I thought we were agreed on it!" he said, confused. "I just wanted to talk to your father before making a proper proposal."

Alex held back tears of joy. "Oh, of course!"

"Would you two concentrate on the issue at hand?" Vice Admiral Luray requested, wounding his opponent with a well-aimed strike. Turning to glance at Alex, he saw someone had managed to get over the rail behind her. Leaping up, he bodychecked the man back over, but not before the assailant flailed his blade around, cutting open his forearm.

"Oh! Papa! Are you badly injured?" Alex asked.

"Sir?" Monroe asked as respectfully as possible.

"Keep at it, lad!" he answered, gesturing to a scoundrel running up the steps. "I've had worse in my time."

"Aye, sir!"

Panting, Barend scowled at Mr. Bibbs. "Who are you, old man? Not one of Carloff's. I'd know."

"I am Mr. Charles Bibbs," he replied. "Unfortunately for you, you have attacked some dear friends of mine, and they do not take kindly to that type of thing. In fact, I might suggest you select a different profession altogether, young man."

"Don't waste your breath, ya gaffer. I care not for your opinion," Barend retorted.

"Are you new to it? That would certainly explain why you're not very good at it," Bibbs returned matter-of-factly.

Increasingly vexed with the old man, Barend growled as he took another swipe at him.

As a sort of pause quieted the room, the defenders frantically tried to assess their status. Though there were wounded on both sides, odds weren't improving as Gbeke received a blow to the head, rendering him unconscious. No thanks to his previous wounds, Rackham was beginning to fade, and now the vice admiral was weakened with the gash in his arm.

Jacq and Murtaugh stood shoulder to shoulder, doing their best to protect Rackham. Likewise, Alex and Monroe did what they could to maintain the stairs. Turner, Bibbs, and Carloff were completely surrounded, and of Bahari's group, only Olsegun and Kukoyi were still standing and able with Bahari guarding Akinlabi.

Just as they were beginning to feel their situation had taken an irreversible turn for the worse, they were dismayed when additional men came pouring in from the street, brandishing weapons and hollering. However, they began assaulting Barend's men with all the mettle they could muster, surprising all those already engaged.

"Oi!" Murtaugh called out. "Who are these chaps?"

"Captain!" one man shouted. "Captain, we hope ya don't mind sharin' the fun!"

"They're my lads!" Captain Turner yelled, waving at the man.

"And mine!" Vice Admiral Luray shouted, spotting Mr. Ellard among them.

"We heard the shouting and gunfire, sir! I hope we're not intruding!" the first mate called.

"We're pleased to have you join us, Mr. Ellard!" the vice admiral yelled back.

With varying degrees of shock and displeasure, Barend's men began turning to take on this new wave of men, but it did not last long. With the obvious strength in numbers now firmly not on their side, Barend's men began surrendering their weapons until the lone person left standing was Barend himself.

Upon noticing this, he flourished his sword, his blood boiling in his veins. Looking past Mr. Bibbs, he pointed an accusatory finger at Carloff. "You! Ya fraud of a businessman! Ya trickster! Ya dishonest coward!" He turned to his surrendered associates. "Yer cowards, all of ya! The whole lot of ya! Is it so wrong for a man to fight for that which is rightfully his?" He looked at the twins. "And you… the two frocks who ruined it all. And for what? To find some pitiful native family? To feel better about yerselves? For a spot of adventure that is otherwise looked down upon in yer polite society?" He scoffed.

"Mr. Barend!" Vice Admiral Luray said in a sharp, reprimanding timbre. "It is you who is breaking the law today. It is you who shall stand trial for your actions. You're a fool to think you'll not pay for your misdeeds. Now, I—"

Barend chortled. "It is you," he whispered in a mentally unstable tone, as Ellard came forward and relieved him of his weapon, "who is a fool." He glanced at Carloff. "I'm sure if ya think back to his behavior, ya shall see. He is not the genteel businessman he puts on the airs of being. He hired me to attack yer ship."

Luray stopped. "What?"

"Aye, sir. He hired me for it. For the sum of twenty pounds, I was to blow a few holes in your ship. Of course, it all went bloody sideways when Bakker failed to declare your colors and then those lout Frenchman caught her on fire, but it weren't by fault of mine, see? But then"—Barend laughed in frustration—"but then the turncoat wouldn't pay. I have proof."

While Barend relayed his side of things, the vice admiral watched Carloff, who, after noticing his stare, grew increasingly anxious. Suddenly, all the oddities came flooding back—his awkwardness, his behavior with the letter, how Barend knew of persons in his employ. Vice Admiral Luray's countenance turned black.

As soon as Barend finished his retelling, the vice admiral marched up to Carloff as displeased and fierce as a lion tends to a hyena going after his lunch. "Is it true?" he questioned, his tone and manner demanding that the truth be told.

"Anything that man said is a lie!" Carloff shouted. "He has designs against me for reasons I do not know!"

"Don't you, Mr. Carloff? There are two things I can tell you for certain, Mr. Carloff," he replied firmly. "I have a sense about folk, and I don't stand for injustice. You smell of a liar and a cheat, Mr. Carloff. I thought so since the moment we'd arrived. I don't appreciate my family being put in harm's way as you poorly attempt to better your name at the expense and misfortune of others." He held up Barend's letter.

Carloff gulped. "Vice Admiral Luray, you must understand, I-I-It wasn't… th-there's not—"

"Understand this, Mr. Carloff. If Barend speaks the truth of your schemes, I swear to you, you will pay for your treachery. I will do everything in my power to ensure you will not take advantage of anyone *ever* again."

Before Carloff could respond, however, Kukoyi's voice shouted, "Kehinde! Kehinde! Help us! My father and brother! They are bleeding! Help us!"

Jacq and her father exchanged glances.

"Help them!" she called, trying to swim through the crowd.

The vice admiral turned back to Carloff. "Fetch Dr. Lindgren, Mr. Carloff. Be quick about it."

"Aye, sir," Carloff said in agreement, hurrying away.

"Mr. Monroe," the vice admiral continued, "let the others know it is safe to come out."

As Jacq reached Kukoyi and tried to help him stop the bleeding on Bahari while he tended to his brother, James mounted the stairs with ease. Bounding agily to the top of the staircase, he trotted down the hall and jiggled at the lock of the door behind which everyone else was hiding. "Hello! It's James Monroe here. Open up! It's safe to come out."

There was a clicking of the lock, and then the door was barely cracked open, and a poker was thrust at his face.

"Mr. Monroe? Is it truly you?" Amy asked.

Grabbing the poker and directing it away from his eyes, he nodded. "It is, miss. And only me."

Letting the door swing wide, she sighed. "What a relief. Mr. O'Keeffe, it is only Mr. Monroe," she said.

"I… I be seein' him," Miata said with a breathy laugh. "I be seein' Mr. Monroe!"

As Amy squealed with glee and ran to Miata, James looked over all the rest huddled together in the room. "Come on then. It's safe now. It's over."

As James ushered Aladia and the family out, Alex hovered on the steps, trying to account for the wounded. Olsegun had his father sitting up with his eyes open, though he was still groggy. Bibbs and Turner stood with her father. Barend was still going on about his sordid dealings with Mr. Carloff. She could not see Bahari or his sons from where she stood, but she watched Murtaugh follow after a limping Jacq, a cut on his arm seeping blood onto his sleeve. Behind them, a hurting and exhausted Rackham slumped into a chair, holding his side.

Catching up to Jacq, Murtaugh cringed at what he saw. Akinlabi was sprawled in a pool of blood, with Kukoyi crouched beside him. Durosinmi was a few feet away, lifelessly impaled on a broken chair leg, and Bahari was hunched over holding his arm as Jacq fretted about his shoulder with a cloth.

Looking up and finding him, she gasped with relief. "Oh, Murtaugh! Hold this cloth here on Bahari's shoulder! I have to help Kukoyi!"

Obligingly, he knelt beside Bahari and took over for her. "Of course, Jacq. Anything you need."

They traded sober, concerned expressions before she turned and scurried over to Akinlabi. As she left and Murtaugh looked after her, Bahari, using his uninjured arm, grabbed him by the front of his shirt and pulled him close. "Murtaugh, be the blackbird."

Murtaugh's face scrunched in confusion. "Wha—?"

"Murtaugh, do not make any promises you can't keep, but…" Bahari gazed at him with a severity that made the Irishman uncomfortable. "*Be* the blackbird."

Understanding dawned on Murtaugh's face, but before he could respond, the doctor was rushing up to them.

"Move aside! Move aside!" Dr. Lindgren glanced about, assessing the situation. "You!" He pointed to Bahari. "Tell me what happened here." Then he moved over to the unconscious boy.

"Of course, sir." Staggering to his feet, Bahari gave Murtaugh one more insistent stare. "*Be the blackbird.*"

Chapter 14

Looking out the window, Alex touched at her long, undone hair. It spilled about her shoulders like honey and glistened like new silk. Sighing, she ran her fingers down her throat, which was devoid of any sort of necklace. Pulling the robe tighter around her shoulders, she sniffled and turned away from the window. Across from her hung a red satin gown with a long pointed bodice and a white silk petticoat. A white sheer scarf was to be fastened into a collar around her shoulders by a gold clasp set with sapphires and emeralds. It was a beautiful dress, fit for a princess.

"Alex!" Amy shouted, bursting into the room. "Alex, your hair! I'll fetch Lydia. Lydia!" Practically bouncing with energy, she crossed over to Alex and giggled. "Can you believe it? Both of us to be married!"

Alex smiled, nodding. "It is certainly a wonder."

"I remember my proposal as if it was yesterday," Amy said, sighing in delight.

"Indeed. Though perhaps not quite the same as the rest of us," Alex said, smiling.

"What do you mean by that?" Amy asked.

"Only that you have a propensity for romanticizing the event whereas Alex recalls a very exact rendition of it," Jacq said from the doorway.

"Oh, and you remember it so keenly?" Amy asked, smirking.

"In fact, I rather think I do! Shall I regale my two bride-to-be sisters of their proposals just two short months ago?" Jacq asked, entering the room and eyeing Alex's wedding dress.

"You do not have to," Alex spoke up instantly.

"Oh, no. I insist!" Amy said enthusiastically, seating herself on the chair.

Alex frowned. "Jacq—"

"It's quite fine, truly," Jacq said, smiling. "Now, let's see. It was two days after we had returned from Africa. Akinlabi was sent to hospital, but the rest of us were trying to settle back to normal. Well, except Mr. Monroe, of course, who was eager to ask our Miss Alex a very particular question."

Giggling, Amy clapped her hands. Alex, however, watched Jacq with a skeptical eye.

"Well, one evening after supper, Mr. Monroe took Miss Alex out for a walk at her father's estate. The dusk had settled, and the sky was orange with a warm breeze tugging at them as they walked. Surely he thought she had never looked so beautiful—a thought he often thinks."

"Jacq!" Alex said, blushing and twirling her hair.

"It must be true!" Amy exclaimed in agreement.

Jacq nodded in faux seriousness. "Aye, it must be true! For as they walked, he bade her pause, took her hands, and knelt on both knees. He gazed up at her and said, 'Miss Alex, for as long as I've known you, I have loved you. Will you allow me to show you this love, to be my companion, all the rest of our lives? Will you do me the honor of becoming my wife?' Then Miss Alex gasped and shed three tears."

"I did not cry!" Alex protested.

"There were tears," Jacq said, unpersuaded.

"Of joy," Alex said adamantly.

Amy giggled, clapping. "Go on! Go on!"

Sending Alex a teasing glare, Jacq continued, "Well, after he asked and Miss Alex regained her statuesque posture, she smiled and replied, 'Yes. I am honored. I feared you might never ask.' Of course, we know that to be preposterous."

Scoffing, Alex gave her a wry smile. "You mock my lack of confidence, but you are no better."

"Ah! But we are not speaking of me, are we?" Jacq asked, maintaining a straight face. "Now, where was I? Oh, Miss Alex accepted Mr. Monroe's proposal with the rest of us watching in great anticipation through the window. When he stood with an enormous smile on his face and scooped Miss Alex into his arms, there was no doubt of Miss Alex's answer. That is when Miss Amy turned to Mr. O'Keeffe and said, 'If you were to ask me, I would not reject you.' Which then prompted an astonished Mr. O'Keeffe to ask, 'Would you be willin' to be marryin' me?' And though some of us supposed it to be a question in want of affirmation, Miss Amy—"

"I threw my arms about him and said, 'Oh, Mr. O'Keeffe! I would love to be your wife!' And we were all a jolly company, were we not?" Amy giggled and bounced over to the mirror. "I think I should love some flowers in my hair."

"I'll go and find Lydia," Jacq said. She glanced over at Alex, who was still watching her with a rueful expression.

"Where are Frank and Bill?" Alex asked.

"I've left them with Mr. Talbot," Jacq answered. "I thought we mightn't like them to attend the wedding at the church."

As Jacq slipped away, Amy noticed the doleful look on her sister's face. "Alex! What is the matter? It is our wedding day! Are we not supposed to be all manner of happiness and joy?"

Sighing, Alex nodded. "But of course you are right. Only I worry for Jacq."

"She will come round. You'll see," Amy said, bright and optimistic.

Glancing once more at the door, Alex nodded. "I am sure she will." Then she joined Amy in the mirror, toying with her hair.

Downstairs, Jacq found Lydia and sent her up to her sisters. As she gazed about the grand house, decorated with flowers and drapings, she felt as if she were living in a palace. In fact, she'd been afraid of touching anything for a week, so she ducked out into the garden, as had become her habit.

Once outside, she took a deep breath of the fresh air, no longer feeling suffocated by the perfect beauty of the interior of the house. However, as she stared at the tree where she and Murtaugh had gazed out toward the city that night a year and a half ago, her heart tore, and she crumpled onto the nearby bench.

Sniffling and fighting to push her emotions back into the corner of her mind, she muttered to herself, "It's fine, Jacq. Everyone's getting married except you, but it's fine. We need to get through today, and then everything will be—"

As she lifted her eyes, she stopped talking.

In the doorway, Murtaugh stood uncomfortably, fidgeting with a hat. He was shaven again, mostly healed, with a fresh haircut. His clothes were sharp and clean; his father's coin was still bound around his neck. He was every bit as handsome as he ever was while she—with her braided hair, puffy eyes, and red nose—more closely resembled a weeping child.

Wishing she could hide the fact she'd been crying, Jacq rose from the bench, angry and embarrassed. "Murtaugh. What are you doing here? The ceremony is not for hours."

"I… I had to see you," he began with apprehension. "I wanted to apologize." He took a nervous step forward. "But I see you're upset."

Sniffling, she stared at him in silence.

"Right. Well… well, I-I wanted to apologize. When you told me about the commission—"

"That was *weeks* ago, Murtaugh! *Weeks* ago!" She took a long, ragged breath to calm herself.

"I know, Jacq! I know! But I didn't think… you talked about Swansea, and then you said you were—all of you were… going with your father to the Caribbean! How's a lad supposed to know how he fits into a plan such as that, eh? I'd been working on making arrangements to have a job here for weeks when you told me."

"I understand that now, and I am sorry," she returned. "Truly. It was thoughtless of me to assume you would have an easy response to the news. It only took me so long to tell you because I wanted to be sure and have the particulars sorted."

"And I wasn't one of the particulars?" he asked, scowling.

"No!" she answered. "I wanted it to be your choice! I wanted to present you with all the facts and afford you the chance to choose."

He observed her a moment before walking forward to stand in front of her. "Jacq, I don't like it. I don't like any of it. The more I've thought on it, the less I like it."

She looked up at him in teary-eyed confusion.

Gesturing for them to sit, he sighed. "I don't like the prospect of you leaving England. I don't like the prospect of leaving

England myself. But what vexes me most is the prospect of you leaving England without me."

"Well, I don't much like it either," she said softly. "To be perfectly honest, I rather loathe the very notion of it."

A rueful chuckle escaping his lungs, he smiled in relief.

Glancing up at the window for Alex's room, she motioned toward the house. "Would you like to discuss this in the sitting room?" she asked, wiping at her eyes and feeling her bitter spirits lift slightly on hopeful wings.

Following her gaze, he nodded then followed her into the large house.

"So, what are we to do about it?" she asked as they reentered the house, headed for the sitting room in the back. "I thought you had quite clearly made up your mind."

"Well, that was why I came to see you," he began. "I—"

Knock, knock, knock! Knock, knock, knock!

"Oh, please excuse me! The servants are spread thin with the wedding. I told Edward I'd assist with the door, though he was entirely displeased with the idea," she said, pausing in the corridor that led to the sitting room.

"Of course you did," he said, smiling at the continuity of her personality and independence.

Knock, knock, knock! Knock, knock, knock!

"Well, go on then," he said, standing aside.

Appreciative of his understanding, she led the way to the door.

"What do you suppose that was all about?" Amy asked from where she and Alex stood by the window.

A sly smile played onto Alex's lips. "I do not know, but it is most intriguing, is it not?"

Below, Jacq and Murtaugh reached the entry hall just as Edward was closing the door.

"Oh, Edward!" Jacq exclaimed. "My apologies!"

"On the contrary, Miss Jacqueline," he said, glancing uneasily at Murtaugh, "I take pride in performing my own duties."

Murtaugh stifled a smile. "Miss Jacqueline's persistence is difficult to resist."

"Indeed," Edward agreed. "Though I try diligently, sir."

Noticing a little envelope in his hand, Jacq's countenance lit up. "Is that a letter? To whom is it posted?"

"It… Oh, it-it is to the vice admiral," he answered tensely.

"Edward, might I take it to him?" she requested.

Edward looked to Murtaugh, who smiled and shrugged.

"Well, this is highly irregular, but… very well, Miss Jacqueline, but I'll not have you taking over my duties, you understand?" he said, reluctantly holding out the card.

Snatching it up, she smiled. "Of course not, Edward." Then she grinned over at Murtaugh. "Come on. Let's fetch this over to Papa."

Murtaugh gave Edward a nod and followed Jacq around the stairs toward the study. Knocking as she pushed the door open, she called, "Papa? You've a post just arrived."

As they slipped into the room, they were met by a tall man, immaculately groomed and attired. Everything in his bearing was entirely flawless, from his glistening brass buttons to his crisp white pants and dark blue coat. His tanned skin and salt-and-pepper hair made him the picture of the perfect navy man. With impeccable poise, he gave them a nod. "Good day, Mr. Murtaugh. Nice to see you!"

"Sir," the Irishman returned.

"It's not time for the ceremony yet, is it?" the vice admiral asked, glancing at the clock.

"No, no," Jacq said, gazing in amazement at his appearance.

"Well, what is it then?" he asked, clueless to her admiration.

"Oh! You-you... you've a post—a letter," she answered, offering it to him.

"Do I? Oh. Edward usually brings it in for me," he said, accepting it from her.

"Oh, he meant to," Jacq said as she watched him open the envelope. "Only I insisted on bringing it to you."

"Oh, Edward won't like that one bit," he said, chuckling.

"Miss Jacqueline can be very persuasive," Murtaugh commented, smirking knowingly.

Nodding, Vice Admiral Luray unfolded the note and began reading silently. After just a few seconds, a handsome grin breached his face. "Oh! They've got Mr. Carloff."

"Have they?" Jacq asked, her eyes lighting up. She sent Murtaugh a giddy glance. "What does it say? And what of Barend?"

"Barend acted immorally and faces jail time for it, but he'll not be hanged for piracy, despite his declarations. It seems his eagerness to assist in the apprehension of Mr. Carloff earned him favor with the judge. Though I pity his situation, I do not know that I would have granted him eventual freedom.

"As for this, it reads that Carloff was apprehended fleeing Cabo Corso on his ship, *Christina*. He was taken to London Tower for examination where they confiscated gold, ivory, and other valuables. It seems the company he claimed to represent, the Swedish Africa Company, is now also under examination. They hope to have it sorted by the end of the season." Vice Admiral Luray grinned broader. "This day has gone from wonderful to perfect," he said, folding the letter up and tucking it back into the envelope.

"It certainly has," Jacq said, glancing at Murtaugh, who nodded in agreement.

Looking between the two young people, the vice admiral's eyebrows came together. "And what of you two?"

"What of us?" Jacq asked, instantly uncomfortable.

"About what I said before, Jacq, as I have said several times, I may have been a bit hasty in my suggestion to you." He glanced at Murtaugh. "If my previous sentiments of concern are at all giving you pause—"

"No, no," Jacq said, casting a wary look at Murtaugh. "I assure you, any pauses we may have are strictly of our own making."

Studying them once again, the vice admiral nodded. "Right. I'll leave you to it. A walk in the garden will do me good."

They stood quietly apart as he walked out, closing the door to the room.

As soon as it clicked shut, Murtaugh took a deep breath and sighed. "He didn't approve of me."

"But he does now," she replied. "More or less."

"But that's not an issue?"

"No."

"So, what is it?"

Exhaling a weary sigh, Jacq shrugged. "You don't want me to leave England, but I must. My father is leaving Bahari as overseer of his estate until they are entirely settled or we return, but he doesn't believe we'll return for years, if ever. And that is why I've determined I must accompany them to the Caribbean. I don't want to miss years of their lives." She watched him frown and nod, defeat overtaking his countenance. "And to be perfectly honest, I'd rather not miss years of yours either."

Lifting his gaze to her, he sighed. "So we are at an impasse?"

Knock, knock!

"Miss Jacqueline?" Lydia called, opening the door and peeking into the study. Seeing them standing an awkward distance from each other—too close to be strangers and too far to be intimate— she gasped. "Oh! My apologies, Miss Jacqueline! Miss Alexandria sent me to retrieve you. It is time to do your hair."

"Oh!" Jacq glanced at the clock then back at Murtaugh. "I…" She stared down at her blouse, jerkin, pants, and boots. "I…"

"Go," Murtaugh said, smirking. "I need to go ready myself. I'll be here when the wedding's through."

"I should certainly hope so," she said, moving toward the door. "I don't feel as though we are resolved."

"I am Miata's best man, don't forget. Let us enjoy their wedding, eh? I'll think of something," he said kindly, following her out. "Besides, I'd not pass up the opportunity to see you adorned and decorated for such an elaborate occasion."

Nodding, she offered up a sarcastic expression. "I'd fancy to see you in a dress wearing a bloomin' corset, barely able to breathe."

"I daresay I haven't the figure for it," he said, heading for the door.

Smirking, she turned and hurried up the stairs.

Jacq and Amy stood behind Lydia, watching her put the final touches on Alex's hair. They themselves already readied, watched in happy approval.

When Lydia stepped back, signifying her work was complete, Jacq sighed. "You and I, dear sister, we are supposed to be twins. Yet here you are looking far more beautiful than I, as you so often do."

Turning around, Alex gifted them an elated smile. "Well, you are all niceness, but I must say, I think the both of you are two of the loveliest girls I have ever seen."

"I'm mostly astonished at Jacq being in such a posh dress," Amy said in a teasing tone. "These are the latest fashion, you know."

"Well, she must convince Mr. Murtaugh he absolutely cannot live without her in every way possible," Alex said with an impish smile.

Gasping at Alex's brash statement, Jacq looked down at her soft gray skirt folds and taught cerulean bodice with a bursting bosom. "I'd like to think he would be interested in me no matter what clothes I happen to be wearing! Perhaps I'll take the scarf, after all!"

Admiring her own slim figure encased in a rich eggplant gown, Amy giggled. "You are right, of course. But there is something to be said for reminding a man every now and then of *all* one's assets."

Scoffing, Jacq shook her head. "A fine pair of sisters you are! Trying to auction me off!"

"I do not know that it qualifies as an auction if there is only one person doing the bidding," Alex returned.

"Stop it!" Jacq retorted, giggling and snatching up a scarf to put around her shoulders. "We should focus on marrying off the two of you who have had a real proposal, should we not, Lydia?"

"Indeed, miss," Lydia said, smiling kindly.

"So what was that in the garden?" Amy asked.

Jacq's eyes narrowed. "That was two mates trying to sort out some…" She struggled for words. "Some unresolved issues."

The two brides stood smirking, entirely pleased with themselves.

"What do you think, Lydia?" Amy asked.

Shaking her head, Lydia shrugged. "I think each of you has her opinions. Seems you are all very keen to keep them. Now, we have a ceremony to attend." She glanced over each girl once more. "Are you ready? We need to be off to the church."

The sisters all smiled among themselves, fidgeting and biting their lips and smoothing and straightening.

"I do believe we are," Alex said, taking a deep breath.

"I can scarcely wait," Amy said, giggling.

"If we wait any longer, I might have second thoughts," Jacq noted in a grumble, pulling the scarf together with a silver clasp Alex handed her.

"Can I have a moment with her, just we two?" Alex requested, gesturing to Jacq.

Lydia nodded. "Of course, miss. I'll walk Miss Amy down to the carriage, and then I'll be back to fetch you."

As Amy and Lydia went downstairs, Alex turned to Jacq, adjusting her scarf. "I just want to say how marvelous it has been, this journey with you." She took Jacq's hands in hers. "I know I have not always been keen on your notions—"

"I'd say," Jacq remarked, smirking.

"And we each have our own type of stubbornness," Alex continued, giving Jacq a good-natured glare. "But I always cherish every moment of our time together. Every ridiculous argument, every brilliant scheme, our adventures, and our struggles. Beginning from the moment we were thrust back into each other's lives and you told me you would rather mop than wash the dishes, you have been there for me in ways I never could have imagined."

"Alex, nothing will change for us," Jacq said softly.

"But they *will*," Alex returned, sniffling. "Things *will* change. Things *will* be different. We are ending one chapter of our lives and beginning another. It would be foolish to convince ourselves otherwise. But what I wanted to say... the truth is, I would not be here, preparing to spend my life with this wonderful man, if it were not for you. You have made my life horribly chaotic, but wholly beautiful." She squeezed Jacq's hands and smiled with eyes wet with tears that never fell onto her perfect face. "I love you, Jacq."

"Always so eloquent within and without," Jacq returned with a sad sort of smile. "You are both my sister and my friend. Your joy and your sorrow are mine. I know today we will begin more separate lives than we've had in years, but it will not diminish what we share. I am so, so happy for you, Alex. I truly, truly am. And though I do not say it enough to anyone, I love you too, and I am blessed to share this day with you."

As Jacq gave Alex's fingers a return squeeze, Lydia poked her head in. "Are we ready, miss?"

"We are," Jacq spoke up. "Any more sentimentality expressed in this room might cause our teeth to rot."

"Jacq! Unbelievable!" Alex huffed in exasperation as she headed out the door. "I think perhaps all those sailor friends of yours have tainted your feminine sensibilities."

"I prefer to think of myself as being logical," Jacq returned, helping her down the stairs.

Scoffing, Alex shook her head. "Please! Of the two of us I am the logical one, and I question even that these days."

They continued going back and forth as they climbed into the waiting carriage with Amy. Once they were all packed inside, the driver guided them down to the main town and through the streets of Swansea. They were lined with banners and jubilant townsfolk, waving flags and throwing petals, happy to have one last thing to celebrate before serious effects of the war reached them.

The carriage came to a stop in front of the church Jacq had left Father George Brandon's poem in a year and a half ago. Their father, Vice Admiral Luray, in all his prestigious and honorable glory, stood waiting for them at the start of the walk up to the building. Captain Turner stood across from him, looking equally as statuesque.

When the carriage came to a halt, both men came forward to help the girls out. Exiting first, Jacq made her way to the bottom of the stairs before turning back to watch Alex get out, taking Captain Turner's arm, and Amy join her, taking their father's. They looked like pure nobility, and the way the townspeople cheered, one would have thought them to be princesses.

Just as they had practiced numerous times before, Jacq entered first, walking alone down the aisle. She passed by many faces she did not know—friends of the Luray family with whom she'd yet to be properly acquainted. However, nearer the front, she found relief at seeing Mr. Bibbs with Bahari and his family: Aladia, Kukoyi, the recovering Akinlabi, Nuru, little Bakari, Moyo, Morenike, Adunni, Ayotunde, Enitan, Gbeke, Olusegun, and Iremide—the whole lot from Tenkodogo, save Durosinmi.

James Monroe and Miata O'Keeffe stood anxiously at the front beside the minister, looking dapper and grand in their long-sleeved ruffled shirts, petticoat breeches, slash-sleeved coats, and falling collars, fidgeting as she approached.

Dante Rackham and Michael Murtaugh stood beside them as their best men, giving the handsome grooms a bit of competition—especially Murtaugh, who had done his best to merge his own sense of style with what was trending. Upon seeing Jacq, though, he nearly forgot he was there for a wedding until the music swelled and all in attendance pushed reverently to their feet.

Amy and the vice admiral proceeded down the aisle first, Amy hardly able to keep herself contained, looking as though she might suddenly begin to skip. With the long, semicathedral train trailing behind her and her dainty shoulders exposed by the modern-style neckline, she appeared as though she might burst with happiness.

When she saw how Miata gaped at her in awestruck wonder, she glowed.

Lastly came Alex, escorted by Captain Turner, who passed her off to her father before she was given to a completely enamored James Monroe. Her beauty was only rivaled by her poise. From the trendy hair adornments to her highly fashionable gown to the carefully selected shoes on her feet, she was everyone's idea of what a royal lady must look like. The sparkle in her eyes and the delicate curve of her lips were all that gave away how thoroughly sated she truly was.

After speaking about the character of love, the duties and blessings of marriage, and the holy nature of such a contract between two people, bound to struggle with their innate bents for selfishness, the minister turned first to Mr. James Monroe. "Will you repeat after me?"

Nodding, somberly, James replied, "I will."

Together, they recited, "I, James Ross Monroe, take thee, Alexandria Thorpe Luray, to be my wedded wife, to have and to hold from this day forward, for better for worse, for richer for poorer, in sickness and in health, to love and to cherish, till death us do part, according to God's holy ordinance, and thereto I plight thee my troth."

The minister then turned to Alex, who was standing tall and contained. "Will you repeat after me?"

Taking a long, shaky breath, she looked James directly in the eyes. "I will."

Together, they recited, "I, Alexandria Thorpe Luray, take thee, James Ross Monroe, to be my wedded husband, to have and to hold from this day forward, for better for worse, for richer for poorer, in sickness and in health, to love, to cherish, and to obey, till death us do part, according to God's holy ordinance, and thereto I give thee my troth."

Giving her a smile, he then turned to Miata as James and Alex gazed at each other in mutual adoration. "Will you repeat after me?"

Miata glanced about nervously. He fidgeted, and his eyes began darting around the room. People began to murmur, and as they did, his breathing began to quicken.

Murtaugh and Jacq both began to feel anxious, praying he wouldn't have a panic attack or flee. Noticing his fretfulness, however, Amy sweetly reached out and took his hand. His eyes were instantly drawn back to her, and his breathing slowed.

She gave him a small smile and silently mouthed, "I love you."

Taking a deep breath, he faced the minister. "I will."

Together, they recited, "I, Miata O'Keeffe, take thee, Amy Luray, to be my wedded wife, to have and to hold from this day forward, for better for worse, for richer for poorer, in sickness and in health, to love and to cherish, till death us do part, according to God's holy ordinance, and thereto I plight thee my troth."

Sending Miata a reassuring smile, the minister turned to Amy. "And will you repeat after me?"

Gleefully grinning, she answered, "I will!"

Though he recited the same vow as he had for Alex, Amy embellished as she repeated, "I, Amy Luray, take thee, wonderful Miata O'Keeffe, the man I love, to be my wedded husband, to have and to hold from this day forward, for better for worse, for richer for poorer, in sickness and in health, to love, to cherish, and to obey, till death us do part, according to God's holy ordinance, and thereto I give thee my troth with all my heart."

"And have you the rings?" the minister asked.

Each best man fished out the ring he'd been given charge of and gave it to his respective groom.

"Place it on her thumb, each of you," the minister instructed.

As the grooms obeyed, Jacq snuck a glance over at Murtaugh, only to find him doing the same to her. They listened to the minister but couldn't look away from each other as James and Miata recited in turn, "With this ring I thee wed, with my body I thee worship, and with all my worldly goods I thee endow: in the name of the Father, and of the Son, and of the Holy Ghost. Amen."

As the grooms took the ring from finger to finger, finally securing it on their brides' ring fingers, Jacq and Murtaugh each suffered a tingling sensation that seemed to pulsate from their heart and run sparking through their veins.

"I now pronounce you man and wife," the minister said first to Alex and James. "And you man and wife." He looked second to Amy and Miata. "You may, each of you, kiss your bride!"

Cheers and wild applause rose up as James eagerly pulled Alex in for a heartfelt kiss, while Amy had to restrain herself as Miata leaned down to modestly press his lips to hers.

The noise jarring Jacq and Murtaugh back to reality, they joined in the clapping, authentically thrilled for their dear friends and family. Dante glanced between them, unaware of their wordless exchange but thought something was odd about Jacq's expression. Still, everyone smiled, delighted for the two sets of lovebirds.

"I now introduce to you," the minister shouted, "for the first time, Mr. and Mrs. James Monroe and Mr. and Mrs. Miata O'Keeffe! May God bless your lives!"

"Hear! Hear!" everyone shouted as the two couples hurried down the aisle to the two carriages waiting to take them back to the vice admiral's estate for the reception banquet.

Watching them go, Jacq was suddenly overcome with sadness, like a sudden nausea had taken hold of her stomach. Embarrassed for the unexpected bout of self-pity, she turned and went out the side door to the churchyard.

Both Rackham and Murtaugh, who'd hardly been able to take his eyes off her, saw her go. Dante started to go after her, but Murtaugh caught his arm. "Please. Allow me?"

Moving aside, Rackham said sternly, "Do right by her, mate."

Taking a deep breath, Murtaugh nodded. Following her into the yard, he found her leaning her back against the building, holding her head in her hands. Her hair, trussed up, shone like gold, and her svelte figure, generally downplayed by her usual attire, was exceedingly distracting. However, he pushed it aside and walked over to her.

Hearing his approach, she looked up and sighed. "I am an idiot, you know? Completely daft." She turned away.

He said nothing, unsure what he could say and wanting her to continue.

"She was right. Of course it will be different. I was a fool to suppose otherwise. A daft child. Logical, indeed." She paused and rotated back to face him. "I am alone now."

"No, you're not," he said gently.

"Oh, but I am! And I am so selfish and pathetic to realize it at my sisters' wedding! But we leave in a week's time. Rackham is going off to court Miss Wallace, and you're staying here!" she said. "Mr. Bibbs is joining us, but he's like an uncle, or-or a grandfather! So just-just let me alone. Leave me to my misery."

She spun to stalk away, but Murtaugh lunged forward and caught her round the waist, pulling her close. "Jackie."

She closed her eyes at the feel of his arm about her and the sound of his Irish accented voice. "Michael. Don't..."

"I think we both know that though I haven't quite said so, I have a deep affection for you. So to be fair, I will tell it to you plain so you'll have no doubts," he said.

She looked up into his blue eyes and found she could barely breathe. "Wha-what?"

"Jacq, I want to be with you. I want to be with you every day for the rest of my life. The truth is, I'm in love with you, Jackie. I have been since the moment you first smiled when we met at the harbor these six years past. I wanted to do things proper with you, but this is what I've got. Bahari warned me not to make any promises to you I couldn't keep, and though he didn't say as much, I'm certain it was on pain of death."

Gasping and laughing, Jacq touched at his face. "Michael—"

"I-I can't promise you much, but I will love you until the day I die, and if you would have me, I will do everything in my power to make you the happiest lass alive. For you, I can be a blackbird," he said, intense and earnest.

"W-w-what are you saying?" she asked, hope soaring in her heart and pushing tears into her eyes.

"I'm asking," he said, sliding down to his knee. "Will you marry me, Jacq? I don't care where we live. Ireland isn't my home. England isn't my home. But you, Jacq, you're it."

She covered her mouth, sniffling.

"So, will you?" he continued. "Will you marry me?"

Chewing on her lip, she sniffled. "I will."

He inhaled in excited relief. "May I kiss you?"

A coy smile played her expression. "Just once."

His face lighting up like the sun on the first day of summer, he jumped to his feet, cradled her face between his hands, and pulled her mouth to his.

As their lips touched, an electric energy ran between them, and she grabbed onto his arms to steady herself. They savored the intimacy a few moments before they each took a small step back, staring at each other in astonishment.

Breathless, he cleared his throat. "I-I never…" He touched at his lips and then ran his hand through his hair.

"Nor I," she said, fanning herself with her hand. "At least, not with so much…" She put her hand over her heart.

"Aye, exactly," he agreed, rubbing the back of his neck. Taking a deep breath, he looked her up and down. "Have I told you that you're beautiful?"

A shy but very flattered glow washed over her countenance. "Not recently. Should I compliment you in return? Tell you that somehow you make all those ribbons and lace look beguiling?"

"I will allow it if you believe it and no one else hears of it," he said, grinning. He took a moment more to observe her. "You have my heart, you know?"

Exhaling in a happy sigh, she smiled. "And you have mine." Then inhaling sharply, she motioned toward the street. "I… that is, *we* have a banquet to attend!"

"So we do. Come on then," he said, holding out his arm.

Threading her hand around his arm, she beamed at him. "You know, you make a fine gentleman."

"And you a fine lady," he returned. "I'll not tell if you don't."

Her blissful expression grew. "An excellent proposition."

After finding a wagon to take them back to the estate, they snuck into the garden as the banquet was already well underway and they hoped not to bring attention to themselves.

"There you are!" Amy exclaimed, walking out of the house. "We've been wondering where you were off to! You'll never guess who's here!" She latched onto Jacq, tugging and pulling her to the dining room where a group of people bunched around the rest of the wedding party. "Here she is!"

As everyone shuffled around to see Amy, Murtaugh came up from behind. There, beside Miata, stood a pale average man with a meticulously preened exterior but an untamed gleam in his eyes.

He smiled at Jacq. "Oh, you all look so gorgeous! Miata could not have found himself a finer family to marry into."

She smiled. "Mr. Pierce. You look well. How do you do, sir?"

"I am getting on," he said, maintaining his pleased countenance. "Married life has proved a fascinating challenge."

Turning around, she motioned between Murtaugh and Pierce. "Mr. Pierce, this is Mr. Murtaugh. Mr. Pierce financed our voyage to Martinique Isle. It seems like a lifetime ago."

"It certainly does," Pierce agreed, chuckling. "And Mr. Murtaugh is a friend of yours?"

A demure smile commandeered Jacq's countenance. "Mr. Murtaugh is, in fact, my fiancé."

Everyone gasped.

"We are engaged to be married," she said, her grin so broad she could hardly speak.

A tidal wave of applause and cheers rippled through the crowd.

Smirking and shaking his head, Rackham gripped Murtaugh's hand. "Well done, mate."

"Thank you," he said, returning the handshake.

Rackham smiled over at Jacq. "You take care of yourself, Miss Luray."

"And you, Mr. Rackham. Best of luck with Miss Wallace," she said, nodding. "And thank you for taking me to Africa."

"Stay true to yourself, Miss Luray. Your sentiments will hopefully do me well. I leave for London in the morning. I actually should leave to check on a few arrangements, to be sure everything's settled."

"Safe travels, mate," Murtaugh spoke up.

Stepping forward, Jacq gave Rackham a farewell hug. "Goodbye, mate. Good luck."

"And to you," he returned. Then he vanished into the crowd.

"Shakina," Bahari said, walking up to them with Morenike at his side, "we wanted to bid you well afore returning home with the others. Akinlabi still needs his rest."

"Poor lad. Are you settling in then?" she asked, a hopeful expression overlaying her face.

"We are doing our best. The vice admiral was very generous to put a roof over our heads, but we must earn our keep. Learning to farm these lands is challenging, but not impossible," he returned.

"But you will also serve as an overseer of the property while we are away," Alex spoke up. "And that is not a light task."

"Very true," Bahari agreed, sighing. "But we are eager to find our own way in this new world."

"We will miss you," Morenike spoke up, smiling. "You know, with Akinlabi on the mend, Kukoyi and Iremide have begun making plans to marry too."

"Oh!" Jacq clasped her hands in delight. "Why did he wait so long to ask?"

Clearing his throat, Murtaugh commented, "You know, sometimes a lad likes to be doubly certain a lass fancies him afore he makes a fool of himself asking."

"Aye, that's the truth of it," James agreed.

"And sometimes a lass be practically askin' for herself," Miata added, chuckling until he glanced at Amy, who was lightly scowling at him.

"You will all be missed," Captain Turner remarked, looking over the jolly group. "I rather envy Mr. Bibbs's accompanying you to the Caribbean."

"Perhaps you should give us a visit," Jacq suggested.

"I don't see how! I've lost my first mate and my boatswain all in the same day," he said, gesturing to James.

"In truth, he might not be able to persuade himself to part with us if he did," Murtaugh said, chuckling.

Everyone laughed along with him.

"It shall be a new adventure," Vice Admiral Luray said. "I am honored and blessed to have such a family to share it with."

"Jacq," Alex started, worry coloring her face. "We leave in just a week's time. How will you be married?"

"Oh. How right you are!" Jacq frowned in thought. "Well, we—I had not—" She turned to Murtaugh. "Alex is right. What are we to do?"

"Actually," Murtaugh said, eyeing the vice admiral, "I have a plan."

Watching the ring slide down her slender finger, Jacq took a deep breath and looked up at Murtaugh, that wonderful lopsided smile forming his expression.

So this is it, she thought to herself. *Good days and bad days shall follow, but this day is mine. This day is ours.*

"I now pronounce you man and wife. You may kiss the bride," the minister announced.

On the dock, at the foot of the ramp up to the ship full of cheering spectators, Murtaugh swept Jacq into his arms, planting a kiss on her that declared to all present that he was absolutely taken with her.

When they straightened, hands clasped and staring dewy-eyed at each other, the minister suppressed a smile and shouted, "I now introduce to you, for the first time, Mr. and Mrs. Michael Murtaugh! I wish you both the very best. May God bless you!"

Edging on the ramp was everyone leaving for the Caribbean while the harbor was lined with those who were not. Waving one final time at their friends on the dock, the newlyweds climbed the gangplank to board the ship, hugging and gathering those on the ramp as they went up.

Being one of the ones nearest the bottom, Vice Admiral Luray shook hands with the minister. "Thank you again, sir."

"It was my pleasure," the minister said, nodding. "It's good of them to be wedded before the voyage. We needn't put ourselves in temptation's way any more than necessary. Lord knows we find ourselves there often enough as it is."

"Strange that two years ago I didn't know they were still alive. Now I've gained two daughters and married all three of them off in a year and a half's time. That, Pastor, is an achievement," he said.

"That, sir, is an act of God. One to certainly be thankful for," the minister said with a chuckle.

"Indeed. Well, we must be off. Good day to you, sir. And again, thank you." The vice admiral offered his hand once more.

Gripping it in a solid shake, the minister nodded. "And to you, sir. Godspeed on your travels."

Taking one last look around, Vice Admiral Luray waved at those on the dock then ascended the gangplank, shouting, "Mr. Ellard! A report, if you please!"

That evening, as they sailed ever into the horizon, chasing the sun across the water, Michael Murtaugh was walking toward the prow when he bumped into a bucket, spilling it onto the deck.

"Oh! My apologies, sir!" a young man said, coming up to him holding a mop.

"What are you doing? Why are you mopping now?" Murtaugh asked.

"I weren't. I mean, I am, but I weren't meant to. I sat down for just a minute and next thing I know…" He motioned to the bucket.

"Listen… well, what's your name, lad?" he asked, hiding his amusement.

"Morgan, sir. Henry Morgan," he answered eagerly.

"Is this your first time on a crew, Mr. Morgan?" Murtaugh asked.

"It is, sir," he answered.

"Well, Mr. Morgan, you'll find the vice admiral to be a fair and decent man, but he doesn't take kindly to slothfulness, savvy?" the Irishman said.

"Aye, sir. I'll aim to do better, sir," he replied.

"It's a good practice to have if you ever expect to be captain of your own ship someday. Now get on with it," Murtaugh said, shooing him away.

"Aye, sir!" No sooner had he said the words than he was scampering away.

"Giving orders, are we, Mr. Murtaugh?" Jacq asked, approaching him from his destination with her blue macaw on her shoulder.

"I'm the boss's son-in-law. That gives me some credit, doesn't it?" he asked playfully.

"I don't know." She smiled as he sashayed up to her. "I'd hate for all that power to go to your head."

"Right you be," Miata said, showing up with Amy in tow. "We be turnin' in for the night."

"As are we," Alex said, appearing with James, a monkey perched on his arm. "We thought you might enjoy a few moments of privacy."

"On this ship?" Jacq scoffed.

"Look at us, all married," Amy said, nearly choking up. "I could cry it's so wonderful."

"Please don't, darlin'," Miata said, ushering her away.

They all took turns bidding each other a fair night as everyone but Jacq and Murtaugh went off to bed.

Once alone, the Irishman took her by the hand and led her to the prow. "I hope you're as happy as I am, Jackie."

"I can't imagine why I wouldn't be," she said with a satiated sigh. "In this moment, all is right for those I care for most." She stared out at the water, listening to Bill click his tongue.

The sun was nearly gone from the crimson sky, and the stars were beginning to shine. The weather was not yet unbearably cold, and the ocean before them was nearly as smooth as glass. Everything was perfect.

"Michael?" She took hold of his arm and squeezed.

"Hmm?" Hearing her say his name immediately brought a smile to his face.

"Have I told you that I love you?" she asked.

His expression broadened. "Aye, but I shall never tire of hearing it."

Giggling, she leaned her head on his shoulder. "Michael, I've been meaning to ask you… what did you mean when you said you can be a blackbird?"

"Oh." He should have known she'd remember and be curious, but he had been hoping she'd forget. "Oh, I just… it's an old Irish song… it's just… just—"

"I think you should sing it for me," she said in a playful tone. "I should like to know about this blackbird of mine."

"Sing it for you?" he asked, rethinking the words.

She nodded, and Bill clicked approval.

"Blackbird of yours?" he reiterated, smiling down at her.

She peered up at his face. "Aye."

"Well…" He paused, thinking as she toyed with his fingers. "I'll revise it just a bit to make it yours." Clearing his throat, he pulled her into his arms while staring out across the water.

I am a young sailor, my story is glad
for once I was carefree, and a brave sailor lad.
I courted a maiden by night and by day,
ah, but now she has asked me to sail far away.
For her I'll be a blackbird, aim to whistle and sing,
I'll follow the vessel my true love sails in.
And in the top rigging, I will there build my nest,
and with her I'll finally be able to rest.
And if I were a scholar and could handle a pen,
one sincere love letter to my true love I'd send.
And I'd tell of the sorrow, the grief and the pain
that would have been mine if she had left me again.
For her I'll be a blackbird, aim to whistle and sing,
I'll follow the vessel my true love sails in.
And in the top rigging, I will there build my nest,
and with her I'll finally be able to rest.